The child who died is the king who will be.

The king who died will slay the king who would be.

The son of three mothers will father three sons, and with their hands on his blood they will shake the world when they are long dead and gone to dust.

Thus was foretold the coming of King Ambescand.

To Graymantle, a mighty warrior in service to Lord Duarin, the words of the prophecy were no more understandable than the gibberings of the southern nomads. He was more interested in living a good, simple life with his family. But it was not to be. Graymantle's fate was inexorably bound to the fate of Ambescand, for *he was Ambescand*—and he did not know it.

GRAYMANTLE is the prequel to **IRONBRAND**, "a great big epic that deserves to be read."

—Andrew J. Offutt

JOHN MORRESSY

GRAYMANTLE

ACE FANTASY BOOKS
NEW YORK

GRAYMANTLE

An Ace Fantasy Book / published by arrangement with
the author

PRINTING HISTORY
Playboy edition / September 1981
Ace edition / November 1984

ISBN: 0-441-30199-1

Ace Fantasy Books are published by The Berkley Publishing Group,
200 Madison Avenue, New York, New York 10016.
PRINTED IN THE UNITED STATES OF AMERICA

For Stan and Do Walters

I tell you naught for your comfort,
  Yea, naught for your desire,
Save that the sky grows darker yet
  And the sea rises higher.

Night shall be thrice night over you,
  And heaven an iron cope.
Do you have joy without a cause,
  Yea, faith without a hope?
                              —G. K. Chesterton

THE HEADLAND

CAPE OF MISTS

THE CRYSTAL HILLS

NORTHMARK

THE FASTNESS

THE PLAIN

LONG WOOD

THE FOOL'S HEAD

THE STONE HAND

THE HIGH CITY

THE SISTERS

THE BROTHERS

SOUTHMARK

MISTLANDS

THE SOUTHERN FOREST

THE CITADEL

CHAPTER ONE

BANHEEN'S BARGAIN

*For a power bound in stony sleep from an age when
    earth was young
Rose secretly, and moved unknown to those it walked
    among,
And it touched the world, and it savored life, and its
    timeless hunger grew;
But far beyond all human ken, a greater Power knew.
  It wove a web of destiny, and for working of Its plan
  It chose from times unborn such men as grace the name
    of man. . . .*

— From *The Last Deed Of Ambescand*

He watched at the window till the last light died; then he
turned and began to pace the cell. It was a sizable cell: eleven
paces along each of the three inner walls, twelve along the
curving outer wall. This part of the prison was quiet, and he
was alone. For these things he was grateful. He did not wish
to pass this night listening to the laments and cries of
strangers.

The rusted gyves rubbed raw the flesh of his ankles, but
still he walked. This was to be the last night of his life, and
he preferred to spend it awake, and moving, and possessed
of his senses. The flagon of wine they had brought with his
dinner stood untouched by the door. One sniff had been
enough to tell him it was drugged—whether out of his keepers'
compassion or for their convenience, he could not tell, nor
did it much matter to him. He only hoped that they had not
treated the food, as well. That seemed unlikely; he had eaten
before sunset, and his senses were as alert now as ever.

He walked his circumscribed path, thinking and remembering and trying vainly to keep his mind from the morning. His
prospects were grim, utterly hopeless. At daybreak he would
be led from his cell—carried out like a sack of meal, more

likely, if he gave in and downed the flagon of wine—and taken to the platform by the western gate of the High City. Here he would be denounced and cursed by the spokesman of the law, and his hands would be struck off and burned before him. His head would then be removed and placed on a spike above the gate as a warning to thieves.

Along the outer wall he paced, trying to drive off the pain in his ankles by thinking of good times past, but without success. Remembered triumphs could not comfort him now.

He became aware of an acute thirst. A score of times he had passed the flagon without pausing. The next time around, he hesitated, but then he walked on firmly and resolutely, and for several circuits he kept up his former pace. Finally, heartsick and weary, weighted down with despair, ankles running blood, he surrendered. He stopped by the thick oaken door and lifted the heavy clay flagon to his lips.

"Do not drink," said a deep, commanding voice.

He gave a startled cry and dropped the flagon, which shattered to bits on the stone floor. Turning quickly, clumsily, painfully, he looked hard into the darkness. He saw no one.

So they had drugged the food after all.

"Banheen Quickhand, you are to die a thief's death at sunrise," said the same voice. "Do you wish to be spared?"

"Who's there?" Banheen cried.

"Do you wish to be spared?" the voice demanded.

"Of course I do! Who are you?" Banheen said desperately, stepping first to one side and then to another, peering fruitlessly into the black corners of the cell.

By the faint starshine from the window, he saw a brief motion. As he watched, a tall, hooded figure came into view, illuminated by the waxing glow of a formless white light at the top of a long staff in its left hand.

"Who are you?" Banheen repeated, more softly now, with a touch of fear in his voice.

"I am one who requires the services of a skilled thief this night, and I will pay for those services with freedom," said the intruder.

"Then I'm your man. What must I steal?"

"A child."

Banheen's chains clinked as he started back. "Wait, now. Just wait. I'd do almost anything to be free, but I've heard tales. . . . What are you going to do to the child?"

The intruder moved forward. Banheen retreated until he

backed up against the wall, and the intruder stopped close before him. In the light, Banheen could see two slender white hands clasped on the staff. No other feature was distinguishable. His visitor was enshrouded in dense, unreflecting black from head to foot, and a cowl was drawn forward to keep his face in shadow. When the dark apparition did not respond to his question, Banheen proceeded to qualify his objection.

"Any wizard with magic enough to penetrate these walls and bring me out—that much power must come from somewhere. I've heard of rites, of sacrifices . . ."

"And so you assume at once that I am a wizard. Have you never heard of keys? Of bribery?"

"Yes. Certainly, I have. But the way you appeared, so suddenly, out of nowhere . . . and asking me to steal a child . . ."

Banheen broke off and turned away as the staff was lowered to shed its light full upon his face. It glared red through his tight-shut eyelids for a moment; then it was withdrawn. He heard his visitor give a soft, low breath of laughter.

"Your misgivings do you credit, Banheen. For a thief, you have a tender conscience," said the hooded figure.

"I'm strictly a thief. I've never slain anyone."

"And you need not. Indeed, by stealing the child, you save his life. If he is not taken to safety, the child will be dead before you are dragged from this cell at sunrise. Even now, the assassin is within the palace."

"The palace? Would you have me steal a child from the palace?" Banheen asked in horror.

The intruder sighed and leaned wearily on his staff. "I see I chose poorly," he said. "Very well. Remain here and die. I will go to the House of All Keys. Iosmut will do what I ask, or perhaps Thode will have the courage."

Banheen's professional pride was stung. "Iosmut and Thode?" He snorted in contempt. "Those two are nothing but stupid bullies. They couldn't steal mud from the gutter."

"Perhaps not. But they could steal a child from the palace. And since you prefer to die a thief's death than to live a thief's life . . ."

"Wait, now. Will I really save the child's life?"

"You will."

"And then I'll be free?"

"You will be free."

"And there'll be no tricks? You won't take my soul, or bend my will?"

"I have no need of your soul, or your will, or anything else about you, Banheen, but your thieving skill. This is a business matter. Once you are done, I will assist you in escaping from the city."

Banheen took a deep breath and stuck out his hands. "I'll do it. Get these chains off, and I'll do it."

The visitor produced a dark key and tossed it to Banheen. At once the thief removed the manacles on his wrists and set them gently on the floor, making scarcely a sound. He did the same with the gyves on his ankles. As he reached down to touch the tender flesh, the visitor extended a hand. On his open palm lay a round box.

"Rub this on the raw places. It will ease the pain and stop the blood."

The salve worked swiftly and well. When he finished and looked up, Banheen saw his visitor standing in the doorway of the cell. The door stood open.

Dark-cloaked rescuer in the lead, the two men passed with wary speed down wide corridors and narrow passages. Locked doors fell open at the cloaked man's touch and swung silently shut behind them. They descended, and rose, and descended once again, lower than before; Banheen heard the great subterranean waterways of the city coursing over their heads at one point, and he had a vision of water cascading down upon them through a rupture in the stone. He started at each drop that fell on him from the slick, niter-coated ceiling, but there was no mishap. Their path turned and branched and bent at sharp angles, and before long the thief had lost all sense of direction and could only follow his rescuer blindly.

Even these obscure ways were guarded, and the two were forced to make their way with caution. Twice they passed within touching distance of an armed watcher, but they were not seen.

At last they emerged into a vaulted cellar, where casks of food and wine were stored in long rows that vanished in the far darkness. Here they stopped. The man in the black cloak looked about as if expecting to see someone, and then he drew Banheen into a little alcove where a torch burned. He slid a slender, tightly rolled tube of vellum from his sleeve and thrust it at the thief.

"Study this. It's a plan of the palace. The child is in the chamber marked with the red crown," he said.

Banheen followed the order. The map was very old, and

very detailed, and he had ample time to choose a safe route
to the child's chamber. Having worked out his approach and
his escape, the thief turned his attention to other portions of
the map, pleased to find two tunnels leading to the royal
treasury. But even as he studied them, the other seemed to
read his mind.

"You're to take the child and nothing else, do you hear?"
he said.

"Yes, certainly. I was only. . . . This is a very complete
map."

"The tunnels leading to the treasury are very well guarded.
Do you remember the Society of the Silent Hands? No, no,
you wouldn't. That was before you were born."

"I've heard of them. Nine master thieves, the best of their
time. They all disappeared mysteriously in a single night."

"That's right," said the man in black. "They tried to rob
the vaults; took one of those tunnels you were looking at so
hungrily, the one leading to the river bank. They got into the
treasury easily enough, but when they tried to leave, the door
was barred."

When he said no more, Banheen cautiously asked, "What
. . . happened to them?"

"Still there, I suppose," said the other carelessly. "How
should I know?"

Banheen nodded solemnly and said nothing. He returned
his attention to the map and retraced his routes carefully,
paying particular heed to alternate paths of retreat. His rescuer, meanwhile, maintained a watch on the entrance to their
alcove.

"Are we waiting for someone?" Banheen asked.

"Yes."

"I don't want any help. I always work alone."

"You'll work alone—have no fear of that."

They stood silently for a time, until the cloaked man
suddenly said, "Come along, quickly."

He followed through the dimly torch-lit cellar to where a
lantern flickered at a small postern. The man in black opened
the door and reached out his hands; a tiny bundle was thrust
into them, and the door shut. He hurried off once again,
Banheen at his heels, through a passage that led off the cellar,
and they did not stop until they were at the foot of a narrow
staircase.

"Do you recognize this from the map?" he asked.

"Yes. It leads to the upper passage—the one that goes directly to the marked chamber."

"Good. Here, take this," the man in black said, handing him the bundle.

"It's a baby!" said Banheen, shocked.

"You're to place it in the cradle when you take the other. You must do this, do you understand? If they suspect that the child has been taken, they'll search the kingdom and torture everyone they suspect until he's found. Wrap this one in the other's blanket, and leave him exactly where the other was."

"But they'll kill this one! I can't—it's an awful thing!"

"The child in your arms is dead, Banheen. See for yourself. He's been in a fever since the first day of Ripentide, and he died this evening. And this night he'll serve his rightful lord better than the bravest guardsman. Now go, and be quick."

Banheen left him. The staircase curved as it rose, and soon he was in utter darkness. Only by counting the steps could he keep track of his progress. At the third landing, he left the stairs and felt along the wall until he came upon a narrow opening. He made his cautious way, scraping the walls on either side, counting his footsteps, until he had reached the designated spot. Brushing his sensitive fingertips over the stone, he at last found the pressure point. An easy push and the stone slab pivoted noiselessly, opening a small aperture to the chimney-corner. A low fire burned, but the heat barely reached him.

Licking his dry lips, Banheen squeezed through the opening. Bracing his back against the slab, he removed his shoes and wedged them in the crack to make certain that his avenue of escape would remain open. Then he peeped cautiously into the room—and his heart sank. The interior was brightly torch-lit. Half a dozen paces from the fire stood a cradle. Next to it, between Banheen and his objective, was a chair, and in the chair, wide awake, sewing busily, was a young servant.

Banheen drew back into the farthest recess of the chimney-corner, tucking his feet up, making himself small, thinking furiously. Clearly, his mission could not now be accomplished. Perhaps it was all a test—not only of courage, but of prudence and judgment. And trust. Even now, the man in black might be waiting for him to return with word of the unexpected situation, to ask for his advice.

But the more he thought on it, the more uncomfortably certain he was that the man in the black cloak expected him to return not with an excuse or an appeal, but with the child from the cradle.

He eased forward for another look. The girl sat upright, tapping her foot, singing a foolish song about a fisherman and his bride. He cursed her alertness. Why couldn't the witless wench nod off like any decent servant?

Suddenly, she threw aside her work, sprang to her feet, and ran to the door. Presumably someone had knocked, too softly for Banheen to hear. The girl opened the door and ran to the arms of a tall man who stood outside. In the bright light, Banheen could see the man's clothing clearly. This was no page or servant; only a noble could dress so richly.

They spoke too softly for Banheen to distinguish their words, and their tone had the warmth of lovers' conversation. He heard the man's low laughter joined by hers, and then they embraced once more. They were just at the edge of the doorway now, out of sight of the cradle. It was Banheen's chance. He swallowed, took a deep breath, and sprang into action.

On silent, bare feet, he hurried to the cradle. Quickly he stripped the blankets from the sleeping child, wrapped them about the still form in his arms, and laid the dead infant in the cradle, placing his head in the indentation on the richly embroidered pillow where the other's head had lain. As he turned to make his escape, the living child awoke, and, feeling the chill on his uncovered skin, he began to cry.

Banheen made a desperate dive for the chimney-corner. Once concealed, he stuck the tip of his finger in the squalling infant's mouth. At once the tiny hands closed on his, and the baby began to suck contentedly on the dirty finger.

Banheen breathed a sigh of relief. He was ready to enter the passage, but before he could move, he heard the creaking of the door. He peeped out and saw the man and the girl enter. He dared not move now for fear of giving his presence away.

The lovers kissed, and the man said, "Let's make certain no one disturbs us tonight. Go and bar the door at the far end of the passage."

"I hate to leave you even for so short a time, now that you're here."

"You must, love. If any of my family should find us together, they'd make you suffer for it. We must be secret for a while longer."

"Will we ever be able to declare our love openly?"

"One day I'll be Lord of the High City, and I'll choose for myself. I can promise you that, my dear. Go now, and make us secure."

The instant she left the room, the man leaned over the cradle, took the tiny pillow from under the child's head, and pressed it down over its face. He held it there firmly for the time it might take one to count to two hundred at moderate speed. Removing the pillow and replacing it, he put his ear to the child's breast. He listened for a time, and then he straightened, smiling, and looked down on the still little figure.

"An easy death for you, cousin. And now the throne is one step nearer," he said.

Banheen looked on, horrified. He wanted only the opportunity to escape, but at the same time, he found the sight of such remorseless evil fascinating. The child in his arms, warmed by the fire, had gone to sleep once more; but Banheen did not feel secure.

The girl returned. Banheen made ready to move, expecting that her presence would distract the man long enough for him to make his escape. But more horror was in store for him.

She ran to the man and threw her arms around his neck. He clasped her tight with one arm, burying the other hand in her thick, dark hair. They kissed long. He took his hand from her hair, and Banheen saw her suddenly stiffen and then go completely limp, head lolling back, arms dangling loose at her sides. The man jerked his hand back, and she slumped and fell to the floor, where she lay still. He knelt and wiped his dagger on her skirt.

When the murderer went to the doorway, Banheen moved quickly. He eased the slab closed and hurried barefoot down the narrow passage. He leaned against the smooth wall at the end of the passage, pausing to put on his shoes.

The sound of grating stone startled him. There was a flicker of faint light from the passage he had just left. After a time, there came a soft thud, and the light vanished.

Banheen stood frozen, listening, but no other sound came. He was not being pursued by that wellborn murderer. It came to him in a flash that the sound he had heard was that of the girl's body being deposited in the passage. The corpse would be carried away, and in the morning, when the child was found dead and the girl missing, blame would naturally fall on her, either for murdering the child or for allowing it to die by her own negligence. Her disappearance would be sufficient proof of guilt, and no one else would be suspected.

Heartsick at all this treachery, Banheen made his way to the place where he and his rescuer had parted. He longed to be out of this palace, this city. Corruption among the nobility was one thing—he could not bring himself to condemn a bit of stealing, even by amateurs—but murdering infants and foolish servants was quite another. He wanted no part of it.

One last surprise awaited him. When he came to the foot of the staircase, the cloaked man was nowhere in sight. A candle burned on the last step. A note was wedged under it, and a purse lay beside it.

Banheen took up the purse. It was heavy. He reached in and drew out a five-oak piece. The purse was packed with them—no less than thirty, surely, and perhaps more. Stowing it safely inside his shirt, he stooped to pick up the note and read it.

The gold is your reward. Take the passage under the staircase. Leave by the third door on the left. Go to Long Wood by the Northern Road and take up an honest life there, as a widower with a son. Name the boy Genlon, and raise him well.

I will find him when the time is right.

Banheen frowned, surprised and angered by the message. Raising a child had been no part of the agreement, nor had an arduous trip over the Plain, into the mountains, and west to Long Wood. This was hardly fair.

On the other hand, Long Wood was far away and safe, and a man could live well there on a purse full of golden oaks. He would never have to steal again. He might buy himself a mill, or a tannery, or a farm, and if he prospered, he would have no fear of thieves because he knew all their tricks plus a few of his own. And this poor, naked child could not be abandoned; that would be inhuman.

Banheen took up the candle. Wrapping the child in a bit of sacking, he ducked into the passage under the staircase.

Banheen traveled by night, avoiding all contact with others until he reached Northern Road. Posing as a widower merchant from the Crystal Hills, he joined a caravan on its way to the Fastness. It proved to be a pleasant journey. The women in the caravan doted on the poor, motherless child and were sympathetic to the bereaved father. Most sympathetic of all was a handsome widow, a slim, fine-looking, soft-voiced woman with dark brown eyes and hair the color of honey. In her brief marriage there had been no children, and she spoke lovingly to Banheen's little son and begged to hold him as often as she could. The boy, in turn, seemed to like her. Banheen liked her very much.

The widow's name was Ketial. She was on her way home to the western reaches of Long Wood, having lost her husband in the mines of the Crystal Hills. When Banheen learned that she was leaving the caravan when they reached the Fastness, he was greatly pleased at the prospect of her extended company.

The Fastness was a great, forbidding pile of stone, deep in the mountains that divided the Plain from Long Wood. High, concentric walls ringed a cluster of massive towers and rugged buildings, all raised ages ago, by unknown hands, to protect against some long-forgotten enemy. It now served as the westernmost outpost of the High City, a garrison for the guards who patrolled the mountain routes, and a resting place for the caravans.

Banheen gallantly took upon himself all the arrangements for Ketial's stay, making certain that he had a room near hers. When her few possessions were safely stowed, Banheen excused himself, claiming that he needed to see to some business affairs. At Ketial's insistence, the child remained with her.

Banheen sought out a quiet corner in the crowded, noisy caravansary that occupied the space between the third and fourth walls of the Fastness, and in his seclusion he thought deeply and seriously on his situation. He was a man of substance now, with a hundred and fifty golden oaks in his purse. There was no need for him ever to steal again, and that was a good thing, for thieving was a young man's trade, and the nimble days of Banheen's youth were behind him. He was also a man with responsibilities. The child required a home, and a proper home required the presence of a woman. Perhaps some people could be father and mother to a child, but that was beyond Banheen's ability. He foresaw enough difficulty simply in becoming a law-abiding citizen.

Ketial was as fine a woman as Banheen had ever known. She and the child seemed fond of each other, and Banheen was becoming increasingly fond of Ketial. He realized, to his astonishment, that he might very well be in love with her. Not that it was astonishing that a man would love such a woman—indeed, it was the most natural thing in the world—but Banheen was a thief and a fugitive, a man who only days before had been chained in a cell awaiting his ignominious death, and for him now to be contemplating marriage to such a fine, beautiful, kindly woman as Ketial was something close to miraculous.

He raised his glass of wine in a silent, private salute to the man in the black cloak. Whoever he was, wizard, conspirator, or spy, he had opened a new life to Banheen and earned a thief's thanks for doing it. Banheen drained his glass, made his decision, and set about the necessities.

That evening, freshly barbered and dressed in fine new clothes, he dined with Ketial in her chamber, a small room in the third wall. It was at the highest level, clean and bright, and the noise and dust of the caravansary seemed very far away. When the last traces of the meal had been removed, Banheen poured two thumb-sized glasses of sweet wine and turned the talk to Ketial's plans.

"I'll stay at the inn. My father will need my help. He's all alone now," she said.

"Where is this inn of your father's?"

"Three days' travel to the south and west of the Fool's Head. It won't be his much longer, though. He's gone into debt, you see, and there's no hope of his paying. But he's found a man who'll buy the inn for enough to pay all the debts, and even let us stay on and work there."

"Is that what you want to do?" Banheen asked.

"It's what I must do."

"Yes, but if you could choose, would you choose to do that?"

She weighed the question for a time; then she said, "I would return to the inn, I think, though I'd not want it in the hands of others. It's a lovely old place, Banheen, and the woods around are beautiful. There's a little pond, and a stream, and an orchard on the hillside. I always hoped we'd return and raise our children there." She sighed and lowered her eyes.

"You might do so yet."

Ketial looked up, startled. "How?"

"Well, you're young . . ."

"My husband is dead, Banheen, and we had no children. With my father to care for, I'll have no chance for marriage. I'm not happy to think of it, but that's how it must be."

"No, it isn't. It could be different."

"I couldn't leave the old man alone. That would be cruel."

"No, I don't mean that. What I mean . . . well, you seem to like Genlon, and the little fellow is fond of you."

"I hope so, Banheen. He's a fine child."

"And I must tell you, Ketial," Banheen said, plunging ahead, "that from the very moment I saw you in the caravan, walking by yourself in the early sunshine, all the sadness seemed to drop from me, and I knew I could be a happy man again. And when I spoke to you, and saw how you and Genlon got on, I just knew. I want you to marry me, Ketial. We'll raise Genlon at the inn, just as you wanted, and we'll have children of our own to keep him company."

"But Banheen, it's so soon for you to remarry—are you sure?"

Banheen had not thought of this objection, but he paused only a moment before taking her hands in his and saying, "All I know is that I could search for half my life and more and not find anyone else like you. I love you, Ketial, and I want to marry you."

Her dawning smile made his heart beat faster, but when the smile turned to a sudden look of dismay, his heart almost stopped. "But how can we, Banheen? The inn will be ours no longer, and there'll be my father to care for."

Banheen sighed with relief. Squeezing her hands reassuringly, he said, "You need not worry about that, my love. I'll see to it."

"He owes at least ten oaks, Banheen! That's more money than he ever saw at one time!"

"Ket, my dearest, when I set out upon this journey I promised myself I'd take up a new life. I've settled all my affairs, and I can think of nothing I'd rather do than pay your father's debts and set about learning the innkeeper's trade."

Again she looked troubled by his words. "My father is a proud man, Banheen. He might think you were buying me."

"Do you think that, Ket?"

"No, I do not. I believe you do love me, for I had the same feeling for you when first I saw you."

"Then between us we'll convince your father. It's as well for me to buy his inn as for a stranger, isn't it? We'll run it together, the three of us, until he's ready to let you and me go it alone."

Ketial thought for a time about that, while Banheen looked lovingly at her studious profile in the fading light from the window. She turned to him, and with a smile that made him weak with joy she said, "Then I will marry you, Banheen."

Banheen was all for marrying that very night, in the Fastness, but Ketial insisted that her father be present at the wedding. Accordingly, Banheen made every effort to get them on their way at once. They were less than halfway to their destination, and travel along the forest paths of Long Wood could be maddeningly slow in the autumn storms, which would soon be upon them.

They left the Fastness the very next morning, traveling through the mountains with a caravan bound for the Headland. At the edge of Long Wood, they set out on their own. Inns and small homesteads were more frequent as they moved westward, and many of the innkeepers knew Ketial's father, and they made the couple and the child welcome. At every inn, there was conversation until late into the night, Ketial giving all the news of the lands beyond the river and catching up on events in Long Wood, while Banheen listened, tempering his impatience with the consolation that he was learning in the best and quickest way the manners of his future home.

They crossed the Fool's Head on a crisp, clear day. The water was calm as a mirror, and the first touch of autumn blazed in the woods all around the lake, redoubled in reflection. Banheen, who had spent all his life in the High City and come to believe that no man could ask for more beauty than was found within its walls, was humbled and moved by the sight. This was indeed a lovely place. He looked on Ketial, who sat before him in the bow of the narrow boat with Genlon in her arms, and he smiled in pure contentment. He had a beautiful wife-to-be who loved him as much as he loved her, a healthy young child to be his son, a purse of oaks in his shirt, and pleasant life ahead in this magnificent forest, far from the scenes of the past. He sighed and blessed his unknown benefactor, the man in the black cloak.

Ketial's father turned out to have more debts and less pride than either of them had anticipated, and he accepted Banheen's offer without cavil; indeed, he did so with great enthusiasm, for there was an immediate affinity on both sides. The wedding took place twelve days after their return.

Banheen found, to his continuous surprise, that the life of a forest innkeeper suited him perfectly; and he learned, to his delight, that married life was not the unrelenting warfare that some of his old companions had called it, nor a cage, nor a wasteland, but a very comfortable and pleasant way of life. He worked hard, took pride in his family, and prospered. He became known throughout the region for his fair dealing.

The years were not without their share of sorrow. Ketial's father died suddenly one winter morning as he rose from his bed. Her third and fourth children were stillborn, and she nearly lost her own life giving birth to a son, their last child, whom they named Feron. But the sorrows passed, and the good things softened the bad memories.

Their greatest source of happiness was Genlon, who grew into a splendid youth. By his twelfth summer, he was as tall as Banheen. At sixteen, he had to stoop to walk through the door of the inn. He was the tallest man for greatmarks around, and very probably the strongest. It was difficult to be certain, for he seemed inclined rather to conceal his strength than to display it. He was cheerful and easygoing, quick to smile at his occasional clumsiness. With his auburn hair and clear green eyes, he bore no resemblance to his supposed father, who was dark-haired, blue-eyed, and slight of build. Banheen, whenever the subject arose, attributed the boy's coloring to his mother and his stature to the healthy life of the forest.

Banheen had his own explanation, and he kept it close to himself. He well recalled the single close look he had had at Iytrigon, ninth lord of the High City. The ruler's hair and beard were white then, but they had once been auburn; his eyes were icy green, and he towered over his tallest guardsmen. Banheen had no doubt about the parentage of the child he had rescued, and no qualms about keeping it a secret from him. Here, as Genlon Banheenson, the boy was loved and admired. He lived a happy life, worked hard, and had good friends. If he were ever to return to the High City and reveal himself as Ambescand, rightful lord, happiness and friendship would be gone from his life, and he would be in constant danger. To know the truth would do him no service; it would almost certainly do him harm.

Banheen remembered, from time to time, the promise of his deliverer concerning the boy: "I will find him when the time is right." He told himself that on that day—if it ever came—he would tell Genlon all, and not before. The years passed, and no visitor came to ask for the boy. Genlon completed his seventeenth summer, pondered his situation, and announced to his parents that he was ready to set out on his faring year.

CHAPTER TWO

THE SHAPING OF
THE KINGDOM

The death of his infant son was the blow that broke the spirit of Pytrigon, ninth lord of the High City. He had suffered other losses in his life, deep and wounding ones, but none that affected him as this did. His two eldest sons had died in battle; his daughter had been taken by a sudden illness nine days before she was to marry; his first wife and his second had died in childbirth. He had mourned them all, as befit his bond, and then he had taken up his duties as a ruler once more. But the death of Ambescand, the child of his old age, was more than he could bear.

Once the child had been interred, Pytrigon withdrew almost completely from public life. On the rare occasions when he appeared before the people, the crowds sorrowed at the speed with which age and feebleness had come upon him. He mumbled to himself and glanced fitfully about during even the most solemn of ceremonies. Oftentimes he would start, as if awakened from a dream, or as if he had heard unexpectedly a familiar voice close by. He never smiled, and he was seldom heard to speak to others.

It was said by some and believed by many that in his last days he had turned to magic, whether for consolation or for remedy, no one could say. This was taken as a sure sign of his decay, for in his strength, Pytrigon had been a merciless enemy of the sorcery that had once again risen in the northern lands and had even made its way to the High City. But now, said rumor, adepts of the dark art came to his chamber by secret ways and practiced their magic at his bidding. What price they exacted from their old adversary could not be guessed. On the night the ninth lord died, clutching in his dry, bony hands the tiny blanket that had wrapped the infant Ambescand, thunder rolled, and lightning struck the walls of the High City, reaching down out of a cloudless sky. There

26

were those who believed that these were signs that something more than human had come to collect its due.

The mourning time was brief, for the affairs of state had been too long neglected. Pytrigon's brother Qunlac succeeded him as tenth lord of the High City.

Qunlac was a hard man, of no more than ordinary intelligence but of great determination. He believed in force, displayed it prominently, and used it at will. On the very day of his accession, he dispatched forces to all the frontiers. He enlarged the garrisons at Northmark and Southmark, and he strengthened the walls of the Fastness, the great fortress deep in the mountains to the west. Within the High City, he took up the old struggle against the practitioners of the dark mysteries. Men and women suspected or accused of sorcery were broken on the wheel, beheaded, or burned with their books and implements.

Qunlac was never loved, and he never sought to be. He had the fear and respect of his subjects, and, most important, he had their obedience. If his reign brought suffering to a few, it brought a welcome sense of order to most.

His death was sudden. It came in the fourth year of his reign, at a great banquet, when he was seized by a choking fit. Those who were near when it happened never spoke of what they had seen, and many of the people of the High City believed that the sorcerers had at last taken their revenge on Qunlac.

Far worse, in the people's minds, than the death itself was the chief result of Qunlac's passing: since he left no heir of his body, his brother Guldergance became eleventh lord of the High City. He was a weak and foolish man who had come to middle age in the shadow of two strong brothers. He had never dreamed of the possibility of succession, and the fact of it overwhelmed him. Guldergance died less than a year after his brother, having accomplished nothing in his brief reign, and the rule passed to the last known surviving member of the family, his son Duarin.

Duarin took his place with manifest pleasure, and despite his youth, he set about his duties like a man assuming a well-rehearsed role. He was different from his father in every way; so very different that there was much speculation about his true parentage. He had the cold intelligence of Pytrigon and the decisive will of Qunlac, and in appearance he was said to resemble his father's father, the mighty eighth lord,

Tallisan. Of Guldergance's timidity and indecisiveness he showed no trace.

One of Duarin's early edicts ended the persecution of the sorcerers. It was recalled that his mother had been banished from the High City under pain of death in the reign of Pytrigon, and that there had been rumors at the time that she had plotted against him by sorcery. But if Duarin sought to befriend the sorcerers, he showed no evidence of his intent. He displayed no further sympathy to practitioners of magic, nor did he extend them his favor. It appeared that his toleration was based on a wise expediency and nothing more. The twelfth lord of the High City had far-reaching plans, and he wanted no domestic distractions while he carried them out.

In time, Duarin's ambition was clear to all; but in those early days, he confided in no one. He built his scheme slowly, piece by piece, and he carried it out methodically. Only when it had succeeded was it apparent.

First, he summoned the historian of the High City and bade him recite his official account of the ancient times. For twelve successive nights the old man spoke, telling of deeds and men and events from the times of legend until the days of Tallisan. When the historian had told all he knew, Duarin went himself to the archives, where he read much and pondered long on what he found. Then he called the historian to him once more.

"I am lord of the High City, twelfth to reign under that title," he said. "But there was a time when the one who sat in my place was known as king of the Northern Lands. Why did this change?"

"It befell in the time of Aluca, as my lord must know," said the historian.

"I know the fact. I ask the reason."

"Aluca, and the five Alucan lords who succeeded him, were known for their love of peace and their generosity toward their subjects. They chose to rule over the city and allow the outer territories to govern themselves, provided that they remained loyal to the lord of the city."

"Is this what you believe?" Duarin asked.

"This is what has been said and recorded, my lord. All men believe it."

"Then all men are very foolish, and so are you. No ruler gives up so easily what has been won by war and bloodshed.

It took a long time to build the northern kingdom, and Aluca dissolved it in a single day. Has no one ever wondered why?"

"He reached his destiny at a tender age, my lord. In the purity and innocence of youth, he—"

"Purity and innocence? Use the proper term, old man. *Weakness.*"

The historian averted his eyes and gestured uncertainly. He could not speak ill of a past lord in the presence of a successor, and so he remained silent.

"Certain facts are obvious," Duarin went on. "Aluca's claim to the throne was disputed by his cousin, a warrior of formidable achievements. Yet all those of influence united behind this sickly boy to destroy his rival. And Aluca's first act on coming to power was to grant them the independence they could not have wrung from his cousin in a lifetime of battle."

"Aluca was generous in his gratitude, my lord."

"Aluca was a stupid child who grew into a stupid man, and his descendants followed his example. The whole dynasty was rotten and weak—not a true leader in four generations. Tallisan was the first lord with the courage and the will to reclaim the kingdom, but by then, there were other problems to face."

"Indeed so, my lord. All his reign, he fought the sea-raiders," said the historian, warming to this safer topic. "Not until the days of Pytrigon were they finally driven off."

Duarin nodded. "And by then, the nomads were starting to move north. It took all the city's strength to turn them back."

"Costly victories they were, too, my lord," said the historian solemnly. "They claimed the lives of the two oldest sons of Pytrigon."

Duarin smiled; then he laughed softly. "A cost I bear willingly. An excellent bargain." Still laughing, he dismissed the historian.

Soon afterward, he conferred with the keeper of the treasury and studied the accounts of the city's dealings. He was thorough, going over transactions from the earliest days to those recorded in Pytrigon's time. What he found when he perused the records of the last king's reign confirmed his suspicion.

"Tell me," he demanded of the treasurer, "when did we last receive tin from the mines in the Crystal Hills?"

"The tin trade has been most irregular of late, my lord. The last to arrive was in the twenty-sixth summer of Pytrigon's reign."

"And did we pay?"

"We paid for it in grain, my lord. The entry is here, in my own hand."

"Did they send any silver?"

"No silver has arrived since the reign of Tallisan, my lord, and very little then. Those were troubled times."

"What of hides, and preserved meat and fish, from the Headland? Trade is brisk, I believe."

The treasurer brightened. "It is indeed, my lord. We purchased a good supply at the end of Yellowleaf last, and more is promised by early Barebranch."

Duarin nodded and repeated, "And did we pay?"

"We paid in the services of our artisans, my lord."

"And the timber from Long Wood and the Southern Forest . . . the stone from the mountain quarries . . . have these been duly purchased and paid for from the city treasury?"

"They have, my lord."

Duarin was silent for a time. The treasurer stood before him expectantly. He was a methodical, unimaginative man, scrupulously honest out of fear of the consequences of dishonesty, and these questions made him uneasy. His apprehension increased as the silence drew on. At last, Duarin said, "Did you know that when the last king was on his throne, a hundred grandweights of tin—two hundred ingots of the highest purity—were brought to him from the Crystal Hills on the first day of each Ripentide?"

"I know nothing of that, my lord," the treasurer confessed, mystified.

"The custom was ancient then, and unbroken. And now it is forgotten. And did you know of the timber brought over the mountains from Long Wood, and the fine logs floated upriver from the Southern Forest? The three hundred skids of building stone, shaped and dressed, from the mountains? And the silver from the Crystal Hills, and gold from the mountains north of the Fastness?"

"It was long ago, my lord."

"It was. And were you aware that all this was not bought with grain, or the skills of our artisans, but was given, in fear and respect, as tribute? Yet now, we purchase. The palace of a king has become the house of a merchant. What do you think of this, treasurer? Tell me."

The treasurer looked at him helplessly. "We do have need of all these things, my lord. We must obtain them somehow."

Duarin looked at him with obvious displeasure, but he nodded in agreement with his words. Without further talk, he dismissed the man.

After this, Duarin began to show a great interest in the city guard. He had decided to form a small personal bodyguard, and he intended to select the men himself. There were to be thirty-six men and three junior officers; Duarin himself would be their commander.

Selection was a slow and careful process, in the course of which Duarin came to know every man in the guard by name. They were a well-trained, highly disciplined force, armed with the finest weapons available, trained by master swordsmen from the lands far to the west, where the blade was a more common weapon; but their number was small, and the younger men had never faced an enemy.

Duarin dined frequently with the guards, and he often stayed at their quarters until late in the night, drinking ordinary wine and listening to old campaigners' stories. On occasion, he had the senior officers to his own quarters. One evening, when the guard commander and his aide were dining with Duarin, he asked the commander's opinion of his choices for the bodyguard.

"You've picked the best men, my lord. Fine soldiers, every one, and loyal to the death," said the commander.

"I'm glad you think so. I only have to choose four more, and I'll have my thirty-nine. By the way, once that's done, I'll be taking them with me to inspect the frontiers. I'd like you to come with us."

"I'd be honored, my lord."

Duarin smiled and pushed the wine jug to the old soldier. "It's not just an honor. I'll need you. From what I've heard, no one knows the outposts as well as you."

"I've served at all of them; it's true."

"And you're something of a historian, as well."

The commander, embarrassed, murmured, "Oh, I've learned to read a bit, my lord, and I've heard the stories the old campaigners told. Not much of a historian, really. Just interested in the guard and what it's done, that's all."

"I've heard differently. Some of the men told me you know

all about the old times, before Aluca. I've often wondered about our strength in those days."

"It was great, my lord."

"Northmark and Southmark, I've heard, were garrisons on a busy trade route, not the remote outposts they are now."

"That's true, my lord. And the Fastness, as well. It was used to protect the trail leading to Long Wood and then north, toward the Headland."

"It still is, isn't it?"

"Yes. But there's only a handful of troops there now."

"That's interesting," Duarin said, taking a sip of his wine and sitting thoughtfully silent for a time. Abruptly, he said, "Tell me, commander, how many men would be stationed at the garrisons in those days?"

"In the days of the kings, as far as I've been able to learn, there were a hundred men at Northmark, a bit more than that—say, a hundred ten or so—at Southmark, and close to five hundred at the Fastness. And, of course, there were regular patrols along the frontiers."

Duarin nodded. "The High City must have had a good-sized force in those days."

"We were a kingdom then, my lord. There was a longer frontier and a lot more territory to protect, and now and then there were heads to knock together. Every few years a hothead would turn up in the Crystal Hills, or the Southern Forest, and complain about the tribute." The commander smiled, wistfully, and went on, "Nothing to do but send up a force of guardsmen to bang some sense into people. The tribute kept coming."

"I wonder, commander . . . could it ever be that way again?"

"I don't think so, my lord. Lord Qunlac asked the same question of us when he came to power, I recall."

"What did you tell him?" Duarin asked.

"We could do it if we had the men, but we haven't, and I don't know where we can get them."

"Mercenaries?" Duarin suggested.

The commander frowned and shook his head. "Mercenaries are bad business, my lord. There's always a chance the other side will make them a better offer."

"True," said Duarin thoughtfully.

"You see, my lord, with a kingdom you've got a sizable pool of manpower to draw on, and a treasury to fund an army. But we're a city now, and a lot of our people are merchants and artisans. Decent people, but not the stuff of an army. They want to be protected, not do the fighting."

"We've got good, strong men in the settlements on the plain."

"We do, my lord," the commander conceded, "but we can't draw off too many of them. We need the food they produce. A starving army's no good to anyone."

"Certainly not," Duarin agreed. "Tell me this, then: how big a force do you think we could assemble from our present resources?"

After à moment's consideration, the commander said, "We could double the size of the guard before summer. We'd have to lower standards a bit—wouldn't get men like the ones you're picking for the bodyguard, that's certain—but we could do it."

"I don't think you'd be happy with that kind of a force under you—am I right, commander?"

"Not for me to say, my lord. I could toughen them up, given time. But the best way to make an army out of a bunch of recruits is to have a reason for them to be an army. We're in no danger now. The sea-raiders have been slain to the last man, and the nomads won't soon forget what we did to them at Southmark. There's work for everyone now, and people are leading good lives. They're contented. To put it simply, my lord, it's hard to take contented men, with no enemy threatening their homes, and turn them into an army."

"Well said, commander. You make sense," said Duarin. Turning to the aide, he said, "If there's anything you'd like to add, we'll both listen."

"The commander's said it all, my lord," said the younger man without hesitation. "We have a good force of guardsmen now, because we've picked the best and given them the best training. Unless there's a clear threat to the city, I don't think we'd improve the guard by enlarging it."

"Not from our present resources, certainly. I think we're all agreed on that," said Duarin. "But what if we were to look elsewhere? Not mercenaries, no, I'm thinking of some of the strong youth of Long Wood, or the Headland, or the Crystal Hills. Their lives are hard, and they might be glad of a chance to enlist in the city guard."

The commander took a draft of wine and thought for a

time before saying, "We might find the makings of some fine guardsmen out there, my lord, it's true. But could we trust their loyalty?"

Duarin refilled his mug and raised it to the commander. "I trust you to teach them where their loyalty lies."

Early in the following spring, little groups of guardsmen from the High City began to visit the inns and markets of the neighboring lands. They were fine-looking men, tall and strong, and their helmets and breastplates shone like silver. Long swords hung at their sides, but the blades remained sheathed, for these men came in friendship. The pouches at their sides were heavy with coin, and they spent freely.

To the young men who looked upon them with an uneasy mixture of envy and admiration, they told of Lord Duarin's enterprise. The twelfth lord of the High City, they said, had received word that the nomadic tribes of the far south had found a bold new leader. Under him, they were gathering to unite and march against the High City and all the peaceful lands of the north. Duarin was organizing an army to march against the nomads and smash them before they reached the River Issalt; then they would go on to level the nomads' homeland from frontier to frontier. Here was an opportunity for a few good men—strong and smart, with the courage to strike deep into an enemy's homeland and the toughness to endure forced marches to a faraway battlefield—to win honor and rich prizes, and to be part of an enterprise whose fame would live as long as the deeds of Tallisan.

The young men listened eagerly, and they left the company of these splendid swordsmen befuddled as much by dreams of glory and adventure as by the drink they had downed. In the light of morning, when they considered the prospect, most of them chose to remain at home, to marry the girls they had walked with since childhood, who might not wait for their return, all covered with glory, from the wars, and to live the lives their fathers, and their fathers' fathers, and all the past generations of their families had lived. The security of the familiar had too great an appeal for them. But a few, the best and the bravest among them, laid down their tools, and said their farewells, and followed the way to the High City.

For a long time, there was no glory for them, and no plunder—only hard work, day after grueling day, as they trained under the commander's cold eye. Some were found wanting and were sent back to their farms and cottages. A few slipped from the High City in darkness and set out to wander the world and make what they could of their lives. The rest stayed, and learned, and grew harder, and at last they became guardsmen.

In their first encounter, they turned back the nomads. They pursued, and they fought three more battles, and finally they sent the nomad forces into helpless flight. With that enemy defeated, they sought new ones. Farther south they pressed, into arid lands where all was strange and different, and they saw sights and took prizes undreamed of in the lands of their birth.

When they marched back along the coast road, marked with battle, fewer in number but as close and well coordinated as the fingers of a hand, nine years had passed. They were an army second to none. They remembered little of the scenes of their youth. They longed to return to the High City—their city, now—where a hero's welcome awaited them.

Duarin was not idle while his army was in the field. He was seen much about the High City, more than the other lords had ever been. Always he went in his war armor, accompanied by a squad of his personal bodyguard.

He restored certain practices forgotten since the days of the kings. Regular announcements of the army's progress were made from the steps of the palace. Whenever a train of wagons arrived from the south, with litters of the wounded and a cargo of plunder, a great holiday was declared in the High City. The treasures of the south were set out for display to all, and the wounded warriors were feted as heroes. The relief column of replacements was sent off to the cheers of all the people, and the men departed eager for glory.

Something was reborn in the High City. A pride, a sense of destiny unknown since the days of Aluca, the first lord, could be felt wherever citizens gathered. Visitors noticed it at once, for they were sure to be told by everyone they met that this was the best and most beautiful of cities: its army was the bravest, its scholars the wisest, its artisans the most skillful in all the lands of the north. And the visitors found themselves agreeing. Many chose to stay.

Not all of Duarin's activity in this time was public; some of it was conducted in the utmost privacy. Only a handful of people were involved in his most secret undertaking, and none knew more of it than his particular role, nor did any man dare to ask what more there was.

The keeper of the prison knew only that an unnamed man was authorized to visit a certain dungeon at irregular intervals, perhaps a score of times during the years of the southern campaign. Each time he visited, a small group of the worst criminals—all of them condemned—disappeared from the prison and were never seen or heard of again. The turnkey of the lower dungeon knew only that he was to admit the hooded man and the four armed guards who walked behind him, two by two, swords drawn, and to allow them to depart with whatever prisoners they chose to bring with them. All the executioner knew was that when the man in the dark hood came, he was to be ready for work. Sometimes there was none; but more often, one or two men were dragged to him for his immediate attention.

Duarin's visitations all followed the same pattern. Each was preceded by careful study of the prisoner list and a comparison of that list with the city rolls. A new list of prisoners was then drawn up, by Duarin himself, and delivered in secret to the keeper. The men whose names appeared on that list were taken from their cells and assembled in a dungeon apart from all the others. There they waited for they knew not what.

Duarin's last visit, made just two days before the victorious return of the southern army, was typical of all. With his face concealed, he arrived at the prison after midnight, traveling through passages known to no one but but himself, and went directly to the lower portion. The turnkey and four guards were waiting. At his signal, they proceeded to the far dungeon, the turnkey in the lead, Duarin at the center of a quincunx, four guards forming the corners.

The clatter of bolts and crash of doors at this unexpected hour jolted the prisoners into fearful wakefulness. When the great door of the dungeon was flung wide, and four burly men clutching torches and swords appeared at the top of the steps, they were sure their last moment had come. They waited, breathless with fear, for an agonizing interval, until a fifth man entered and came partway down the steps. He was not so big as the swordsmen, but he was a tall man all the same, and he walked with a confident and dignified bear-

ing. At a signal from him, two of the swordsmen descended
to the step above him and raised their torches.

The prisoners gasped at the sight. Their visitor wore a tight-
fitting hood that concealed all but his eyes and mouth. It was
all too similar to the hood worn by the executioner. One man
began to weep and cry for mercy.

"Be still, scum," said the man on the steps. When there
was silence, he went on, "You are the dregs of the High
City. Twelve of you lie in this cell, every one a thief. Some
are murderers, rapists, and arsonists as well. You're all condemned to die a thief's death—or worse, if the Lord Duarin
chooses to inflict worse. And you know you deserve no better,
do you not? Answer me!"

They murmured their grudging assent, and he went on,
"But some of you may be spared."

For a moment they were stunned into absolute silence;
then a babble of questions burst forth. The hooded man
stood impassive until the prisoners were still once more; then
he descended two steps more before speaking.

"I have it in my power to deliver you this very night. If I
do, you must go far from here, across the plain, through the
mountains, and deep into the part of Long Wood that lies
beyond the Fool's Head. On your way, you must see no one,
speak to no one—above all, you must claim no victims. You
will be given provisions sufficient for the journey." He paused
then, waiting for the question he knew must come.

"Why?" said one of the prisoners.

"Yes, why do you do this?" another called out.

A third, a slim, wiry thief with grizzled hair, said, "What
do you ask in return?"

"I require only that you take up your trade in Long Wood.
Kill, steal, rape, plunder, burn . . . do what you will. The
worse your deeds, the more pleased I'll be," said the hooded
man.

There was an outburst of confusion, amazement, and wild,
unbelieving hilarity. When the hubbub had subsided, he went
on, "You will be subject to two inflexible conditions. You
must remain together without increasing the size of your
band beyond the number who leave the prison tonight. And
you must never return to the city—never, under any circumstances whatever. If you should be found in the city after
tonight, you'll be flayed alive—after you've watched all your
kinfolk die. Is that understood?"

The wiry thief stood and peered hard at the hooded man. "I understand well enough, and I will accept. But who are you?"

"I am one who is not deceived. If you think to cheat on this bargain, and escape to the west or south, think of it no more. Each of you has ties to the city." Pointing to the wiry thief with the grizzled hair, he said, "You, Iosmut, have three children. You've been a poor father to them, but all the same I doubt that you'd like to see them at the end of a rope." To the man at Iosmut's side, he said, "Your parents are sick, but not too sick to climb the scaffold." And then he encompassed the rest in a gesture and said, "You all have kin in the city. Do as I bid you, and they'll be protected and provided for, better than you could ever hope to do it yourself."

Iosmut and the men beside him exchanged glances. "We're your men," said Iosmut.

"If any man prefers to trust to luck, or the mercy of the Lord Duarin, let him speak."

A young man pushed his way forward and stopped at the foot of the steps. Ducking his head respectfully, he said, "Sir, I'm grateful to you for your offer of freedom—"

The hooded man broke in, "But you do not wish your life and freedom under my conditions."

"Oh, no, sir, I do. But this is my first crime. My brother has won great honor against the nomads. . . . My wife is going to appeal direct to Lord Duarin. She's certain I'll be shown mercy," the man said falteringly.

"Perhaps you will. Go, then. The guard will return you to your cell," said the hooded man. "Are there any others?"

No others stepped forth. A guard took the young man from the dungeon and led him away, deep into the prison. The executioner was waiting in a little cell. The others in the prison never heard the young man's despairing cry.

The prisoners were securely blindfolded. When the fourth guard returned, they were led from the dungeon, and each was given a scrip of food and a waterbag. Iosmut was given extra of each and told to share it with the others when they were safely out of the city. Then prisoners and guards, led by the hooded man, set forth on a long, intricate track that wound upon itself, rose, descended, and twisted until no man but the guide could have guessed whether they were halfway to the plain or back where they had started. At last, they stopped, and at the order of the hooded man, the blindfolds were removed from the two biggest prisoners. They blinked and rubbed their eyes and looked down at a ring sunk in the floor of the corridor. The hooded man pointed to a rope fastened on the wall.

"Lower the hook and fix it in the ring. Haul up the door and push it to one side. Quickly," he said.

At their first tug, nothing moved. Then the floor quivered slightly under the ring, and the faint outline of a circle appeared in the dust. A few hard tugs and the round door was raised high enough to be moved aside. The sound of flowing water rose from the opening.

"Head downstream. Keep to the right at every branching. You'll come out on the plain by daybreak. Remember, you're to have no contact with anyone until you're west of the Fool's Head," said the hooded man.

"How deep is it down there? I'm no swimmer," said one man nervously.

"There's been no rain for five days. It's no more than knee-deep. You two go down first," the hooded man said to the two who had raised the stone.

The others dropped down as soon as their blindfolds were removed. When the last one was on his way, holding high the torch the guard had thrown to him, two guards replaced the stone. Duarin then blindfolded the guards with his own hand and led them back to the palace by a different route.

This was the last band he planned to loose. At least four packs of desperate brigands were now at large in each of the neighboring lands. His victorious army was on its way home. Duarin knew that he had only to be patient for a little longer.

CHAPTER THREE

THE BARROW AND THE BLADE

Beware, beware, the barrow-wight
Who comes to life in darkest night!
Beware, beware his grinding jaws,
Beware his curving, catching claws!
Beware the barrow where he sleeps,
And shun the treasure that he keeps,
And let the sea-kings slumber still,
Or barrow-wight will wake and kill!
        —Song of the northern mountain people

The faring year was a custom observed throughout Long Wood. No one knew its true origin, only that it had begun long ago, in the hunting times, before the taming of Long Wood to the uses of men. Every region had its own legend, and half the families in Long Wood claimed that one of their remote forebears had been the first farer.

No inflexible rules governed the faring year, and there was no authority but that of custom and conscience to guide one in the observance. The proper time was left to the individual. For practical reasons, it usually fell between the fifteenth and twentieth years. In theory, every firstborn child, whether male or female, sound or sickly, timid or venturesome, was obliged to spend a year away from home, wandering in solitude, seeking some token of the direction his or her future life would take. In practice, this was not always so. A few sought diligently and found something that changed their lives in unexpected ways, but most youths passed the year in desultory roving. For some, the faring year was an obstacle looming between childhood and a settled adult life, and these did little more than camp in a distant corner of their families' land, eat as many meals as they could under the familiar roofs, and return to their accustomed lives at the first touch of inclement weather. A very few wandered far

and returned long after, much changed, or never returned
at all. Of these last, sad tales were told and melancholy songs
sung on the long winter nights.

As the month of Longdays ended and Greenblade drew
on, bringing his seventeenth birthday near, Genlon Banheenson decided that the time for his faring year had come.
He was not unhappy with his present life, nor restless to
change it; but he had a growing suspicion that this was not
the life he was destined to lead. He, who had never been
known to lose his temper nor to strike a blow in anger, had
in recent months had dreams of leading men into battle.
Several times, the chill of the sweat drying on his chest and
back had roused him from a fantasy of war against some un-
imaginable inhuman power to find himself standing idle
with ax in hand. There were no armies in Long Wood, and
the only demons he knew were those in the tales told at the
fireside. Yet the visions were clear, and they troubled Genlon.

Once, long ago, when he was a child, a pair of guardsmen
from the High City, splendid in their gleaming silver breastplates, scarlet cloaks, and plumed helmets, had visited his
parents' inn. All the local young men had clustered around to
hear them speak of a great expedition to the south, against
marauding nomads. Genlon had listened in awe to words he
did not fully comprehend, and he had looked on with fascination. There was glory to be won, and treasure to be taken, if
a man were brave enough and strong enough to earn a place
in the guard. And there was a promise of something else,
something fierce and yet joyous, that could not be put into
words but shone in the guardsmen's eyes as they clapped
their hands on their sword hilts and remembered long-ago
battles. The Polter brothers had gone with the guardsmen, he
recalled, and other youths had traveled to the High City in
the years that followed. Perhaps he was remembering those
things now as a sign that his destiny lay in the martial life,
defending the honor and beauty of the great city that had
once ruled all the lands of the north.

And yet he loved the forests and the waters and the sun-
dappled trails of Long Wood. He had good friends here, and
a loving, close-knit family. With his strength and skill, he
could be a master woodward, a farmer, or a fisherman on
the Fool's Head; he might even make a good innkeeper one
day, but he preferred to leave that to the others, who seemed
to enjoy the life more. Already the older girl, Kettijan, was

married to the son of an innkeeper a day's walk to the south, on the road to Mistlands, and the other children, Ketinella and Feron, were busy assisting their parents in the day-to-day work of the inn. Only Genlon worked in the forest, pitting his strength and woodland skill against the giant trees of Long Wood.

He thought on his dilemma all through the summer and concluded that his faring year would resolve it. For some inexplicable reason, he felt that he must go north, to the barren mountains on the Cape of Mists, in search of the answers to his questions. Since autumn was drawing near, he would be wise to leave as soon as possible.

His mother, born and raised in Long Wood, accepted Genlon's announcement calmly, but it seemed to trouble his father. Banheen had traveled much in the world, and he had an exaggerated idea of the dangers and pitfalls awaiting a young man faring on his own for the first time. He spent many hours over the ensuing days warning Genlon against every possible contingency. The young man listened respectfully, though not without inner reservations. He could not bring himself to believe that the world was as perilous, or he himself as helpless, as his father depicted.

At the traditional feast of faring, neighbors and family joined in wishing Genlon well. Those who had returned from their own faring years offered advice, but it was always of the most practical nature, regarding food, clothing, or trail conditions, or else vague and general. They knew that each faring was unique, and that Genlon would learn the important things for himself.

He left on a misty morning in the month of Gleaning, late in summer, and made his way due north, to the limits of Long Wood. When his food ran out, he worked for a day to earn a new stock. At the last settlement, he worked for twenty days with a team of woodwards. In return for his labors, they gave him provisions and a warm traveling-cloak for the journey north. They praised his work and invited him to join them when his year was done. He thanked them and went on.

At the northern edge of Long Wood, he turned to the east. Soon the high cliffs of the Headland loomed on his left hand, and the booming roar of the waters of the Fissure drifted to his ears. Genlon knew a little about the Headland —a neighbor had once lived there—and felt no urge to see it. He headed toward the single bridge that linked the Headland and the mainland.

The bridge had stood unguarded for generations, but as he neared it, Genlon saw that it was unguarded no longer. A small stone hut now stood at either end, and outside the nearer hut was a man with a short spear. Curious, Genlon approached him. When he was still a good twenty paces distant, he waved a friendly greeting. The man, instead of returning the salute, sprang to the guard position.

"Halt there and identify yourself!" he shouted.

"I'm Genlon Banheenson, of Riverfield Inn in Long Wood."

"State your business," the guard called loudly, brandishing his spear.

"I'm on my faring year, bound for the Cape of Mists."

"Alone?"

"All farers set out alone."

The guard made no immediate reply, but he grounded his spear. A moment later, he said, "You'd be wise to seek companions. You look well able to take care of yourself, but even a man your size couldn't do much against an armed band."

"What do you mean?"

"Robbers. Brigands. They murdered a family of good crofters six nights past, and that was not their first work," said the guard.

"Are they in Long Wood, or on the Cape of Mists?"

"They're still on the Headland. We're hunting them down. We want to be sure no more come over. From what we've heard from travelers, there are other such bands about."

"We've had no trouble in Long Wood," said Genlon.

"Then you're fortunate. The cape may be safe. Nothing up there to rob but the barrows, and no man dares disturb them. But if you see a band of men, you'd best avoid them."

"I will. Thank you for the warning."

Genlon was more watchful now. He cooked his midday meal over a low, smokeless fire and slept with no fire at all by night, in places where no one could approach unheard. Twice he saw solitary men, and once he saw a group of three. Each time, he took cover quickly and remained unseen. By early Yellowleaf he had reached the Cape of Mists, and here he felt safe.

There were many who would not have felt safe anywhere on the Cape of Mists; many who would, indeed, have preferred to face alone and unarmed a bloody-handed gang of cutthroats than stand with an army against the unseen menace of the northern cape. Genlon did not share this fear. He had heard of the barrows, the crumbling grave mounds that dotted the coast here, but he saw no reason to fear piles of stone. The legends of barrow-wights he discounted; the dead were dead, and they could not harm him here or anywhere. No monstrous guardians prowled the burial grounds of Long Wood, and he saw no reason to believe that things should be different here.

He came upon the first barrow at sunset of a gloomy day. It was a hillock about twice a man's height, perfectly circular, with steeply rising sides and a flattened top. Moss and tough grass grew thickly over the ancient stones. Genlon circled it three times, slowly, studying it in the waning twilight; he could see no sign that it had ever been breached. It appeared to have stood untouched through all the ages since those unknown sea-people had erected it, stone by stone.

He withdrew to a sheltered spot in the rocks where he could look down on the barrow, and here he made camp for the night. He ate lightly, all the while watching the barrow. A feeling of uneasiness had come over him, and he could not understand why. This was a gloomy place, and a grave mound was no cheery sight; but that did not explain the fear that he could sense closing in around him.

It was not a time for fear, but for clear thinking, and his own weakness angered him. Something had drawn him here, to this stony waste and these barrows; the key to his future lay here, and he ought to be alert and receptive, not befuddled by superstitions and fantastic terrors. He unslung the double-bit woodward's ax that he carried at his back and hefted it in his hands. The mass of it reassured him. If anything attacked, he was ready.

"That won't help. Get a fire going, and hurry," said a deep voice close behind him.

Genlon whirled around, ax raised to strike, and beheld a white-haired man in a long traveling-cloak of black, much stained and besmutted. He was seated comfortably on Genlon's own pack, legs straight out before him and crossed at the ankles, and he was eating a piece of dried fruit, licking a finger clean as Genlon stared at him in astonishment.

"You can gape at me later, Genlon, by the light of a good

fire. Right now, you'd better start gathering driftwood," said the man in black.

"But the robbers will see it," Genlon said.

"There isn't a robber within a hundred greatmarks. They're terrified of the barrow-wights, which makes them a lot more sensible than either of us, I suppose."

"Barrow-wights . . . ? There's no such thing. That's all superstition."

The man in black raised a finger and pointed accusingly. "Now, listen to me, Genlon. You're a young man with a lot to learn, and your first lesson will be your last if you don't hurry and get a fire going. It's getting dark fast, and the barrow-wights are creatures of darkness. Hurry!"

Genlon responded to the note of urgency. Eager as he was to learn some answers, he slung his ax and scrambled down to the water's edge. In a short time he returned with a heaping armful of wood.

"Bring another load. The nights are getting long," said the stranger.

When Genlon came back the second time, the man in black had a small blaze going. He pointed and said, "Drop it over there."

Tossing the wood down, Genlon said, "You have your fire now, and I want to know a few things. How do you know my name? And how did you get here? Were you here all along, waiting for me? I didn't hear anyone—where were you hiding? And how did you know I'd come here when I didn't even know myself where I was heading?"

The other man took a stick from the pile and laid it on the fire. Without looking up, he said, "None of that's important. What matters is that I know more about you than anyone else on earth does." Laying another, larger piece of wood on the growing blaze, he glanced up and said, "I'm going to help you find a few things, and learn a few things, that will better enable you to make the right decision about your future. That's important to a lot of people. I hope you're strong enough to move that rock."

"What? What rock?" Genlon asked, bewildered.

"That one right there, between the two big ones. It's in the way."

"Where do you want it?"

"Just get it out of the way, in a hurry."

Genlon tugged the rock free and heaved it aside, down

the slope. The stranger reached quickly inside his tight-drawn cloak. Genlon saw a flash of silver at his breast, and then the cloak fell back into place. In the stranger's hand was a small, curved mirror. He set it in the open space between the rocks so that it reflected a beam of firelight onto the barrow. "There. Now we're safe," he said when he was done.

"Why does it matter to anyone whether I become a woodward or a fisherman, or help my family at the inn? How can that be important to a lot of people?" Genlon demanded.

"It is. You'll just have to believe that. There's a lot I can't tell you now, but I'll explain everything when the right time comes."

"Can't you tell me anything?"

The man frowned and scratched thoughtfully in his white beard. "We're going to find a certain barrow, a much bigger one, farther north. I can tell you that much. And I'll be staying with you for a time, teaching you, so I suppose you'd better know my name. I'm Cathwar," he said.

Genlon nodded respectfully. He was uncertain how to respond. His visitor put more wood on the fire, placing it with great care, and then he seated himself against a boulder. "Go to sleep," he said. "I'll care for the fire now. I'll wake you when it's your turn."

Genlon gladly did as Cathwar ordered. He rolled himself up in his cloak, using his pack as a headrest, and fell almost at once into a deep, untroubled sleep. He awoke with a start to see the fire burning low and the wood almost all gone. The first faint light of dawn was rising in the east. Cathwar sat where he had settled himself at nightfall, looking coolly into Genlon's eyes.

"You never woke me," Genlon said.

"No reason to. I don't need much sleep. Are you ready to move? We have a long journey ahead."

Genlon yawned and stretched; then he climbed to his feet and stretched once again. "Let's eat before we start out," he said.

"We'll eat as we walk. This dried fruit of yours is vile stuff, anyway."

"I've got some dried meat."

"That's worse," said Cathwar, scowling. "You can catch some fish on our way north. Let's go."

All that day and the next, they traveled through a wilderness of barren stone, silent but for the wind and the rhythmic mumbling of the waves on the rocky strand. The place was literally trackless, and yet Cathwar walked with the purposeful step and alert eye of one who follows a marked path. He answered every question with a curt phrase that gave no information at all, and he rebuffed every attempt at conversation. Finally, when Genlon had asked about their destination for the tenth time, he stopped in his tracks, turned on the youth, and said angrily, "We're getting closer to it with every step, and I have a lot of thinking and remembering to do before we get there. If I don't remember certain things exactly right, we may both be in trouble, do you understand? Now, don't disturb me any more. I'll tell you everything you have to know when we get there." With that, he turned and started walking on.

Genlon held his tongue. He had been taught to respect age and learning; that was the way of Long Wood. And besides, he had a growing suspicion that Cathwar was more than just a wise old man. Genlon had heard of wizards and sorcerers, but he had never met one, and he had never really been persuaded that they existed. But if there were such persons, then Cathwar might well be one. He seemed to know things he had no right to know, and he had appeared from nowhere, as wizards were said to do. That trick with the mirror on the barrow had seemed like sorcerer's work.

Late in the morning of the third day, as they reached the peak of a long rise, Cathwar laughed aloud and pointed. Below them, on a lower rise that kept it out of the tide's reach, guarded on three sides by high, concealing rock walls, stood a barrow bigger than the biggest structure Genlon had ever seen.

"That's our destination," Cathwar said. Shading his eyes and looking skyward, he went on, "We've got half a day's light left, and that should be plenty. Get a fire going. We'll eat, and then we'll go to work."

Genlon did as he was bade, but when the fire was burning and he was seated opposite Cathwar, chewing on a piece of dried meat from his pack, he could hold back no longer. Gulping down the half-chewed meat, he blurted, "What work are we going to do, Cathwar? You said you'd tell me, and I want to know."

"Something I need and something you need are down there in the barrow. We're going to take them," the white-haired man said offhandedly.

"Despoil a grave? That's a terrible thing to do!"

"We're not despoiling anything or stealing from anybody. Do you know who lies under that heap of stones?"

"No. How could I know?"

"Then don't get so righteous. His name was Skobo. The Torch from the Sea, people called him. He was a sea-raider, a pirate, one of the worst there ever was, until his very last years. Everything in that barrow is stolen, most of it from people who had stolen it themselves."

"It's still stealing from a grave," Genlon said.

Cathwar looked at him darkly for a moment. Then he said, "Banheen's certainly brought you up right."

"My father taught me to be honest."

"That's what I mean." Cathwar smiled and looked for an instant as if he wanted to say more. Instead, he scratched in his beard and said, "I suppose it won't hurt to tell you a few things. Mind you, Genlon, there's nobody else alive on earth who knows what I'm going to tell you, and you're never to speak a word of it to anyone. Not anyone, not for any reason. It concerns things that happened long ago, but it explains why you and I are here now."

"That's what I want to know."

"Listen, then. And don't interrupt me with a lot of questions." Cathwar settled himself and began. "Once, long ago, in a land that no longer exists, a great empire flourished on the earth. It had enemies, of course. But its might was so great, and, once provoked, it was so swift to retaliate, and so merciless, that there was peace for a long, long time, and the empire grew and flourished, acquiring ever greater power, knowledge, and wealth. Eventually, its enemies realized that they could not hope to survive alone; and since their envy and hatred of the empire, and their greed for its wealth and splendor, had by this time grown much greater than their enmity for one another, they formed an alliance. Slowly, in secret, they gathered a mighty army. It's said that that army was a thousand times greater than any army that had ever been assembled before."

"How is that possible, Cathwar?" Genlon blurted.

Cathwar shook his head and made a little indifferent gesture with his hand. "In legends, anything is possible. But I told you, no interruptions."

"I'm sorry, Cathwar. Go on, please."

Cathwar gave him a hard, disapproving look, grunted irritably, and then resumed his account. "The war was terrible, and it went on and on. For the first time in all its history, the empire was not immediately victorious. The enemy held, and then they counterattacked, and then they began to press forward. Outposts fell, and conquered territories were abandoned, and the imperial army was driven back on all fronts. Finally, the wise men who counseled the emperor realized that the war was lost, and the empire doomed, unless they resorted to magic. They feared magic, and they had always avoided using it, but now it was their only hope. And while they debated, their enemies learned of their deliberations and feared that victory might be snatched from their grasp. And so, in a very short time, both sides brought powerful magic to bear against each other. The war was soon over, but there was no victory; only destruction so complete that there was no hope of rebuilding. That great civilization collapsed, and the world sank into a savagery that lasted for ages. Our own world has risen, very slowly, out of that long savagery."

Cathwar fell silent, his eyes closed and his head bowed. Genlon sat motionless, enraptured, waiting for the old man to continue. At that Cathwar sighed, opened his eyes, and, with a glance at the youth, went on.

"In all the world, only one man—a good man, a mage of great power—perceived the true nature of the struggle. It was not merely a clash of rivals for land, or treasure, or any of the things for which men go to war. There was something deeper, some all-pervading evil power that influenced leaders on both sides, filling them with unreasoning hatred, making them cruel and unforgiving, making them drive their followers to horrible deeds. While this power existed, there could be no peace, ever, on the earth. So the wizard sought out this power, and learned its ways, and discovered its weakness. When the clash came, he turned all his power against it, and he defeated it. But the price of his victory, as I told you, was universal destruction. The unleashed power of magic is . . . it's beyond anything I can describe or you can imagine. The wizard himself was brought to the brink of death."

Cathwar turned and looked hard at Genlon. "He knew— but he could tell no one, for there was no one left to tell—that this evil force might one day return from where his magic had hurled it, as strong and as wicked as ever, hungry for revenge. So he infused all his remaining magic into—into a certain object—and left it to make its way about the world, all unknown, until it was needed. And now it's needed. The old evil has begun to stir, and there's a terrible power moving on the earth. Those who would confront it need the help of the ancient mage."

"Is it—is the object—in the barrow?"

"It is."

"How do you know?"

"The old wizard knew where it would be when the day came, and he left a message."

"He knew? Ages ago?"

Cathwar laughed softly. "He probably knew that you and I would be sitting here, arguing. He was a very great mage."

"And will you turn back the evil with his magic?"

"I didn't say that. I hope I will, but I don't know if I'm strong enough. But without his magic, there's no hope at all, so I have to try."

"You said there was something I need, too."

"There is. A sword. It's lying right on Skobo's chest, in a black scabbard."

Genlon looked at the old man and shook his head slowly in bewilderment. "What need have I for a sword, Cathwar? I'm not a swordsman. I don't know anything about using one, and there's nobody in Long Wood who can teach me."

"I'll teach you what you have to know. You may not need a sword now, but you'll need one before very long, and this is a particularly fine one. The blade was made at the forge of Zixil, by Zixil himself, the greatest swordsmith who ever walked the earth."

Genlon thought for a moment; then he said, "This is really important, isn't it, Cathwar?"

"It's the most important thing that's ever happened in your life, and you know it is. It might turn out to be the most important thing in a hundred generations," Cathwar replied without hesitation.

"But why would I need a sword?"

"Remember your dreams," said Cathwar. He quickly went on to ask, "How good are you with that ax?"

"I'm as good as any man in Long Wood. So I'm told, anyway."

"I hope that's good enough. Let me see it."

Genlon unslung the ax and handed it to Cathwar. The

older man inspected it and laid it near the fire. With the tip of his dagger, he knocked a glowing ember free; then he looked up at Genlon. "Hold out your finger. I'm going to take a few drops of blood."

"What for?"

"To save us both, I hope. Well, come on."

Cathwar held the youth's hand steady so that the drops of blood fell on the ember, which spat and sizzled as they hit. Picking up the ember gingerly, he laid it in the palm of his hand, spat on it, and with his forefinger began to mash it into a thick black paste. He then inscribed a symbol on each side of the ax blade, using the paste.

"Why did you do that?"

"The only way to stop a barrow-wight is to cut off his head. But an ordinary ax might not be enough for what we'll encounter in this barrow. So I gave you a little help."

Cathwar smiled at Genlon's horrified expression. "Starting to believe in them? Go on, tell me—what have you heard about barrow-wights?"

"They're ghosts—the ghosts of the people in the barrow—only they have bodies."

Cathwar snorted angrily and shook his head. "That's a pack of nonsense. Think, boy! If a barrow-wight is the ghost of the person in the grave, then there ought to be barrow-wights everywhere! But you've never heard of them anywhere but here, on the Cape of Mists, in the barrows of the sea-raiders, have you?"

"No, I haven't," Genlon admitted.

"Well, that ought to make you think. About time you started doing some thinking. Your muscles won't always be enough to do the job."

"Then there must be something special about these barrows. Maybe there's something in them that mustn't be disturbed, and the barrow-wights act as a sort of guard. Is that it, Cathwar?"

"You're close. These barrows were all built to hold the loot of sea-kings. It was a tradition of their people. They'd lay out the dead king on a pile of treasure, put his sword and shield on his chest, and then cover him with an overturned boat, dismasted and stove in. If any of his family and followers wanted to make the last voyage with him, they'd sit around the boat and kill themselves; just put a dagger right into their hearts. Then the servants and slaves would build the barrow over them." Cathwar looked down on Skobo's barrow and was silent for a moment before going on with his story. "A lot of people knew where these barrows were, and what was in them, but that didn't bother the sea-people, not at first. Among them, looting a barrow was such an awful crime that it just wasn't thought of. You could do almost anything else, but if you disturbed a barrow you were an outcast in life and a tortured spirit afterward."

"But what about other people?" Genlon asked.

Cathwar's expression brightened. "Now you're thinking, my boy. Of course, once others found out about them, people who didn't live by the code of the sea-people, the barrows and their treasure were in danger. So the sea-kings had their priests summon up the spirits of all those who had been barrow-robbers in life and were now suffering torment in the Valley of Cold Fire. They offered them release if they'd dwell in the barrows and protect them against intruders." He rose from the fireside, wiping his blackened hands on his robe, and said, "This is the richest barrow of them all. There might be more than one guardian—might be a whole army of them. But we have to go in. Scared?"

"Yes," said Genlon at once.

"Good. That shows you're not a fool."

"Do you really believe I can hold off an army of barrow-wights alone?"

"You're not alone. I'll have a torch, and that will keep them back. They hate light. If we move fast enough, we can be in and out before they attack."

"What if they attack?"

"Lop off their heads."

"Is it that easy to kill a barrow-wight?" Genlon asked, incredulous.

"Well, you're not really killing them. They're long dead. And I wouldn't call it easy. It's possible, if you don't panic and try to run. That's how they get everyone. They don't expect anyone to stand and fight. They all have long necks and big heads, so you'll have a clean target. Sometimes they have a spell to protect them against weapons, but the markings I put on your ax will overcome any spell I know. Ready?"

Genlon wanted very much to know what would happen if the barrow-wights had a protective spell unknown to Cathwar, but he was afraid that he might not be able to speak without his voice cracking. He gripped his ax in both hands and nodded. The wizard led off, picking his precarious way among the boulders and loose scree of the steep hillside. They made a slow circuit of the barrow; then Cathwar backtracked and stopped .

"Right here. Sling your ax and start pulling those rocks away," he said.

"What if we're attacked?"

"They won't come out into the light. They're waiting in the heart of the barrow. Go on, get to work."

As Genlon pried loose the mossy rocks, Cathwar searched the strand for something to use as a torch. By the time the youth had made an opening large enough to admit them to the dank-smelling darkness of the barrow, the wizard had found a sizable chunk of dry wood and anointed the end of it with oil from a vial.

"I'll go in first. You stay right behind me. Remember, the important thing is to get what we came for and get out. Don't attack if you're not attacked. But if something comes at you, strike for the neck," said Cathwar.

"I understand."

"Good," said the wizard. He stepped to the black opening and blew on the torch. It burst into flame. Holding it before him, he entered the barrow.

Genlon followed, into a narrow passage that curved to his right, leading inward. The walls were of stone, and the low roof was of spongy, rotting logs. The air was still, heavy with the sweetish stink of decay and death, and Cathwar's torch burned without a flutter. Genlon was alert for every sound, but he heard nothing except their own muted footfalls on the moist earth.

Cathwar stopped when they reached a large chamber. By the light of his raised torch, they could see the outline of an overturned boat. Three skeletons in rotting robes grinned up from where they sat cross-legged against the side.

The wizard pointed to a spot in the center of the boat. "Smash it in," he directed.

Using the ax-head as a ram, Genlon drove a blow into the side of the boat. The wood crumbled like a moldy oatcake and fell in moist fragments. The torchlight glinted off gold.

"Take the sword," said Cathwar.

Under a crumpled shield of wood and leather lay a long sword in a black scabbard. Genlon reached in, pushed aside the ruined shield, and gripped the scabbard. To his surprise, it was firm beneath his hand, as though it had somehow escaped the decay that consumed all around it. He drew it out and thrust it through his belt.

He heard a scuffling sound and turned in time to see the torch struck from Cathwar's hand. At the same time, something burned across his face, and a sickening, foul breath closed on him. Dimly, in the dying torchlight, he saw a misshapen figure lurching closer, and he set his feet and aimed a smooth, level stroke at the thing's neck. His ax sheared the grotesque, long-jawed head free, and he turned to Cathwar's aid.

The wizard's hand was on the torch, but before he could lift it, another of the barrow-wights kicked it away, scattering sparks across the damp earth. Genlon sprang at him and beheaded him with a stroke; then he reached down to help Cathwar to his feet.

"Get out. I'll be right behind you," the wizard said.

With the sound of tearing cloth, the rotting boat before them burst asunder, and a new and terrifying presence made itself felt in the darkness. Tugging Cathwar to his feet, Genlon cocked his ax and moved to confront it. A powerful blow took him in the chest and sent him staggering back, and he fell over the twitching, headless corpse of one of the barrow-wights. He climbed to his feet, gasping with pain, and started forward again.

Suddenly, a brilliant light flooded the chamber. Cathwar stood with his hands cupped above his head. A glow of white light, painfully pure and bright, shone from his hands. The creature from the shattered boat gave an awful cry, a moist, broken sound like something torn from a rotting throat, and flung long arms before its face. Cathwar spoke in an unknown tongue, and the thing writhed and howled, lashing out a taloned hand vainly. Genlon ducked under the flailing arm and dispatched the barrow-wight.

When they were safely outside, Genlon sprawled full-length on the ground, clutching his ribs. His cheek burned, and his chest felt as though it had been smashed in like the rotting boat in the barrow. Cathwar squatted by his side.

"You did well, Genlon," said the wizard when he had regained his breath.

Genlon did not respond for a time. He was taking shallow,

cautious breaths, pressing on his ribs. "I don't feel as though I did well," he said weakly.

"Spit. Go ahead, spit," the wizard ordered. When the youth had done so, he inspected the sputum and said, "No blood in it. You'll be fine. Get your shirt off. I'll look at those ribs." After a close inspection, he announced cheerfully, "Nothing broken, as far as I can tell. Just bruises. You'd better go and wash those cuts on your face."

When Genlon returned from the shore, Cathwar took out a small, round, stone box. Dipping his finger into it, he drew a coating of salve over each of the three ragged cuts in Genlon's cheek. Handing the jar to him, he said, "Rub this on your ribs. It will stop the pain, and the bruises will heal more quickly. Then get some rest. I'll watch."

"Is it safe here?"

"There's nothing to fear now."

Genlon slept soundly until late in the day, awakening to the smell of fish broiling over a fire. He ate ravenously, in silence. Only afterward, as he sat by the fire chewing on a piece of dried fruit, did he ask Cathwar what was to become of the barrow-wights.

"According to the beliefs of the sea-people, they've redeemed themselves by dying for a king. Their spirits will be taken to the Hills of Silence, and they'll enter the sleep of good dreams," said the wizard.

"I'm glad. I pitied them."

"You're free with your pity. They would have killed us."

"They did what they had to do. We were intruders."

"You do have a fine moral sense," Cathwar said, and his tone suggested that such a quality in others made him uneasy. When Genlon shrugged the remark off and looked away, embarrassed, the wizard said, "Well, you do. Don't act as if you're ashamed of it. You didn't run when that thing knocked the torch out of my hand."

"I couldn't leave you there to die. I thought you were hurt. Where did that light come from?"

Cathwar's fingertips slipped inside his cloak to touch the silver disc that hung around his neck and lay on his breast. He withdrew his hand quickly and muttered, "Just something I keep with me."

"You saved me from the third barrow-wight."

"Fair is fair. Were you afraid?"

Genlon looked at him and said levelly, "I don't think I was ever so afraid in my life as I was inside that barrow."

Cathwar nodded and smiled with evident satisfaction. "You'll be all right," he said confidently. "You were afraid, but you did what you had to do, and when it was done, you showed pity for your enemy. That's good. Banheen raised you well."

"Are you a good friend of my father?"

"I only met him once. We had business together a long time ago. He wouldn't remember me, and I'd prefer that you not mention my name to him when you go back."

"If you like," Genlon said.

"Tomorrow we have to repair the barrow. It has to look untouched. And when that's done, we'll start south. Your faring year is passing, and you have a lot still to learn."

"Tell me, Cathwar—will we be doing this again?"

The wizard frowned, scratched his beard, and pondered that question for a time. Then he shook his head. "No, you'll never have to do this again in your life. But when we get down to work, you may wish all you had to do was easy little chores like fighting off barrow-wights. Think about that while you're watching. I'm going to get some rest now."

CHAPTER FOUR

CLASH AT RIVERFIELD

Genlon returned to Riverfield Inn on the day his faring year ended. He was little changed in appearance save for the three thin scars that ran across his left cheek from jawbone to nose. They had healed cleanly and were scarcely visible unless one was close and the light was bright.

In his manner, though, he was not the same youth who had left Long Wood a year earlier. He was more thoughtful, less talkative. He carried a long sword, and he practiced with it every day. He would say nothing about the events of his faring year or his plans for the future. He seemed to be waiting. It often appeared to his parents that he had reached some decision but was determined not to reveal it to anyone; but at times they were equally certain that he had settled nothing. He worked as hard as ever, and he was as helpful around the inn as he had been in the old days, even after a strenuous day's work in the forest and a hard practice session with his sword. But Ketial and Banheen both sensed a reserve that had not existed before the faring year.

The full extent of the change in Genlon was made clear to all on the first night of Barebranch, when the robbers came to Long Wood.

The evening began quietly, after a warm autumn day. Ketial and Ketinella were seated in the arbor behind the inn, conversing in low voices and laughing frequently, softly, like friends sharing a private joke. Feron and a boy from a neighboring farm were sitting at Banheen's feet as he smoked his pipe and told a long, leisurely tale about a famous thief he had once met in his travels. Outside the inn, Genlon and three young men were discussing a neighbor's forthcoming wedding and speculating on the feast he would give.

Feron's friend Darste was the first to notice something out of the ordinary. He glanced out the doorway of the inn, looked for a moment, and then said to Banheen, "Someone's coming up the southern path."

Banheen leaned forward, squinting into the distance. He followed Darste's pointing finger and said, "Too far for my eyes. Can you make out who it is?"

"No," said the boy, shaking his head.

"I can't think who it would be, unless it's one of your sisters come to call you home."

"They know I'm staying with Feron tonight. It must be a traveler," the boy replied.

"Travelers from the south don't use that path. They come by—wait a minute—something's wrong!"

Banheen's cry carried outside. Before anyone reached the door, Genlon was heading for the southern path at an all-out run, and the others were behind him. The traveler staggered and fell; then she rose again, took a few tottering steps, and collapsed. Genlon lifted the fallen figure and carried her to the inn.

"It's my sister!" Darste cried, running to them.

The child was sobbing hysterically, clutching at Genlon's shirt with both hands in a desperate grip. Once at the inn, Genlon sat and held her cradled in his arms. He rocked slowly back and forth, speaking in a soft, soothing voice until her sobbing was under control.

"Run. We must all run," she said, in a taut, toneless voice. "We must run away before they come."

"Who, Dareene?"

"The bad men."

"What men, Dareene? What did they do?"

Genlon's question sent the child into a fit of sobbing, and it was only with great patience that he was able to coax the story from her. When she was through, he rose and set her on her feet. Enfolding her little hands tightly in his, he dropped to one knee before her and said, "I know you're very tired, Dareene, but you have to walk on a way before you rest. You and my mother and father, and Feron and Darste, are all going up north, to Polters' farm. You'll be safe there. In a few days, you'll all come back, and then you and Darste will live here with us."

Ketial, who had come up beside the still-weeping little girl, asked in a low voice, "And what of you?"

"I'm staying here."

"But the robbers are coming this way!"

"They'll be tired and hungry from long travel, and they'll expect no resistance. We'll stop them here."

"Can we do it?" one of the young men asked.

Genlon nodded, but he said nothing more. When Ketial had taken Dareene and the others inside to prepare for the flight to safety, he explained. "These are the marauders who killed the band of travelers on the west road and beat old Gossman and his wife to death. They're not a band of fighters."

"Neither are we, Genlon," another of the youths pointed out.

"You can split an apple in two at a hundred paces, three shots out of four, Thaxter," Genlon replied. To the others, he said, "And I've seen you do just as well. Together, you can cut down half of them before they reach the inn. I'll be waiting inside."

"We don't have our bows," Thaxter said.

Banheen said, "We have three bows inside, and plenty of arrows."

Thaxter nodded. "Dareene said there were eleven of them. Even if we get five or six, can you handle the rest alone?" he asked Genlon.

"Yes."

"Then get us the bows and tell us what to do."

By the time darkness fell, all was ready. The three bowmen were in position. All the southern windows of Riverfield Inn were lighted, reflectors behind the lanterns directing all the light so as to silhouette anyone approaching the door. Luckily for the defenders, and for the little group heading north to seek refuge at Polters' farm, the moon was only two days from full.

A tense hour passed. Then Genlon, waiting by the door, heard the signal. Soon he could make out voices, loud and utterly confident. A man laughed, and others joined in until a harsh voice ordered them silent. Genlon took up his position and waited.

There was a shout; then cries of pain and alarm were heard, and then no voices at all, only the drumming of heavy feet and one last choked outcry before six men, breathing heavily, burst into the inn, the last one slamming and bolting the door behind them.

"There's an army out there!" one cried.

"We'll think of a way out. Where's Iosmut?" another asked.

"He went down. I heard him yell."

"Then I'm taking charge," said the second speaker. By this time, he had glanced around the inn, but he did not see anything odd, because lanterns had been placed so as to dazzle the eyes of anyone who entered. The edges of the room lay in shadow. The stools and tables and benches had all been pushed to the walls, and the center of the big room was as open and as brightly lit as an arena.

Before the self-proclaimed leader could realize that they had entered a trap and shout a warning, Genlon was upon them. Two men fell before they could even utter a sound, and then the third went down, slashed nearly in two.

Quickly the remaining three spread out to form a wide triangle, bobbing from side to side, trying to work one man behind their adversary. All carried long daggers, and one wielded a club as well. At close quarters, so armed, they could overwhelm a swordsman. But Genlon was as quick as they, and well taught; he was wise to their tactics. He kept his back to the wall, thrusting to hold his assailants at a distance. When they were positioned properly, he moved quickly, striking the fourth robber just below the shoulder, shearing off his arm and cutting deeply into his chest.

Genlon's blow lodged his sword in the man's rib cage. As he tugged at the blade, another robber darted behind him and struck with his dagger. Had he thrust, Genlon might have been killed with that single blow; but in his haste and rage, the robber slashed downward, and his dagger glanced off Genlon's shoulder blade.

The sword came free, and Genlon brought it around backhanded. It caught the fifth of the robbers under the ear and sank deep into his skull, nearly severing the jawbone.

The last of the six was at the door, tugging frantically at the bolts he had slammed home for safety only moments before. He turned in time to take Genlon's thrust under his breastbone. He gasped and looked with wild eyes at his executioner, and, with his last strength, he flung his dagger into Genlon's face. Genlon ducked aside. The robber sagged, pinned to the door like a beetle on a thorn.

Genlon tugged the door open wide enough to slip out and signal his friends. They ran to him, shouting exultantly in the joy of their victory, but when they entered the inn and saw the carnage they were shocked into silence. Firing arrows at a distant figure silhouetted against lamplight was one thing; the sight of hacked and bloody corpses strewn about a well-lit, familiar room was quite another, and they were unprepared for it. The bodies that lay in grotesque contortions, weltered in blood, were real men, not anonymous manifestations of evil.

They looked on the sight with growing horror and revulsion, and one by one they turned their eyes to Genlon and saw him as a frightening stranger. This friend of their youth, the peaceful giant who had grown up with them, worked at their sides, joked and laughed and shared food with them and their families, had done a brave and terrible deed, something unparalleled in the oldest legends of Long Wood. They had all known of Genlon's strength, and none had ever doubted his courage. But they had never suspected that Genlon was capable of a deed like this.

They all jumped at the sound of someone at the door. Banheen slipped in, looked at them and at the bloody scene, and said, "I had to come back. My son, and my inn . . . it wasn't right for me to leave."

"It's all over now," Genlon said.

"What about the others? There were eleven."

Thaxter spoke up ."We got five before they could reach the door."

"Let's go out and look them over," Genlon said. He took a lantern in each hand and gave one to Thaxter and another friend. As he turned to take two more, the others saw that the left side of Genlon's shirt was soaked with blood from the shoulder to the waist.

"You're hurt, son," said Banheen. "Sit down and let me look at it."

"We'll take care of this lot, Genlon. You get that shoulder fixed," Thaxter said. "We'll drag these outside and put them where Ketial and the children won't see them."

It took two of them to pry the sword free from the door. They carried the six corpses outside and laid them side by side on a mound beyond the woodpile, and then they went to seek out the five who had fallen to their arrows. While they were gone, Banheen cleaned the gash on his son's shoulder.

"It's long, but it's not so deep. A good clean cut. I'm going to tie up your left arm for a few days, so you don't open this up again," Banheen said.

"I ought to help dig the graves."

"We'll do that. You've done enough." Banheen was silent for a time; then he said with animation, "You certainly have done enough! People will tell of this night for generations to come."

"I killed six men," Genlon said softly.

"They deserved killing."

"They probably did. All the same, I'm the one who killed them, and I helped plan the deaths of the others."

"You don't feel guilt over it, do you, son?"

Genlon did not answer at once. When he spoke, the words came slowly, as if he were working out a difficult problem. "It isn't guilt, exactly. I'm confused. We condemned those men, and we called them brutes and savages, because they killed. And I killed them, brutally, without warning, and peope will call what I did a brave deed. But killing is killing, isn't it?"

"If you hadn't been here, if Dareene hadn't brought us warning—how would you feel now if your friends and your family were dead, and those robbers still lived?"

"I'd feel terrible, father. I know that. But I don't feel good now, or proud of what I did. I saw the expressions on my friends' faces. It's a bad thing to take life, whatever the reason."

"They're just shaken up, son. They've never done anything like this, either. We're none of us warriors here in Long Wood," Banheen said.

"Maybe that's changing. Think how many of the men we knew have gone to the High City to become guardsmen."

"Yes," Banheen said disapprovingly. "We need guarding here as much as they do in the High City, it appears. It's as though a new spirit is moving in the north—a cruel spirit. Life was never like this before. Robbers on the Headland, here in Long Wood . . . just last spring, a man told me about bands of marauders in the mountains. I don't know what's—"

"One of them's alive," Thaxter announced, pushing open the door. His two companions entered, bearing between them a slim, wiry man with grizzled hair.

Two arrows protruded from the man's body. One was lodged deep in his groin, near the hipbone, and the wound was bleeding badly. The other had penetrated his chest at elbow level and pierced his lungs. His breath came out in bloody foam.

"Lay him by the fire," Genlon said.

"Ought to put him in head first," one of the men carrying him muttered.

"Yes, let him roast, and think about the people he's killed," said the other.

"He's dying. That's enough," Genlon said. "It will do us no good to become as cruel as our enemies."

Banheen, finished binding his son's shoulder, knelt beside the dying robber. He recognized the man's face, though he could not put a name to it. This was someone from his old life, in the days before Long Wood; a thief from the High City.

Slowly, snatches of memory came back. Banheen recalled the man boasting loudly in a croaking voice after too much drink at the House of All Keys, the tavern where the thieves congregated. He was a robber and a brute who would slit a throat or smash a skull on the chance of a few coins. The better class of thieves, the skilled professionals like Banheen, had always looked down on him. And here he was, having stepped out of the past to die at Riverfield. Banheen was shaken by the sight of him.

"Can you do anything for him?" Genlon asked.

"I can try to make him comfortable for the little time he has left. That's all."

"Will he be able to talk?"

"No," Banheen and flatly. He rose and turned to his son. "A man with an arrow through his lungs can't do much talking."

"Too bad. We might find out something."

"Not from this one. Son, there's something you can do. I don't want you lifting corpses or trying to clean up this place, not with that shoulder, but you could go after your mother and the children," Banheen said, drawing Genlon away from the dying robber. "They're waiting by the first footbridge. They'll stay there until moonset, so you have time to catch them before they've gone all the way to Polters'."

"Are you sure you won't need me here?"

"No. You can't be moving that left arm. Besides, you can cover ground faster than any of us. You'll save your mother a night's worry."

"You're right, father. I'll go at once."

With Genlon gone, Banheen again knelt by the robber's side. He wiped the dying man's brow, listening all the while to the shallow, strained breathing. When the man's eyes opened, he spoke quickly, close to his ear.

"Why did you come to Long Wood?"

The man's eyes were glazed; they did not focus on Banheen's face. In a faint voice, he said, "The man in black . . . sent us . . ."

"Listen to me," Banheen said. "You're dying. No one can help you. Maybe if you tell me why you've come here, and who sent you, it will be easier."

"He came to the dungeon . . . set us free . . . said we must go . . . Long Wood . . ."

"Why?"

"Kill . . . steal . . . freed us to . . ." The robber coughed dark blood, and his features twisted in pain. Banheen wiped the man's lips and bent closer to hear his fading voice. "We do this . . . man in black protects . . . families. . . . Tell him . . . I kept my bargain."

The man drew a broken breath and coughed up a gout of blood. With an awful choking sound, he shuddered and lay still.

Banheen climbed slowly to his feet, mystified and frightened at the robber's words. He had all but forgotten the man in black who had freed him from the cell in the High City, and the story told by this robber bore some tantalizing similarities.

Iosmut—that was his name. The man in the black cloak had spoken of him on that long-ago night. Banheen was certain of that, but there was little else he felt certain of. On that night, the man in black had freed a prisoner to save a child's life, and he had been most generous with his reward. If Iosmut had told the truth, the man in black had now released a band of robbers with orders to go to Long Wood and kill. It made no sense at all, yet Banheen could not make himself believe that a dying man would lie.

What was there to steal in Long Wood? Surely the High City held more riches, if all the tales of loot from the south were true. And why the killing? Whom could the man in black wish dead in Long Wood?

The shocking answer came to Banheen in a flash—these marauders had been sent in the hope that they would find, and kill, the child rescued eighteen years earlier. Absurd as it was, no other possibility made even this much sense. The man in black had had a change of heart—or a change of plan—and wanted Pytrigon's heir removed. Perhaps he had entered into league with that murderer in the upper chamber or had come into power himself. He might even have gone mad.

Banheen did not want to believe any of this. As he turned it all over in his mind, he realized that none of his conjectures could explain the sudden appearance of the robbers in other sections of the north. The man in black had no reason to believe that Genlon was anywhere but in Long Wood, so why would he send his agents elsewhere? And yet Banheen found it difficult to believe that there were two men in black, both of whom helped condemned thieves to escape, but for opposite reasons.

He worried over this until Thaxter and his companions returned, and then he forced it to the back of his mind while he celebrated the victory with them. The return of Genlon with Ketial and the children started a new round of celebration, and it was past midnight before Banheen crawled into bed, physically exhausted but with his mind working busily.

He could reach no conclusions about the mystery of Iosmut's release and the motives of the man in the black cloak. The only decision he could make was that he would keep the truth of Genlon's origins secret from the boy forever and help him to reach safety before the man in black could come for him or send a more effective group of assassins to do his work. He resolved to speak to Genlon as soon as he had things worked out. Not tomorrow; but very soon, he promised himself. Definitely very soon.

Before Banheen could take Genlon aside and advise him, the youth made an announcement that at once surprised and greatly relieved him. It came on the day that Genlon's wound was sufficiently healed for him to wield his ax and sword once more. When dinner was over, and the children had gone to their chores, he told his parents that he was leaving Riverfield.

"How long will you be away?" Ketial asked.

"I don't know. It may be a long time."

"Is it because of what happened with the robbers?"

"Partly, mother. But I've known since I returned that I'd have to leave again before long."

"Can't you tell us where you're going, or give us some idea of how long you'll be away?"

"I don't know myself, mother."

"But this isn't faring year. You're a man now. You can't just wander off aimlessly, Genlon!"

Banheen laid his hand on hers. "He's a man now, Ket. You said it yourself. He must do what he thinks right."

"It's not safe—not for him or for us. If he comes on a band of robbers while he's alone in the forest, or if another band attacks Riverfield, it will be slaughter. We have to keep together, Banny!"

"There are no other marauders in Long Wood, mother," Genlon said.

"But they may come."

"If they do, they'll regret it. Thaxter has already begun organizing the best archers into a home guard."

Ketial seemed slightly comforted by that news, but there was still concern in her voice. "What about you, Genlon? You'll have no guard with you. If you leave Long Wood you may meet worse men than the ones you fought."

"I survived my faring year, mother. I know how to be careful. I'll be safe."

She glanced at the faint scars on his cheek, but she said nothing more. Banheen squeezed her hand to reassure her. "Genlon's well able to look after himself, Ket. If he says he must go, then we should trust his judgment."

"You sound as though you want him to go."

Banheen laughed uncomfortably. "I care as much as you do, Ket, but I can remember when I was his age. It was important to me to have the chance to be out on my own. He can't stay here with us forever."

"He's only just returned from faring year, and now he wants to be off again."

Banheen was troubled. He knew that Ketial loved Genlon as if he were the son of her own flesh, but he had never seen her act so possessive toward him and show such concern for his safety. He told himself that this was all the result of the shock of recent events, and that his Ket would soon be her levelheaded self again. But he, too, was concerned for Genlon. The youth had changed since he left on faring year; there was no doubting that now. The battle at the inn might have forced the decision, but Genlon had been planning his departure for some time. Of this, Banheen was certain.

"He'll be back here before you know it," he said to his wife. "Nobody stays away from Riverfield for long, we all know that. You'll be back, won't you, son?"

"I'll come back. I promise," said Genlon.

"There, Ket. Now, let's be about our work," Banheen

said, rising briskly. Ketial sighed and followed, leaving Genlon alone. He remained at the table for a time, thinking.

He could sense his mother's confusion, and it saddened him to know that he had caused it. But he had no choice, and no way of explaining. A sign had been given him. Prophetic words of Cathwar's had come about, and he must start on his way to an unknown destination. He could delay no longer.

He remembered the day Cathwar had said the words. Genlon had just had his first lesson in swordsmanship, and a grueling lesson it had been. When Genlon lay sprawled on the grass, stiff and aching, resting between exercises, he asked the wizard how long it would be before he was a decent swordsman.

"Not long, if you pay attention and practice faithfully. You have all the natural ability. One day you'll take on six armed men all by yourself," Cathwar said.

Genlon raised his head and looked at the wizard in disbelief. "Six armed men?"

"There'll be more, but you'll only have to deal with six."

"Kill them?"

"Every one. A single blow for each."

"But I don't want to kill anyone, Cathwar!"

"No choice with this lot. If you don't kill them, they'll kill you and those dear to you."

"If that's why you're teaching me swordsmanship, then I don't want to learn any more. I don't want to be a killer," Genlon said flatly.

"I told you to think, and you're not thinking. Don't be trapped by words. What's the penalty for robbery and murder in Long Wood?"

"Death."

"Then you'll be an executioner, not a killer. Don't brood on it, Genlon. It will come. And when it does, you'll do what you must, because you must. All right, now, on your feet. There's plenty to learn before the day arrives."

And now it had come about, just as Cathwar had predicted, bringing a turning point in Genlon's life. There had been other hints of changes to come. Some had seemed absurd, some flatly impossible; but as he recalled them now, after one had been fulfilled, they seemed inevitable.

For the first time, Genlon clearly saw that he had a destiny, and one which he could not escape.

CHAPTER FIVE

THE SIGN OF
THE WALKING MAN

It was the season of bright, crisp days, when the air was intoxicating as wine and seemed, like a wizard's glass, to delineate distant objects—a stand of golden birch on a river islet, a tuft of red maple on a far hilltop—with supernatural clarity. Nights were dry and chill, coming on a bit sooner each afternoon and lingering later into every dawn. The world was resplendent in these days before the first stilling touch of winter.

The skies, too, were at their most beautiful. Often Genlon rose at night to stand in a clearing, in the utter silence, and look up at the stars brilliant in the black and moonless heavens. It was a good time to be traveling.

The trails and byways of Long Wood were busy. Little groups of travelers were heading in all directions. Their mood was cheerful, and they exchanged news with everyone they encountered. Genlon was surprised to find that half of them were bursting to recount the true story of the great battle against a band of brigands that had taken place recently in the west, at an inn near a river. He heard the tale half a dozen times each day, and he listened each time with a suitable show of alarm, amazement, and righteous enthusiasm. It amused him to find that no two versions agreed, but he kept his amusement to himself and allowed the storytellers the pleasure of their inventions.

He made his slow way eastward until he reached the shore of the Fool's Head. Here he turned north, the lake on his right hand, and began the half-circuit that would take him to the northern trail into the mountains. He wandered at an easy pace, stopping at night in the small stone faring-houses that stood along the lake shore for the comfort of travelers, setting himself no goals of time or distance for his day's walking. Even his northward direction was without clear purpose; given a reason, he would have turned aside in a moment. What he was seeking he did not know, but he felt a growing certainty that it would find him when the moment came, for he was the sought as well as the seeker.

In the northernmost faring-house, he met two merchants and their four servants. The group was silent for a moment when Genlon's big frame filled the doorway, but when, in the traditional gesture, he laid his waterbag by the door and passed his scrip of food to the nearest man, one of the merchants greeted him.

"Good faring, friend. Come, share this shelter with us," he said, making room by the fire.

"Thanks to you all. There's a cool night coming, and a good fire is most inviting," Genlon responded. He remained near the doorway.

"What news have you heard?" the other merchant asked.

"There have been heavy rains to the south. The waters are high all through Mistlands."

The merchants laughed. One of them said, "Not high enough to suit us, my friend. We've both had bad experiences in Mistlands. We were talking about that just before you entered."

Genlon nodded. "I've never seen Mistlands. It's a place best avoided, from what men say."

"If men say, 'avoid Mistlands,' they say wisely. But have you not heard of the great massacre of brigands at the hostel in Long Wood?"

"A few people have spoken of it. Since every account is different, I'm inclined to doubt them all."

"Very sensible," said the merchant. "I think it's all imagination, myself. One man does not defeat two score armed bandits, all of whom have sworn to shed his blood!"

"And with a broken sword!" the other added.

"I've not heard that version," Genlon said, smiling with them. He loosed the clasp of his traveling cloak and moved to settle in the offered place.

"It's the sword that makes a joke of it," the merchant went on. "The woodwards of Long Wood use the double-bit ax. Why, there hasn't been a swordsman in Long Wood . . ." His eyes fell on the sword at Genlon's side, and the handle of the double-bit ax that he still wore slung behind him, and he fell silent.

His fellow merchant, after a moment's pause, said, "There never was. They're fine, strong men in Long Wood, brave as

you could wish, but they know no more about swordsmanship ... what's the matter, Hathil?"

The other merchant's frantic facial contortions had not
alerted his partner, and only when Genlon shifted his position, revealing the sword, did the man fall into an embarrassed and uncomfortable silence.

"We had no idea ... we intended no ... it was absolutely ..." Hathil fumbled, while his partner nodded desperately.

"You meant no offense, and you gave none," Genlon said.
On an impulse, he told them what he had told no one else
he had met on this journey. "In fact, there were eleven robbers and four of us. My three companions were archers, and
good ones." He glanced from one merchant to the other and
smiled. "We use the bow in Long Wood, as well as the ax.
The robbers, as far as we know, had sworn no oaths. They
were robbers out for plunder, nothing more. They killed for
their convenience, their pleasure ... for whatever reasons
such men kill. We stopped them for the sake of our families
and our neighbors."

"How many did you kill?" a servant asked.

Without looking at him, Genlon said, "Killing is not a
thing to boast about."

"Of course not," Hathil heartily agreed. "Well, you must
be on your way to the High City, then."

"Why would I go to the High City?"

"I thought you'd be joining Lord Duarin's guard. He's
recruiting the best fighting men in the north for his guard."

"Is he recruiting still? I thought all the High City's enemies
were defeated by now," Genlon said.

"Small bands of nomads still roam in the south. There are
robbers in the mountains, and on the Headland."

"And you just fought them in Long Wood," Hathil's partner added.

"True. But we had no help from the guard. We've seen
and heard nothing of them since they came to Long Wood to
recruit, many summers past. Just as well, I suppose. We
solve our own problems."

That statement was beyond dispute. There was a brief
silence; then Hathil said, "If you're going to the High City,
we welcome you to travel with us. We'd be safer with your
sword, and you'd be safer with six of us than alone."

"The mountains are dangerous. A man traveling alone—

even a good swordsman—takes a grave chance," his partner said.

"Are there no guards to protect travelers?"

Hathil shrugged. "The guards pursue the robbers once they've attacked. That does the victims little good."

Another indisputable statement. Genlon nodded, and at last he said, "I'll tell you in the morning."

"Good enough, friend. Meanwhile, let's eat," Hathil said.

Genlon spoke little while they dined, and when they were done, he went outside and stood alone by the door as the night came on. He badly wanted time to think on the merchants' offer.

He had come all this way seeking a sign to guide him, and now he wondered if this chance meeting was what he sought. He had never pictured himself in the High City, never thought of himself as a swordsman or warrior, but the events of recent days seemed to be pushing him in that direction. Yet this could all be coincidence. The significance of this meeting might lie in his over-eager imagination. He longed for a clear sign to follow.

A sound far up the road brought him out of his reverie and into instant alertness. It was a repeated two-beat rhythm; not footfalls, but something else, and it was approaching the faring-house.

Genlon stepped to the margin of the road. He was in deep shadow here, and there was no chance of his being seen. He peered up the road and saw a solitary figure moving toward him with an odd, teetering motion. As the figure drew nearer, and the double beat grew louder, Genlon saw that it was a one-legged man, making swift, steady progress along the road on a pair of crutches.

Even as he started forward to greet the man, memory of certain words spoken by Cathwar came back to him. With the realization of their significance, he stopped in his tracks, joy, fear, and expectation flooding over him. He knew it beyond a doubt: the one-legged man with his two crutches was the sign that Cathwar had promised.

Cathwar, like all the wizards Genlon had ever heard of, was reluctant to speak plainly of things to be. Instead, he spoke cryptically, embedding his meaning in the heart of a thicket of riddling words. Whoever sought the future had to penetrate the labyrinth, sift the truth from the teasing false clues, and dig up the knowledge from where it had been deeply buried. If one looked backward after the event, the message was always clear—now that it was of no use at all. When one hungered for it, the knowledge was so well concealed that its hinted presence taunted more than ignorance.

Genlon remembered the wizard's exact words. He had spoken them near the end of their time together, when Genlon had learned swordsmanship and a few other skills of less obvious value which the wizard had insisted on his mastering. The youth had asked why he was learning these things, which would be of little use to him in Long Wood.

"You'll be leaving Long Wood soon after you return. Don't act surprised—you've known that for a long time," Cathwar said.

"I've suspected it, but it never made sense. Why would I leave? Everything I have is there."

"You have more to do with your life than fell trees and pour out beer, my boy. Much more."

"Where will I go? What will I do?"

"No need for you to know that until the time comes. When you need to know, you'll hear it from someone."

"Who? You, Cathwar?"

"I'm not a messenger," the wizard said testily. "You'll learn it—if you're wise enough—from a man who walks on more than two legs and yet has fewer than two. Listen to him and decide."

"Will he speak in riddles, too?" Genlon asked with some exasperation.

"Everything is a riddle to the stupid man. Use your brain. Think. I keep telling you, think. That's what will save you when everything else fails."

And now, here by this faring-house, he saw the man who walked on more than two legs and yet had only one—a sign so plain any child would have seen it.

The one-legged man was bony and dirty and well past his youth. His waterbag was plump, but the scrip he passed around held only crumbs and crusts.

As last-comer, Genlon offered the greeting. He waited until the one-legged man had settled in his empty place, and then he sat down beside him.

"What news have you heard, friend?" Hathil asked.

"Floods in Mistlands, trouble in the High City, a great feat of arms in the west of Long Wood," the newcomer said rapidly, like a peddler announcing his wares. "The hunt goes on for the brigands of the Headland, but most men think they tried to cross the Fissure and were lost."

"There's no way in or out of the Headland but over the bridge," said Hathil's companion flatly, and the others all nodded.

"True," said the one-legged man, hitching closer to the small fire and holding grimy fingers out for warmth. "But at least the Headlanders use their bridge now and then. The people of the Crystal Hills seem to have given up all trade and travel. I've met no one from the Crystal Hills, nor anyone who's been there, for these three summers past."

"We met a small party heading for the Crystal Hills when we were trading up north. Early in Longdays, it was, as I recall."

"I hope they made it," said the one-legged man.

"Don't the guards keep the roads safe? They've strengthened the Northmark garrison, and there are patrols in the mountains and on the Plain."

"Not enough. And the best men don't get sent out on patrol." The man turned to inspect Genlon more closely, and then he said to the company, "What they need is men like this. If he's any good with that sword, he can be commander of the guard before ten summers pass. Lord Duarin rewards good men."

Hathil and his partner both looked expectantly at Genlon. He said nothing of his deed at the inn, and his frown and the slight movement of the head told them unmistakably that he wished them to remain silent, as well.

After an awkward pause, Hathil cleared his throat and asked, "What's the trouble in the High City? Surely no brigands have dared attack there."

"No, no, the High City is as safe as sunshine. The trouble is all in the future, if you believe in prophecies. Lord Duarin doesn't, but there are those who do."

"What is the prophecy?"

"I can tell you what I heard from a man who swore he heard it from a woman who swore she heard it from the lips of the prophet herself. For my part, I believe the words are accurate, but I no more understand them than I do the gibbering of the southern nomads. Here's the prophecy:

> *The child who died is the king who will be;*
> *The king who died will slay the king who would be;*

*The son of three mothers will father three sons, and
with their hands on his blood they will shake the world
when they are dead and gone to dust."*

The one-legged man looked around the circle of puzzled
faces. He appeared proud of the confusion he had caused.
"Those are the words as I heard them, friends. I don't understand them, and if any man here does, Lord Duarin will
reward him for his wisdom, I tell you that."

"I thought Lord Duarin didn't believe in prophecies," Genlon observed.

"He does not. But he believes very much in removing anything that might confuse his people, and this prophecy is
troubling to some. There are those who say it foretells the
fall of Duarin at the hands of Pytrigon's ghost."

"How do they explain that?" Hathil asked.

The one-legged man shrugged. "As I said before, friends,
I understand none of it. I only say what I heard said."

Genlon offered food from his pack. The one-legged man
accepted it gratefully and gobbled it down like a starveling.
Even as he crammed bits of dried meat into his mouth, he
kept on talking, regaling the company with gossip from all
the regions of the north.

Genlon excused himself from the fireside while the others
were still exchanging tidbits of gossip and morsels of food.
He neither needed nor wished to hear more; his decision was
made, and his mind was clear.

The prophecy was unintelligible to him, but he was not
troubled about that. He had understood Cathwar's riddle
not at first, but when the moment of its fulfillment came. If
the prophecy related to him and he was meant to fathom its
meaning, he would understand it, too, when the time was
ripe. If it had nothing to do with him, his ignorance made
no difference.

More significant to Genlon was the one-legged man's mention of the High City and Lord Duarin. That fact, added to
what the merchants had said and their invitation to join
them on their journey, was a clear indication to him that his
destiny, whatever it might be, lay in the High City. With his
immediate future settled, he slept soundly through the night.
When he awoke, the others were already stirring. The one-
legged man was gone.

The journey to the Fastness was uneventful. The little

band of travelers enjoyed excellent weather. Soft rains fell on two nights, but the mornings were always clear and the days bright, and they made rapid progress.

Two days into the mountains, they caught up with a large caravan. Their arrival caused something of a stir among the travelers, who were already much alarmed by rumors of bandits lurking on the road. The merchants and their servants could have frightened no one, but Genlon, armed as he was and towering over his companions, was a fearful sight to them. Four caravan guards, keeping a cautious distance, conducted him and Hathil to the caravan master. While Hathil parleyed, Genlon looked over the caravan.

Ahead of them were a handful of brawny, sullen-looking guards; to Genlon's eye, they were as hard a lot as the brigands of Long Wood, but the caravan master appeared to trust them, and so did the other travelers.

About two score travelers walked ahead of the master; the rest followed. Most were on foot, as was the custom in the northern lands, but in this caravan were six wagons drawn by tall, sturdy-looking creatures with wide horns, great dust-colored brutes bigger than any animals Genlon had ever seen before. They moved with a ponderous, slow step that magnified the impression of strength their bulk conveyed, and Genlon studied them with fascination. He had heard of such creatures, but he had never known of them in the north until this moment.

The wagons they drew were identical save for the first of the six. That was the same size as all the others, but more richly made; even from his present distance Genlon could perceive that. The others were made of dark-painted wood, with iron fittings, and they were covered in a plain, canvas-like material. The first wagon was covered with a canopy of dark, soft-looking cloth. The wood was polished; brass fittings shone on the wagon and glinted on the harness of the beasts that drew it, the largest pair of all. A man wearing a short cloak of the same color as the wagon cover walked beside the oxen, and a similarly dressed man kept watch at each corner of the wagon. Such caution made Genlon curious about the occupant, and he determined to ask his first acquaintance in the caravan who it might be.

Five days later, when they arrived at the Fastness, he had learned nothing. Everyone in the caravan was as curious as he, and not one of them could satisfy that curiosity. Not even the master of the caravan, it was rumored, knew the mighty personage who rode in the dark wagon; and no one thought it wise to ask.

Once inside the gates of the Fastness, the caravan scattered like a broken string of beads, for this was the site of the great caravansary of the north, where travelers met and caravans rested and re-formed. Some of the travelers planned to leave this caravan and join another; others had come to complete some business at the Fastness and then return whence they had come; a few had no plans at all and were waiting to see what befell them amid the colorful activity and the crowds that swarmed between the third and fourth ring of walls.

Deeper in the Fastness, life was somber and tightly disciplined. The daily traffic of guards and relief columns brought with it a sobering air of iron and darkness. But in the caravansary, all was bright and brisk and joyous.

Genlon wandered wide-eyed through the swirl of color and the din of many voices, seeing sights he had never dreamed of, sights as astonishing as the great horned beasts that had drawn the mysterious wagon. There were dark-eyed people from the lands to the south, dressed in loose robes as colorful as rainbows. Goods were displayed everywhere—rich cloths, objects of gleaming brass and silver and gold, bright-colored pottery, jewels, unknown foodstuffs of pungent scent, unfamiliar weapons of exquisite workmanship, boots of leather supple as silk. There were unfamiliar sounds in the dusty air, cries and conversations in many languages, some guttural, some soft and liquid, all utterly strange.

More women walked in the caravansary than he had seen in all his life. He had heard from travelers at his parents' inn that this was so, but he had never quite believed it. Not only were they here in plenty, but they were young, and they were lovely. Each appeared different from all the others, yet all were beautiful to his appreciative eyes. They were not like the girls of Long Wood, who seemed to look on all males as nuisances and necessary evils. These girls were free with their smiles and their laughter. They spoke to him and to everyone with easy familiarity. Several of them brushed against him and gave him inviting glances as he passed.

He was utterly bewildered. Marriages in Long Wood were business matters, arranged with great care by parents; courtship was unknown, and the contacts between young

men and women were always well chaperoned. Amid this
plenitude of beauty, Genlon did not know how to act. He
felt as awkward as a small boy being talked about in the
presence of elders. He was unable to think of anything to
say, and he was afraid even to return their smiles. His solemnity seemed only to make them smile the more. He began to
think that Riverfield Inn, which he had once considered the
center of a busy, exciting world, was a very small and backward place indeed, and that he himself, for all his great
stature, and his strength, and his deeds, was hardly more
than a boy.

He felt a touch on his arm, turned, and sighed with relief
at the sight of Hathil. The merchant gestured for him to step
into a nearby establishment that appeared to be a small and
very crowded inn, covered with a gaudy canopy and open
on three sides.

"Come. Eat with me," Hathil said.

Genlon's thoughts had not been on food. But the mention
of eating, and the aroma that drifted from under the canopy,
reminded him that he had not eaten since morning.

"I will, Hathil. I'm starving," he announced cheerfully.

"You must try some seven-savor. It's very good here. And
while we eat, I want to talk to you. There are some things
about the Fastness that I think you should know."

The food was delicious, seasoned with spices unknown in
Long Wood. But as Hathil explained the ways of the caravansary and its people, Genlon found his appetite fading. He
began to feel very much the fool. Hathil was a kindly man,
and he refrained from criticism or mockery, but his message
was clear: a young, inexperienced traveler was looked upon
as fair game by these smiling ladies. Genlon was very fortunate to have his purse intact, and he would be wise to
choose his companions carefully and avoid the press of
crowds for the rest of his stay at the Fastness. When he spoke
of Genlon's stay, Hathil's voice faltered, as if the subject
made him uncomfortable.

"The thing is, Genlon, we've met an old acquaintance," he
went on in a sudden rush, looking intently down on his
empty dish. "He stopped here in Earlygreen, on one of the
first caravans after the snows melted, and he's been here
since, trading with the caravans that pass through. He's done
very well, and he's invited us to come in with him." Hathil
looked up squarely at Genlon and said, "I know you're plan-

ning to go to the High City, but if you'd like to stay with us for a while, we could find work for you. Good work, too, where you could do well. Then we'd all go on to the High City with a good bit of coin in our purses."

"How long would we stay here?"

Hathil shrugged. "Until next autumn, most likely. Perhaps longer."

Genlon said nothing for a time. Then he shook his head and said, "I don't know, Hathil. I never thought of anything like this."

"Think about it," the merchant said. "I know you don't make hasty decisions. There's no hurry."

"I'll do that, then."

"And if you want a place to stay, go to the Twin Oaks Inn. It's built into the outer wall, about a longmark to the right of the gate. A good clean place, and cheap, too. The innkeeper knows us well. Tell him you're with us, and he'll find you a room near ours."

After the meal, they separated, Hathil to attend to his business with his new partner and Genlon to seek out the Twin Oaks. As he retraced his way to the gate, Genlon looked with quite different eyes on the smiling faces that turned to him from every side. The smiles were all for sale, he thought with new cynicism, exactly as the trinkets thrust at him in eager hands were for sale. The falsity of it all was repellent to him; yet he still felt a perverse fascination for the life and color and movement of the caravansary even as he yearned for the familiar ways of Long Wood. He wished that the smiles were honest, and that he was truly welcome here.

The revelation of his own gullibility would have been depressing enough; now he had the additional care of reconsidering a decision he had thought to be final. To stay here for a time, learning the ways of trade, might be interesting and would surely be profitable. His father had once been a merchant; perhaps his own true talents lay in that field. He could enter the High City in a summer or two, a man of substance, and fulfill his destiny then as well as now—if, indeed, his destiny lay in the High City. And surely a merchant's life was better than the life of a guardsman.

He turned the question over in his mind a dozen times on the way to the inn, but he could not resolve it. The innkeeper, a gruff-looking little man with a pleasant manner

that belied his appearance, showed him to a small room just
below Hathil's. It was a shady, quiet chamber, high in the
eastern face of the wall—a place conducive to thinking. When
the innkeeper left him, Genlon sprawled on the too-small
bed and sank into a reverie.

A guardsman's life meant travel to far lands, long absence
from all those he knew. It meant periods of weariness and
boredom interspersed with times of intense action and ex-
citement. It meant, too,. the likelihood of killing and the risk
of death.

More than anything else, the thought of using his sword
against other men troubled Genlon, for it raised a perplexing
question that he could not answer. He had taken no pride
nor pleasure in the victory at Riverfield Inn. He had not
fought for glory or riches, but purely from necessity; still,
he had taken the lives of six men. They were bad men, to
be sure, and they would have killed him with no more
thought than they would have given to plucking a handful of
stingberries from a bush; but they were men, all the same,
living men, and now they were dead. That could never be a
good thing.

And yet he knew that if he had not led his friends in making a stand, others would have died as surely as the eleven
brigands had died. Those other deaths would have been
painful and degrading, and utterly pointless, the side issue of
a casual brute greed. He had prevented that; perhaps he had
saved scores of lives.

It seemed to him that when he had taken up the sword
of Skobo, he had taken up, all unaware, a life in which a
man must sometimes do terrible things in order to avoid
worse. He did not want that to be his future. But he could
not imagine himself as a merchant, accumulating coins and
smiling at strangers as the ladies and hawkers of the caravansary did.

A heavy knock at the door of the room broke his concentration. He swung his legs to the floor and buckled on
his sword as the door opened and a stocky man in a short
cloak stood silhouetted in the doorway.

"My mistress would speak to you," the man said.

"And who is your mistress?"

"She's a wise and powerful woman, and she's taken an
interest in you."

"That tells me nothing."

"She'll tell you more when you meet her."

Genlon was not in a mood to oblige anyone. He still smarted from the day's revelations and perplexities, and this intrusion came as the last straw. He hooked a thumb into his belt, laid his hand lightly on the hilt of his sword, and said, "I've met enough people for one day."

"My mistress expects to see you," the other replied, making no move either to attack or to withdraw. His voice was even.

"Then your mistress will be disappointed."

The intruder was silent for a time, as if waiting for Genlon to go on. When Genlon did not speak, the man sighed and said, "It will be uncomfortable for me if she is. Listen, I'll tell you no lies. My mistress has far to go, and she's heard of robbers and brigands on the way ahead. Five of us guard her now. She thinks five may not be enough. But with you for a sixth, she believes we could turn back any attackers. I agree with her." He paused, and when Genlon still made no reply, he went on, "She's very generous, and very influential. It's a good place, and you can go far if you please her."

"Where is she bound?"

The other man hesitated; then he said, "You must give me your word that you'll tell no one."

"You have my word."

"We go to the High City."

Genlon let out a great sigh of relief and smiled on the man as on a newfound friend. "Then take me to her," he said.

In the bright afternoon light, Genlon recognized the man as one of the escorts of the mysterious dark wagon. He appeared to be about twice Genlon's age, with a face lined and coppered by exposure to all weathers and blond hair that was almost white. A head shorter than the forest youth, he was equally broad in the chest and a bit thick-waisted without any suggestion of flabbiness. He walked with a brisk step, like a man accustomed to covering his set distance regardless of conditions, and he talked freely as they made their way through the crowds to the inner gate. His name was Cade.

"This place never gets any better," he said, with a gesture that at once encompassed and dismissed their surroundings. "I've been through here a score of times, and each time it's noisier and more crowded than the time before. They're all thieves here, too. You have to keep your purse well hidden. At that, there are some here who could steal ten oaks out of your closed fist and you'd not know it was gone until the next day."

"I was warned about thieves," Genlon said.

"All the same, you're lucky to have anything left. A young lad like you, still wearing your Long Wood colors, is fair game for this crowd. While you're looking at one pretty girl, another one plucks the purse right out of your shirt, and then they both disappear into the crowd, and you're left to beg for your dinner and sleep in any corner you can find. I remember the first time I came through the Fastness. Thieves stole everything but the clothes I had on my back, and they probably would have stolen them, too, if they hadn't been so ragged and filthy. I was only a boy, then, on the run. I hadn't seen so many people in one place at the same time in all my life, and I walked along gaping and staring like a fool. It didn't take them long to spot me."

Cade smiled and shook his head slowly, as if at some bittersweet memory. "First a girl bumped into me, and while I was trying to think of something clever to say to her— pretty little thing she was—another brushed past me. Then a man nearly knocked me down, and when I went for him, two others jumped in to break it up, and then a girl came over and took my arm and asked me if I had a place to stay for the night. Well, I got all tongue-tied at that, and I didn't know what to say or how to say it, and she just walked away, laughing at me. And when I went to have dinner, I found my purse gone. I still haven't figured out which one of them did it." He laughed softly and glanced at Genlon. "That was a long time ago, half a lifetime and more, but I remember it all. I'd know their faces if I saw them today."

"I think people tried to do the same to me this morning," Genlon said.

"They can spot a first-timer while he's still below the horizon, this crowd can. Now, you don't look all that green to me, but you can't fool thieves. I was just a ragged boy, fifteen summers old, with a dagger in my belt and a traveling-staff in my hand. I tried to swagger in here like an old warrior, and I must have looked quite a clown. That ax, and your Long Wood colors, give you away, but your sword must have confused them. Not many swordsmen in Long

Wood that anyone's heard of. None, most people say. Where'd you get it?"

"In the north, on my faring year."

"And you care to say no more. I see." Cade laughed aloud and looked at Genlon with a conspiratorial glint in his eye. "Well, when you're ready to tell the story of that blade, I want to hear it. I'm sure you didn't buy it from a peddler, or find it lying by the road. Have you ever used it?"

"Yes."

"You're still alive, not missing ears or fingers, and you don't limp, so you must have used it properly."

"I was well taught," Genlon said.

Cade nodded. He said, "You must have gone far in your faring year. There's no one in the northern lands can teach you proper use of a sword like that. There's a real fear of swords and swordsmen in this part of the world, clear from the Cape of Mists to well south of the Issalt. The memory of the sea-raiders is still very much alive, and the sword was their weapon. The ax and bow and pike drove the sea-raiders off, and they've been the favored weapons ever since in these parts. But from what I hear, Lord Duarin has no dislike for the blade. His guardsmen all carry swords like yours, and they use them well. You may find your fortune in the High City."

They had reached the inner gate, and here they stopped. The crowd around them watched with interest, for transients seldom passed beyond the third wall, and the guards who came and went were not talkative. These two men did not have the look of nobles; clearly they were not prisoners, and they did not walk like servants. They were a puzzle.

The guard recognized Cade and nodded to him as he unlocked the gate and swung it open. He looked closely at Genlon, but he said nothing to the youth. As Cade and Genlon passed under the archway of the inner gate and walked the dark passage through the thick wall, the uproar of the caravansary faded. When they emerged into the court behind the third wall, they were in a place of silence. The next wall lay beyond fields of rich dark earth, bare at this time of year. Genlon looked on that blackish brown soil with amazement. It was not the soil of this barren place; it had been brought here, every clod of it, to make the Fastness self-sufficient. At the thought of the effort involved, an effort commensurate with the immensity of the Fastness, he felt dwarfed. Such an undertaking was beyond his wildest imaginings, and yet it had been conceived and carried out long ago, and maintained ever since, by the keepers of the Fastness. He was aware once again of how far he had come from Long Wood and his old life.

"It's impressive, isn't it?" Cade observed. "I never saw it myself before this, for all my times through here. I never traveled in such exalted company before. The inner gate was always closed to me. Of course, this place doesn't compare with the High City, but it's still the biggest fortress I've ever heard of. I'd hate to have the task of laying siege to it, I'll tell you that."

"How old is it?" Genlon asked.

Cade shrugged. "The keep and the inmost wall are older than anyone knows. They were old when the High City was founded and the calendar was begun. No one's quite sure when the other walls went up, either, except the outer wall. That was built in the days of the last king. Everything else is just old, very old."

"There must have been a powerful enemy in those days, to make anyone want to build such a stronghold."

"So there was, if the tales are true." Cade pointed to a compound on their left ahead, a large building surrounded by a dozen smaller ones, and said, "My mistress is there. See the two middle-sized buildings beside the big one? She's in the far one, she and her waiting-woman. The rest of us are in the small hut just ahead of hers."

"She must be very powerful, to be entitled to such quarters."

"She is," Cade said. With that, he fell silent and said no more until they reached the quarters of his mistress. When they passed the hut where her guards were quartered, he waved to two who sat before the door, lounging lazily in the afternoon sun, but they exchanged no greetings. At his mistress's doorway, he instructed Genlon to wait. He entered and emerged soon afterward. "Go in. She's waiting for you. Good luck, Genlon," he said, and he took up a post by the entrance to wait.

Genlon brushed aside a heavy, dark cloth and then a second, and when they fell into place behind him he found himself in darkness. The air was warm and close, like that of a room long sealed, and it carried a faint, sweet scent. He sniffed it cautiously, and he remembered the smoke of dried firesong leaves: they were crumbled into powder and sifted onto embers, and the smoke gave deep sleep and pleasant dreams when inhaled. It was said that old people found it relaxing. So this powerful woman, whoever she was, might be old, he reasoned.

He strained his ears but could hear nothing. Reaching out gingerly, he walked slowly forward until his fingers touched cloth. He felt around; the walls were all draped heavily with layers of thick, soft cloth.

Turning and setting his back to the wall, Genlon said in a conversational tone, without challenge or disrespect, "I've come as you asked, lady. What is your business with me?"

About ten paces before him, a figure suddenly appeared, seated on cushions, a brazier of burning coals at either hand. She had been waiting there, silent, concealed by draperies. In the faint light, Genlon could see only that her head was covered and her face was in shadow. She was very small, and she appeared frail, but her voice was strong and clear.

"I had my doubts about you, child. I thought you might be a mindless, muscle-bound warrior who'd lash out with his sword at the first hint of anything unfamiliar. But you kept your wits. That's good. Weren't you afraid?" she asked.

"I have no enemies, lady," he replied.

She laughed a high, thin laugh, not of mockery but of genuine amusement. "How very young you must be to say such a thing!" she exclaimed. She burst into fresh laughter. Then she said, "You're very fortunate, Genlon Banheenson. It won't be long before you have enemies all around you, so enjoy your freedom while you can. Come closer now." She snapped her fingers and called out, "Tupaji, bring me light."

A woman appeared from behind her, carrying candles which she set in stands on either side of the spot where Genlon had stopped two paces before the old woman. She was on a kind of dais, so that she reclined at about the level of Genlon's chest. He saw her staring intently into his face.

"Step closer to the candles. I want to see what you look like," she ordered. He did so, and after she had studied him carefully, she asked, "Which of your parents do you resemble more, child?"

"My mother, lady. Her hair and eyes were the color of mine, and everyone in her family was tall."

"Is your mother living?"

"No, lady. She died giving birth to me."

"And your father? Is he alive?"

"He is, lady."

"You wear the clothing of Long Wood. Were both your parents from Long Wood?"

"They were from the Crystal Hills, lady. My father sold all he had and left when my mother died. He remarried, to a woman of Long Wood, and they keep an inn at Riverfield, as her father and his father before him did."

"Ah, yes, the inn at Riverfield. This is where you performed your great feat of arms, is it not?" When she saw the look of surprise on Genlon's face, she went on, "Your merchant friends kept your secret. I learned it from their servants. Servants are always eager to give away secrets. All except Tupaji," she said more gently, turning to smile at the silent dark woman beside her, who bowed and left them. "Tupaji is mute. She neither reads nor writes," she explained when the woman was gone.

"I'm not a seasoned warrior, lady. At the inn, I was defending my home and my family, and I had old friends to help me. If the way to the High City is dangerous, you may need more help than I can give," Genlon said.

"You are not boastful, either. Another good trait. I might grow to like you very much, child."

"Thank you, lady."

"Enter my service, Genlon. If you serve me well, I'll see to it that you go far. I can be very helpful to those I like."

"I will serve you, lady. Again, I thank you," Genlon said.

"Then it's done. Go and have Cade buy you decent clothes. Say your farewells, but tell no one our destination. You are welcome to the service of the Lady Ammaranza."

CHAPTER SIX

THE HOUSE ON THE PLAIN

They left the Fastness at first light. Genlon, in a new gray traveling-cloak, tunic and tight-fitting trousers of deep maroon, and the softest, most comfortable boots he had ever worn, walked at the side of their little caravan.

One of the wagons had been left at the Fastness, and they traveled now with five. Cade was far ahead of them, scouting the trail. Half the time he was lost to their sight. Levvo, a slim, dark-haired man eleven years in Ammaranza's service, walked beside her wagon. Genlon walked behind him, on the other side, between the second and third wagons. Another guard walked between the fourth and fifth, and two more brought up the rear.

Inexperienced though he was, Genlon could see that he was in the position of least importance. He was not certain why, and he sensed that it would do him little good to ask. Perhaps he had been given the easiest post because he was young, and a new hand; but more likely he had been placed here because anyone in this post could be kept under the eye of other guards at all times. Genlon was not much given to suspicion, and he resented falling under the suspicion of others. But he kept his doubts to himself, confident that he would prove his trustworthiness when the moment came.

On the first day, they covered sixteen greatmarks between dawn and late afternoon. Cade and the others seemed satisfied with this pace. To Genlon it was little better than crawling, but it appeared that the oxen could move no faster. They camped for the night in a recess with high, overhanging rock walls on two sides and clear ground sloping away in front. Cade judged that a single guard would suffice, and he sent Joast, one of the rear guards, to take the first turn. Genlon was to take the midnight watch, sharing it with Levvo and then Cade.

To Genlon, this sounded like one more manifestation of their distrust. He said nothing, but his expression or his manner must have betrayed his feelings, for Cade raised the subject while they ate.

"I don't want you standing watch alone for the first few nights," he said. "There are things you have to know, and if you don't know them we can all end up dead. Standing watch isn't just a matter of keeping awake and listening. You have to know what you're listening for."

"I've watched nights in Long Wood."

"Long Wood isn't the mountains," Levvo said without raising his eyes.

"You didn't have brigands stalking you in Long Wood. All you had to do was keep the fire going and see to it that nothing ran off with the food. It's a lot different here," Cade added.

"Whatever you say, Cade. I'm willing to learn what I have to learn."

"You think we don't trust you. Don't deny it—I can tell just by looking at you. Now, listen to me," Cade said earnestly. "I'm a pretty fair judge of men, and I think you can be trusted. And the Lady Ammaranza is a better judge of people than you and I are ever going to meet, and she thinks you're trustworthy. So there's no question in our minds about that. We're not afraid you're going to lead us into a trap. But we don't know how good a guard you'll be until we see you working at it. I wouldn't sleep soundly while another man stands watch until I've seen how he works."

"The man on watch is responsible for the whole caravan," Levvo said.

"Levvo's right. Now finish eating and get some sleep. He'll wake you in the middle of his watch," said Cade.

There was no more talk during dinner. The others were neither friendly nor unfriendly toward Genlon, nor were they any more talkative among themselves than they were with the newcomer. Their conversational resources seemed limited to groans, yawns, and halfhearted complaints about the cold food and the hard ground. Such talk as there was all came from Cade, but even he seemed subdued. Genlon wondered if this was a sign that they anticipated trouble; but he did not ask.

Levvo was a taciturn watch companion, but Cade was more his voluble self as they sat in the darkness. He seemed able to talk and yet at the same time listen attentively to his surroundings. At any noise, he stopped abruptly, and then he went on to explain the significance of the sound to Genlon.

The next day, Genlon marched in the fourth position, and that night he shared guard with Fomdey and Cade. As they moved out the next morning, Cade told him that he would take his turn alone that night.

On the third day, Genlon shared rear guard with Neff, a husky fellow with long, thick arms and a big half-bald head set solidly on his shoulders with scarcely a hint of a neck intervening. Neff was from a land far to the southwest, and Genlon tried to get him to talk about his homeland, but Neff preferred to complain about the uneven trail and his sore feet. Genlon listened patiently, with an occasional grunt or monosyllable to indicate his continued attention and sympathy.

The attack came at mid-morning. Neff suddenly stopped in his tracks and then took an unsteady step forward. He clutched at Genlon's arm and turned to him, wide-eyed, with an almost childlike whimper of pain. Then he fell to his knees and collapsed on his side. Genlon stared down on him, mystified; he had heard and seen nothing. Then he felt something strike his foot and looked down to see an arrow jutting from the heel of his boot. He hauled Neff to his shoulder and ran forward, shouting the alarm.

Suddenly the air was thick with arrows. In actuality there were no more than three or four score launched in the entire attack, but it seemed then as if they were flying thick as hail. Fomdey went down with an arrow in his leg, and two more sank in his ribs before he could drag himself to cover. Joast took an arrow in the back of the neck as he tried to climb into the nearest wagon; he toppled backward and crashed to the ground, where he lay still.

Genlon laid Neff's body in the last wagon and ran the gauntlet to the front of the column. His duty was to protect the Lady Ammaranza, and he meant to do it. The sight of three fallen comrades, the whisper of the arrows that zipped past him as he ran, the threat of the coming onslaught—all these excited him. He felt no fear; he knew only a desire to close with the invisible enemy and prove himself to his mistress and his companions.

He dove under the leading cart and lay flat, taking cover

behind a rear wheel. Cade was already there, kneeling behind one of the front wheels and peering cautiously out at the boulder-strewn slopes whence the arrows had come. Not a soul was in sight. He had a short bow in his hands, one arrow nocked and ready and about a score more lying close at hand.

"Take the other side," he ordered. "They must have men over there, too."

Without a word, Genlon sallied forth from their shelter. Stooping low, his sword drawn, he made for the nearest cluster of rocks at a lope. The ground on this side of the road fell away sharply, and he was moving at a good speed when the two men slipped out from their cover, unaware of his approach. One of them quickly raised a bow, but Genlon was too close; he crashed into the bowman and knocked him sprawling. The second lunged at him with a hatchet, shouting a warning to unseen comrades. Genlon jabbed the point of his sword in just under the man's chin, drew it out quickly, and turned to cut at the bowman, who was scrambling to his feet. His blow landed high on the man's thigh, just below the hip, nearly severing the leg. The man screamed in pain and shock and went down in a bright spray of blood.

At the sound of movement, Genlon turned again to face the rocks, and an arrow hissed by his face so close he blinked and jerked his head back. The attacker fitted a second arrow to his bow. Genlon charged into him, sword arm fully extended like a lance, and impaled the archer before he could take aim. The arrow struck sparks from the rock at Genlon's feet.

As Genlon strained to draw out the deep-thrust blade, a fourth brigand attacked from behind the shield of his comrade's body, reaching over the man's shoulder to stab downward with a long, broad-bladed dagger. Genlon blocked the blow with his wrist and caught his attacker's elbow with his other hand; with a hard twist he wrenched the man's shoulder out of joint. He dispatched him with his own dagger.

All was quiet now. He pulled his blade free, and with sword in one hand and his captured dagger in the other, he made a swift reconnaissance of the few hiding places nearby. In the midst of his searching, he heard an outburst of wild cries from above, on the road.

The brigands did not see Genlon coming. He did not hesitate or break his stride, but he came around the rear of the wagon at a run and fell on them like an avalanche, scything down the nearest man and cleaving the skull of a second before the rest were even aware of his presence.

Thy turned from the fallen Cade to deal with Genlon. He cut down two more with his sword before their rush forced him to use the sword as his shield and the dagger as his weapon. He batted aside a thrust and drove the pommel into one attacker's face, felling him; he deflected a hatchet blow and slashed the man's belly open with his dagger. His swarming enemies could not reach him. Twisting and dodging with a speed and agility they had never seen in a man his size, he worked the brigands to a rage of frustration that a lone swordsman should deprive them of what had seemed such easy prey.

Cade, though injured, could still protect Genlon's back. The brigands had no choice but to face their enemy head-on, and each onslaught cost them another man. The odds against him fell quickly in the furious encounter, and soon only two men stood before him. As one of the brigands raised his long, metal-tipped club, and the other, dagger low and extended before him, moved to Genlon's other side, Cade loosed an arrow that sank deep into the second man's neck just below the ear. Genlon moved into the open, and, feinting a sword cut to the legs, he thrust his dagger under the robber's breastbone as the club descended. The last attacker was down. The attack was over, and his mistress was safe.

Genlon lowered his weapons and stood silent, panting, for a time. His shoulders ached, and his hands were so tightly clenched around his weapons that the wrappings of the hilts were imprinted in his palms. He stooped to tear free a cloak with which to clean his blades. When he rose again, sword in one hand, cloak in the other, dagger thrust in his belt, he stood motionless, like a man transfixed. At Cade's voice, he started.

"Thanks, Genlon. If you hadn't come back, they'd have cut me up for meat pie," Cade said.

"My thanks to you. You covered my back."

"You're good, Genlon. I've seen a lot of swordplay in my time, and you're the best. I don't understand how a man from Long Wood, of all places . . ." Cade broke off and gave a laugh of sheer exhilaration. "You're the best! Whoever taught you, he certainly taught you well." Still laughing, he pulled himself to his feet, leaning heavily on the wheel.

"Are you hurt?"

"My legs. I won't be able to walk for a while."

"Let me help you into the wagon."

Cade waved the offer aside. "See how the others are. Be careful. One of the brigands may be playing dead."

Warily, Genlon picked his way through the carnage to seek out Fomdey and Joast. Both were dead, as was Neff, who lay in the wagon where Genlon had flung him. Three of the drivers were dead, and the fourth was slightly injured. The fifth driver had escaped unhurt only by diving back into his wagon at the first outcry.

Genlon found Levvo's body about half a greatmark ahead. He was bristling with arrows, but he had dragged himself to a rock by the roadside, and he lay with his back to it, his dagger and hatchet in his hands.

When Genlon returned, the Lady Ammaranza was seated in the driver's place on her wagon. Tupaji knelt over Cade, who was seated against the wheel while she tended to his injuries.

"You fought bravely, Genlon," his mistress greeted him.

"I did my duty, lady."

"And did it well. Are any of our attackers still alive?"

"I think so, lady."

"Bring one here. I wish to question him."

In a short time, Genlon dragged a lean, yellow-haired youth before Ammaranza. The fellow's left cheek was purple, and blood flowed from his nostrils and his puffed lips where Genlon had battered him with the pommel of his sword. The clotted gore on his chin and throat and chest made his injury appear more serious than it actually was, but Ammaranza seemed to perceive his true condition at once.

She stared down on him without speaking. Her eyes were large and dark, ageless in her small, pale, old woman's face. She raised her hand and turned it so the light glinted from the stone in her ring and lanced into the captive's eyes, and he winced and turned his face aside. When at last she addressed the youth, her voice was soft, almost caressing.

"How many were in your band?" she asked.

"Sixteen, lady. Only sixteen, no more, I swear it."

"And why did you attack us?"

"Our leader had heard of your caravan. Wagons full of treasure, and only five guards. Some great lord or lady to hold for ransom, too, he said. We were sure that sixteen of us, striking from ambush, could take you easily."

"You were wrong about many things. Who told your leader about us?"

"He has a spy in the Fastness. I don't know who it is, lady, I swear! He told no one."

"How many other bands of robbers are between here and the plain?"

"No others, only us. I've heard of other bands up north, but none to the east of us," the prisoner said.

"Genlon, count the dead and fallen. See that there are fifteen of them," Ammaranza instructed.

"Yes, lady. What of the prisoner?"

"He will not move," Ammaranza assured him. She fixed her gaze once again on the yellow-haired youth and gestured with her right hand, moving her lips silently.

Genlon did as he was ordered. The four he had fought on the hillside were all dead, and nine lay dead or dying by the wagon. Cade pointed out two more on the uphill slope, downed by his arrows as they charged. Genlon reported the total to his mistress, who nodded, satisfied with the tally, and turned her attention to the prisoner once again. The young man stood as if paralyzed.

"Most of the caravans that pass along this road are much larger than ours. You could not hope to attack them with sixteen men. Where are the rest of your band?" Ammaranza said.

"There are no more. I swear it, lady!"

"Are they waiting ahead?"

"No, lady! We could never have more than sixteen. It was forbidden!"

Ammaranza laughed her high, thin laugh, like rustling silk. She said, "So, there are rules among you brigands. Your bands are not to exceed sixteen. Do you think me a fool, to believe such a story, little boy?"

"It's true, lady," the youth said desperately. He strained to move but remained as still as a man bound to a post. "The hooded man forbade us ever to number more than we were when he set us free."

"Tell me more of this hooded man."

"All I know is that he came to our cell and offered to set us free if we'd swear to go to the mountains and rob and kill those who passed. We were never to return to the High City."

"So you come from the High City. All of you?"

"Yes, lady, all. We were to die for thievery. For murder, some of us. I had only stolen food for my wife and child, I swear, but some of the others were lifelong robbers. The hooded man came to us late one night with his offer. It was a chance to escape death. I agreed. I had to, lady!"

"Of course you did," Ammaranza said, and her voice was soothing, but the very tenderness of her voice and manner was somehow menacing. Cade and Genlon looked on as the young prisoner tried again to move but failed to stir even a finger. From the neck down, he might have been a statue.

"Spare me, lady, please! I'll go far away. I'll go anywhere you say. I'll serve you till I die, if you want me, but spare my life!" he said frantically.

"I will spare your life. But you will go nowhere. You'll stay right here, with your friends, until the wolves and the ravens come," Ammaranza said. She lifted her hand, and the prisoner jerked as if a puppet master had twitched his strings. She pointed to a high rock by the roadside, and at her gesture the young robber began to walk stiffly toward it. He rounded the rock, and when he had reached the summit, Ammaranza dropped her hand. He stopped and stood rigid, screaming for mercy.

There was much work to be done before they moved on. Three of the wagons held fodder for the oxen; the fourth held food and water for the members of the caravan. On Cade's instructions, three wagons were abandoned and the other two overloaded as much as they dared. The oxen were set to eat their fill while Genlon and the uninjured driver did the unloading and reloading under Cade's direction.

All the time they worked, the crying and pleading of the last brigand filled the air. Genlon steeled himself against it as long as he could, but at last he went to where Cade lay and squatted at his side.

"That's a terrible punishment, even for a robber," he said.

"What should we do? Cut his throat?"

"I don't know. It seems so cruel to leave him there to die slowly. How did she do it?"

"Our mistress knows a few things, Genlon. I sometimes think she could take good care of herself without any help from us. Anyway, don't interfere. She's decided on that robber's punishment, and it's not for you to question it. Did you ever stop to think of what they would have done to us if they'd won? We'd have died a worse death than he will, that's certain."

Genlon remembered the story told by a sobbing, trembling child in Long Wood on the night he first wielded his sword in earnest. He nodded, forced to agree with Cade, but he was still troubled. It seemed to him that it was wrong to use the cruelty of one's enemies to justify one's own cruelty; but he knew that he was young and inexperienced in such things, and he had no right to oppose his mistress's decisions. His duty was to obey.

As Genlon rose, Cade said, "When you get the wagons unloaded, put our men's bodies in one of them. We'll burn them."

"What about the robbers?"

"Let them feed the ravens."

When all else was done, Genlon laid the bodies of Neff, Fomdey, and Joast in an empty wagon. The two extra wagons he had smashed apart to furnish wood for their pyre. Before the flames had begun to sink, the little caravan was on its way east. Over the crackling of the funeral pyre, slowly receding, came the broken, hoarse pleading of the solitary brigand, rooted to his perch.

Genlon was the forward guard now, and he worked himself to exhaustion each day, ranging far ahead of the wagons, searching up into the roadside hills for danger, seeking out a safe resting place for the night. Cade, unable to walk, slept during the day and kept the night watch, with Tupaji to relieve him.

One evening, as Genlon wolfed down his supper, Cade began to reminisce about the fallen guards. Listening, Genlon realized that he had never thought of them as men with past lives, families and friends, lovers and children; men who had eaten and drunk, laughed and sorrowed, sat by a thousand or five thousand or ten thousand trail-side fires like this one and talked about the small, ordinary things of life. He had scarcely known them. They had worked together for a few days, but only he and Cade had shared the experience of battle and survived. Now he felt the bond of mutual dependence and trust with Cade, even more strongly than he had felt it with his companions of the battle at Riverfield, for he and Cade had fought side by side, each defending the other. Cade was a friend like no other he had ever known, he realized.

"How do your legs feel?" he asked with sudden concern. "Are they healing well?"

"I'll walk through the gates of the High City without help. No bones broken, and everything's closing up clean. Tupaji's a good healer."

"I'm glad to hear that. Do you want me to help with the night watch?"

"I can handle it. I may not be able to walk, but I can listen, and I can shout. I feel a lot better knowing you go out there in the morning well rested and alert."

"Can I do anything else to help?" Genlon asked.

"Not a thing. Why so worried about me?"

Genlon shrugged and mumbled something vague. He did not know how to express his feelings. It was not customary in Long Wood to speak openly of friendship and admiration; one kept such things to oneself.

"Do you know, Genlon, it never occurred to me to ask, but did you come out of that brawl without a single scratch on you?" Cade asked. "You never complained, and you seemed unhurt, but it's hard to believe you fought all those men and weren't even touched."

"I took a cut on the arm and a few bruises."

Cade gave a low, whistling exhalation of breath and shook his head slowly. "You're better than I thought. And luckier," he said solemnly.

Genlon had been too busy to reflect on his luck; now, as he looked back, it seemed a miracle that he had come through this clash almost unscathed. At Riverfield, too, he had vanquished his enemies with only a slight injury to himself. He knew that Cathwar had taught him well, and he was aware of his own ability; even so, he had no illusions about mortal combat. Victories were not easily won, and often they cost the victor as dearly as the vanquished.

Yet twice he had fought and won against impossible odds; and both times he had confronted his enemies fortified by an inner certainty of victory. He, who had never held a sword in his hand before his faring year, never confronted an armed enemy until the assault on Riverfield Inn, had known that he was unconquerable. As he thought back on the grueling days of learning under Cathwar's all-observing and highly critical eye, he wondered if the old wizard had done more than merely teach him. He had heard of victory-spells, of magic that protected against harm. Such things were certainly within Cathwar's power.

He stretched out beside the fire and stared up at the stars, thinking of the wizard, wondering about the future. He was more certain than ever that he had interpreted the signs correctly and was on the right path. Already he had done a good thing: if he had not decided to go to the High City, the Lady Ammaranza and all her household might now be dead, and the band of brigands would still roam the mountain ways.

The thought of the young robber—younger than Genlon, hardly more than a boy—disturbed him. Perhaps Ammaranza had the right to judge and the power to impose such a death, but such rights and powers were always harsh in execution. To be rent and devoured alive by scavengers, or to die slowly of hunger and thirst under the sun by day and in the cold night wind, immobilized, able only to shriek in pain and desperation—it was an awful death. Better a single swift blow and oblivion, thought Genlon. A sword was clean and direct. Magic was subtle, and full of surprises, even to those who appeared to be masters of it. The thought of the magic that had become interwoven with his life made Genlon uneasy. He went to sleep quickly that night, exhausted by the day's exertions, but his dreams were troubled.

He awoke to a drizzling rain. For the next three days, rain and heavy, clinging mist slowed their progress and made them cold and uncomfortable. Their food was dangerously low by the time they saw the Plain stretching golden green before them, unrolling eastward as far as the eye could follow into the barely risen sun. But the trail was clear, and they met no brigands, so their chief feeling was relief.

They first set foot on the Plain at midday, and by early afternoon they were within sight of an inn. The oxen were balky from hunger, and Genlon felt his own stomach grind on its emptiness, but Ammaranza ordered him on. Late in the day, they reached a crossroad, and here she directed him to take the left-hand way. About a greatmark down the path, they could see the first signs of a settlement, and when they rounded a turn, it burst upon their view. Beyond cultivated fields and arbors rose a palisade that extended, in Genlon's estimate, more than two longmarks—two hundred times the reach of a tall man, by northland measurements—and nearly half a greatmark. Apart from the Fastness, it was the largest construction Genlon had ever seen. Just over the rim of the palisade, a pitched roof and chimneys were visible. It was hard to estimate the full size of the building within those protecting walls, but Genlon knew it must be huge.

Ammaranza called a halt and summoned Genlon. She drew back the flap of her wagon ever so slightly and extended one pale, spidery hand, clutching a ring in her fingers.

"Go to the house and ask for Darra Jhan. He is an aged man with a withered hand. Speak to no one else of our coming. When you see him, tell him that an old friend has returned, and give him this," she instructed, dropping the ring into Genlon's palm and withdrawing her hand.

Genlon passed down the path and entered the wide-swung gates unhindered. He saw no guards and heard no challenge. The courtyard within was green and still, and he walked to the house on a path lined with trees and flowers all unfamiliar to him. Their fruits and blossoms were strange in shape and color, and the aroma that filled the air was rich and sweet. It was too sweet to be pleasant; there was a suggestion of some familiar scent in it that made Genlon ill at ease. His empty stomach growled, but his appetite vanished at the exotic aroma.

The door was firmly barred. He pounded on it, waited, and then pounded again, harder and longer. At last he heard the creak and clang of bolts being drawn, and the door opened a crack.

"Who are you? What do you seek here?" a dry voice demanded.

"I must speak with Darra Jhan."

"My master speaks with no stranger," said the voice, and the door swung to.

Genlon threw his weight against the door and forced it wide. A little man, thin-limbed, totally hairless, gaped up at him, opening and shutting his mouth in mixed outrage and terror. Genlon folded his arms, looked down on him sternly, and said, "I've been sent to see Darra Jhan. Take me to him."

The hairless man hesitated for a moment; then he said, "I'll ask him. You must wait outside."

"Don't bolt the door, or I'll break it down."

The little man glowered at him, but he clearly believed that this giant intruder could, and would, do as he threatened. He shut the door again, but Genlon heard no bolt shot.

Waiting on the broad threshold, he set his back to the door and took a second, closer look at the garden that filled the courtyard. Under the slanting sun, much of the ground was in shadow, and the treetops glowed where the light hit their leaves and fruits. Figures moved among the greenery, but they were indistinct, and Genlon could not tell what they were about.

A flowering vine rose on both sides of the doorway and arched over the entry. It was a growth unfamiliar to Genlon, and he turned to study it more closely. The vine was thickly covered with flowers about the size of his thumb, of a red so deep it was close to purple. The edges of the flowers curled inward, and as Genlon moved closer to inhale the sweet odor that they gave forth, the vine rustled, and the flowers nearest him surged forward as if to clutch at him. He drew back quickly, and the flowers twitched, strained toward him for a moment like hungry mouths, and then sagged back into place. Genlon stepped from the threshold and stood well away from the vine.

The door opened again, and this time a woman stood in the entry. She was dark-haired and dark-eyed, with skin as pale as milk. Her dress was a simple gown of shimmering black, and a pendant containing a single large diamond hung around her neck. She was beautiful, as the diamond was beautiful: she was sharp-featured, glittering, cold. Genlon felt an actual physical chill pour forth from her, but it passed in an instant, like a gust of northern wind.

"Darra Jhan will see you. Come with me," she said. As he walked at her side, she asked his name and his profession.

"I'm Genlon Banheenson, lady. I serve one of high birth."

"You are a messenger."

"I bear a message to Darra Jhan. I have other duties."

"You're a swordsman, I see. Are you brave?"

It was not the way of Long Wood to proclaim one's own courage. "I've never fled from battle," Genlon responded lamely.

"Never? Not even when the enemy is stronger, and you're outnumbered, and there is no hope? Don't you think you'd turn and run if you lost all hope?" she asked.

"I hope I wouldn't, lady," he replied.

She laughed, and her laughter was cool and metallic. She said no more to him, but as they passed a window, Genlon caught her amused sidelong glance. He saw a cruelty in it that sent a chill down his spine.

They stopped before the door of a room at the center of the house. The woman tapped on the door and pushed it open, gesturing for Genlon to enter. He did so, and the door closed behind him.

At a table facing the door sat a man with grizzled hair that fell to his shoulders. A thick volume lay open before him, and his left hand rested on the page, shrunken and brown as a leaf, fingers twisted together into a gnarled hook. He was not as old as Genlon had expected him to be; he looked little older than Banheen. When he raised his head and silently studied his visitor, Genlon saw in his eyes a cold intelligence that could judge the price of everything it scrutinized down to the smallest fraction of an oak.

"What have you for me?" Darra Jhan said in a deep, flat voice.

"I'm to tell you that an old friend has returned and give you this." Genlon held up the ring; then he stepped forward and laid it on the table.

The red stone gleamed in the candlelight, and an answering gleam lit Darra Jhan's eyes as he picked up the ring. He glanced at Genlon with a quick, cold slash of a smile, a smile of pure avarice, and with his clawlike left hand he urged the ring onto his finger, where he looked on it hungrily.

"The Lady Ammaranza is welcome," he said, not removing his eyes from the ring. "A chamber will be made ready for her and her waiting-woman. The rest of you will be quartered in the building beyond the kitchen garden. Go now, and conduct your mistress here." As Genlon moved to obey, Darra Jhan added in a sharp voice, "Say nothing to Skelbanda. I will tell her what it is fit for her to know."

The dark-haired woman was waiting outside the door. Her arms were folded, tightly clutched across her breast, and she was frowning.

"Have you delivered your message?" she asked sharply.

"I have, lady."

"Tell it to me."

"I cannot."

"Tell it to me," she repeated. She looked up, and her dark eyes turned full upon him, dazzling as Ammaranza's. He felt his will falter.

"I must not tell you, lady."

"But you will. You cannot deny me. Your will is too weak to withstand mine." She raised a hand and beckoned him closer. "You cannot hope to resist me. Tell me all you said to Darra Jhan."

Genlon broke his gaze from hers with a great effort and turned his eyes to a grotesque mask of gold and silver that hung on the wall. He concentrated on the twisted features while he said, "I must go, lady. Show me the way, please."

"Tell me all."

He felt her eyes drawing his, and he feared that he could not resist her will if again their gazes met. His hand fell on the hilt of his sword, and he grasped it tightly, in desperation. The familiar touch of cold metal was comforting and real; he felt his will grow stronger. He turned and met her gaze fully, and he said, "I must return. Show me the way or stand aside, lady."

For a moment she did not move or speak. At last, with no apparent disappointment, she murmured, "Your master has shielded you well. I look forward to meeting so powerful a man. Or is it a woman you serve?"

He did not reply, and his eyes did not waver. She turned and walked with brisk steps down the corridor, and he followed at a few paces' distance. As they turned a corner, something scuttled into a dark doorway. Genlon had only a glimpse of wide yellow eyes and a lumpy form about the size of a child, but much misshapen. Whether it was a child or not, he was unable to tell. From other rooms, as they passed, strange sounds issued—the breathing of some huge creature, tiny claws scratching at smooth stone, a low murmuring that might have been laughter or sobbing, or both commingled. He had heard none of this when he passed these rooms on his way to see Darra Jhan; the house, and all who dwelt in it, seemed to have come to life. He kept his hand on his sword and his eyes on the woman who walked ahead of him, and he was glad that he would not have to sleep within these walls.

They remained at the settlement for ten days, during which time they saw no sign of Ammaranza or Tupaji, nor of Darra Jhan or the woman Skelbanda. Though Cade and Genlon frequently glimpsed distant figures in the gardens and arbors, the only servant they spoke with was the cook, a sour, red-faced woman with a bitter, grating voice and a temper to match. She told them little. They gathered, from her disconnected grumbling, that a good many people were assembled in the mysterious house, and that they demanded unusual services from her at unreasonable hours. In one outburst, on a morning when they had had her up working for most of the night, she condemned them as a pack of nasty, wicked sorcerers and wizards, and wished them all to the coldest, darkest, bleakest depths of Shagghya, where the spirits of the restless dead wander for all time. No sooner had she spoken than she looked fearfully around her, as if shocked by her own words. She would say no more.

For the rest of their stay, the cook said not a word to either of them. They met no other servants. It was with relief that they left the house on the Plain, with its magics and mysteries, and set their path for the High City.

It rose before them on the last day's traveling like something carved from sunset and studded with gold, its beauty doubled against the backdrop of the deepening blue sky. Genlon was silent, dazzled by the sight, and when they passed through the western gate at last, he was awed anew by the splendor within those walls of honey-colored stone.

His amazement grew as they went on, without a halt, until their wagon stood before the palace of Lord Duarin. The last and greatest surprise of all was the sight of the lord of the High City himself bursting from his escort of guardsmen and torchbearers to welcome and embrace his mother, the Lady Ammaranza.

CHAPTER SEVEN

AMMARANZA'S QUEST

Mother and son dined privately in a room on the upper level of the palace. A pair of Duarin's personal guards stood on duty outside each closed door, and another pair watched inside the open door through which the servants came and went. Tupaji sat unmoving near them, by the wall, arms folded, looking straight ahead.

Ammaranza and Duarin sat in cushioned comfort before a lively fire, dining out of carved bowls of goldenband, a rare wood from the south, and drinking wine from golden vessels. They were well out of earshot of the guards, and they conversed freely, but habit made them keep their voices low.

"It's good to have you here, mother. I had given up hope of seeing you again. I sent my messengers everywhere, and they found no trace of you," Duarin said.

"I could not return sooner," Ammaranza replied.

"Did you know I was seeking you?"

"Yes, of course. I've always kept watch on events in the High City."

"But how?" when Ammaranza dismissed the question with a wave of her hand, he said, "Are you really a sorceress, mother? I've heard it said."

"I have certain skills," she said, with an oddly innocent smile, like that of a child embarrassed by praise and yet delighted to receive it. "They've acquired a bad reputation in the northern lands, but I find them useful."

"It was said that Pytrigon banished you because he feared you'd place an enchantment on him. Is that true?"

"Oh, Pytrigon," she said, with the same smile. "There was never a need to use magic on him. I could make Pytrigon do anything I pleased . . . except where you were concerned. He was always afraid of you. Did you know that?"

"Of me?"

"He thought you'd kill him and seize the throne when his two oldest sons were dead, and he assumed I'd help you."

Duarin looked at her, bemused. "What good would that have done me? Qunlac still lived, and so did my father."

"Yes, your father." Ammaranza seemed to be on the verge of saying more, but she remained silent, looking thoughtfully into the depths of her goblet.

"As it turned out, I had no need to seize the throne, even if I'd been planning to. Four years after Pytrigon's death, I became lord of the High City by right of descent."

"You were very fortunate."

"Very," said Duarin, complacently sipping his wine.

"Particularly fortunate that Pytrigon's last child—the son by his third wife—died in infancy. When I heard of that child's birth, I expected to hear of your death within a few days."

"You did?" Duarin said, startled. "Why?"

"I knew how Pytrigon's mind operated. The death of his first two sons changed him. He lost his trust in everything and everybody. He saw plots everywhere. He simply could not believe that you would have allowed an infant to become ruler of the city."

"That was foolish of him. At best, I was third in line for the lordship."

Ammaranza made a little scoffing sound and waved that objection aside. "You were the dangerous one. Qunlac was a simpleton and Guldergance was a weakling. All Qunlac ever cared for was strutting about in his fighting gear and burning sorcerers." She flashed a triumphant glance at her son and added, "Little good that did him, though."

After a brief silence, Duarin said, "Pytrigon shouldn't have wasted time worrying about his family. He should have paid attention to his servants. If he hadn't trusted the child to a stupid slut, the boy might be alive and ruling today. She let him smother, and when she saw what she'd done, she fled."

"The servant was never found, was she?"

"No. There was a rumor that she had sought refuge far to the south, but the guards found no trace of her."

"How unfortunate. She might have given helpful information."

Duarin gave a scornful laugh. "What could she have told?"

"She had a lover in the palace. Didn't you know? His identity was never discovered, but he was a member of the ruling family."

"How could you know that?" Duarin demanded angrily. She said nothing in reply. She met his eyes coolly and enigmatically and then turned to gaze into the fire. He calmed himself and said, "Well, what of it?"

"Perhaps nothing. But it's possible that the servant girl smothered the infant to benefit her lover. Perhaps he persuaded her to do it—promised to reward her, perhaps even to marry her. If that were the case, then of course he'd have had to kill her." Ammaranza smiled at her son and said, "But as you pointed out, she's rumored to have fled to the south, so all this is pure speculation."

"You speculate a good deal, mother."

"I'm curious in all things that concern my son. The child's name was Ambescand, was it not?" Duarin nodded, and she went on, "That's an interesting name. Ambescand was one of the early kings, in the days before Aluca gave up power over the north. I've often wondered why Pytrigon gave such a name to the child of his old age. Perhaps he dreamed that Ambescand would one day reunite the northern lands under his rule and reestablish the kingdom."

"That would not be an easy task."

"No. But not impossible." Ammaranza took a sip of wine, set down her goblet, and observed offhandedly, without looking at her son, "You've been making good progress at it, until now."

Duarin did not respond at once. He emptied his goblet, and when it had been refilled, and the servant had left them, he drank from it deeply and then asked, "Exactly why have you come here, mother?"

"Don't be suspicious, child. You need help. At the rate things are going, every part of the north will have its own army in a very few years, and there'll be no unifying them once that's happened."

"If I'd been able to build a decent army—"

"But you haven't," Ammaranza broke in. "It was a very clever plan, and I haven't a word to say in criticism. Sending those brigands out to terrorize the other regions was a sound idea. Your mistake—"

"How did you know it was I who did that?" Duarin exclaimed.

"Really, child, I'm not a fool. When I learned of the man in the black hood, I knew it had to be you."

Duarin frowned. "I don't see that it's so obvious. The man

in the black hood might be some conspirator—an enemy of mine, seeking to disrupt the north and undermine my rule."

Ammaranza shook her head slowly and emphatically. "If you had an enemy so resourceful and so determined, you would now be dead." When he continued to glower at her, she said, "Is it so easy to gain access to your dungeons? Can anyone who pleases free a score of prisoners? Does anyone but you have this power?"

"No," Duarin grunted. He raised his goblet and drank deeply.

"Very well, then." Softening her tone a bit, she added, "I must say, it's probably the only workable stratagem, if you want them to leave the city completely and permanently. How do you force obedience? Do you keep hostages?"

"I only free men with families in the city."

"Very sensible. Surely you don't expect them to keep their numbers down, though."

Duarin pondered her words for a time; then he said irritably, "Why not? If they increase their band, I'll kill their families. I don't want an outlaw army growing out there."

"How will you know? Their victims don't stop to count how many attacked them. Any reports you get are bound to be inaccurate."

"Well . . . if I think they're adding new men, I'll go ahead and kill their families."

"Then you'll have no hold over them at all. That's another mistake."

"Another . . . you still haven't told me my first mistake, mother."

"Don't be surly. Your first mistake was in not moving more quickly with your guardsmen. If they'd come marching to the rescue after the first few raids, they'd have been hailed as saviors. You would have had the people of the outer regions begging to be taken under your protection. It's too late for that now. In parts of Long Wood, and on the Headland, people have started to organize for their own defense. Your men might be looked upon as invaders."

"I couldn't have been sure of my men if I'd moved sooner. I had to take louts and bumpkins from out there in the wild and build them into an army loyal to the High City and not to their birthlands. That took a long time."

"Too long, I think," Ammaranza said. "But there may still be a way."

"Well, tell me what it is. You seem to have given this a great deal of thought."

"Don't be so cross," she chided him. "You need a leader whom your men will follow into battle even against their own birthland."

"I'm their leader."

"Oh, don't talk like Qunlac, please," she said testily. "Your place is here, ruling and making plans, not risking your life in battle. You must have someone to lead your troops."

Duarin scowled and shook his head. "There's no man like that in the High City. My best commanders have never enjoyed that kind of loyalty."

"Did you notice that big swordsman who walked before my wagon when we arrived?" Ammaranza asked.

"Yes."

"Well?"

"Him?" Duarin laughed loudly and scornfully. "Do you think my veterans would accept a boy as their leader and give him their loyalty?"

"What do your veterans respect in a leader?" Ammaranza asked patiently.

"Courage. Daring. Experience of battle. They want a man who leads them to good loot and divides it fairly. A man who keeps his word."

"Genlon is such a man."

"He's a boy. He's not half my age. Oh, he's big, I grant you that, and probably as strong as those ugly beasts of yours. But he's still a boy, and my veterans won't follow him."

"On the way here, we were attacked by a band of robbers. There were sixteen of them, and I had six guards," Ammaranza began in a calm voice.

"You should not travel with such a small guard, mother."

"I'm well protected, child. If I may resume . . . ?"

"Go on."

"Four of the guards were slain from ambush before we even saw an attacker. The fifth was injured. Genlon, alone, slew thirteen of the brigands. He showed courage and daring such as I've never seen before. He burst upon those robbers like a man cutting grain. And he did it because he had given his word to protect me."

Duarin gave a low grunt of approval. "Impressive, I admit. Still, it's a single encounter."

"In Long Wood, he and three companions slew eleven robbers who attacked his father's inn," Ammaranza added.

Duarin raised an eyebrow. "If this fellow's so good, I might do better to keep him here, in my personal guard."

"That would be very foolish."

With a considerable effort, Duarin retained his composure. He had long been unquestioned ruler of the High City and the Plain, obeyed and feared by all within his dominion; and now he was being checked and chided like a boy. He did not welcome questions or criticism, and yet he had received little else from this frail wisp of a woman ever since her arrival in the city.

It was not love for his mother that gave him patience. Ammaranza was almost a stranger to him, and love was not a strong force in this man who measured every relationship by a calculus of utility. It was Duarin's recognition of his mother's usefulness that made him submit to her censure without protest; that and the aura of cool, self-confident power that surrounded her tiny form like invisible and impenetrable armor. He was not convinced that he would fail without her help; but he was certain that with her help and advice, however unpalatable they might be at the time, he would succeed. A little stooping seemed a small price to pay for the certainty of kingship.

"Why foolish, mother? I don't understand," he said.

"You don't want the people seeing too much of him. They're liable to make comparisons."

"Let them. I'm not afraid of being compared to any man."

"You should be. You have a long, hard struggle ahead before you can be king of the Northern Lands. You'll enjoy victories, but there may be setbacks along the way. And people are very fickle, child. When things look bad, they forget all the good you've done for them and get troublesome ideas about new leadership. They start looking around, and if they see someone who catches their fancy, they'll tear down everything and make him their leader."

Duarin thought on this, and he nodded in agreement. "I see the point, mother. But if there's a chance that this great bumpkin might be a rival one day—even against his own will —why should I keep him around at all? I can easily get rid of him, and it might avoid trouble later on."

"Any tool is dangerous if one does not use it properly. You must learn to use things properly, that's all. Genlon's proper use is on the battlefield, leading your army. You'll be here in your palace, to announce his victories and take credit for them. If he suffers defeat, you can denounce him and be rid of him," Ammaranza said.

"Yes . . . and I'll surround him with men I can rely on."

"Well, of course. You'll want to know what he does and says. Start him off with a small command, and increase his responsibility slowly. There's no need to go too fast. You want to be completely sure of him. I think it would be wise to get him married, as well. If he has a wife and children here in the High City, he'll be more reliable."

"A good idea, mother. We'll find some servant girl from the palace, and—"

"No, no, no," Ammaranza broke in wearily. "Don't waste the marriage, child, use it. Pick the woman from one of the powerful families of the plain around Southmark. You'll have a hostage against Genlon and a guarantee of her family's loyalty."

Duarin broke into a broad smile of appreciation and approval. "You're right, mother. Absolutely right. I know exactly the family."

"I thought you'd agree. Perhaps we ought to discuss this further before you make your final decision."

"Anything you say, mother."

She smiled at him fondly. "You're being very gracious about this, child. I hope you realize that I'm only doing these things for your sake. You have a good mind and a good imagination, but there's an impulsive side to you that you must learn to control."

"I'll try, mother."

"Please do."

Duarin emptied his goblet and summoned the servant to refill it with wine. Ammaranza, whose wine stood scarcely touched, dismissed the servant with a wave of her hand. While Duarin drank, she settled back and stared silently into the glowing fire.

"Something you said, mother . . ." Duarin began, hesitantly, as if reluctant to speak further.

"Yes, child? Go on, I'm listening."

"What you said about people sometimes turning on their ruler, and setting up a new one . . . how does such a thing come about? Is it sudden? Are there any warnings?"

"There are no rules, child. It's different every time. The

last Alucan ruler was overthrown in a matter of hours, but
Tallisan fought the usurper for years before he won the
throne."

"Are there signs? Do prophecies mean anything?"

"Prophecies always mean something, but they seldom mean
what people think they mean."

"There's a prophecy being spoken in the city. It's probably
all nonsense, but there are those who claim that it foretells
the near future."

"What is this prophecy?" Ammaranza asked.

"I've heard it so often that I know it by heart:

> *The child who died is the king who will be;*
> *The king who died will slay the king who would be;*
> *The son of three mothers will father three sons, and*
> with their hands on his blood they will shake the world
> when they are long dead and gone to dust."

She listened with eyes closed. Her lips moved slightly as
she repeated the words to herself. After a time, without opening her eyes, she asked, "Can you find any meaning in it?"

"Well . . . Pytrigon had three sons . . . but I never heard
about Pytrigon having three mothers. How can anyone have
three mothers? That part makes no sense at all," Duarin said,
perplexed.

"It seems impossible," Ammaranza said softly.

"If the part about 'the king who would be' means anything, I think it must refer to me. I certainly intend to regain
the kingship. And since the last king died long ago, that
part sounds reassuring."

"Reassuring? It speaks of his slaying."

"If the only enemy I have is a dead king, I don't see much
to worry about. That's almost like promising me a long life,
isn't it? It could mean that no man living can slay me."
When Ammaranza made no reply, he went on, "I can't make
sense out of the first part, though. A dead child can't become
a king, or anything else. When you're dead, you're dead."

"The dead child might be Ambescand."

"It might. It could be one of my children, too. None of
them has survived beyond the first summer. Maybe˙. . . it
could be a way of predicting that I'll become king. Do you
think so? One of my sons was named after me, so that could
mean that he'd have the name of a king. So, in a sense, the

dead child would become king. I think that's what it means. Don't you think that's possible, mother?" Duarin asked eagerly.

"Are you certain that Ambescand is dead?"

He looked at her, puzzled; then, firmly, he said, "Yes."

"Certain beyond all doubt?"

"I saw him put in a coffin and buried between his brothers. Ambescand is dead."

"Then perhaps the prophecy means what you say it means. Or perhaps it means nothing." Ammaranza covered a yawn. "Tomorrow we must plan Genlon's marriage. It would be well to settle that quickly."

"As you say, mother," Duarin said cheerfully.

"And now, you must excuse me. Sleep well, child," she said, rising and beckoning to Tupaji, who sat with folded arms, as she had sat all evening. They left the room and made their way through the corridors to Ammaranza's chambers.

The old woman lay awake for a long time in the darkness. She slept very little now. Night was her time for thinking, remembering the things she had seen and heard during the day, turning them over in her mind, evaluating them and fitting them into precise patterns. The light and noise of day obscured the truth; in silence and darkness one could follow the threads of events to their ends, observe the crossing and weaving, unravel the tangles, and grasp the design.

Duarin was promising. His ideas were subtle, and he had planned well. But he needed direction. Years of power had softened him. He enjoyed food and wine far too much, and he was already showing the effects of his indulgence. Unquestioned and uncriticized, he could easily fall prey to caprice and undo everything in one arbitrary gesture. He needed someone to shake his complacency if he were to regain the kingship.

Genlon would be a useful foil. At her first glimpse of him, she had seen how well he would suit her plans, and events had borne out her judgment.

Several things about Genlon troubled her, though. There was an uncertainty in her mind, and she disliked uncertainty. His build, a way he had of turning his head, his green eyes, all raised disturbing questions.

She remembered Pytrigon well. They had been lovers from

the day she first visited the castle until her banishment. Even when he drove her from the High City in fear of her dark power, he loved her more than he had ever loved his wives —of that she was certain. And when she looked at Genlon, she saw Pytrigon live again.

He was about the right age, and he had the right physical characteristics. He could be the child called Ambescand. But that child was dead and buried. Duarin had been positive on that point, and she did not doubt that he had played a part in the child's death; probably he had slain him with his own hand, to be absolutely certain of the deed.

Even if Genlon were not Ambescand, he might still be Pytrigon's child, and any son of Pytrigon would be useful. She resolved to seek the truth of his origins in the Crystal Hills. It might require magic—more magic, perhaps, than she wished to expend—but the knowledge could be helpful. The essential thing was to unify the northern lands under a single ruler; whether that ruler was Duarin or Genlon made little difference to her. Only unification was important, because once the north was unified, her quest could begin. And to Ammaranza and her fellowship, only the quest mattered. Every other aspect of their lives was subordinate to it.

She had come far and learned much, but her real task was yet to begin. She and her fellow sorcerers labored in utter darkness. They knew only that the object of their search was hidden somewhere north of the River Issalt. They were ignorant even of the exact form that long-dead wizard had given it. It might be an ancient ruin, a mountain, a single grain of sand on an isolated beach, a precious stone in a prince's ring, or a rock to hold back a farmer's door; it might be anything under the sun. But the fellowship was determined to find this object, for it was the key to a magic greater than any that had worked in the world for ages, a power beside which their combined magic would be no more significant than a child's breath against a hurricane.

To learn even that much had cost their fellowship lives and lifetimes. The object of their quest had been buried under the forgetfulness of ages, guarded by obscuring spells of infinite potency. The one who had concealed it—they knew him only as the Iron Mage—had meant it to be hidden forever, unless his old enemy should somehow revive. Until then, it was to lie in obscurity, accumulating ever-greater power against the day of need, when its existence and its whereabouts would be made known to one chosen soul.

Ammaranza stared up into the darkness and drew a long, shallow breath. She was old, inhumanly old; without a new source of power she would soon begin to weaken, and when she was weak enough, her power would be seized from her. She was not certain which of them would do it: Darra Jhan, or Skelbanda, who hated her, or skulking Korang; but she was well aware of the danger. All those in the fellowship had sworn oaths of fidelity under awesome penalties, but she knew that these oaths were meaningless. Given the power of the Iron Mage, no oath could be used to bind one, no promise held against one, no punishment inflicted.

The old enemy, whatever it had been, was as dead and forgotten as the ancient world that had held them both, as the civilization it had crushed in the moment of its downfall. It would never return, and the power of the Iron Mage would never come forth to confront it. The power they sought must be discovered and seized.

She quelled the hunger that racked her at the thought of all that would come about once the power was in her grasp. Calm and control were essential; the goal was remote and uncertain. There was work to be done, and her mind had to be kept free of interference.

As a discipline, she turned her mind to the prophecy Duarin had recounted. It was a puzzle, and though it had no apparent connection to her quest, she knew she must overlook nothing. She had first heard this prophecy in Long Wood, and she had heard it again at the Fastness. Three of those assembled at the house of Darra Jhan had known it, but they could not unravel its meaning.

Again it came to her that "the child who died" might refer to Ambescand. It made no sense—Ambescand's death was as certain as anything could be—and yet the thought returned to trouble her. Perhaps the presence of Genlon, reminding her as it did of Pytrigon, was the cause; or perhaps the old rage and hatred smoldered in her still, even after all these years.

She remembered the day she had learned of the child's birth. She was far away then, alone and almost powerless. The illusion of youth and beauty she had maintained for so long in Pytrigon's realm had cost her dearly. Though she was then many times Pytrigon's age, she appeared as fresh and virginal as a maid of sixteen summers. Pytrigon could not resist her; she made all other women seem plain, as dull as dust.

Duarin had been her victory. In her exile, she had followed his fortunes, tracing his inevitable rise as the line of Pytrigon's legitimate descendants dwindled. The daughter Ciantha died —of a sudden sickness, they all believed—before she could marry. The second son, and then the first, died in battle without leaving an heir. Pytrigon, despite the urging of his counselors, was too despondent to remarry. Already he had begun to read significance into his misfortunes. Two wives had died in childbirth, his children had all died childless—to him, this was clearly the working of a higher will, and he dared not defy it further.

Twice it seemed that he was on the verge of admitting his liaison with Ammaranza and declaring Duarin his successor; but without Ammaranza present to urge him, he faltered. It would have been easy, if he had been determined. Qunlac would happily have accepted the post of commander of the guard, and Guldergance would simply have gone on nodding his head and looking bewildered. Even open knowledge of his cuckolding could not have roused that sorry man to anger. If others had objected to Pytrigon's misconduct with his brother's wife, they could soon have been silenced. All it took was decisiveness.

Summer followed summer, and still Pytrigon made no announcement. And then, working on his loneliness and his growing doubts, a pair of his advisers gulled him into marriage with a stupid child from one of the prominent city families. A year later, Ambescand was born.

The child meant ruination of all Ammaranza's plans, years of work undone, Duarin's life in danger. She was too old and too weak now to begin again. She might be able to recreate the illusion of youth and beauty, but there was no time to build the magic that would enable her to bear another child. If Pytrigon were to die, she might return to the High City and begin working to gain influence over the child; but whatever happened would take time, and for her, time was running out. While Duarin was ascendant, she held sway over the fellowship of sorcerers. His fall would bring about her own. The quest would pass to others, and her hope of possessing the power of the Iron Mage would be lost forever. And all because of the birth of Ambescand.

She realized that she was clutching at her light coverlet with a grip that pained her fingers, and she released it at once, smiling to herself somewhat shamefacedly at her surge of feeling. It was all over now. Ambescand was dead, Pytrigon was dead, and Duarin was lord of the High City. Before long, if he followed her bidding, he would be king of the Northern Lands. It would be as she had planned.

She directed her thoughts once again to the prophecy. If "the child who died" were not Ambescand, who could it be? After some reflection, she had a thought. That part of the prophecy might be put to good use if somewhere in the city's history there was an heir apparent named Duarin who died before he could become king. Duarin had even suggested something like that, she recalled. It would be easy to persuade him to investigate the possibility.

The second part of the prophecy was definitely a warning and not, as Duarin would have it, a promise of immunity. Some person, or some object, connected with the olden kings represented a danger to Duarin; that much was clear. But who or what the danger could be remained as mysterious as the goal of her quest.

She turned her mind to the last part of the prophecy. "Son of three mothers . . . father of three sons." Again she thought of Ambescand. He had been the child of his father's third wife; perhaps the reference to three mothers signified that. But a dead infant cannot become father of three sons. She shook her head, annoyed at the constant intrusion of Ambescand into her thoughts, and set to the prophecy once more. Pytrigon had been father of three sons; so had his own father, Tallisan. In the history of the High City, perhaps a score of kings and lords had had three sons. The prophecy might refer to any one of them; it might refer to someone far distant, or yet unborn, but that seemed unlikely. Ammaranza felt that if the prophecy had any meaning, it must be in terms of the High City and its destiny.

Long she lay gazing into the darkness, turning over the puzzle in her mind and reaching no satisfactory solution. This prophecy might be significant to her quest, but she could not see how.

The sky outside her window showed the first faint glow of dawn. There was much to be done this day. She drove all thoughts from her mind and settled into sleep.

CHAPTER EIGHT

THE FORTUNES OF GENLON

From darkness came their swift attack,
And blood and ashes marked their track—
They filled the north with dread,
For no man in the northern lands
Could say whence came those hate-filled bands
That struck them down with bloody hands
And took, and slew, and fled. . . .

Lord Duarin heard their cries of woe,
And at the melting of the snow
He sent his guardsmen forth.
Through the high gate that fronts the west,
Thirty, the bravest and the best,
Led by one greater than the rest,
Set out to save the north. . . .
          —From *The Hammer Of The North*

For a time after their arrival in the High City, Genlon and
Cade were at complete liberty. The Lady Ammaranza had
no need of their protection here. They took a day to rest
from their journey and then set about exploring the city.

Genlon could not conceal his awe at the size and mag-
nificence of the High City. He had heard much about it from
Cade, and he had expected much, but the reality dwarfed his
anticipations. The walls were high and thick, in stone the
color of sunset, enfolding in their massive guardianship a
crown of gleaming domes and rooftops. A broad avenue ran
from the main gate, in the western wall, to a fountain that
rose like a shimmering crystal flower in the center of the
city. Genlon had never dreamed of such a thing in his life.
He stood gaping at it until his gray cloak was dark with
blown spray, and when Cade, laughing, dragged him off to

seek out an inn, he turned and looked back with wondering eyes at the crest gilded by the setting sun.

On each side of the avenue was a grassy slope, gently rising, threaded by a narrow stream. These streams flowed from smaller fountains, one on each side of the gate, and emptied at last into two reservoirs, one on each side of the city, in the wooded palace grounds behind the central fountain. Beyond the parklike strips of greenery stood rows of splendid buildings, some towering eight or nine marks high, with four floors, one atop another. The smallest building Genlon saw was twice the size of the inn at Riverfield.

The avenue itself was paved with blocks of stone, each the size of a platter, so closely fitted that there was scarcely room to insert a fingernail between them. And Genlon learned that not only the main avenue, but every street of the High City, even the narrow alleys of the workers' district in the north end, was paved with stone.

Because he wore the colors of Lord Duarin's mother and was quartered in the palace precincts, Genlon was able to see more of the city, and learn more about it, than most visitors. Its beauty stimulated his eager curiosity. This curiosity, and his openness of manner—together with the popular interest in his feat of arms—made him welcome everywhere. Before nine days had passed, he had explored most of the city and was greeted gladly wherever he went. He had begun to overcome his native diffidence and move more confidently in his new surroundings. Then, on the tenth day, he was summoned to the presence of Lord Duarin, and his life took a new turn.

Duarin received him in the early afternoon, in a large room at the upper level of the palace. As he passed down the high halls, up the broad staircase of carven stone, and along corridors lined with the accumulated treasures of long dominion, Genlon's sense of wonder was newly roused by the splendor of his new home. He began to feel once again like an overgrown woodsman far out of his comfortable place. If it were his destiny to serve the ruler who dwelt in such a palace, he reflected, his was a high destiny indeed; too high, perhaps, for him to achieve at this stage in his life.

The twelfth lord of the High City was seated on a plain wooden stool behind a long table covered with maps and documents. At Genlon's entry, he rose, smiling in welcome, and stepped around the table. Before the astonished youth could execute his carefully rehearsed bow and greeting, Duarin had clasped his hand in a firm grip and clapped him on the shoulder in comradely fashion; not as his master, but as his friend.

Duarin was a big man. He stood almost as tall as Genlon, and his shoulders were broad and well muscled. His short, trim beard was streaked with white, and gray flecks glimmered in his close-cropped dark hair, but the strength of a man in his prime was in Duarin's hand-grip, and the power of youth was in those bulging arms. He was a formidable man. But in the pouches under his eyes, and in the sagging paunch that stretched his tunic as taut at the belly as it was around his burly chest, Genlon saw the signs of Duarin's decline. Genlon judged him to be about the same age as Cade, or perhaps a bit younger; but Duarin was beginning to soften as Cade was not.

Genlon checked his thoughts quickly, with a feeling of sudden shame. This was a ruler, lord of the greatest city in the world; he was not a soldier, or a woodcutter, working with his muscles in every kind of weather. He was a man apart, with the weight of high affairs on his shoulders, worn by the care of thousands, and it was not Genlon's right to judge such a man—particularly when he was in the very act of showing him special favor.

"You saved my mother from a vile death and brought her safely to me," Duarin said in a deep, strong voice. "There is no way I can reward you properly, but I mean to be as generous as my power permits."

"I did my duty, Lord Duarin, and no more."

Duarin laughed and clapped him again on the shoulder. "If I had fifty men who did their duty as well as you, I'd soon have no enemies left from here to the Upland Sea."

"Thank you, my lord."

"Save your thanks. I've done nothing yet." Duarin snapped his fingers and gestured toward the window. Two guards, whom Genlon had not noticed on entering, brought a small table and a tray bearing wine and drinking vessels to the window. Duarin guided his guest to the table and poured two measures of wine.

"To your future, Genlon," he said, raising the golden goblet. "May you meet ever worthier foemen and be always the victor." He drained the wine, set his goblet down with a clang, and said briskly, "Now, to business. You come from Long Wood, do you not?"

"I do, my lord."

"But the men of Long Wood are not swordsmen. Aside from my own guard, there are no swordsmen in the north worthy of the name. Where did you learn to use that blade?"

"On my faring year, I went to the Cape of Mists. There I learned the use of the sword from a master."

"This master might be a useful addition to my guard."

"I have not seen him or heard from him since my faring year. He left the Cape of Mists and did not tell me his destination."

"Unfortunate. But you're here, and you'll have a chance to put your skills to good use. Have you ever led men into battle?"

"Never, my lord."

"You will before long. Not married, are you?"

"I'm too young for marriage, my lord."

Duarin laughed again and said, "In Long Wood you may be too young, but you're in the High City now. You're going to be a commander in my guard, and I want all my guardsmen to have someone in the city to defend besides myself. My mother has chosen a wife for you."

"A . . . wife, my lord?" Genlon said weakly.

"Yes. My mother will give you the necessary details. She'll be here in a little while. Before she comes, I want to tell you something about your duties. I'm giving you a very special mission, Genlon. Come, I want to show you something." Duarin returned to the long table where his papers lay. He pushed aside several documents heavy with seals, disclosing a large, well-detailed map. "Do you understand maps?" he asked.

"A little, my lord."

"You'll learn to be an expert. Here, look at this. This is a map of the Kingdom of the North at its height, back in the days before Aluca threw it all away."

As Genlon stepped to his side and bent his head to study the time-darkened vellum, the two guards quietly took up positions at either end of the table and set their watchful eyes on him. All unaware, he followed Duarin's pointing finger. "Here's the High City, right on the coast. Here's the Fastness, deep in the mountains to the north and west. You fought the brigands just about . . . here. Directly north of the

Fastness is the Cape of Mists. Far off to the southwest," Duarin went on, sweeping his thick finger halfway across the fanciful mountains and forests, "is Long Wood, where you come from, directly between the headland in the north and Mislands to the south."

"Where are Southmark and Northmark, my lord?"

"Here, on the coast," Duarin said, recrossing the map with his finger. "Southmark guards the approach from the Southern Forest and Drylands beyond. Northmark protects the way to the Crystal Hills." He straightened and looked Genlon in the eye. "Once, all of this was under the protection of the king of the Northern Lands, who ruled from the High City. People traveled and traded freely from one end of the kingdom to the other. They feared no brigands or marauders. Wealth poured into the High City, and life was good for everyone. But the boy king Aluca ended that. He released all his subjects from their obligations, and he took for himself the title of lord of the High City. I'm the twelfth to hold that title, Genlon. And with your help, I'll be the last."

"I don't understand, my lord."

"The people of the north need leadership and protection, Genlon. Things are not as they were in Aluca's time. No man knows that better than you," said Duarin, putting his arm paternally around the youth's shoulders and drawing him toward the window. "They've lived through generations of war, first against the sea-raiders, and then against the southern nomads. Now, when our outside enemies are crushed, we have bands of marauders attacking from within, and few good men left to fight them. It's partly my fault, Genlon —mine and my predecessors'—for bringing the best men to the city to join the guard. We had to do it if the nomads were to be driven off, but by taking their strength we left the other regions weakened."

"I think some good men remain, my lord."

"Of course they do," Duarin said heartily. "You're proof of that. But there aren't enough of them to prevent outrages like the raid on Riverfield or the attack on my mother's caravan. Some atrocious deeds have been done in the north in recent years, Genlon. The people of the outer regions are almost helpless. And things might get worse. We don't know how many of these outlaw bands exist, or where they come from, or why they've appeared so suddenly."

"One we questioned said he came from the High City, my lord," Genlon said.

Duarin jerked his head and turned to stare, astonished, at the youth. "From here?"

"Yes, my lord. The Lady Ammaranza questioned him, and he swore that a hooded man had released him and his companions from a dungeon and sent them to the mountains to kill and steal."

Duarin scratched his beard in bewilderment. "My mother said nothing to me of prisoners. Most likely she chose not to waste my time with such obvious lies. Who was this hooded man—some friend of the robbers?"

"He said it was a stranger, my lord."

Duarin narrowed his eyes and shook his head in anger. "That scum would say anything to squeeze out a few more minutes of life. I hope you weren't fooled."

"His story made no sense to me, my lord."

"A hooded man . . . in the High City . . ." Duarin was silent for a moment; then he gave a little grunt of disgust. "Well, whoever sends them, wherever they come from, these brigands would have destroyed your home and family if you hadn't been there to defend them. Now, I want you to do the same for others. With your help, Genlon, I'll restore peace and unity to the north."

Genlon thought of his parents, and his sister and brother, at the inn without his sword to protect them. The men of Long Wood were beginning to band together to defend their homes, but they were not warriors, and they might prove no match for a desperate, well-armed band of raiders. The danger was lessened, but it still threatened. Here was a task he could undertake gladly, and with some confidence of success.

"I'll do whatever you command, my lord," he said.

"You'll be my right arm—the hammer of my justice. I'll give you a force of picked men, the best of my guards, and your mission will be to rid the north of these marauding bands. You'll report in the morning to the guard commander, Eksaar; he'll see that you get whatever training you need. I want you ready to start for the outer regions by the first day of Flowerdown." Duarin clapped his hands together loudly and said, "We'll show the people of the north that they need a king once again. There'll be trade, and travel. People will prosper and be able to enjoy their prosperity. The High City will know its old days of glory. And it will all be your doing, Genlon. And mine." Before Genlon could respond, Duarin turned toward the doorway, gave a slight nod, and said, "Good afternoon, mother. I'm glad you came."

Ammaranza strode past the towering guards, who bowed as she walked by, and stopped directly before Duarin. "Have you informed Genlon of your plans for him?" she asked.

"I have. But I don't think he's as eager to marry as he is to fight," said Duarin with a faint smile.

"Is that true, Genlon? Are you reluctant to marry?"

"I'll do as you and Lord Duarin bid me do, my lady."

"But not with all your heart?"

"We of Long Wood marry late in life. It is our custom."

"This is not Long Wood, Genlon. Those of Long Wood marry late because they are too poor—most of them—to marry young. They have made a tradition out of a necessity. You're out in the world now, and you'll soon find that there are other ways than the ways of Long Wood, and a wise man follows the ways of those around him. I've chosen a good wife for you. She is Meragrand, daughter of Ordred of Goldengrange, by Southmark."

"That's a good family. Ordred fought at Pytrigon's side when he crushed the nomads at Southmark. And his father served with Tallisan," Duarin said.

"They are loyal, brave people. Meragrand is said to be a great beauty," Ammaranza added.

Genlon, who by now could think of nothing to say, merely murmured, "Thank you, my lady."

"And I must give you this, Genlon, lest you think me ungrateful," Ammaranza said. She drew from her sleeve a small dagger, its scabbard exquisitely worked in gold and silver. A single red jewel was set in the pommel. She took his hand and laid the gleaming prize in it. "Trust this dagger, and heed it," she, said, closing his fingers around the hilt. "Carry it always with you, and remember the one who gave it. From this time, I look upon you as my second son."

The dagger was at Genlon's side when he went next morning to report to the guard commander. Eksaar was a short, thick-set man with a face bearing a tracery of old scars and the marks of exposure and endurance. His coppery skull was clean-shaven. His nose was flattened and bent, his brows thick, his hands big and raw-looking. He received Genlon coldly.

"I have orders to make a leader out of you. I'll do it if I have to skin you alive and sew you back up again. You'll work until I'm satisfied that you're perfect, and then you'll work until you're better. Weapons practice in the morning and again in the evening until dark, command training at midday, field training when and where I decide you need it. That will go on until I think you're ready. Do you understand?" Eksaar said in a voice like grinding stones.

"Yes, commander."

"I've heard the stories going around. You're supposed to be good. Come along, and we'll see how good you are," Eksaar said. The tone of his voice made it clear that he did not expect Genlon to impress him.

They walked around the main guard building, past a row of small barracks, and into an open court where about two score men were gathered. Half the men wore only short trousers and carried heavy training weapons. Most of the others were dressed in heavily padded tunics and wore basket-like helmets over their heads. A tall, sinewy man, red-haired and red-faced, carrying a long, slender cane, walked among them and observed their exercises. Now and then he laid a stroke of the cane across a man's bare shoulders or legs to urge him to better efforts.

Eksaar barked a command, and all action ceased. He beckoned to the tall man, who trotted forth at once and snapped to a rigid halt before him. The eyes of all the rest were on Genlon.

"Walman, this is the big woodcutter who killed that mountain scum and saved the Lady Ammaranza. I'm supposed to train him to command a special force of guardsmen. Match him with someone so I can see how he handles a sword," said the commander.

"Yes, sir," Walman replied crisply.

"Wait, Walman." Eksaar turned to Genlon and asked, "How many of them did you fight? Fifty? A hundred? Nobody seems to know for sure."

"Thirteen, commander."

"Only thirteen?" Eksaar replied with mock astonishment. "What did you do, surround them?"

Genlon ignored the scattered laughter and said, "I couldn't do that, but I was able to surprise them."

The men laughed louder, but Eksaar's face was unmoving. "You won't surprise anyone here, woodcutter. But just to give you a fair chance to show what you've got, maybe you ought to take on two men."

"Whatever you think is best, commander."

"Walman, pick two men. Get this fellow an outfit and a practice blade. You, woodcutter, give me that sword. I don't want you losing your temper and thinking you're back in the mountains first time someone cracks you on the head," said Eksaar.

Genlon unbuckled his sword and stripped off his tunic and shirt. The padded tunic that Walman tossed to him was tight across the chest and shoulders; he fastened it as loosely as he could, but still he felt it pull as he raised the heavy, blunted training sword. Eksaar settled the helmet on the youth's head and guided him to where two men in similar gear stood waiting. He positioned the three combatants at the points of an equilateral triangle; then he stepped back to join the ring of watchers.

At his command, the two guards moved swiftly to entrap Genlon, but he eluded them, slipping aside with the quick grace of a cat, keeping them always before him. Some of their blows he fended off with what looked effortless strokes, but most of them he simply dodged. Eksaar studied the skirmish for a time; then he gave a command to halt. He strode forward and stood before Genlon.

"What did you do to those thirteen crippled beggars, woodcutter—dance them to death?" he roared into the barred opening of Genlon's helmet. "I brought you here to see how you fight, and all I've seen you do is duck and dodge and weave. If there was a place out here to hide, I believe you'd be hiding in it. If you want to be a guardsman, you'd better show some fight, do you understand me? That's what the guard does. We don't duck away, we fight!"

"Yes, commander."

"Then let's see some swordplay. Or have you been in the city too long and gotten soft? Have you forgotten all you knew?"

"No, commander. I only . . ."

"You only what, woodcutter?" Eksaar growled.

"I didn't want to hurt anyone."

Eksaar's weathered face turned red and then white. His eyes narrowed, and the cords of his thick neck stood out in high relief. With his arms folded, he stood in silence, breathing deeply and slowly. Then he said in an unexpectedly gentle voice, "Well, don't you worry about that any more, woodcutter. If you can hurt one of my men, he deserves hurting. So just go right to it. Let's see what you can do when you're not afraid of hurting somebody." He started back to the ring on onlookers, all of whom were silent; then he stopped and turned back to Genlon. "I'll make it easier for you not to worry. I'll send in a third man to keep you busy."

The men sensed Eksaar's anger, and there was no shortage of volunteers. A third man was quickly made ready, and Eksaar again positioned the participants, setting the guardsmen in a half circle facing Genlon and equidistant from one another. He rejoined the watchers and gave the command to begin.

Exactly what happened was perennially disputed by those who saw it. The participants were reluctant to discuss it, and the witnesses could not agree. It was all over too quickly—a blur of movement, a few thudding blows, the clang of metal on metal, and Genlon was standing alone. Two of the guardsmen lay motionless. The third sat dazed for a moment; then he fell back and lay supine. Two of the exercise blades were badly bent. The third had been sent flying over the bystanders' heads.

"See to them," Eksaar said, snatching Genlon's shirt and tunic from Walman's hands. Pointing to Genlon, he snapped, "Woodcutter, you come with me!"

"These men may be hurt, commander. I tried not to—"

"If they aren't hurt now, they will be when I'm done with them. Now get that gear off and follow me, do you hear?" Eksaar bellowed, red with rage. Still clutching Genlon's shirt and tunic, with Genlon's sword under his arm, he stalked off. The guardsmen parted with alacrity for his passage.

Walman ran to Genlon's side and helped him remove the helmet. The tunic, now split down the back, came off easily. "You did well," Walman said as he worked. "Not many men could stand up to those three."

"I hope I didn't hurt them."

"Knocked the wind out of them, that's all. Did them a good turn, in the long run. It will teach them to be careful next time. You'd best follow the commander now. At a run."

"I will. Tell the men I'm sorry, will you?"

Genlon trotted off, leaving Walman staring bemusedly after him. Whoever this young fellow was, wherever he came from, he was unlike any man Walman had ever trained or —and he breathed a brief thanksgiving for this—fought. He was fast and deadly, strong as a team of oxen, and oddly enough, he was likable. He would make a terrible enemy, but a good friend.

Eksaar showed no sign of amity when Genlon drew up beside him. He marched in silence to the building where Genlon had first presented himself. Once inside, he flung the shirt and tunic at the youth, growling, "Put these on and be quick about it." When Genlon was dressed, the commander tossed his sword and belt at him angrily. "Get this on."

Eksaar paced the floor in silence for a time, stopping twice to look hard at the youth, but not speaking. At last, he planted himself squarely before Genlon, scowled up at him fiercely, and said, "All right, I want the truth. How many of those men do you think you could have handled?"

"Not more than five, commander. They're very good."

Eksaar's voice was bitter. "Are they, now? Well, we all thank you for the compliment. They're very good, but you're as good as five of them. Nobody taught you to be humble in Long Wood, that's plain."

"I don't mean to boast. The sword is my best weapon. I was taught by a master."

Eksaar grunted sourly. "What are your other weapons?"

"I've been using an ax since I was a boy."

"Cutting down men is a lot different from cutting down trees. Have you ever used an ax in battle?"

"Only in mock battles, on festival days."

"What about the bow? From what I've heard and seen, Long Wood is full of bowmen, and some of them are good."

"I'm as good as any of them for distance, but many are more accurate."

Eksaar's manner relaxed a bit, and he said almost pleasantly, "It's comforting to find that there's something you can't do better than five picked men. Maybe we can teach you a few things, after all. I'll have you at the archery butts every day. You'll learn to be accurate, I promise you. And you'll spend mornings working with sword and ax. You've still got a few things to learn."

"I'll work, commander."

"You start today. Get your things and report here at midday. We'll take our meal, and you'll meet the men. Then you'll start learning how to use a bow."

From that day on, Genlon worked harder than he had ever worked before in his life. Days grew shorter, and the sun lay lower in the skies. The first snows fell, and the sea wind numbed his fingers on the bowstring, and still the daily round of training went on.

His new companions were a harder breed of men than any he had known before. A few were veterans of the southern campaign, and the rest had been in skirmishes against the marauding bands in the outlying territories. They were not quick to accept a newcomer, and Genlon's first appearance among them had made them even more cautious.

Their first reaction to him was ambivalent. On the one hand, he was a valuable comrade-in-arms. Like him or not, he was as good a fighting man as any guardsman had ever seen or expected to see. He was not boastful, nor did he use his abilities to make others appear the worse. Where he could be helpful, he offered his help freely, and where his skill was the lesser, he took instruction willingly.

But on the other hand, many of the guards felt—though they said nothing openly—that this young swordsman was being shown favor even beyond his undeniable merits. It was soon common knowledge that he was to be placed in command of a special unit, leading men older and more experienced than he, and this troubled the men who had given years to the guard, shed blood, endured hardship, and received little advancement in return. Even Eksaar, for whom loyalty to the Lord Duarin was as natural as breath, doubted the wisdom of this decision—not because of any failings he perceived in Genlon, but because the next man so favored might not be Genlon's match.

But Genlon slowly overcame all objections. Tolerance melted to acceptance and warmed at last to admiration and friendship. When the month of Flowerdown arrived, and Lord Duarin himself came to name the men who would serve under Genlon, every man in the guard hoped for the honor of being among the chosen thirty.

Springtime was always a beautiful season in the High City, but this year's month of Flowerdown brought a new beauty to the city in the person of Meragrand, daughter of Ordred of Goldengrange. Though she arrived at night, and her coming was unheralded, she was glimpsed by people in the city and in the palace, and rumor of her beauty quickly spread. Genlon listened eagerly and anxiously, not daring to believe what he heard. But when he first saw her, on the day they joined hands before the lord of the High City to pledge their loyalty to him and their fidelity to each other throughout their lives, Genlon knew that no description could hope to capture the beauty of this small and graceful girl who stretched out her hand to him.

Her hair was as black and gleaming as the rare nightwood, her eyes the pale blue of midday skies in the month of Ripentide, with a light in them he had never seen in a woman's eyes before. As he enfolded her small hand in his, Genlon felt clumsy and overgrown, like some great beast of burden. He became acutely aware that he was not a handsome man. His features were coarse, rough-hewn. The glass showed him a nose too thick, cheekbones too prominent, eyes too narrowed, a hulking body, toughened and hard. Holding her soft, fair flesh to his would be like bruising the petals of a flower with a bludgeon. Yet he wanted her, passionately, with an all-consuming desire he had never felt before, a desire so strong that it created a fear in him even as it burned in his blood.

This was indeed love, the rare sensation told of in song and legend, attributed to men and women of far lands and forgotten ages, but never of the here and now. In Long Wood, "love" was an unruly emotion that led to ruin, dividing families and causing feuds that endured for generations. It played no part in marriage or married life. There, weddings were family pacts—Kettijan's had been just such an arrangement, an alliance in which family interests were paramount and the chief participants had little to do but comply with others' instructions.

And yet his own father had not seemed to feel this way. Banheen had asked Kettijan and her betrothed about their feelings once in Genlon's presence, and he had seemed a bit disappointed—so Genlon now recalled—when they did not seem particularly fond of each other. Genlon knew that his father was not native to Long Wood. Perhaps it was true, then, that people from different places felt differently about things, and that different ways were not necessarily bad or foolish ways. Perhaps the sensations that now overmastered him were rightful and good, after all. Whatever they were, he could not resist them. He had no wish to.

As Genlon knelt before Duarin, at Meragrand's side, he felt that every eye in the room was on him, and that he was certain to do or say something that would bring their mockery upon him. Then Meragrand squeezed his hand gently, reassuringly, and gave him a quick, sidelong smile. All his fears vanished, and he knew that she understood his wild feelings, and that everything would be well.

The Lady Ammaranza provided them a suite in the palace, and there they passed the first three days of their married life in seclusion together, as was the custom of the High City. Then Genlon returned to his duties, and Meragrand attended the Lady Ammaranza, and the month of Flowerdown drew to a close. On the last day, having said his farewells, Genlon assembled his force of thirty guardsmen, picked by the lord of the High City and named by him "Duarin's Hammer," and as the sun rose at their backs, he led them out the western gate.

CHAPTER NINE

A STONE FOR
THOSE WHO FALL

They headed north, along the coast road, to the Crystal Hills, covering forty greatmarks a day at their steady marching pace. Word of their coming preceded them, and on the far side of the long, many-arched bridge that linked the Crystal Hills to the mainland, they were met by two very apprehensive sentries. Genlon halted his men and went forward, alone, for a parley.

He showed his commission, sealed with the mark of the lord of the High City; but the sentries could not read, and the scratchings meant nothing to them. He displayed the medallion around his neck, which bore the likeness of his master; but they had never seen Lord Duarin, and they cared nothing for the tiny image of an unknown man. He stood frustrated, scratching the stubble of his new-sprouted beard, wanting to offer his help but unable to convince these frightened men that he was indeed a friend, and not an ally of the marauders or some new, unsuspected enemy.

"You've seen the Lord Duarin's guardsmen before. They've come north to help you hunt down the brigands," he said.

"No outsiders came to help us," said one of the sentries. "The only outsiders who came were the brigands, and we'll let in no more."

The older man said, "Guardsmen came from the High City once, I remember. But they offered no help—they asked it of us. And they were not like the men you lead. They wore other colors."

"We're a new force. We've been sent to hunt down the brigands and punish them," Genlon said.

"How do we know you're not brigands yourselves? What do marks on a piece of vellum mean, or a man's face stamped in silver?" the first sentry said.

"Take me to someone who can read—someone who knows Lord Duarin's face."

The sentries conferred, and the older one said, "That we cannot do. One of us would have to go with you. You could kill him on the way, and your men would overcome the other before he could give the alarm."

Genlon folded his hands before him and looked patiently down on the ground. In a calm, even voice, free of boast or threat, he said, "If we wished to attack, you would both be dead by now, and my men and I would be a greatmark deep in your homeland. You know that, and I know it. Why do you hinder us?"

The younger of the two glanced uneasily from Genlon to the band of dark-clad men who waited, seemingly relaxed, within call. The other man stared hard at Genlon; suddenly his eyes widened. He pointed at him, nodding.

"I've heard of a man—a giant in a gray cloak—who roams the north slaying whole bands of brigands single-handed. A traveler from the High City told of him."

As a courtesy to Lady Ammaranza, Genlon was permitted to wear her colors. Therefore, his cloak was gray and his shirt maroon. His other garments were of the dark blue that Duarin had chosen for his special force. He hooked his thumbs in his broad belt and smiled on the grizzled sentry.

"Your traveler exaggerated. I fought two bands of brigands, no more, and neither time was I alone. But I won, and now I serve the lord of the High City, and he has sent me to help rid you of the marauders in your land."

"That's what the traveler said—you went to the High City to serve the ruler there," the older sentry said, wonder in his voice. He paused for a moment, furrowing his brow in deep concentration; then he said abruptly, "Come. I'll bring you and your men to the chief assayer."

"Wait, now!" the younger one blurted. "We can't be sure—"

"This is the man. I'm sure of it. A giant in a gray mantle, bearing a long sword. You stay here and keep alert. I'll send relief as soon as I can."

The sun was high, and the white-capped peaks of the inland mountains flashed and glimmered under the clear sky as the little band marched along the winding road to the main settlement. Genlon saw apprehension on the faces of those they passed, but their guide shouted reassurance to the onlookers, and the expressions changed to relief and welcome. Word raced ahead of the marchers, and as they neared the gates of the settlement—huge slabs of dull metal set into a stone wall more than a mark high—people poured out to watch their entrance.

The chief assayer of the settlement was a wiry old man named Rosobal. He heard Genlon's story, perused his commission, studied the medallion bearing Duarin's profile, inspected his thirty companions, and declared the group welcome in the name of the people of the settlement. His word was final. They were received as friends.

Rosobal offered the gathering hall as quarters for Genlon and his men. Putting his subordinates in charge, Genlon went with the chief assayer to his neat stone house, directly beside the hall, and watched Rosobal unroll a map of the Crystal Hills preparatory to explaining the situation.

The chief business of the settlement was mining. It had been named Generosity because of the wealth of the earth on which it rested. Veins of tin and silver ran directly beneath it. In the far hills, men dug in the ground for coal. Genlon had heard of this strange black stone that burned like well-dried wood, but he had never seen it; trade from the Crystal Hills had all but ceased in the years of Duarin's rule. A small traffic in precious metals was carried on, but the production of coal had dwindled to no more than was sufficient for the needs of the people of the Crystal Hills; none reached the mainland.

Generosity was the largest settlement in the region, and it had been growing steadily as people abandoned the small outlying camps to seek safety behind its walls. But once there, the coal miners found little means to sustain themselves, for the chief business of Generosity was raising food and processing metal for use and trade, and the miners had no skill in these matters. Worse still, diminished coal supplies meant less refining and processing of metal, and this increased the numbers of the idle. Already, whole families had left to seek new work in the mountains around the Fastness, or on the Headland. Rosobal confessed his growing fear that unless the brigands were driven out, the Crystal Hills might be an unpeopled wasteland within two generations' time.

"Can't the miners band together for protection?" Genlon asked. "Are the brigands so many that there's no opposing them?"

"Now you speak like a stranger. There's only one band of brigands, and it numbers no more than thirty or so. If the miners could work together, they'd be safe. But that's not the way these people are," said Rosobal.

"They must work together in the mines."

"Oh, they do, they do, but only a few of them. Blood and tradition are very strong in the Crystal Hills, my friend, and they make it impossible for us to band together, even against an enemy that threatens us all alike. The mines in the coal camps are family mines, and no family will let an outsider set foot in their mines. Tin miners will not work with silver miners, and neither of them would ever think of mining coal. Farmers have nothing to do with miners or smelters or merchants, and so it goes," Rosobal said, throwing up his hands.

"I'm surprised it's so peaceful here in Generosity."

"We're not a fighting people. We don't like one another very much, but we need one another, so we get along."

"Only one band of brigands, you say?"

"As far as we can tell. Let me show you," Rosobal said, peering closely at the map, moving to the extreme edges the smooth rocks that held it flat. "Here's where they've done the worst, up here by Three Springs. They destroyed two camps, killed everyone they could find . . . killed some of them in ways I never thought I'd see used on helpless people."

"Is that the only place they've struck?"

"We're sure of one other raid. They attacked a camp near Blackwater, over here," Rosobal said, pointing to a spot on the far coast.

"They range far. How long have they been here?"

Rosobal shook his head. "Nobody knows. Could have been a long time before we ever suspected. The kind of work people do out in those hills, it's not unusual for a whole camp to disappear and never be heard of again. We don't generally ask after people."

"Didn't help come from the High City?"

"No help. Men came up to ask if anyone wanted to be a guard, fight strangers for the sake of other strangers somewhere far away. Foolish business."

"That was long ago. Has no one come since then?"

"The brigands. Now you."

"How did the brigands get past the sentries? Kill them?"

"We didn't keep sentries on the bridge before. Didn't need them."

"I can understand why they were so suspicious."

"They still are. So am I, to be truthful. But we need help, and maybe you can help us. I've heard the same stories as the others: a big man in a gray cloak, dark blade at his side. I'm willing to take a chance and trust you."

"We'll rid you of the marauders."

Rosobal nodded, looking down at the map, and both men were silent for a time. Then Rosobal looked up at Genlon and asked, "Why?"

"I don't understand."

"Why should you do this? What do you, or your men, or the lord of the High City care about us? Better for you if we all die or wander off. Then you can come up here and take the wealth for yourselves. I tell you this—some people say that the brigands were sent here from the High City for that purpose."

"Do you believe them?"

Rosobal shook his head slowly. "It doesn't make sense for the High City to send marauders and then send men to hunt them down. But I still don't understand why you're here."

"A long time ago, when all the lands of the north were joined in a single kingdom, people traveled freely, and traded freely, and lived their lives free from fear. But the kingdom broke apart in the time of Aluca, because some men said that life would be better if each region went its own way and ruled itself. Those men were wrong. Since Aluca's time, there have been attacks by sea-raiders, by nomad armies from the south, now by these bands of brigands. Travel has all but ceased, and no one is prosperous. Fear seems to be everywhere—men even fear those who would help them."

"All true, but what does it matter to the lord of the High City? He's in no danger."

"The High City has a trained fighting force. Lord Duarin wants to use it to restore peace and order in the north, for the benefit of all who live here."

Rosobal grunted thoughtfully. "He may want to restore the old tribute, as well. Maybe even the kingdom."

"Whatever he plans to do, he trained us and sent us here to help you, if you want us."

Rosobal held out a leathery hand. "We need you. We'll take your help, friend, and worry about the future when it comes."

Genlon spent the next few days with his lieutenants, studying maps, questioning refugees from Three Springs and the outlying camps, provisioning for the trip north, and choosing a guide. On the sixth day after their arrival, they left Generosity. Their guide was a lanky, gray-bearded man named Cloap, sole survivor of the raid on Blackwater.

They headed northwest, toward Blackwater, but on the third day of travel, Genlon ordered a turn eastward, toward Three Springs. If the brigands had spies in Generosity, their information would be no help.

The weather turned cold and raw as they moved farther north and into the mountains. On the twelfth day of searching, they found the first trace of the marauders. Two days later, they came upon a deserted camp. Cloap went over the ground on his hands and knees, studying the site as a scholar pores over a text. Genlon's own trackers did likewise. As Cloap reported, they stood silently by, listening unobtrusively but attentively.

"Twenty-six of them, at least, and maybe as many as thirty. They're hungry and ragged. The food they took in the last raid got them through the winter, but it's gone now. They stayed here two nights and ate nothing," Cloap said.

"Where's the nearest food?" Genlon asked.

"There are fisher folk in the north cove. They'll be taking good catches this time of year. And there are wild sheep in the upland valleys."

They followed the trail to where it divided and found signs that the brigands had split their forces, the larger group heading for the coast while four continued to the upland valley. Genlon detached six men to hunt down the smaller group, and he took the rest eastward; the brigands who were on their way to the fishing settlement were an immediate threat to life.

The path to the coast was narrow and twisting. Every turn and rise was the setting for a potential ambush. They moved as quickly as caution allowed, traveling through the night, and they reached the cliff overlooking the north cove some hours after midnight, Setting four men to guard the trail, Genlon and the rest began the descent. The night grew bitter cold. The wind rose, and snow began to fall. Their descent became slow, dangerous going, but they managed it safely, in silence. At first light, the guards were ranged in a broad semicircle around two stone huts that stood about forty marks back from the sandy cove, just above the point where the land dipped to the shore.

The entrances to the two huts faced each other. Each was covered by a thick hide that hung to the ground.

"Do they have any other way in or out?" Genlon asked Cloap.

Cloap shook his head. He lay on his belly at Genlon's left side, cloak drawn tightly around him, shivering. Edging closer, he whispered, "I think they're in there, Graymantle. Leastways, something's wrong here."

"How can you tell?"

"No dogs. All these people keep guard dogs. We'd never have got this close if the dogs were alive."

Genlon returned his attention to the little settlement as Cloap blew on his chilled fingers. The sky was growing brighter, and he could distinguish faint outlines through the blowing snow. As he watched, details became clearer, and he saw that Cloap had judged correctly. Things were very wrong here.

Two mounds by the side of the larger house—he had thought them smooth stones—were the bloody carcasses of huge dogs. Beyond the house, just at the edge of the level ground, stood a drying rack for preserving the catch. A human form was spread out on it like a bundle of bloody rags.

The sun glared dully through the morning mist and the last swirls of snow, and still there was no sound or sign of life. Genlon studied the scene intently; then he turned to Cloap.

"Are they still here? It's very quiet."

"There's nowhere else to go but out to sea."

"But they posted no guards."

"They're not afraid of us. No one's ever fought back before," Cloap said simply.

Even as Cloap spoke these words, a wisp of smoke arose from the smoke-hole of the larger house. He tapped Genlon on the forearm and pointed to it, but Genlon had already seen. He raised his hand, and at the signal his men began to work forward, tightening the semicircle to close in around the huts.

Genlon, at their center, drew ahead of his companions and reached the larger stone hut first. It was not so rudely made a structure as it had first appeared. The walls were solid, the rocks neatly and tightly fitted, the interstices plugged with moss. Sword in hand, Genlon drew the little dagger given him by Ammaranza. As he did so, the jewel in the handle gave a sudden flash of red. At that instant, the door-hide of the opposite hut was flung aside and three men rushed out, armed, closing on him from two marks' distance.

He met their charge, deflecting an ax blow with his sword and ripping the axman from belly to breastbone with his dagger. The second attacker lunged with a short pike, and Genlon slipped the stroke and thrust the sword point into his teeth. As he tugged his blade free, a numbing blow struck his shoulder. His feet went out from under him on the snow-slick muck, and he fell. The dagger dropped from his limp fingers. He rolled to one side and scrambled to his feet just as a guardsman spitted the club-wielding brigand.

His men were in the huts now, and the brief battle gave way to a methodical slaughter. The brigands, desperate and cornered, killed three guardsmen; but before the sun cleared the horizon, every one of the brigands was dead.

Genlon had a huge purple welt on his shoulder two hand-spans broad, and his arm ached to the fingertips, but no bones were broken. He sheathed his weapons and assembled his men. A few had been injured, but none seriously. All could travel unassisted.

He set his healers to binding their comrades' wounds, and he gave the others a rest while he inspected the site. The huts were filthy, and they stank. He had the bodies of the brigands hauled to the water's edge and thrust into the current, to be carried out to sea. The body on the drying rack, swollen and blackened, was dressed in the fisher folk's garb; he had it buried.

The absence of other bodies puzzled him, until Cloap came upon a crevice in the rocks behind the huts. There they found what was left of the other settlers.

They had no wish to remain on this grim, death-haunted spot, and once they had buried their comrades and covered the remains of the fisher folk with stones, they ascended the cliff and made camp at the top, in the lee of a low outcropping. Here, at sundown, arrived their six companions. One was limping badly, his lower leg opened to the bone by an ax blow. Another was being carried, unconscious. His head was wrapped in a blood-soaked shirt. The left side of his skull had been crushed. He died during the night, without speaking.

The weather improved and remained clear and fair, with a warm sun, all day. Genlon kept his men at the campsite for five days. It had been the first taste of battle for many, and it had shaken them. Oddly, the four who died had all been battle-tested veterans. The inexperienced men had suffered only minor injuries, though they had fought as hard as any.

For the rest of the summer, Genlon and his men combed the northern reaches of the Crystal Hills for survivors of the brigand band. At first, the guardsmen were greeted with hostility and fear by everyone, and Cloap had to display considerable powers of persuasion to keep the people of the tiny, isolated settlements from fleeing or barricading themselves in against the armed strangers. But slowly the word of their mission spread, and when they left the settlement at Hawkscliff on the last day of Greenblade, they were sent on their way with the thanks and good wishes of all. Even the dogs trotted by their sides amicably, protecting the protectors.

Early in the month of Ripentide, Genlon and his men returned to Generosity. They were welcomed now, and their arrival was the signal for a festival in which most of the settlement partook wholeheartedly.

Genlon's joy at a successful mission was blunted by the loss of his four companions, and though he said nothing of his feelings, he resented the mean spirit of these people who could celebrate their liberation without giving a thought to their fallen liberators. Not one resident of Generosity seemed even to notice that fewer men returned than had left. They hailed him as Genlon Graymantle, their protector and deliverer, and they proclaimed their eternal gratitude. But in his heart, Genlon wondered if they would recall his name, or his men's deeds, when a summer had passed and no marauders threatened.

He left ten men behind to hunt down any brigand who might somehow have escaped this force. They were to remain in the Crystal Hills until the next winter had passed. As a tribute to Duarin, he accepted a richly worked silver chest set with precious stones and lined with aromatic sweetwood, reputed to neutralize all poisons. For himself and his men he accepted no reward: they had done their bounden duty. His only request to the people of Generosity was that a stone be raised at the roadside, near the gate. It was to be a mark high and a mark broad, and these words were to be cut in its front surface for all to see: "To the memory of four who died so that you who read might walk this way in peace."

He returned to the High City by a roundabout way, going westward to the Inn of the Three Branches, where he and his sixteen men rested for three days, and then turning south on the Shadow Trail, westernmost of the ways that followed the mountains. They left the main road often, to visit remote hamlets and farms, and everywhere they went they spread the word of their mission, as they had in the Crystal Hills. When they entered the western gate of the High City, the month of Yellowleaf was nearly over, and the first chill days of Barebranch were near at hand.

At the sight of Meragrand, Genlon shouted aloud his joy, for he could see that she was to bear a child. And in the month of Whitefall, Meragrand gave birth to a dark-haired daughter whom she named Meradaina.

That winter was a happy, busy time for the young family. It passed quickly. Genlon spent his days training, studying, and working his new men into shape. In the evenings, he was content to sit by the fire with Meragrand close at his side, talking easily of small things while Meradaina slept in her cradle.

Sometimes, as he gazed dreamily into the flames, his mind went back to his faring year, and he thought of Cathwar, and the magic that had touched his life so briefly and yet changed it forever. Because of Cathwar, he had his sword and his battle-skill; they had saved the lives of his family and won him the favor of a powerful lord and the love and fidelity of a beautiful woman. He was the right arm of Duarin, protecting those in the northern lands who could not protect themselves, bringing Duarin's peace and justice wherever he traveled. It was a high calling, with great rewards, and he was grateful to that short-tempered old wizard who had made it possible.

He would gladly have thanked Cathwar in person, but he did not expect to see him ever again. If half-remembered phrases now and then came back to him, and unanswerable questions sometimes troubled his sleep, he did his best not to dwell on them. He had found his destiny; and when Meragrand was in his arms, he wanted to know no other magic but the spell of her love.

CHAPTER TEN

THE FELLOWSHIP ASSEMBLED

The room was lit by a pale glow from the globe that stood in the center of the table. Walls and ceiling were draped in thick folds of soft black cloth, and the shadows sank into the blackness as mist sinks on still water. The table seemed to hang suspended in some unbounded void which held only itself, and the unwavering light, and the twelve figures that sat unmoving around it.

Ammaranza knew them all by name and reputation, as they knew her, and some of them she had seen before, in this very room. All too well, she knew Skelbanda, the cold beauty whose subtle magic could congeal a man's soul with despair, and Darra Jhan, who could stir up ambitious envy in the hearts of twin brothers. They, and the stunted, twisted little man called Korang, the Warmaker, had met in this room before, and once they had been joined by innocent-seeming, wide-eyed Taerhael, who could befuddle will and memory with enchantment stronger than drink or opiates. But the others were new to her, and she observed them closely and carefully even as they studied her.

At her right sat a tall man whose dark robes hung like a shroud on his wasted frame. His face was skull-like, his large, dark eyes rimmed in red. His bony hands poised like pale spiders on the arms of his chair, and the flesh of them was as gray and leprous as the flesh of his corpse's face. This was Bellenzor, the Blightbringer, whose magic struck down men and animals and all things that grow, who left in his silent wake disease and famine and death. Next to him sat Hane, dark-browed and frowning. Hane's touch shriveled healthy limbs and bodies to dry husks. Beside Hane was Jashoone of the Frost and Flame, fiery-haired and icy-eyed and ageless, her hands covered with the cold fire of precious stones, rubies burning on the fingers of her left hand, diamonds glinting on the fingers of her right. At her side, in a chair three times the size of any other in the room, was a great, bloated mountain of fat. He was known as Ulowadjaa, the Twister of Bones. His gleaming, hairless head seemed to float on billowing collars of flesh; his swarthy face was creased in a broad, empty smile, but his eyes, under thick tangles of brow, were alert and busy.

To the left of Ammaranza sat a slight man, plainly dressed, unadorned by rings or amulet. His tawny, gray-flecked beard and brown hair were neatly trimmed; his blue eyes were mild, his voice gentle, his manner courteous. This was Rombonole, whose unleashed power could make the earth tremble and split asunder. Beside him, smiling vacantly, sat Taerhael, and next to him, like a child among her elders, sat Aoea, the Windwraith, her tiny figure cloaked in a fall of long hair so golden pale it was almost white. Her wide, gray eyes peered out innocently, and her full red lips were parted as if in wonder. With her magic, Aoea could summon winds to level forests, tear the growing grain from the earth, and raise rushing mountains on the surface of calm waters.

Next to little Aoea sat the stony-faced Cei Shalpan, the Stormlord, master of weathers. Beyond him, completing the circle, were Korang, Skelbanda, and Darra Jhan.

The twelve sat in watchful silence. They had not greeted one another as they took their places, and now, as they awaited the explanation of the summons that had brought them together for the first time, they felt no need to exchange pleasantries as ordinary mortals do.

They were not ordinary mortals. Every one of them, even the childlike Aoea, had lived for many mortal lifetimes, and they faced the new with the caution of survivors. Each looked on all with a wary eye. They were now met as partners in an undertaking beyond the power of any individual among them, and while their quest endured they were sworn to deal openly with one another; nevertheless, each had worked protective magic against the power of the others, as much out of habit as out of suspicion.

Not one of them, not even the ancient, mighty Cei Shalpan, could have withstood the combined attack of that circle. If all were to turn their magic against an individual, that one would perish horribly, with no hope of escape. But there was as yet no reason for any to fear such an onslaught, and each of the sorcerers present was capable of resisting any other individual. They all knew, too, how the use of magic drains one's power and vitality—that, indeed, was one of the factors that had drawn them to unite in this quest—and they did not anticipate its use in caprice, or sudden anger.

The light of the globe flared up briefly; then it dimmed. Darra Jhan, in a voice as flat as beaten metal, droned an invocation in a long-dead language, and all eyes turned and fixed upon him.

"The lord of the High City grows stronger," he said. "Soon all the lands of the north will be united under his hand, and our quest will be a step nearer fulfillment. We are assembled here to plan for that day."

Jashoone's voice broke the ensuing silence. "Duarin is an ambitious man."

"We have made him so," Rombonole pointed out gently.

"No matter why, he is ambitious, and he is strong, and I think it might serve us better to have a weaker one in his place."

A mirthless, acrid laugh burst from Korang. He cocked his large head and gave Jashoone a crooked glance. "A weaker man could never unite the northern lands. We have helped make Duarin ambitious, and strong, and resourceful. He believes he serves only himself—and in doing so, he serves us."

"Nevertheless, let us hear our sister's words," said Darra Jhan.

Jashoone laid her hands on the table, spreading the long, white fingers wide and tapping them rhythmically, sending forth an aurora of shimmering light. Hane, clearing his throat, turned to her and said softly, "Really, Jashoone, there is no point . . ."

She stopped, drew back her hands, and folded them demurely in her lap. With lowered eyes, she said, "I believe Duarin's ambition might prove a danger—perhaps cause our downfall and utter destruction. If he were to learn our true purpose and turn all his energies to finding the object we seek, he might well succeed. If he did, he would be more powerful than all of us together."

Into the silence that followed this statement came the rasping voice of Bellenzor. "Duarin is a common mortal. It is childish to fear that he will achieve what we cannot."

"Hardly a common mortal, my brother," Darra Jhan pointed out. "His mother is one of us, and his father . . . his father was a son of the valiant Tallisan."

"That does not make him worthy of our fear. We might

as well fear that some wandering beggar will chance upon the talisman and make himself our overlord," croaked Bellenzor.

"Duarin is not a wandering beggar. He is lord of the High City. With our assistance, he will be king of the Northern Lands. He has other advantages, as well," Jashoone said.

Ammaranza's ringed hand rapped on the table, drawing all attention to her. The dark eyes blazed in her lined and sunken face as she glanced from one of her companions to the next, challenging them with her silent scorn. "Let me say what others seem unable to say. I gave birth to Duarin, and I kept close watch over him even in my exile. Now I live within his palace in the High City, advising him and guiding his actions. And so you think that I mean to betray you, and break my oath, and turn our quest to my own advantage. You think so, but not one of you dares to say it."

"No one accuses you, Ammaranza," said Rombonole.

"They dare to insinuate. I've given more to this quest than any of you—any of you!" she said, darting her accusing glance around the ring of faces.

"Let no one question Ammaranza's devotion to our undertaking, nor the value of her long effort," said Cei Shalpan, in a voice that chilled all present.

"I question Duarin, not his mother," Jashoone replied.

"And our brother Bellenzor has spoken to your question, and his words were wise. Heed them. Duarin is mortal, with all the limitations of mortal men. He will never unravel the secret that still tantalizes us and baffles even our collective power. And if Duarin, by some inconceivable means, were to learn the form of the talisman, and its location, he would be annihilated by its power the instant he set eyes upon it."

"And what if Duarin were assisted? Not by one of us—I accuse no one—but by another as powerful as ourselves?"

"There are none such in the north," Cei Shalpan said.

"Are you so certain?"

"If a power as great as ours were near, I would know."

Jashoone was persistent. "What of cloaking spells? Power can be concealed. We all know that. What of simple restraint? Perhaps a rival sorcerer is waiting, biding her time, letting us seek out the talisman—"

"We are not here to wrangle, Jashoone. We are here to plan. Pursue this matter further—any of you—and you might displease the fellowship." Cei Shalpan glanced about

the table as he said these final words, and his eyes lingered
on Taerhael and Darra Jhan. Having spoken, he sank back
in his chair and peered impassively over the tented fingertips he raised before his lips.

"The Stormlord recalls us to our purpose, and we thank
him," Darra Jhan said coldly. "Without unity and mutual
trust, we cannot hope to succeed. Let us recall the oath that
binds us and have faith in one another. Ammaranza speaks
truly: she has given greatly of herself to further the quest."

In a subdued, contrite voice, Jashoone said, "I assure my
sister Ammaranza and my sworn brothers and sisters that I
speak only out of concern for our quest. To have come so
far and then to risk losing all . . ."

"So, you still fear the interference of men. And not you
alone," said Cei Shalpan with heavy sarcasm. He spoke without stirring or moving his hands. "Then let us hear Ammaranza. No one knows better than she what this fearful
Lord Duarin does, and what he plans to do."

"A wise suggestion," said Ulowadjaa, and other voices
were raised in agreement.

Ammaranza spoke at length, giving a full account of the
progress toward the reunification of the north since her arrival in the High City. She explained Duarin's actions and
acknowledged the valuable assistance already given by Korang, Skelbanda, Bellenzor, and Darra Jhan in smoothing his
way. Her companions listened with rapt attention as she told
of Genlon's victories in the Crystal Hills and on the Headland, his long campaign in the Southern Forest, where brigands and bands of renegade Drylanders had besieged the
Citadel on the Lake Isle, and his excursions into the mountains beyond the Fastness. These triumphs, and the sacrifices
of the guardsmen, had been as effective as any deed of
Duarin's in bringing the northlanders to a new view of the
High City.

"I think it safe to say that the Old Kingdom will be restored within a year," Ammaranza concluded. "The High
City will once again rule the north. People will come and go
freely, and travelers will be a common sight. Information
will be easier to gather in less suspicious times, and our
search will be less noticed."

"You have done well, Ammaranza," said little Aoea in her
soft, childlike voice. "I hope I play my part as successfully
when I am called upon."

"I hope we all do as well as Ammaranza," said Rombonole warmly. "There'll be work for us soon enough, for you and me, and Jashoone, and Cei Shalpan. We may have to level the northern lands to the ground and turn each twig and pebble and grain of sand upside down to find the talisman of the Iron Mage."

Cei Shalpan interjected, "We will do what we must. It seems we owe much to this swordsman from Long Wood: he defeats the enemies of outlanders and wins loyalty for Duarin as Duarin himself could never do."

"They complement each other perfectly. Duarin is a shrewd planner but too impetuous. He suspects everyone. He can command fear but not affection. Genlon can follow instructions without chafing, and he is much loved," said Ammaranza.

"And has this woodcutter-turned-swordsman no ambition?"

"He is a simple man. He thinks himself rewarded far beyond his desert simply by my favor and Duarin's."

Cei Shalpan nodded approvingly. "A useful acquisition, Ammaranza. Is he protected?"

"He bears my protection," Ammaranza said.

"Good. We may need him a while longer. And now that we know the situation, let us proceed with plans for our search," said Cei Shalpan.

As the others explored this topic, Ammaranza, weary from long speaking, gazed blankly into the glowing sphere and let her thoughts turn to Genlon. He had, indeed, been a fortunate find for her and for the company of sorcerers, and she valued him highly. The little dagger that he always wore inside his shirt, the red jewel of its handle near his heart, had been a costly work of magic for her, but she did not regret it. In truth, she was fond of the young man.

Though her power over men's wills was most often turned to their destruction, Ammaranza had at times directed her special magic to gentler ends. Unlike the other women at the table, she had known the love of men, and she had borne children; she appreciated the pleasures of love and its role in human life. She had worked a small spell to draw Genlon and Meragrand ever closer, telling herself as she did so that she was only being practical: a man happy with his wife and children has neither the time nor the inclination to plot for things beyond his reach. But she knew in her heart that she had done it as much for her own pleasure as for the policy of her fellowship. Genlon reminded her of a man who had once loved her deeply and yet had been forced to send her into exile; but Genlon was still young, unclaimed by the needs of state. Forced to the same choice, Genlon, she believed, would choose with his heart. In the happiness of Genlon and Meragrand, she saw mirrored past happiness of her own.

Far to the east, across the windswept winter plain, deep within the frost-encrusted walls of the High City, Genlon was sprawled comfortably on a pile of rugs before a sinking fire, listening to the voice of Meragrand and their two oldest children as they sang a Snow Moon song. He was deeply content, and he lay peacefully, eyes closed, hands folded across his stomach, and let the sweet sounds wash over him.

"You're thoughtful," said Meragrand when the song was done.

"All of a sudden, I thought of the Lady Ammaranza. She's been very good to us," he said, turning his head and gazing into the fire.

"She has, truly. But she would not allow you to go with her, so you must not reproach yourself."

"I don't. But I worry about her. Just she and Tupaji, off on the Plain in this weather . . . she should have taken Cade. Even a driver would have been some help."

"She need have no fear of brigands, Gen. You've seen to that."

"There might be trouble with the wagon."

"If there is, every soul on the Plain would be honored to help the Lord Duarin's mother."

"I suppose so," Genlon said halfheartedly, rising and stretching. He laid a log on the fire, placed another atop the first, and knelt to stare into the glowing bed of embers beneath.

Meragrand came to his side and laid her arm lightly over his shoulder. "You worry about everyone, Gen. I don't think Duarin himself worries more about people's welfare," she said fondly.

"Ammaranza seems so old and frail. I never noticed it before this winter. And yet she sends Cade off to the Lake Isle on some mysterious business and refuses to let me escort her to this place . . . this healing spring. She wouldn't even say where it is, Merry."

"She's very determined, and Tupaji takes good care of her. Don't worry about Ammaranza."

He drew his wife closer and pressed his head on her breast. With his other arm, he enfolded the two children who stood at her side and pulled them to him. "I'm grateful to her, Merry," he said, his voice softened with feeling. "I owe her the most precious people in my life."

Ammaranza drew her eyes from the globe of pale light and glanced quickly around. A lively debate was in progress, and no one appeared to have noticed her momentary inattention.

"Any other action would be foolish," Cei Shalpan said flatly. "We must go to the High City. Once the north is reunited, it will be the center of the kingdom. We will learn more, and learn it sooner, in the High City than if we remain scattered throughout the north."

Skelbanda warmly agreed. She added, "There is a better chance of keeping our quest secret in the High City. Small settlements are fearful places; questions arouse suspicion, and strangers are remembered and discussed."

"Anything may be forgotten," Taerhael said, smiling pleasantly.

"Would you squander your power beclouding the simple minds of peasants? We may yet need all our strength, and more besides," Cei Shalpan warned.

His words silenced the others, and for a moment it seemed that he had overcome all opposition. Then Rombonole, in a subdued voice, said, "No one has spoken of the great hatred shown for sorcerers by the lords of the High City."

"Duarin shows no such hatred, nor did his father before him," Skelbanda said.

"They have shown toleration; nothing more. But the two who ruled before them persecuted sorcerers with zeal and cruelty—broke them on the wheel, burned and dismembered them. Can we feel safe in a city where such things were done within living memory?"

"They were never done to such as us, brother," Cei Shalpan said. "Those who died were petty enchanters—charlatans, most of them—who had not magic enough to protect themselves. The lord of the High City and all his guards—even with this marvelous woodcutter to lead them—could not withstand us."

"Pytrigon burned Nakkarra. She was the equal of any of us in her magic, but he burned her all the same. And he sat watching, drinking wine and joking, while she reviled him with her dying curse."

"Nakkarra was taken in a time of weakness. She had worked a strong magic, and her powers were spent. Otherwise she would have driven the breath from the lungs of all in the city with a word and a gesture," Skelbanda said.

"Nevertheless, she burned," Rombonole said matter-of-factly.

Ulowadjaa, in a high, fearful voice, interjected, "And Zandinell was forced to flee the city for his life. He's powerful, but he had to run."

"Do not speak his name!" cried Korang, his voice cracking with passion. "He rejected the quest. He ridiculed us to our faces!"

"I use him as an example, brother. I am no friend of his."

Darra Jhan gestured for order with his withered hand. "We will attend to Zandinell when our work is done. Meanwhile, let us keep to the question at hand. Some urge that we gather in the High City, but others object to this. We must resolve the question here and now."

Hane, ever frowning, glanced across the table to Rombonole and favored him with a nod, saying, "I agree with my brother who urges caution. It will be difficult to concentrate our energies on the quest if we are in constant danger of unpleasant death."

"Pytrigon and Qunlac died painfully, and their example is remembered. Nakkarra was well avenged. The knowledge serves as a deterrent to those who might otherwise harm us," said Cei Shalpan.

With a genial smile, Rombonole said, "I would rather avoid my death than avenge it. It seems to me that there is something in the High City—some power unknown to us—that is inimical to sorcery and protects those who oppose it. I think this would create, as my brother Hane suggests, a distraction. I recommend that we locate ourselves somewhere within a day's travel of the High City, but not inside the walls."

Aoea's soft, tentative voice broke the tense silence. "Our

sister Ammaranza has lived some years in the High City. She seems unafraid."

"She lives in the ruler's palace," Hane pointed out.

"No mortal ruler could protect her from a power such as Rombonole suggests," Aoea said. She turned to Ammaranza. "Advise us, sister."

Ammaranza nodded. She paused a moment to gather her thoughts; then she said, "In all my years in the High City, in the time of Pytrigon and now in the time of Duarin, I never sensed a power unfriendly to me. The persecutions were the work of men. But Duarin is practical. As long as no magic is used against him, he will not oppose it. Pytrigon persecuted sorcerers out of fear for his life. Nakkarra was known to have practiced against him, and when he learned that her power was weakened, he had her taken and killed. As for the others, it is as Cei Shalpan said: they were neophytes and petty practitioners. They made enemies, and their own folly left them defenseless. We would have no cause for fear."

"Perhaps not. But perhaps if twelve sorcerers assembled in the High City, the people's fear would return—not only Duarin, but all the people might rise up against us," said Hane.

"We would annihilate them," Cei Shalpan declared.

"And in annihilating them, we would consume our power and leave ourselves weakened for the quest."

"No need to speak of annihilation. We will not announce our presence. If we enter the city separately, at intervals, and remain apart except for meetings such as this, we will be unsuspected. A concealing spell is very simple," said Ammaranza.

"Very simple and very easily penetrated," Hane said, turning his dark frown on her. "It takes a greater master than any here to work a perfect concealing spell."

Wearily, Ammaranza sank back into the comforting cushions of her chair, and in a fading voice she said, "I was asked for my advice. I advise going to the High City."

She closed her eyes and let the words of the others fly back and forth across the twelve-sided table without comment or question. Sensing the currents of rivalry and antagonism that ran beneath every utterance, she found herself despairing. Surely their quest could never succeed. They sought an unknown talisman hidden ages ago by a sorcerer more powerful than any who had walked the earth since. To determine its

form, discover its whereabouts, penetrate its defenses, and
learn its secrets would require the utmost concentration of
their collective magic. Some would have to sacrifice as she
had already sacrificed. And here they sat, squabbling like
common soldiers over loot, full of suspicion and old fears
and longing to revenge ancient injuries. The oath they had
sworn seemed forgotten as each thought only of personal
gain and personal safety.

But as Ammaranza reclined, quiescent, against the soft,
dark cushions, the tone of the discussion changed. Agreement seemed at hand, and she felt a stirring of hope. It was
as if the quest had come to life in their minds, asserting its
importance to each, and to the fellowship, and had stilled all
doubts. When they dissolved the assembly, they were agreed:
one year from the day that Duarin became king of the Northern Lands, they would gather in the High City, not to depart
until the talisman of the Iron Mage was in their grasp.

CHAPTER ELEVEN

RESURRECTION

At the last rise before the outskirts of the great Southern Forest, Genlon turned, and, shielding his eyes from the midday sun, he looked to the north. The tower at Southmark, two days' march behind them, could no longer be seen, nor could the pale walls of Goldengrange, where Meragrand and their three children waited. Only the coastal plain, decked in pale early green, lay before his gaze.

The slender, gray-haired man who stood at his side turned to him and said, "Have no fear for them, son. They'll be safe and happy until you return."

"I know they will, Ordred. Merry was so eager to visit you that she's talked of little else since Whitefall," said Genlon, his eyes still fixed on the far horizon.

"It's good to have her back. Almost like having her mother with me again," Ordred said wistfully. "And good to have children at Goldengrange once again, too," he added more brightly.

"They like the place. It's quite a change from the High City."

"I hope you like it, too. It will be yours before long. I like to think of you and Merry living there, raising children where I and my children were raised."

"Don't talk so, Ordred. You'll live to see our children's children grow."

"I doubt that. But I'll hang on until you return, I promise you that," the older man said, extending his hand. Genlon took it firmly, and Ordred added, "You've made my daughter very happy, and you've been the son I always hoped for. I'm grateful to you, Genlon."

"She's a wonderful wife. I'm sorry to have to leave her."

"You might be back before the first snow falls."

"I might also be gone for years. This is not a mission like the others."

150

Ordred looked at him somberly. "Do you have forebodings? If you do, Genlon . . ."

"No, nothing like that," Genlon assured him, waving off all such ideas. "It's only that you've made us all so welcome at Goldengrange that I hate the thought of leaving. But 'the sooner the dark, the sooner the dawn,' as the mountain people say. Farewell, friend, and care for those we both love."

They parted, Ordred and his men returning north, Genlon and his little troop proceeding south, into the forest. Only nine men marched with Genlon. He needed no more; they traveled through friendly lands, and theirs was a peaceful mission.

Out of the burnt and broken aftermath of war, a new leader had emerged among the nomads of the dry lands to the south. His name was Daun Sheem. He was a warrior from a tribe of warriors, but the message he sent to his northern neighbors was one of peace. He expressed his and his people's wish to forget old enmities and let the wounds heal. As proof of his good will, he invited Duarin to come with all his court and visit him as an honored guest, or to send an emissary of his choice. And if the lord of the High City and king of the Northern Lands preferred, Daun Sheem proclaimed his willingness to travel north himself.

The message took Duarin by surprise. His attention had been so tightly concentrated on the progress of his northern venture that he had paid little heed to word from elsewhere. An enemy in the south was no longer useful; a strong ally was what he wanted now, and Daun Sheem's message was welcome. But success had made Duarin no less suspicious; if anything, he was more watchful and less trusting than before. In the two years since he had assumed the old title abandoned by Aluca, he had uncovered four plots against his throne and dealt with the accused conspirators summarily and brutally.

Duarin pondered the unexpected overture from the land of the old enemy, and he came only slowly to a decision. It would be reckless for him to visit Daun Sheem, for this might be a plot to lure him far from home and assassinate him. And it would be imprudent to let Daun Sheem visit the High City until it was completely under control. But a visit from Genlon, the legendary Graymantle, accompanied by a small honor guard, would be an effective display of force as well as a gesture of good will.

This seemed the wisest course of action, but it was not an

easy choice for Duarin. It required investing Genlon with considerable authority, and Duarin had no wish to share power or authority with anyone. Genlon had been loyal and dependable since the day he entered Duarin's service, and he had risked his life repeatedly for the good of the High City. But even that could not allay Duarin's suspicions. There still remained uncertainty about his true origins: all the inquiries made—and liberally paid for—had produced only vague information about Genlon's mother and none at all about his father. Such obscurity was not comforting to Duarin.

And Ammaranza had been showing entirely too much interest in Genlon and his family, treating him with the generosity and indulgence she seldom showed her own son. This, too, disturbed Duarin. She was old, and growing feeble, and her behavior might be no more than the whims of age; on the other hand, she had powers that were more than human. She knew no master but her own will, and her will was unfathomable. If she were working some design of her own, he would not know of it until too late. If Genlon were a party to it, there would be great danger indeed.

As he brooded in his solitude upon the possibilities, Duarin alternated between the conviction that all those around him were betraying him and an equal certainty that his subjects were loyal and all the plotting was in his imagination. He thought, and drank more wine, and went on brooding. In the end, he sent Genlon off to greet Daun Sheem and sound him out. He stood atop the western gate and raised his hand in a last farewell, and he even permitted Meragrand and the children to travel as far as Goldengrange and visit there while Genlon was away. But despite these gestures of trust, his mind was not at ease.

Genlon spoke seldom to his companions on the long journey south. He remained apart and was often deep in thought, for he, too, was troubled in his mind. He knew nothing of Duarin's suspicions, and had he been warned of them he would have dismissed the warning as fantasy. His problem involved only himself and his own deeds. He had not mentioned it even to Meragrand, although she had noticed his preoccupied manner and sought to comfort him all through the winter.

It had all begun when the last battle was over, and the last and fiercest band of brigands was no more. They were tough, experienced fighters, and when the last' of them fell, only Genlon and six companions were on their feet, bloodspattered and arm-weary. Upon their return to the High City, Duarin had declared a special festival day to honor them. Representatives of all the northern regions came to pay tribute to their defenders and show their gratitude with generous gifts. For a time, the High City was theirs. But by the first day of Whitefall, people's minds had returned to their own affairs.

In spite of recognitions and rewards, Genlon felt a sense of emptiness, and it grew in him as the days darkened. Accomplished, his mission did not seem quite so glorious or so noble as it had in prospect, and even in the doing. To bring a peaceful life to defenseless people, he had shed a sea of blood, and good men had died at his side. Yet these same people whose lives and homes he had saved looked on him and the guards almost as fearfully as they had looked on the brigands; he had seen the fear in their faces. They shouted their thanks, and they set up memorial stones—sometimes with prodding—but they were clearly relieved that these swordsmen from a land beyond their own had proven mortal, as if their vulnerability, in some paradoxical way, made the weaker people strong.

Genlon tried to rouse his spirits by thinking back on the long string of victories in his years of service to Duarin, the innocent lives saved, the pain and suffering prevented, the evil punished. Nothing helped. For the first time, he doubted the worth of his deeds and wondered if he had somehow gone astray in pursuing his destiny and turned his life into an ongoing ritual of slaughter in the name of a high purpose. He longed to speak with Cathwar and hear the old wizard's advice, but he knew no way to summon him. So he did nothing, and he sank deeper into gloom every day.

In the depths of his despondency, he was summoned to Duarin and informed of the mission to the south. It seemed providential: just when he had lost all belief in his destiny as a warrior, he was given the opportunity to become an agent of peace between old enemies. He could perform this mission successfully without drawing his sword against any man.

His spirits improved at once, and even Meragrand remarked that he was becoming his old self. But as he marched ever nearer the appointed rendezvous, he felt the weight of

his mission more acutely than he had ever felt a burden
before.

They followed the River Issalt to the southeast, where it
left Hidden Lake. After a short rest among the netters of the
lake shore, they continued south, still following the river.
The landscape began to change. Trees were smaller and
more scattered. Open meadows and ever-greater stretches of
grassland began to intrude on the oaks, beeches, and maples
of the hardwood forest, and the sun was ever more oppressive
overhead. When they came to Golden Lake, glittering under
a clear blue sky, they could scarcely wait to plunge into its
mild waters and refresh themselves. From here on, the forest
was behind them, and the land was open on both sides of
the river. They proceeded southward, keeping to the river
bank and the shade of the tall, strange-looking trees that ran
like a living fence along the water's edge. At the mouth of
the Issalt, where it left its parent river, the Irachmé, they
found their guides waiting. In three days' travel over the
stony uplands, they reached Daun Sheem's settlement.
Genlon had taken no part in the wars against the nomads,
and he had no firsthand knowledge of their land or their
ways. His first sight of Daun Sheem's settlement surprised
and impressed him. It lacked the splendor of the High City,
but it had a bleak beauty unlike anything he had ever seen
before.
The settlement stood in the middle of a sandy waste, about
five greatmarks from the river bank. It was a single enor-
mous unit composed of hundreds of domes of varied sizes
flowing smoothly into one another. The whole structure
seemed to rise out of the ground, as bubbles rise in a thick
porridge, the undulating, vaulted roofs like a sea of dunes
arrested in their leeward motion. Other than the low gateway, Genlon saw no openings except the narrow slits—
archers' posts, he assumed—that punctuated the outer wall
in an irregular row about one mark from the ground. The
wall was otherwise smooth and seamless, matching in color
and texture the ground on which it stood.
Passing through the gateway of the domed city, the visitors
entered a cool refuge from the sun's heat and glare. Covered
streets, tapestried with lacy shadows from the trellises overhead, ran in three directions from the dappled courtyard before the entrance. Their guides walked on, silent and imper-

turbable, until they reached a great well surrounded by a low wall of stone carved in intricate openwork. Above them soared a pierced vault in the same pattern, a full five marks from the water's surface at its high point. Men and women were seated around the well, all wearing loose-fitting, hooded garments of a pale sand color. At the entrance of the visitors, they rose and silently departed, drifting into the shadows, their robes blending with the walls. The chief guide motioned for Genlon and his men to be seated, and he gave orders in his own tongue to his men. They, in turn, hastened to fetch food and water for the visitors, and when these had been supplied, the chief guide left them. Neither he nor his men had spoken a word to the northerners since the brief exchange of greetings three days before.

The water was cold and clear. Genlon drank deeply, wiped his lips, and turned to his lieutenant. "What do you think, Jesseman?" he asked.

"Nothing's out of the ordinary, according to what my father told me, commander. They're not a talky people. He was a prisoner for three years, and for the first year and more, no one said a word to him. They didn't mistreat him. Just didn't speak to him."

"Did he escape?"

"No, sir, they set him free. He never knew why. They took him almost to Golden Lake—kept him blindfolded all the time—and just turned him loose. Gave him food and water and his weapons."

Genlon grunted and shook his head uncomprehendingly. He took one of the hard, flat slabs of bread and dipped it into the dish of dark paste. The flavor was rich and nutlike and delicious. He scooped up a second helping and had just put it in his mouth when he saw a lean, bare-headed man burst from an archway to his left, followed by a group of men who were obviously hurrying to keep up with him. The leader was beaming, his arms extended, and as he drew near he cried, "Welcome, my friends from the north! My house is yours, and all in it!"

His eyes fell on the dishes set before the visitors, and the water jars at their sides, and his face darkened. Glowering, he turned on his followers and shouted angrily in his own language, and as he berated them, he emphasized his message by hurling dishes of the dark paste at their heads and smashing water jars. He turned back to Genlon, and his smile flashed again. He opened his arms and said in a husky voice, "I am Daun Sheem, and I am ashamed of the food you have been given within my walls. You are warriors and heroes every one, and you will eat and drink like warriors in the house of Daun Sheem. No more of this old man's food—we will have roast meat, and wine as dark as blood, and we will learn to be friends as strong as we once were enemies."

He embraced Genlon and then the other visitors, and his men did the same. The northerners, uncertain how to accept the welcome, smiled and nodded uncomfortably until Genlon embraced Daun Sheem, and then there followed another round of embraces, and much laughter, and shouts in both languages affirming friendship and good will.

Daun Sheem stepped back from the press, looked his visitors over with obvious approval, and then, pointing to Genlon, said, "You are the one they call Graymantle. The big man with the dark blade, that's the way they describe you. You move like the wind, and you strike like the lightning, and no blade can pierce your skin. You honor the house of Daun Sheem, you and the men who march with you."

"The honor is ours, Daun Sheem. We bring you the friendship of King Duarin and all the people of the north," Genlon said.

"Good. That's what we want, friendship with the northern people and their kind. No more wars between us. Plenty of fighting, and lots of plunder, but no more wars between us," Daun Sheem said happily, leaving Genlon somewhat confused. "Now you go and wash and rest, and at sundown we have a feast. We have robes for you, so you can be comfortable here and out under the sun. Wear them."

In accordance with Daun Sheem's command, Genlon and his men arrived at the feast wearing hooded robes like those of their hosts. All the robes but Genlon's were of the ordinary sand color; his was of a smoky gray. It felt as light as a cloak of air, and it was as soft as down. He had never seen or felt such cloth before, and he thanked Daun Sheem warmly for the gift.

His host stroked the ends of his long, grizzled moustache; a smile lit his sun-browned face, and the leathery skin near his mouth and eyes creased with pleasure. "That's good stuff —keeps you warm when it's cold, and cool when it's hot. It's made from the hair of a mountain goat that only lives in the peaks beyond the Upland Sea. Very rare animal. Only four

robes like that in the world, and they were all made for me.
One I gave to my bravest fighter when he married my
daughter, two I keep for myself, and the other is for you.
Now, when men speak of Graymantle, they'll be speaking of
the robe I gave my friend."

"It's magnificent, Daun Sheem."

"Good. And what gifts do you bring from your king?"
Daun Sheem asked, smiling expectantly, like a child awaiting
a promised present. Genlon called for the pack they had
brought with them. Setting it before him, he opened it to
reveal a goblet, a dagger, and a coiled armband. The dagger
was set in a black and silver sheath, with a single emerald in
the pommel. The armband was of gold, finely worked in the
form of a dragon with a head at either end, one pair of eyes
elliptical emeralds, and the other round rubies. Each scale
was carefully incised, and every hair on the dragon's two
tiny chins stood out. Daun Sheem cried out with pleasure at
the sight of his gifts, and he displayed them eagerly to his
companions, who marveled.

The old man who sat at Daun Sheem's side had eyes only
for the goblet. It was a beautiful example of the work of the
High City's artisans, with a hunting scene circumscribing its
broad silver base, and golden medallions around the bowl
representing symbols of the northern lands, but the old man's
eager attention was on the lining of the bowl, which had
been carved from a single block of sweetwood. He spoke
urgently to Daun Sheem in the lilting liquid tongue of their
people, and then he took up the goblet eagerly. Daun Sheem
exchanged a few quick phrases with him; then he turned to
Genlon.

"He says the goblet is made of the wood of long life."

"We call it sweetwood. It's only found in the Crystal
Hills."

"Magic?" Daun Sheem asked.

"Some people think so."

Daun Sheem pondered the reply for a moment; then he
laughed and pointed a chiding finger at Genlon. "Some think
so, but not you. What do you think, then?"

"Everyone says that it neutralizes poison. It was highly
valued by the old kings of the north, and Duarin drinks
from such a goblet, so I suppose it works."

Daun Sheem nodded and fell silent. Then he clapped his

hands and gave a command. As the servant departed, he explained to Genlon, "We'll try it."

A man was dragged in between two hard-faced swordsmen. He was bound, and his face was puffed and discolored from a recent beating. He looked about apprehensively, and he started when Daun Sheem addressed him. After a very short speech, Daun Sheem took up the goblet, emptied into it a dark powder provided him by the old man, and bade a servant fill the goblet with wine. The prisoner was freed, and the goblet was presented to him. He rubbed his wrists, glancing about, and only when Daun Sheem gave a low, harsh growl of command did he take the goblet in both hands. He licked his lips, took a deep breath, and downed the contents of the goblet without stopping. The servant took the empty goblet, turned it upside down for all to see, and set it before Daun Sheem. He, in turn, signaled to a group of young men who sat apart from the others. Immediately one of them rose and began a high-pitched, ululating chant.

"If he's still alive when the chant ends, your sweetwood works," Daun Sheem explained.

He said nothing further, and Genlon thought it best not to inquire what would happen if the sweetwood did *not* work. He watched, and listened to the eerie chant, and observed the others, all sitting with eyes fixed on the prisoner. His own men knew nothing of what was going on; but they too, caught up in the fascination of those around them, watched the man.

The chant ended abruptly. Daun Sheem spoke, and the guards stepped aside to allow the prisoner to depart, a free man. Refilling the goblet himself, Daun Sheem drank half the contents; then he handed it to Genlon, who emptied it.

"King Duarin is generous," Daun Sheem said.

"He wants to be your friend."

"Good. Tell me . . . what other magic trees do you have up in the northlands? Are there any that protect from sword points and arrows?"

Genlon was beginning to feel the effects of the wine. He shook his head and said firmly, "Only if a man hides behind them, Daun Sheem."

His host thumped him on the back and laughed wildly. He repeated the exchange in his own language, for all to hear, and set the feast in an uproar. He repeated it again, for Genlon's men, and laughed even louder. After more wine, and the singing of piercing chants, and laughter, and story-telling, Daun Sheem was moved to tell Genlon the reasons behind his sudden change of heart toward the north.

"Your guardsmen were good fighters, but they were care-less. Very careless. Twice they left me for dead, and twice I lived. Look at these scars," he said, pulling open his shirt to display three thick welts of scar tissue on his pale chest. "One quick thrust of a dagger and they'd have been rid of me for good. But they didn't finish their job. The second time they came close. It was a long time before I was ready to fight again. There weren't any other leaders left by then. It was all up to me." He paused to drink from his goblet and refill both his and Genlon's, and then he inclined his head to indicate the old man at his other side. "I went to Kekuda for advice. He knows everything. Reads the stars the way you and I read a map. He can hear them talking to one another, and he understands. Kekuda told me that if I went north I'd fall a third time, and I wouldn't get up. But if I went to the east, I'd have victories, and I'd bring back enough treasure to make everyone in my house rich." He nodded and winked at the old man, who returned the nod with slow dignity.

"So you decided to make peace with Duarin," Genlon observed.

"Not just peace. Alliance," Daun Sheem said, throwing his arm around Genlon's shoulder. "Imagine you and me at the head of an army . . . the best fighters from both our lands . . . we'd go clear to the world's end, and take what we wanted wherever we went."

That sounded suspiciously like brigandage, but Genlon held back the observation, instead asking, "What's out there, Daun Sheem? I've heard some of the veterans talk of wealthy cities."

Daun Sheem laughed loudly at this. He called out to a group of battle-scarred men near at hand, who joined in his laughter. He explained to Genlon, "We fooled your guards-men—led them off to the east, so they never found this place. They came on the border villages of the eastern king-dom—miserable little border villages, my friend!—and they held so much riches that your guardsmen thought they were our high cities!" His face grew serious, and he leaned closer to Genlon. "Think what lies in the treasury at the heart of that kingdom, Graymantle! Their ruler lives in a palace made all of gold. He drinks from a goblet carved out of a single diamond the size of a man's head. The poorest beggars beg with silver bowls!"

"I've heard of great riches, but never anything like that."

"Well . . . maybe the stories were exaggerated a little. But only a little," Daun Sheem said, refilling their goblets.

"With so much wealth, there must be a strong defense. Otherwise, it would have been seized long ago."

"Plenty of defense. Ten men for every one of us. But they're disorganized. Little bands of swordsmen, each band defending its own hill and attacking its neighbors. They'd take one look at our army and run in all directions."

"What if they united?"

Daun Sheem frowned and set his goblet down. "You northerners always look at the bad side of things. They haven't united in fifty generations. They won't for another fifty. In the meantime, we'll take what we want."

"It certainly sounds as though we could," Genlon admitted.

"Daun Sheem and Graymantle can do anything they want. Remember that," said the Drylander. He drank deeply, shouted a command, and told Genlon, "Enough talking. Time for pleasure."

Four young women entered, wearing little more than thin chains of gold, hung with tiny silver bells, around their necks and waists. Their glossy black hair and tawny skin gleamed in the torchlight, and their gold and silver ornaments glittered with their liquid motion. An appreciative murmur arose from the gathering as they formed a loose square, back to back, and began to sway their bodies in unison, moving their hands and feet in slow, intricate patterns. At a gesture from Daun Sheem, the young man who had chanted earlier now rose, joined by two of his companions, and began a soft, low, wordless melody, very sweet and lulling, its harmonies as complex and sensuous as the movements of the dancers. The tinkling of bells, the rhythmic clapping of hands, and the soft patter of bare feet on the earth floor mingled with the soothing chant to weave a hypnotic spell over dancers, chanters, and watchers alike. Only when the dance reached a writhing peak, and the chant had his pulse pounding, was Genlon even aware that he was wildly clapping his hands and shouting along with the rest. When sound and movement ceased abruptly, and the dancers whirled like shadows from the room, it was some time before the assembly ceased to shout and applaud.

"Do you like them?" Daun Sheem asked proudly.

"I've never seen anything like them. We have no such dancers in the High City."

"Good. Which one do you want for tonight?"

"Tonight? Oh, no, thank you," Genlon said quickly.

"I'll have them all bathed and scented," Daun Sheem reassured him. "You can pick one when you're ready. Two, if you like. If you think their dancing is good, wait until you lie down with them."

"You're generous, Daun Sheem, but I can't."

"Are you sick?"

"No, I'm fine. But I have a wife."

Daun Sheem looked bewildered. "She's not here. You're here, and the dancers are here. So enjoy one of them."

Genlon attempted to explain himself, but with little success. Daun Sheem listened for a time; then he silenced Genlon and poured more wine into their goblets. "I can't understand why, but I see you don't like to take pleasure away from home. It's a strange custom, but I respect your ways. Let's talk about our campaign against the east."

Genlon's sleep that night was filled with dreams of dancing girls and Meragrand, of treasure and battle. He awoke in the morning troubled and unrested. His mission of peace threatened to lead to a new outburst of warfare, and for no such high goals as his campaign against the brigands. Fortunately, he could take honest refuge in the fact that he was only an emissary, and he had no authority to speak for his king in a matter of such gravity. When Daun Sheem spoke next of their joint venture to the east, he gave that response, and the nomad leader accepted it. But later remarks showed that he expected Genlon to urge the eastern campaign upon Duarin.

As his stay drew on, Genlon found himself liking Daun Sheem more and more. He was volatile, but his anger passed as quickly as it flared, and he lavished his generosity on anyone he had injured in his wrath. He was proud, but not too proud to recognize an error and learn from it. His most frequent reaction was laughter, sometimes at a joke, sometimes out of pleasure, often out of sheer exuberance and a love of life that exceeded his power of words. Genlon found his set-

tlement a far different and much more enjoyable place to be
than Duarin's gloomy, suspicion-haunted High City.

About midway through the month of Yellowleaf, Daun
Sheem hinted none too subtly that Genlon might be eager to
return to the High City so that Duarin would have the winter
to plan for their great war on the eastern kingdom. Genlon
had enjoyed his stay, but he did wish to rejoin Meragrand
and their children before snowfall. He and his men readied
themselves, said their farewells, and were on their way to the
High City before the last day of Yellowleaf.

The days were pleasant until they passed Golden Lake and
entered the forest, and then the growing chill of the air became noticeable. In his new robe, Genlon was as comfortable
as he could wish to be, and he was glad for the brisk air that
helped them keep up a fast pace, greatmark after greatmark,
day after day, bringing him ever closer to his loved ones.

At the first sight of Southmark, a tiny upright bristle on
the far horizon, his heart leaped in joyous anticipation.
Goldengrange was a day's journey to the west of the tower
on a fine, straight road. He shouted to his men, urging them
on, and they responded with renewed effort. At sundown,
when they made camp, they were half a day's march from
Southmark.

Genlon made it a practice to take a regular turn on watch.
That night, as he sat by the fire, his thoughts were on Meragrand and the children, and the pleasure of home and familiar faces: Ordred with his furrowed brow and perennial
predictions of his own demise which somehow never came
true; Cade, with his prosperous girth and sympathetic ear
and sound common sense; and poor Ammaranza, now so
frail and weak she seldom left her bed except for impulsive
visits to friends in the city. Thinking of his benefactress, he
sighed and shook his head sadly; and at that moment, from
the dagger in his waistband there came a sharp crack, like
the splintering of cold crystal plunged into fire. Startled, he
came at once to his feet and groped inside his shirt.

The red jewel in the handle of the dagger was cracked,
and its color was dull in the firelight. Genlon examined it,
and his heart filled with foreboding. He had told no one,
but he had found that this dagger possessed a strange
power. Three times in his long struggle against the brigands,
the sudden glowing of the red stone had alerted him to unsuspected danger and probably saved his life. And now that

the stone was cracked and dimmed, he feared for Ammaranza, whom he believed responsible for the daggers' warning power.

When they reached Southmark the next day, his fears were
realized. A guardsman greeted him with an order to return
directly to the High City, where the Lady Ammaranza had
need of him. Meragrand and the children, he was informed,
were already with her.

Just at sundown, on the third day of hard marching from
Southmark, the little band entered the High City. While his
men went to the guards' quarters, Genlon and his escort
proceeded directly to the palace. He grew concerned when
they passed by the wing where Ammaranza's suite was
located and went on to the chamber on the upper floor where
Duarin held private conferences.

"Why aren't we going to the Lady Ammaranza?" he asked
his escort.

"I was instructed to bring you directly to King Duarin."

"Is she still alive?"

"I know no more than you, commander," said the man,
not turning to face him.

As always, two of Duarin's private bodyguard stood on
watch outside the chamber doors. Once Genlon had passed
through, the doors thudded shut, and he heard a bar slide
into place. Directly before him, seated on a carved wooden
throne, his face lit by the glow from the four-branched
candlesticks that stood at either side of the throne, was
Duarin. His triumphant look was not that of a man in
mourning.

Exhausted by travel, preoccupied with worry for Ammaranza, Genlon was scarcely aware of the ring of guards
until he felt the pricking of steel at his throat, and in his
back, and under his ribs. The troop leader, a tough old
veteran named Helring, plucked Genlon's blade from the
scabbard with a single quick gesture.

"When I give the command, Helring, run him through,"
said Duarin.

Helring leveled the sword at Genlon's chest and held it
steady. Genlon looked at him; then he looked at Duarin,
and he shook his head helplessly.

"Most conspirators fail because of their impatience. But
you were too patient," Duarin said. "You were overcon-
fident. My mother always thought I was a fool, and she

must have persuaded you to think so, too. But I turned out to be too clever for you all. I know who you are. I suspected it the moment I saw you, but I wanted proof. And I searched, and I questioned, and I found you out."

Genlon, unable to make sense of anything that was happening here, said, "I'm Genlon, son of Banheen and Bilinse of the Crystal Hills, stepson of Ketial of Long Wood. Everybody knows that. I never tried to conceal it."

Duarin listened, nodding, smiling in a superior way, and then his expression clouded, and he rubbed his temple thoughtfully. Suddenly he threw his head back and laughed. Genlon searched the faces of the guards and found them expressionless. Their points held steady scarcely a finger's width from his body. There was no appealing to them and little chance of breaking free.

"She never told you!" Duarin crowed. "She used you, just as she used the others and would have used me, and she never told you the secret!" Again he burst into loud laughter, pounding the arm of the throne with his fist, rocking backward in an ecstasy of glee. It was clear to Genlon that Duarin was close to madness.

"There is no secret, my king," he said calmly.

"Oh, but there is. There are many secrets, and I'll tell them all, but I'll save the best one for last. I'll whisper that one to you as you breathe your final breath, and you'll die knowing who you are and what you might have been. That's fitting punishment for betraying me."

"I never betrayed my king."

"Perhaps not," Duarin admitted. "But you would have, before long. She would have told you the secret, or she would have worked one of her spells on you and had you kill me and seize the throne."

"The Lady Ammaranza is your mother," Genlon protested.

"She was a sorceress. She betrayed every man she ever knew. Father, son, husband, lover—she betrayed them all."

"She was ever kind to me."

"Oh, indeed she was. And she soon would have been kinder. But she's dead. She died in her sleep, four nights past, in the middle of the first watch." Duarin paused, and he then went on, in a subdued voice, "I placed a cushion over her face, very gently, and I held it there for two hundred heartbeats. She never struggled."

The guards' expressions did not waver; neither did the ring of sword points.

"Your own mother," Genlon said faintly.

"She was evil! Evil!" Duarin cried. "Pytrigon drove her from the city for fear she'd steal his will away. She tainted everyone. I didn't want to kill the others, but she made it necessary."

A chill went through Genlon at these words. "What others?" he asked.

"It was her doing, all her doing. If she hadn't sought you out and tried to use you against me, none of this would have happened. She would have used your wife and children one day. She might have turned them against you, in time. I had no choice," Duarin said, his voice as calm and gentle as a man speaking to his own child.

Genlon felt his blood turn to ice and then, as quickly, course like molten fire through his veins. He scarcely heard what Duarin said as he rambled on. He did not care, now, what mad ravings poured from Duarin's lips, for he knew that the king of the Northern Lands was a dead man. With all the self-discipline of his years of campaigning, he kept an outward calm, awaiting cnly the signal for his execution. As soon as Helring set himself for the thrust, Genlon would attack. A quick three strides forward and his hands would be on Duarin's throat, and all the guardsmen in the north could not pry them free. Let them hack the hands from his body; the fingers would be sunk deep in Duarin's flesh, and Meragrand and the children would be avenged. Nothing else mattered.

All his mind and will were focused on his final act. But as he stood statue-still in the ring of sword points, attentive for the cue to action, a little corner of his mind looked ironically on the scene. He had wondered so many times about his true destiny, questioned so often the purpose of his life and all his deeds; and it had come down to this. He would die at the hands of old comrades, at the behest of a mad king, with his fingers in the throat of the man who had covered him with honor and then killed those he loved most. Betrayal, madness, revenge: these were his destiny.

Duarin talked on, his voice rising and falling. He punctuated his words sometimes with laughter, sometimes with tears, and he often fell abruptly silent. At last he turned to

Genlon, weeping, and said, "I do only what I must. Forgive me, brother. She would not let me be!"

Genlon readied himself. He glanced at Helring, and he was surprised to see beads of sweat trickling down the old warrior's forehead, and a muscle twitching in his cheek. The sword point wavered, and Helring's eyes grew glassy, like those of one who hears a voice unheard by those around him. Before Duarin could give the command, Helring took a backward step and then turned and thrust. The sword flicked in and out of Duarin's chest.

Genlon moved then, crashing into Helring, wrenching the sword from his limp hand and sending him into the tall candlestick by Duarin's left side. He hurled the other candlestick to the floor and glided back to the wall to make his stand. Every man in the room was his enemy. That simplified the situation: he need not hesitate to strike for fear of hurting a friend.

In the darkness, he waited for the first contact. Ammaranza's dagger was in one hand, his dark blade in the other. He breathed cautiously, soundlessly, alert to every rustle and every footfall.

Suddenly, a great light filled the room, shadowless and all-illuminating. Its source seemed to be the very air. The barred and bolted doors flew open with a screech of splintering wood, and the light poured into the corridors, dazzling the outer guards, who howled in pain and astonishment. Before Genlon, the guardsmen reeled in agony, hands pressed to their eyes, weapons abandoned. Yet even though he felt the awful intensity of the white light, Genlon could see clearly, and he felt no pain.

"On your knees before the king!" rang out a deep, commanding voice. Genlon recognized it at once: Cathwar had returned at last. "This is Ambescand, son and heir of Pytrigon, rightful lord of the High City and king of the Northern Lands. Receive your king!" said the mighty voice, and the guardsmen obeyed, dropping to their knees in homage.

The light began to fade, and Genlon felt a hand on his shoulder. Dazed, he turned to look on the dark-robed wizard.

"The throne is yours. The first part of our work is done," said Cathwar, lowering his staff.

"You called me Ambescand . . ."

"You are Ambescand. Recall the prophecy: 'the child who died is the king who will be.' It speaks of you."

"I never died," said Ambescand, bewildered.

"Everyone believed that you did. Only Banheen knew, and he kept silent."

"That's the secret Duarin kept babbling about!"

"Yes. He learned it . . . dug out the facts and reasoned it out. He was an intelligent man, in his way."

"He was a murderous madman," said Ambescand, looking down on the figure sprawled at the foot of the throne. "I only wish I'd had the chance to kill him myself."

"His death, too, was part of the prophecy."

"All the same, he should have died at my hands."

"Better he did not. He was your half brother."

"Duarin? Do you mean that Pytrigon deceived his own brother?"

"Ammaranza's magic could rouse the lust of any man. Do not blame your father. He was helpless. Ammaranza wanted her child to rule the north, and she did what she thought necessary."

"And all for a throne. For this," said Ambescand in an empty voice.

"For something more than this, I think. We'll talk of it another time. You're a king now, and there's work to be done," said the wizard. Taking him by the arm and leading him to the doorway, he sent forth the king of the Northern Lands.

The return of Ambescand was a cause for celebration in the High City, but the people's joy was tempered with sorrow for the deaths of so many innocents. One person took no part in the festivities. For four days and nights, Tupaji sat cross-legged and bareheaded before the western gate. Her dark gaze was fixed on the eyelids of the blanched head that perched on a spike above her, and her lips moved unceasingly in a silent curse on the man who had slain her mistress. On the fourth day, late in the afternoon, Tupaji rose stiffly. She spat on the ground, and, taking up her mat, she walked into the west. She was never seen again.

CHAPTER TWELVE

A TIME OF DISCONTENT

A white blade lay in the treasure-house of a king in
*   a weary land;*
A black blade swung at a chieftain's side in a world of
*   sun and sand;*
*   And no man dreamed of the distant day when the*
*   dark blade and the bright*
Would be reborn in sacred flame and purified in
*   light;*
*   And no man knew that the winged blade as ancient*
*   as the sea*
Would loft again in a mortal hand, and set the northland
*   free. . . .*

From *The Last Deed Of Ambescand*

Ambescand was a dour king in the early years of his reign,
but his stern manner and his aloofness did not affect his
standing among the people of the north. He was accepted by
all. Most of them loved him from the very start. They remembered him as Graymantle, the deliverer from fear, and
they sympathized with him for the loss of his wife and children. They did not inquire closely into the details of his accession and Duarin's fall. They felt that the return of the lost
child of Pytrigon fulfilled the prophecy that had been whispered about in recent years and thus somehow restored order
and righteousness to the kingdom, and more than this they
did not care to know. A few feared him, believing in their
hearts that he was a usurper shrewder and even less scrupulous
than Duarin, and therefore more dangerous. But as the years
passed and he levied no new taxes, executed no old friends,
and confiscated no one's property, their suspicion diminished.

It seemed for a time as if the legendary days of the Old
Kingdom were come again. The new king made no demand
for tribute; tribute came nonetheless, freely and generously

rendered. Ingots of tin and silver from the Crystal Hills; building stone and occasional quantities of gold from the mountains; lumber and the rare decorative woods—goldenband, neverburn, and winewood—from Long Wood and the Southern Forest; it all came to the High City in the caravans that now moved freely over the old trade routes.

To Ambescand, the rich tribute was as meaningless as barrels of sand. He would have given it all, and added to it the contents of the High City's treasury, to have his beloved Meragrand and their children before him once again. But they were gone forever. In their place he had a carven throne, a golden crown, a lost name, and a newly gained kingdom. He had things that all men wish for, and they brought him no joy.

He thought often of Cathwar, and he wished that the old wizard had remained longer in the city, to advise and instruct and help him make sense of his new life. Cathwar had left all too soon and told all too little. His explanations raised a score of questions for every one they answered. But that was the way of wizards, and though his presence could be exasperating, Ambescand missed him and wished him back.

No tribute came from Drylands—only a message from Daun Sheem offering congratulations and a renewed invitation to join him in a march to the east. Ambescand lingered over his reply. The thought of a long campaign in a faraway land was attractive. In the stir of battle, he would have no time for memories, and if he fell on some remote field, there would be an end to his sorrows. The kingdom would survive without him.

In the end, he realized his selfishness and sent back a message wishing his friend a successful venture but begging off with the excuse that he was needed in the High City for some time to come. The following spring, a messenger came from Daun Sheem bearing lavish gifts: a silver sword in a black scabbard decked with diamonds set in a web of silver, and a box about two hand-lengths on each side, carved in a design of intertwined serpents. Opening it, he found a bag of soft leather and a note which read, "Accept these gifts from an old friend. When you were Genlon Graymantle, a sword was enough to protect you. Now you are Ambescand, a king, and you need different protection. Live in strength, good friend, and die in battle." Scrawled across the bottom was Daun Sheem's symbol.

Removing the leather bag, Ambescand opened it and saw the sweetwood goblet he had given the Drylander when they first met. He read the message over, nodding, and he sighed at the truth of the words. He was a different man now, living a different life. It would do him no more good to wish his crown away than it did children to wish for the Snow Moon in the middle of Longdays. The only way to peace of mind was to accept things as they were.

Slowly, he tried to force himself to do this. He learned to listen, to sift the truth from a dozen conflicting accounts, to render fair judgment. He studied the history of the kingdom, its laws, the lives of its rulers, and the legends of the ancient days. He familiarized himself with the city, its buildings and streets and parks, the wall and outer defenses, and the labyrinth of waterways and sewers and tunnels, dungeons and treasure-vaults, that ran beneath it; and then he pored over all the maps of the northern lands, checking and comparing, in preparation for a new mapping expedition of his own. He learned how to use the wealth of the city, and how to store food against lean years, and the ways of building and trading; and every day, faithfully, he trained with the guard in the morning before breaking the night's fast.

His closest friends were the two surviving members of Duarin's Hammer, Conquaine and Peramee. Often, of an evening, he would send for them, and the three veterans would drink wine until late in the night and fight old battles over once again, smiling at the memories of fallen comrades. These hours were the only times he allowed himself to think of the past, for with these men he felt somehow secure. Conquaine had lost an eye during an encounter on the Headland, and the sight in his other eye was fading; Peramee had been crippled in the last battle in the mountains. They would not go into battle again. He could not lose them as he had lost all his other friends, and the people who were dearest to him. He was often lonely, but he accepted loneliness as the lesser pain and sought no new friends, nor a new wife. He did not want to risk losing those close to him again.

Banheen came to the High City on a visit, accompanied by Feron. The women of the family remained at home, Ketial in the throes of a fever and too weak to travel, Ketinella caring for her and managing the inn. Ambescand was at the western gate to meet them, and for a moment, upon their arrival, he abandoned all his reserve in a rush of overwhelming feeling

and threw his arms around his adoptive father and brother,
blinking back tears of joy to have them with him.

Banheen's stay was brief. Though he tried to conceal it, his
concern for Ketial was obvious in every gesture and intona-
tion. Ambescand had not the heart to detain him. He loaded
the old man down with gifts and sent him home with the High
City's finest mediciner and surgeon in his train and a guard
of honor to escort him to the door of the inn at Riverfield.
Feron, at his own request, stayed on.

Without Banheen to serve as a link between them, the two
men were awkward with each other at first. Feron kept calling Ambescand by his old name, and Ambescand had constantly to remind himself that this man who looked so different from him was nonetheless his brother, united to him by a
bond of shared memories and experience stronger than the
blind ties of blood.

Feron, now in his twenties, was a younger version of Banheen. He had his father's slender build and narrow shoulders,
and the same manner of listening intently, with pursed lips
and a silent frown, when another spoke to him. His hair was
jet black, as Banheen's had once been. Like Banheen, he had
no skill with weapons, nor did he seek to acquire any. Indeed,
he seemed reluctant to face, or even to hear about, physical
danger, and Ambescand's uncomfortable first impression of
his half brother was that Feron was a somewhat pusillanimous
young man.

But Feron's mind was as quick and agile as his darting
blue eyes, and he could grasp a complex idea with the same
sureness with which Ambescand could grasp a sword. He was
good company and well spoken. Ambescand entrusted him
with matters of some importance, and he was pleased by
Feron's handling of them. By the end of his second summer's stay, Feron had become a trusted aide and a close
friend.

But still Ambescand said nothing of a new marriage, and
this became a matter of concern among his advisers. When
the question was raised in his presence, he silenced the
speaker abruptly. Even Feron was not free to mention this
forbidden subject. In private, however, the king's remarriage
was a matter of endless discussion.

Now that the kingdom was restored, the people of the
north wanted a legitimate blood heir to the throne—two or
three of them, for safety's sake—so that the death of Ambe-

scand would not plunge the north into chaos. This was a king's duty to himself and his people, and now that a decent mourning period had passed, it was time for Ambescand to fulfill it. Yet he refused.

Ambescand himself realized the clear necessity, even the urgent need, to remarry and provide the kingdom with an heir. But what logic and duty made inescapable, his feelings made unendurable. Even the coldest, most politic marriage, intended as nothing more than an arrangement for the breeding of future kings, was sure to create a bond of affection; never such a love as he had felt for Meragrand, for that could not come twice in a man's lifetime, but still a feeling that would make him vulnerable as he never wished to be again. He pondered and postponed. Another summer passed, and though no one spoke openly to him, he sensed the apprehension all around him.

One evening late in winter, as he sat alone studying a difficult passage in the ancient laws, he looked up to see Cathwar standing before him in the glow of the fire. He rose to greet him, but the old wizard, frowning, merely pointed accusingly and said, "It is time for you to marry."

Ambescand was taken aback for a moment; then, angrily, he retorted, "Is that all that anyone in my kingdom is capable of saying?"

"It is something that must be said, even though you forbid it."

Ambescand hesitated; then he said more calmly, "I know my duty, Cathwar, and I'll do it. But I loved Meragrand. I want to mourn her properly."

"You have done so, and you have been faithful to her memory. Now you must keep faith with your people."

"Not yet. In time, yes, but it's too soon now."

The wizard's voice was cold and contemptuous. "You ceased to mourn Meragrand and your children long ago. You mourn for yourself, and you pity yourself. You fear being hurt again."

"Yes, I do," Ambescand said defiantly. "Why should I marry again and give new hostages to the idiotic powers that govern this world? They took the people I loved and threw me an unwanted crown in exchange. What will they do next time?"

"Your words do you little credit. Has kingship blinded you to everything but your own concerns?"

"You know it hasn't. I work hard to be a good king."

"Yet you speak as though you were put in this world only to be happy; as if it were unjust and unnatural for you to undergo the sufferings common to all men. The powers that you so easily condemn have given you much happiness, as well as the sorrow you dwell on. You've had the love of family and friends, of wife and children; the respect and admiration of equals; the honor of those more powerful. You were saved from death as a helpless infant and restored to your rightful throne. You've been given more than any man alive," said the wizard solemnly.

Ambescand sank into his chair and put his head in his hands. He sighed, and in a lowered voice he said, "All you say is true, Cathwar. I've said it to myself, a hundred times and more. Yet I can't seem to get over my love for Meragrand. I never knew love could be like that."

"Have you ever reflected on who arranged the marriage?"

Ambescand looked up, bewildered. "It was Ammaranza."

"With her magic, she could arouse such an overpowering desire in Pytrigon that he betrayed his own brother for her love. Is it not possible that this love for Meragrand that sets you against reason and duty—"

"No!" Ambescand cried, raising his hands as if to ward off physically the very suggestion.

Cathwar was silent for a time. When Ambescand looked up at him in mute appeal, he said gently, "Ammaranza was fond of you. She might have worked a small magic to enhance your happiness with Meragrand and hers with you."

"Then all our closeness . . . our happiness . . . was a deception?"

"Your love was real. Believe that, Ambescand. Not all of Ammaranza's power could create love where there was none. But where it existed, a very small magic could deepen it."

"So . . . I must forget Meragrand."

"Not forget her. Accept that what is past is past. Your obligation is to the future." Cathwar stepped to the king's side. His voice softened, as if a weariness had come over him. "Evil is stirring in the north. It's something vague and inchoate, a dark magic from the far past. I can sense it even within the High City, but I don't dare reveal my own presence as yet. The end is unclear. But I know that you, or your descendants, or their descendants, will one day be called upon to confront it."

Ambescand rose, and his expression was troubled. "If that's true, Cathwar . . ."

"It is true. I wish it were not."

"Then why am I still alive? If this evil power wants to be certain of overcoming, it should kill me now, before I have descendants who might somehow be preserved, as I was."

"Something more powerful protects you."

Ambescand let out his breath in wonderment. He shook his head, and then he said, "What, Cathwar? And why me?"

"I can tell no more now. I have much to learn myself, and the time is short. But what I say is true, that much I know. You must marry soon, and you must be ready for the confrontation, should it come in your lifetime."

"How can I confront magic? I'm not a sorcerer," Ambescand protested.

"When the need comes, the power will come. Believe that," said Cathwar, and before Ambescand could respond, he was gone.

In the first days of Earlygreen, while the spring rains were still falling and snow lay in the shaded places, Ambescand set out to inspect the garrison at Northmark and revisit the Crystal Hills. He was boisterously welcomed at the end of the long bridge, and when the triumphal procession at last entered Generosity—now much enlarged, and looking very prosperous—he was offered the hospitality of the current chief assayer. This turned out to be a big, soft-spoken man named Colberane, totally bald, with a dark red beard that reached to his waist.

He sat down to dinner in Colberane's hall with the chief assayer and his wife and a score of the leading residents of Generosity. But he was scarcely aware of their presence, because Colberane had a daughter. Her name was Ciantha, and she sat four places away from her father's guest. Ambescand noticed her as soon as she entered. She was tall and slender, with a graceful carriage. Her hair was bright red, and her eyes were as green as his own. When their eyes met, and held, he had a blaze of revelation: this was the woman he must marry, and no sorcery would be needed to make him love her.

Ambescand prolonged his stay in the Crystal Hills as long as he could, and when he returned to the High City, his first act was to issue a public announcement of his forthcoming marriage. The people of the city heaved a great collective sigh of relief and set about celebrating. When Ciantha arrived, the celebration resumed, and it continued through the bright day in Greenblade when the king and his new queen pledged their mutual fidelity, and for several days afterward.

In the month of Yellowleaf in the following autumn, Ciantha gave birth to twins, a girl and a boy. Following the tradition of the Crystal Hills, the girl was named Ketial, the boy Colberane. They were perfect miniatures of their parents.

Their second son, whom his father named Ordred, was born little more than a year later, early in Firstfrost. With his bright red hair, he favored his mother and sister. The next two children were a second set of twins, both girls, dark-eyed and dark-haired as was Ciantha's mother. The honor of naming them went to Ciantha's parents, who named the elder Ingionel and the younger Ingellett. Two years later, on a cold day in the month of Whitefall, was born their sixth child, a son, for whom Banheen choose the name Staver.

Ambescand learned to take what joy he was given without dwelling on possible ills to come. He never forgot Meragrand or his slain children, but he slowly overcame his crushing sorrow at their loss. He remembered the words of Cathwar —*what is past is past*—and accepted his obligation to the future. He often found himself happier than he had ever expected to be again.

The evil power Cathwar had warned of did not manifest itself in the northern kingdom in any way that Ambescand could percieve. Year succeeded year, and always the crops were abundant, trade was good, no plagues or sicknesses struck, and there was peace throughout the kingdom and in all the neighboring lands. Banheen came to the High City to stay when his beloved Ketial died. Feron had become a dedicated uncle and brother. The people of the north adored Ambescand and all those close to him. It seemed that the future would be bright, and his reign the beginning of a golden age.

Late one night, Ambescand awoke from a dream in which something was reaching out, clutching at him with inhuman fingers, groping vainly and desperately for him in the darkness. It was a frightening dream, and he rose up chilled with perspiration, his heart racing, his breath rapid. But Ciantha slept on, quite undisturbed, and when he looked in at his children, they were all sleeping peacefully and soundly. It was a dream, and nothing more. He returned to Ciantha's side feeling foolish, like a child afraid of shadows, and he smiled ruefully to himself at the thought of the people's reaction should they learn that their king, Ambescand Graymantle, Blade of the North and Hammer of Justice, had been frightened by a dream.

Unnumbered levels below the streets of the High City, below the waterways and the deepest dungeons, lay a vaulted chamber. No foot had walked in its dust since the days of the early kings, when it had been sealed and its existence stricken from all records and deleted from all maps of the city.

In that chamber, on a starless night when rain swept the streets and the waterways overhead roared, eleven figures assembled around a glowing sphere. One by one, they extinguished their lanterns, their motions provoking the shadows to swoop and swing violently and then to blend into a single entity as they stood unmoving to hear the incantation of Darra Jhan.

Cei Shalpan was the first to speak. Looking into the light of the sphere, his arms folded, his cloak thrown back, the Stormlord said, "Despite all our seeking, we have learned nothing. We have questioned every traveler, sifted every bit of information, traced every story to its source, and we know no more than we did on the day we first set foot in the High City."

"I alone have spoken with more than a hundred travelers, and I have gained not one bit of useful information," said Ulowadjaa in his high, complaining voice. Aoea and Korang spoke after him, and their accounts were similar to his.

"Have my brothers and sisters forgotten the early days of our undertaking?" Rombonole asked. "We formed this fellowship because the quest was beyond the power of any individual among us. It took more than a mortal lifetime merely to ascertain that the talisman lies hidden in the north, and we knew, from the very outset, that to possess it might well cost us ten lifetimes—perhaps hundreds. And now I hear my companions speak despairingly when fewer than a score of summers have passed with no apparent progress."

"I do not despair," said Cei Shalpan coldly.

"Then I have misinterpreted your words, brother. To me, they sound like the words of one who expects to fail."

"I expect to succeed, and I will succeed. But I say that

success will be long delayed, and more of our strength will be consumed, if impediments are placed in our way. And I believe that this has been done."

"Who could oppose us? Who even knows of our existence?" Skelbanda asked. When the Stormlord responded not with words, but with a sweeping gesture that encompassed them all, she cried, "Betrayal? No one would dare!" Other voices were raised in angry denial and denunciation. Cei Shalpan stood impassive amid the outcry, and only when all were still did he say, "I accuse no one present."

"Who, then?" Rombonole demanded.

"Ammaranza. Is it not obvious?"

"It's obvious only that she's dead, brother."

"Think of how she died. She was smothered in her sleep, and she died without offering resistance. That could happen to none of us unless all our power had been spent."

"Ammaranza had given much of her power to our cause. She was greatly weakened," Aoea pointed out.

"Do you all believe that she was still weak from exertions so long past?" Cei Shalpan said scornfully. "It is true that she spent much magic to entice Pytrigon, and to bear his child. But she recouped. No, she was working other magic, and it was not on behalf of the fellowship. She spent all her force, and left herself helpless, but her magic is still working."

"Ammaranza walks the dark ways of Shagghya, and no sorcery is strong enough to call her forth," said Hane.

"Ambescand lives."

"Ambescand? A woodcutter turned king? What have we to fear from Ambescand?" Hane demanded, sneering at the very suggestion.

Without taking his eyes from the glowing sphere, Cei Shalpan said, "Perhaps nothing. Perhaps everything."

"She favored him over her own son. That was clear from the time she took him into her service," said Jashoone thoughtfully.

"She knew his true identity, I'm sure," Darra Jhan added. "She learned it somehow, and she kept it from us. Why would she have done such a thing, except for some private gain?"

Taerhael said softly, "I have seen Ambescand. I once stood within three marks' distance from him, and I sensed no magic in him. His will and vitality are strong, but he has no magic."

"Yet he fought brigands for ten summers and took no injuries. And it was said by his followers that he could foretell danger, and he was always right," said Darra Jhan.

"It's a warrior's business to sense danger. He knew his profession as we know ours. There's no magic in that," Rombonole said.

"What soldier goes through years of battle without an injury?"

Rombonole shrugged the question off carelessly. "Ammaranza told us she was protecting him. As I recall," he said, glancing at Cei Shalpan, "she was encouraged to do so by one of our honored brothers."

"He was useful, and one does not waste a useful tool. But I fear that Ammaranza made too great use of him. Consider," Cei Shalpan said, glancing about the ring of softly lighted faces. "What single man, even though a mere contemptible mortal, could do more to impede our quest than this Ambescand? And if he were cloaked in protective magic, think how much more troublesome he might prove."

"But why would Ammaranza invest a mortal with all her magic? She left herself helpless," Aoea said.

"She was by far the oldest among us. Simply keeping herself alive took much of her power. She may have thought it worth the risk to take what magic remained to her and enfold Ambescand in its protection and its influence. If he should hinder us and find the talisman of the Iron Mage, he would have the power to recall her from Shagghya a thousand times over," said the Stormlord.

"How could he hope to succeed alone?" Hane asked.

"Perhaps he is not alone. I denied that possibility once. Now I am less certain."

In the troubled stillness that followed Cei Shalpan's words, the mild voice of Rombonole was soothing as balm. "I'm not an obstinate man, brother. You've convinced me that there's a reason for concern. How shall we deal with our woodcutter king?"

For the first time, Bellenzor's dry, croaking voice was raised. "Lend me your assistance, all of you, and I will strike him down before the sun rises. If he has allies, we will destroy them as well. Nothing can withstand our conjoined magic."

"A sensible suggestion. I'm willing to join with my brothers and sisters to rid ourselves of this upstart at once," said Rombonole.

"I, too," said Hane. "He may merely be an impediment,

or he may be a rival in our quest. In either case, he is intolerable alive."

"He is a danger. We must be rid of him," Jashoone added.

Before any others could speak, Cei Shalpan raised his hands for silence and said, "Let us not act in haste. I do not doubt that our united power could overwhelm any opposing magic, but why use our power needlessly? Surely we can devise a means to remove this creature in a way that will exhaust all his protective magic and yet require little effort from us."

"Why delay?" Bellenzor rasped.

"Why hurry? Far better to spend time than magic. Let us always remember that there may be demands on our power as the quest proceeds."

The Stormlord's words seemed to sway the company. Rombonole and Jashoone retracted their assent. Bellenzor and Hane, though they did not deny their words, offered no objections to the plan that evolved from the ensuing discussion.

In the end, the task was entrusted to Darra Jhan, Korang, and Taerhael, who accepted it willingly. It called for only a small exercise of each one's special skill. When the others left the chamber, these three remained behind to begin their work.

The messenger's lean, leathery frame sagged with fatigue. His hair and skin and clothing were coated with the dust of his travel, and his voice was harsh and dry. When he had repeated his message a third time, Ambescand called for water, and he bade the man drink and refresh himself while he studied the map.

After a time, he summoned the messenger to the chart table and said, "What was the source of this information?"

"Fugitives from the lands of Daun Sheem, my king. One of them had been a trusted friend of Daun Sheem for many years, but he was set aside by the new men from the east. He resented this treatment, and when he protested, Daun Sheem drove him from his home."

"His name?"

"Lajka, my king."

"Describe him."

The messenger closed his eyes and frowned in concentration. "He was taller than I . . . by perhaps a handbreadth. He had a muffled way of speaking. His face was thin, and he had a black moustache, very long and very thick. The tip of the small finger on his left hand was missing."

Ambescand nodded. "And the others?"

"His son and daughter, my king. They spoke little, and they kept their faces concealed."

"Such is their way. You've done well to remember so clearly. Go, rest or eat or drink, as you please. You'll be in the chamber next to this, in case we need further information," said Ambescand, dismissing the man.

He bent over the map, but he scarcely saw the markings before his eyes. His mind was on the danger gathering around his eastern and southern borders.

This was the third messenger in forty days to arrive with similar news: Daun Sheem had returned from the east at the head of a mighty army. After his first victories, warriors from those far lands had flocked to his standard. The army had rolled like a wave over towns and cities, unresisted after its initial crushing victories, and it had brought all the lands and riches and uncounted peoples of the east under the sway of Daun Sheem. And now, if these reports were to be believed, Daun Sheem was not content with ruling half the known world. His eyes were on the Kingdom of the Northern Lands.

The people of the kingdom were ready to do battle. They had no doubt that with Graymantle to lead them, they would sweep through the Drylanders and their eastern auxiliaries as easily as Duarin's Hammer had smashed the brigands who once menaced the land. And Ambescand believed that the pikemen, archers, and ax-wielding woodsmen who even now were making their way to the High City could stand against any army, if only they were properly led.

That was his problem. For the first time in his life, he felt self-doubt. He had led men into combat many times, and he had always been victorious. But his forces had been small, close-knit groups, and they had fought in friendly territory, as welcome champions, with no need to worry about supply lines, or unfriendly locals ready to attack them or butcher their wounded. It would not be that way on the barren uplands of the south, and he had no idea how it might be if they drove to the east; those lands were unknown. He had studied war, and he had read of the great battles fought in the past, and he had often been struck by how very different the true experience of battle is from the account written on a sheet of vellum in a time of peaceful recollection. In his youth, he had been full of confidence. Now, age and experience had shown him that no man controls his destiny, and even the most powerful king, the greatest warrior, the wisest sage, is small and weak before the onrush of events. He knew that nothing was less certain than the plans of men.

Yet he had to act, and he knew that he would march at the head of his army when the time for battle came. And herein lay a dilemma. As yet there had been not one act of overt aggression. Daun Sheem's mighty army had been seen by only a handful of observers, all of them Dryland fugitives. His own spies had been able to learn nothing. The true size of the army, its makeup and weaponry, its tactics and fighting skills all remained as much a mystery as its leader's intentions.

This was the time when the northland was most vulnerable to an attack from the south. Men and women were busy harvesting, working hard all day, falling exhausted on their pallets at night, unready to resist an invasion. The roads were dry and firm. The Drylanders' army could strike deep into the kingdom before encountering resistance.

Ambescand did not want to wait passively for an army to invade his kingdom. Yet he was reluctant to provoke a war by striking first at men who had done him no injury, set no foot in his kingdom, uttered no threat.

He spoke with his advisers, with the commanders of the guard, with the wise men and women of the High City. Some urged him to attack before the Drylanders could mount a campaign. Others counseled patience, so the kingdom could prepare for a long war while natural rivalries divided and weakened the enemy. Some despaired and urged conciliation toward an enemy so powerful, and others dismissed the threat as a phantom menace spun from the wild tales of barbarians. The people looked to the guard for protection. The guard looked to Ambescand for leadership. He pondered, studied maps, and relived his stay with Daun Sheem, and he could not decide.

In the end, action was forced upon him. Cutters' Ford, a border village on the River Irachmé, was raided and devastated. Every house was smashed down and burnt, every inhabitant, from the oldest to the newborn, was brutally slain, all the livestock slaughtered, all foodstuffs scattered or fouled. There seemed to be no motive for the assault beyond the blind will to destroy. It was all the more inhuman because the village was one in which northerners and Drylanders freely mingled. Indeed, half the residents were Drylanders, who had lived there at peace even during the earlier wars.

His irresolution thrust aside by events, Ambescand moved with eager speed. On the second day following the arrival of the news, he stood under the west gate, cloaked in gray, sword at his side. Behind him, ready to march, was a picked force of three hundred men.

His kingdom and his family he placed under the protection of Feron, as regent, and he charged his brother with readying the remainder of the High City's forces and sending them off in sixty days to an appointed rendezvous. Then, after saying farewells to Ciantha and his children, and to Banheen, he embraced his brother and resumed his place at the head of his men. He himself gave the command to march, and they set forth along the coast road, the sun on their left hand, to avenge their countrymen and preserve the kingdom.

CHAPTER THIRTEEN

THE MAN WHO TURNED

Day succeeded day, and no message from Ambescand reached the High City. Feron grew uneasy. He rather enjoyed the title of regent, but what he liked most about it was its temporary nature. Should anything befall Ambescand, he might find himself a very busy man, regent for a child king. The thought of such responsibility unnerved him, however remote the likelihood.

His friends, sensing his mood, did much to encourage him. They were good friends and lively companions. Ambescand disliked them—he was a very serious-minded man—and Ciantha openly spurned them, but Feron found them bright, clever young fellows. They came from the finest families in the city, nobles with old and honored names and a long history of involvement in the affairs of the city. Their advice seemed sound to him, and their company was pleasant. Now that he was regent, they were often with him.

One evening, after an interminable council session that had resulted in no action at all, Feron sat late in his chambers with two of his good companions, Quernister and Macchal. They were drinking wine from the palace cellars. It was good wine, and his friends were cheerful and merry, but Feron sat gloomily silent.

"Cheer up, Feron," Macchal urged. "It's a fine night, and this is the best wine in the city. Don't look so gloomy."

"I can't help it. I just wish it were over."

"What?" Macchal asked, puzzled.

"This. All of it. I don't like being regent. I wish Ambescand would come back."

"But you're doing a fine job," said Quernister.

"No, I'm not. No one thinks so."

"Many of the nobles think so, Feron."

"Do they? Have you heard anyone say so, Macchal?"

"Yes. Haven't you? Don't you know how pleased everyone is with the way you govern the city?"

"No . . ." said Feron, his voice low and full of doubt. "Are people really pleased?"

"Very much," Macchal assured him.

"The council doesn't think so. Every time I suggest something, they tell me it can't be done. Or else they say it won't work, or Ambescand wouldn't approve of it if he were here."

"They're a pack of old men," said Quernister contemptuously.

"Yes—but they're the council."

"And you're the regent," said Macchal.

"Only the regent. Ambescand is still king, and no matter how far away he goes, they act as if he's still right here. They won't listen to me."

"If anything happens to Ambescand, they'll have no choice but to listen to you," said Quernister.

Macchal added, "And obey."

Feron took a drink of wine and shook his head. "Even then . . ."

"They'll have to, Feron," Quernister said.

"But what if they don't?"

"Throw them in the dungeon!"

Macchal stood up boldly and unsteadily and cried, "Cut off their heads and appoint your own council! Appoint me keeper of the cellarage, and I'll do anything you say."

"And make me your treasurer, Feron!" Quernister said, laughing.

"I will, I will! And I'll make Cotterall . . . I'll make him commander of the guard!" Feron cried. Cotterall was another of their circle, a slightly overweight, extremely fastidious young man who was an abject physical coward. At the nomination, all three howled with laughter.

"What of Imberwick? We must find something for Imberwick in your new council," Macchal insisted.

"I'll make Imberwick my regent," Feron declared with mock solemnity. "Then I'll go off and do as I please, and he can do all the work and all the worrying."

That sent the three of them into another round of laughter,

and for the rest of the evening they amused themselves by assigning various friends and acquaintances—and a few enemies—to posts on the council. When he went at last to bed, his head light and his sides aching, Feron was still grinning at the notion of naming his own council.

It was all a great joke, of course. He could not imagine Ambescand's defeat, much less his death, and he was almost certain that he would never be king. And if by some chance he should be placed on the throne, he could never appoint his friends to positions of power. Someone would be sure to stop him, to point out to everyone that he was not really a king's brother, but only an innkeeper's son from Long Wood, with no right to the throne at all.

But as he drifted off to sleep, he thought that if he were once a king, no one would dare to stop him. He could do whatever he pleased despite the advice of all the old men in the kingdom. Old men did not know everything. Even the council seldom agreed on anything, and they were considered to be the wisest men in the north. There were people in the kingdom who believed he would be a good king. Quernister and Macchal had heard them say so.

He dreamed that night that he was king of the Northern Lands, and that all obeyed him. Ambescand came and tried to thrust him from the throne, but a stranger, a hard-faced man, came and told Ambescand that he was dead, and his power was gone, and even as the man spoke, Ambescand went away, and Feron knew that he would never return. His friends were all around him, praising him and protecting him and shouting, "Good King Feron!"

But when he awoke, he was still the regent. People were waiting to ask him questions and then dispute his answers; to urge action and then force him to delay; to advise delay and then force him to act; to thwart him in every way. He wished that he could be king, even briefly, to pay them all back as they deserved.

A new month began, and still there was no word from Ambescand. Feron grew ever more impatient with the uncertainty. He had not imagined that the regency would be like this. He wanted to be king or nothing. He could not endure this impotent middle state, where all the responsibility was his, but all the power seemed still to reside in the absent Ambescand.

When the man with the withered hand came to the palace, Feron became cautious. The man spoke of important news from the south, and for that, Feron longed to receive him. But he then presumed to lay down conditions. He would not give his name; he insisted on a private audience; he would deliver his message to no one but the regent.

Something about the man made Feron uneasy. His voice was dry, as if the life had been drained from it. The cold, appraising eyes in his gaunt face seemed to penetrate and judge mercilessly everyone he looked upon. His withered hand was as brown and shrunken as a pulled-up root, but he seemed to use it as easily as any healthy hand. When Feron rejected his conditions, he turned and walked from the chamber, and no guard moved to bar his passing.

Two days later, the man returned, and his message was the same. This time, Feron surrendered to his curiosity and received him alone.

"You are not of the blood of Pytrigon and Tallisan," said the man with the withered hand as soon as the doors were shut.

"No, I'm not. Who are you, and what's your news?"

As if Feron had not spoken, the visitor went on, "Do you believe in the knowledge that surpasses all knowledge? In the wisdom beyond all wisdom, and the truth beyond truth?"

"What do you mean?" Feron asked. When the man looked at him with those cold, unnerving eyes and said nothing, he asked, in a lower voice, "Do you speak of sorcery?"

"I speak of knowledge drawn from sources closed to most men. Some of those who once ruled in the High City feared such knowledge and dealt harshly with those who sought it. You seem wiser than they. You seem to be a man unafraid to seek where others turn back."

"I am," Feron said boldly, though the fluttering in his heart made his voice tight and small. "I have no fear of such knowledge."

"Then I may bring you news of the king."

"Is he well? Has he fought?"

The man with the withered hand said, "He has fought, and he lives. But his forces were shattered."

"Ambescand has never been defeated!"

"He is a mighty warrior, but he is a poor leader. He took his men into an ambush, and fewer than a score of them escaped. Even now, he is fleeing to the Red Mountains for his life."

Feron was stunned into silence. This news was impossible, and he had no idea how to react to it. If it were true, he might soon be king. But it could not be true.

"You say this, but what proof do you bring?"

The man's eyes narrowed. "Do you doubt me?"

"I ask for proof."

"If you require proof, you need only be patient. In time, your king's remains may be returned. Perhaps his life will be spared, for a ransom. You will have your proof before long."

"But how do you know this?"

The man studied him for a moment, as if appraising him. Then he said, "I am Darra Jhan. I, and certain colleagues of mine, have ways of learning and seeing that others do not possess. By these ways, we have seen the fate of Ambescand, and we felt it wise to inform you."

"Show me," Feron demanded.

"I cannot do so alone, nor can I do it here."

"Where, then?" When the sorcerer hesitated, Feron went on, "I must see for myself. I must know beyond a doubt, Darra Jhan!"

"You ask for magic, and magic is worked slowly and with great difficulty. Even the king of the Northern Lands cannot command magic—"

"You claim to command magic. Do you say that you're more powerful than the king of the Northern Lands?"

Darra Jhan raised his clawlike hand in a defensive gesture. "I do not command magic. No man does, nor any woman. It is beyond all human control. But some of us, with great effort, can penetrate a little way into the darkness and glimpse fragments of the mystery. Out of concern for the kingdom, we sought to learn the fate of Ambescand. When we saw him defeated and in flight, his state hopeless, we knew we must bring the news to the regent, even at the risk of our lives."

Feron nodded weightily. "You did rightly, and you need not fear. I am no enemy of magic."

"Then perhaps . . . if you place your trust in us . . ."

"I trust you, but I must see proof."

"Are you willing to come alone to a place where our magic can be done? There is a chance that we may be able to show you things we have seen. I can promise nothing—"

"I will come," Feron broke in.

"We must prepare ourselves," said Darra Jhan. "Two nights from this night, when last watch ends, I will await you at the fountain. Come alone. You will be safe, I swear it."

"I will be there," Feron said.

Darra Jhan left, and Feron received no one else that day, nor on the two days that followed. He spent the time alone, struggling with himself to reach a decision.

If Ambescand were dead, then he was king. There could no longer be any question about it. It was his duty to ascend the throne. Colberane, the oldest son of Ambescand, was too young to rule. It would be farcical to crown him king while Feron and the council were the real rulers. That action would only lead ambitious men into courses that would endanger the kingdom. For Colberane's own sake, and the realm's, the boy could not succeed his father.

That was all very clear, but it was not the only possibility. What if Ambescand were alive and badly wounded, or in hiding, or a prisoner? The kingdom would need a leader more than ever, and a regent subject to the former king's council would not serve. Only a new king, with a council loyal to him, could save the kingdom, for only he could act as he saw fit, without delay.

It was time for a new king, Feron reflected, time for one who knew the value of peace and respected the benefits it brought. Ambescand was a warrior. His solution to every crisis was to take up the sword. Such a man had a role in the kingdom, but perhaps his role should not be that of king. A king should be one who listens to all sides but follows his own judgment; one who keeps the peace, encourages prosperity, and does not seek to do battle at every pretext.

If he were king, Feron thought, and a group of rebel nomads destroyed a cluster of filthy hovels somewhere on the fringes of the Southern Forest, he would not risk the lives of guardsmen in seeking revenge. The burning of some insignificant settlement presented no danger to the High City, or

the Fastness, or the Crystal Hills. The expedition was a foolish gesture, the typical reaction of a swordsman and slayer
of brigands. No true king would have acted so.

By the time the appointed night came, Feron was convinced of the necessity for decisive action. Should this sorcerer present proof of his story, make it possible for Feron
to see with his own eyes some testament to Ambescand's
rout and flight, there would be no hesitation. Feron would
proclaim himself king of the Northern Lands. With the help
of his loyal friends, he would overcome any opposition. As
for Ciantha and her children . . . he would treat them fairly,
but firmly. They would not interfere with his destiny.

Darra Jhan, cloaked and hooded against the midnight chill,
was waiting at the fountain when Feron arrived. With only a
word to identify himself, he led the regent off to the workers'
quarters in the northern end of the city; across the green,
through the parklike wood, and into the labyrinth of narrow
streets and alleys, poorly lit, smelling of sweat and food and
refuse. It was a part of the High City that Feron avoided,
and under ordinary circumstances, in the company of another, he would have been apprehensive making his way
through these shadowed passages; but he was completely in
the grip of his desire to know Ambescand's fate, and he was
scarcely aware of anything but the hooded figure walking two
paces before him.

They entered a dark court, and Darra Jhan stopped before
a narrow door that opened at his touch. He entered, and
Feron, with just an instant's hesitation, stepped in behind him.

A cresset hung from the ceiling, burning with a low flame.
Darra Jhan lit two torches from it, handed one to Feron, and
led on, through corridors and empty rooms that wound and
twisted in dizzying complexity until Feron was bewildered,
amazed, and fearful. How could all these involuted ways be
contained within one of the houses he had seen? It was as if
he had entered a tiny cell and found himself on the high
road to the north. Swallowing his fear, he walked on, close
at Darra Jhan's silent heels.

Down flight after long flight of well-worn stone steps they
went, until Feron believed he could hear the beat of the
legendary Earth's-heart and feel the hot breath exhaled by

the indwelling demon at the world's core. And still they
descended. The air grew dank. The way underfoot was pooled
with stagnant water. Waterways roared above them, and their
torchlight glittered off the niter that arched overhead and
crawled in lacy webs down the walls.

They came at last to a door that stood open, and they entered a spacious chamber. A glowing sphere in the center
cast its light downward and around, leaving the upper reaches
of the chamber in darkness. Men and women were assembled
around the light, and when Feron entered, they turned and
bowed in respectful greeting. A tall, broad-shouldered man
with a face expressionless as a stone mask stepped forward
and said, "Hail Feron, king of the Northern Lands! Cei
Shalpan greets you on behalf of your loyal servants."

"I am not king, but regent."

"Ambescand has fallen. For the good of all, you must assume the throne."

Feron took an unsteady step backward, and the torch fell
from his hand. "Dead?" he whispered. "Is Ambescand dead?"

"We have seen his fall."

Feron covered his face for a moment, struggling to compose himself. At length he looked at Cei Shalpan and said,
"I must have proof."

"What power we have, we place at your disposal," said
Cei Shalpan, gesturing to a gap in the circle of figures around
the glowing sphere. Feron took his place, and Cei Shalpan
and Darra Jhan completed the ring. One by one, the others
identified themselves. Feron's mind was racing, and he could
not link names with faces: Aoea, Skelbanda, Rombonole . . .
a twisted, misshapen little man with a huge head; a leprous,
corpselike, red-eyed man; a beautiful woman with hair bright
as flame and eyes pale as ice; other men and women, some
grotesque, some ordinary; they all hailed him as king, proclaimed their loyalty, and placed their power at his service.

"I must have certain knowledge before I proclaim myself
king. I must see the death of Ambescand with my own eyes,"
Feron said when they were done.

"We will do all within our power to satisfy our lord
Feron," said a pale, dark-haired woman at his left hand.
"You must look into the light. Keep your eyes fixed on it.
Do not look away."

Feron nodded and turned his gaze full on the sphere of brightness that hung in the air, just head-high, unsupported by any means that he could see but nevertheless firm and unwavering. The pale woman's hand closed on his left hand, and the moist, soft fingers of an obese giant enfolded his right. Low murmuring filled the room, like a chant heard from far away, and Feron stared fixedly at the pale light.

It grew and filled the space before him. The light became a mist, and the mist churned and swirled, and then of a sudden it thinned and cleared, and Feron saw a figure moving within it, blurred and vague at first, but gradually clearer until he recognized Ambescand. But it was an Ambescand much changed from the proud warrior-king who had marched southward at the head of an elite army.

His right arm was blood-caked from shoulder to fingertips. It hung limp at his side. His face was bruised and haggard, and fear was in his eyes. In his left hand he clutched a hacked and battered sword, not his own. His gray robe—what was left of it—hung about him in dirty tatters as he stood at bay.

The surroundings grew more distinct. Ambescand was in a stony pocket, with no way of retreat. He wiped his brow, put his back to a flat rock wall, and set himself for the last onrush of his enemy. As the first robed figure burst into view, he raised his sword. A second appeared, then two more, and then a mass of nomads erupted into Feron's view, obscuring the figure of the beleaguered king. They closed on Ambescand, and their swords rose and fell in a wild fury. Then the weapons were still, and the nomads backed away from a fallen figure running blood from a score of mortal wounds, and the mist moved in, enshrouding the scene in formless light.

Feron stared blankly into the bright sphere. The chamber was silent, and no one moved. His hands were released, and he looked around to see the others all standing with bowed heads, their breasts heaving with deep breaths.

"Have you seen?" Darra Jhan asked.

"Ambescand is dead."

"And you must be king of the Northern Lands," said Cei Shalpan.

"Yes," said Feron abstractedly. "But if he should return ... if he somehow survived..."

"You saw him fall. Do you doubt your own eyes? Do you doubt the power of magic?" Cei Shalpan asked.

"No, I do not," Feron said with sudden firmness. "Ambescand is dead, and I am king. He must have wished it so —he did make me his regent."

Darra Jhan, coming to his side, said, "Of course he wished it. Who else could rule so well? Who else merits the throne?"

"I must tell Ciantha."

"Be wary, my king. Ciantha may protest your accession, and she has friends. It would be wise to inform her only after the fact," said the pale woman at his left hand.

Darra Jhan added, "Good advice, my king. Ciantha will think of her son Colberane, and not of the kingdom. She must be checked."

"Yes, you're right. I must . . . I'll send them away."

"That might prove dangerous. Better for you to keep them where they can be seen but be sure they communicate with no one," Cei Shalpan said.

Nodding eagerly, Feron said, "I'll keep them in the palace, but under guard. My friends and their men can watch them. I will do so." Looking around the circle, he said, "I thank you for this knowledge and your good counsel. I will not forget you."

"My king, we serve you willingly. Our advice is at your command."

"I may seek it again."

"We will come at your summons," Cei Shalpan said, bowing.

"You will be rewarded."

"To serve our king and the kingdom is reward enough. All we ask is to be allowed to continue our work free from persecution."

"No man will harm you while I rule," said Feron. He started from the room, but at the doorway he halted and said, "It might be well for some of you to come to the palace tomorrow, when I announce the death of Ambescand and my decision to assume the throne."

"We will attend, my king," Cei Shalpan said.

Walking behind Darra Jhan's torch, Feron was scarcely aware of the return to the palace. Darra Jhan went with him to the side gate from which he had slipped some hours before, and he made his way to his chambers unseen. He lay awake, exhausted but unable to relax, until the sky was bright, and then he fell into a fitful doze from which he started awake a score of times before sleep at last overcame him.

At midday, he summoned his council to him. When they entered his chamber, they found two strangers with the regent. One was an innocent-looking, open-faced man of indeterminate age whose features, and whose very presence, seemed to slip from their minds even as they beheld him; the other was a pale, raven-haired woman whose dark and penetrating gaze made them grow cold in their hearts and forced them to turn their own eyes aside. Without preamble, Feron announced that Ambescand had been slain and that he was assuming the throne and placing Ambescand's family under his personal protection.

After a moment of numb silence, the council cried out in protest at his actions. But one by one their voices and their wits and their courage failed them, and they subsided into sheepish silence. In shame and fear, each glanced at his companions, seeking in the others the strength that had deserted him, and finding instead the reflection of his own abasement. When Feron gave the command, they fell to their knees to hail him as their king.

The old council was dissolved that very day, and a new one was soon formed of young nobles close to Feron and in harmony with his ambitions. The hexagon tower, a forbidding pile of stone long unused, was refurbished and put at the disposal of a fellowship of men and women with strange and frightening powers, said to be supporters of the new king. Those who displeased them suffered mysterious afflictions, and the word quickly spread that Feron's sudden rise was the work of sorcery, and the fellowship was responsible.

Some greeted the new regime with enthusiasm; Ambescand had always frightened these, and they looked forward to the reign of a king who preferred pleasure and splendor to constant fighting. Most of the people saw little to praise in Feron and his friends and supporters, but they realized that they could do nothing to change the situation. Resistance meant suffering, and so they did not resist. It was as easy to shout "Hail, King Feron" as "Hail, King Ambescand." In the long run, it did not matter much to them, as long as they were left alone.

There were a few who suspected treachery and vowed to resist it and avenge Ambescand and his family. But soon they were heard of no more, and Feron ruled unquestioned in the High City.

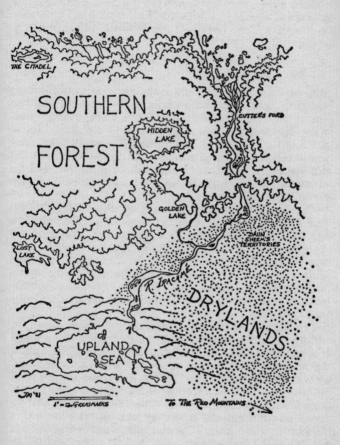

THE CITADEL

SOUTHERN

FOREST

HIDDEN LAKE

CUTTER'S FORD

GOLDEN LAKE

DAUN SHEEN'S TERRITORIES

LOST LAKE

R. IRACINE

DRYLANDS

JM '81

1" = 2 GREATMARKS

UPLAND SEA

TO THE RED MOUNTAINS

CHAPTER FOURTEEN

THE CALL

Ambescand marched directly south and then eastward along the coast road, toward the banks of the Irachmé. His plan was to cross the river above the Sea of Zuma, continue eastward deep into Daun Sheem's lands, and then turn back to strike at the domed city. A surprise raid, just at dawn, from the direction considered most secure, would kill many and demoralize the rest. Daun Sheem himself might fall, and the devastation of his chief settlement would be fitting retaliation for his attack on Cutters' Ford.

There was little chance of returning to the High City before the first snowfall made the ways impassable, but Ambescand intended to leave clear indications of a headlong flight to refuge in the north. Though pursuit might be slow to organize, the Drylanders and their allies would be certain to follow in force. And they would be met, in the woods north of Golden Lake, by the full might of the kingdom, dispatched by Feron to meet the returning raiders. One battle would decide all.

The plan was a bold and simple one: march and fight, and march and fight again, until the enemy was trapped and broken. It was the tactic he had used successfully against the brigands. Now he was employing it on a larger scale, with armies instead of squads. He had taken counsel with his wise men and his experienced warriors, veterans of the nomad wars. Beneath all their bitter disagreement he perceived one fundamental truth: no man knows what makes for victory in the clash of armies. Some said weaponry was the deciding factor; others said mobility, or audacity, or superiority of numbers and training, or discipline, or hatred of the enemy, or the hope of plunder, or fear of defeat, or some two or three of these in combination made for victory. They all said what they had found to be true, in one instance or more, but none had seen the truth whole.

It became clear to Ambescand that he was as much an expert as any of them, and all his experience told him that even the greatest battle was only one armed man against another, multiplied a hundredfold, or a thousandfold, or ten thousandfold. Good men, led by someone they trusted and respected, could accomplish as much as any army that ever drew blades in battle. From this conviction, he had settled on his present plan. Now, as they came each day closer to their enemy's stronghold, he felt his confidence unshaken.

At the estuary of the Irachmé they took half a day's break. The men caught fish and cooked enough for that night and the next day, knowing that there would be no more fires now that they were in the borderlands. Ambescand circulated among his troops, stopping with each group to share a joke or story, take a morsel of bread or a piece of fish, inspect a blistered foot or a sore tendon. He was pleased to find his men holding up so well. More than halfway to their objective, they appeared as eager for battle as they had been when they stepped out of the High City.

Late in the day, they resumed their march, southward along the west bank of the Irachmé. The river narrowed for a time, but it was still too deep for an easy crossing. They camped that night two greatmarks above the first ford, which lay near the border village whose devastation had brought them on this mission.

Ambescand rose in the middle of the night to inspect the watch. When he had made his rounds and spoken with every guard, he felt wide awake and had no desire to return to his blanket. He walked to the trail and marked how clearly it was lit by the Gleaner's Moon, then at its full. It gave him an idea, and he returned to the nearest guard with a message.

"I'm going to visit Cutters' Ford. I'll be back by third watch," he said.

"Does my king wish an escort?"

"I'll be safe alone. The Drylanders left when they finished their murderous business."

"There might be scavengers."

"I doubt it, lad. There's nothing left for them to take."

The truth was that Ambescand felt a sudden desire to visit the ruins alone and see with his own eyes the outrage he was set to avenge. In the presence of others, he would have to react as their king and commander; alone, he could react for himself.

He did not think it foolhardy to make the visit. There was no reason to suspect the presence of Drylanders in the area or to fear his own people, even if they be scavengers. Still, he kept to the shadows, and he walked warily in places where an ambush might be expected.

The desolation of Cutters' Ford was complete. All around him, bathed in the tranquil gold of the Gleaner's Moon, stood jagged walls like the stumps of rotted teeth, splintered beams, and shards of stone. The reek of things burned and rain-soaked, and of foodstuffs slowly putrefying, lay heavily on the cool air, and though all bodies had been removed, the night had the scent of death.

Except for a few blackened roof beams leaning at precarious angles, nothing stood in Cutters' Ford above knee height. Walls and chimneys had been pulled down or battered down, and they lay in a fall of tumbled stone. The dull blackness of charred wood and smoke-darkened stone absorbed the moonlight. Ambescand stood in an eerie lake of brightness with a floor of abyssal black, highlighted by the pools and puddles of stagnant water that lay where once had stood homes, and shops, and taverns.

The sight sickened and enraged him. He walked aimlessly through the debris, setting his feet carefully on the shifting rubble and the char that crunched beneath his boot soles.

His hand went to his sword hilt at a soft clatter of stone close by his side. A tiny form scuttled over a broken wall and vanished into silence: a river rat, come to pick through this unexpected bounty. He paused, hand still resting on the sword hilt. They were the only creatures to benefit from the carnage of battle, he thought. They, and the wolves and ravens, the ants, and finally the worms. We fight for them, not ourselves. He shook his head as if to clear it of such grim thoughts and walked on.

At the edge of the ruins, he stopped and sighed, and for a time he stood unmoving in the moonlight, lost in deep thought. The prospect of a long and bloody war lay before him, as surely as these ruins lay at his feet, and he felt a great revulsion for it, and for all it would bring to his people and his kingdom. He was reluctant to do battle with an old friend, to raise his arm against men with whom he had once shared food and wine and laughter. Good men would fall on both sides, and when all the dying was done, the world would be little changed.

Yet at the same time he felt this deep disgust, something within him lusted for the clash, and he was aware of it as a man is aware of a shameful craving that lures him sweetly to destruction. Here was a challenge to him as a man, as a warrior, and as a king. He ached to confront that tough old campaigner Daun Sheem and his armies and to prove himself the better. Ambescand had been hailed for his victories, but he knew they were small. His father, and his father's father, had fought real wars against real armies. He had fought only brigands and robbers. This was his first true test, and his pride was roused in longing for it despite all reason and judgment and hope for peace in the north. He sighed once more, perceiving his own frailty, rejecting it, cherishing it.

"So, Graymantle, you've come to look at the ruins, too," said a familiar voice near at hand.

Ambescand drew his dark blade with a swift, hushed *whitt* of steel on steel and turned to face Daun Sheem, whose voice he had known at once. He saw no one. The ruins stood empty and silent.

"Come out, Daun Sheem!" he shouted.

"Put up your sword. Let's talk for a while," said Daun Sheem, stepping out from behind a fallen rafter three marks away. His hands were empty.

"What have we to talk about?"

"This," the nomad said, gesturing to encompass the desolation all around them.

"These ruins speak for themselves."

"To you, perhaps. But they don't tell me why a man like you does such a deed."

Ambescand was stunned into silence by the sheer effrontery of such a remark. Finally, with contempt in his voice, he said, "If you're trying to make a fool of me, I won't help you. Half the people in this village were subjects of mine. The rest were Drylanders, but no enemies."

"I know that. And I know you. And it makes me reluctant to believe that you would have them all killed, and the village destroyed. That makes no sense to me. Yet it happened."

"It's you who destroyed Cutters' Ford."

"No, it is not, Graymantle. Whoever tells you so is a liar. Not I, not my men, not anyone under my banner did this deed."

"What about the men from the east who follow you?"

Daun Sheem gave a little snort of disgust. "I sent the last one back to his mountain cave before the harvest."

"But there's no one else. If you didn't do it, and I didn't, there's no one else who could," Ambescand said.

"Why are you so sure I'm behind this? Who saw my men attack the village?"

"Those who saw it happen are all dead. But we knew your forces were massing on our borders. You had thousands of new troops from the east. It was only a matter of time before you marched on the northern kingdom, and the attack on Cutters' Ford—"

Daun Sheem's laughter silenced Ambescand. "This is crazy, old friend! It's all crazy! Who told you such lies?"

"We heard it from Lajka, for one."

"Lajka! Is he with you? Is he well?"

"He's safe enough. Why do you care?"

"You know he's my oldest friend. I owe Lajka my life."

"Then why did you drive him out? Why did you replace him with men from the east? He told all about it."

Daun Sheem flung up his hands and gave a strangled cry in his own tongue. The words were unknown to Ambescand, but their significance was clear enough. When he had calmed a bit, the nomad said, "Now, listen, old friend. I tell you the truth. Lajka disappeared from my settlement, along with his son and daughter. It was just before the last full moon. Like a puff of smoke—gone! We thought it was enchantment, it was so sudden and complete. Now you say he came to you and told you that I want to steal your kingdom. This is crazy!"

"But what about—"

"No, no, no," Daun Sheem said, waving off the question. "Something is wrong here. You heard lies about me, I heard lies about you. Messengers came, told me you were going to march south, claim everything as far as the Upland Sea, and then move east, against my lands. Kekuda read the stars and said that the messengers spoke the truth. And when the raid came, I believed them. But I know you, and you know me. We're friends. Why didn't we talk to each other?"

"I don't know. I don't believe it ever occurred to me."

"Not to me, either. I heard bad things about a friend, and I believed them."

The two men stood silent in the moonlight, reflective. Ambescand at last sheathed his sword, stepped forward, and held out his hand to Daun Sheem. "I did you wrong, and I'm sorry," he said.

Daun Sheem took his hand in a firm grip. "And so am I. But maybe we should be worried. Neither of us destroyed this village, but it's destroyed. We have an enemy we don't even know about."

"Could it be that some easterners formed a brigand band?"

Shaking his head, Daun Sheem sat on a smooth chunk of rubble and motioned Ambescand to a similar seat facing him. "All this talk about easterners . . . how many do you think I had?"

"We were told you had thousands."

"Never more than fifty at one time. Usually a lot less. Do you want some wine?"

"I brought some myself."

Both men drew out their wineskins and unstoppered them. Each offered his to the other at the same instant. They laughed, exchanged wineskins, and drank in silence.

"Just like the old days, before you were a king."

"Yes."

"Do you like it better being a king?"

Ambescand remembered old times, close friends, Meragrand and their children, all gone now, and a darkness filled his soul; and then he thought of Ciantha, and his new family, the good things he hoped to accomplish, and a bitter war now avoided. "It's different. Not better or worse, just different." He raised the wineskin, but before putting it to his lips he turned to Daun Sheem and asked, "What was the eastern campaign like? You were gone a long time."

"Dirt huts, smelly shepherds, stupid farmers trying to grow food in a waste of sand and stone. The little bit they grew was always in danger of being stolen. The robbers would leave them just enough to stay alive for another season."

"And the treasure?"

"Two good handfuls of gold, a small wagon half-filled with booty. I gave more than that away at the feast before we left."

"But the east is rich. You spoke of a king who lived in a golden palace. I've heard old veterans talk of precious stones too big to hold in both hands."

"What we hear is seldom what we find. People are always lying about treasure. I should have known better." Daun Sheem sighed. "It's a sign I'm getting old. Greed is the old man's failing." He fell silent, and after a time, he said, "Those easterners were never any help. They kept joining us and then sneaking off. They'd rather fight one another than strangers, but they couldn't keep up interest in a long campaign. Like children, they were. Strange ways of worship, too. Some of their gods . . ." He shook his head and shuddered.

"The gods are all gone from the north."

Neither man spoke for a time. Finally, Daun Sheem asked, "How does such a thing happen?"

"They failed us. Achalla, Ylveret . . . all of them. Even Wrothag failed us. We invoked them against the sea-raiders, and the sea-raiders kept defeating our best forces. Some in the north even took to worshiping the gods of the sea-raiders." Ambescand took a swallow of wine and passed his wineskin to Daun Sheem.

"I didn't know you had such good wine in the north," the nomad said appreciatively.

"There's a pinch of winewood ash in that. It sweetens the stomach and clears the brain. So people say."

"Delicious. But go on about your gods."

"It was at the third battle of the Cape of Mists. Our forces were led by Bormor. A distant relation of mine," Ambescand said, turning to his companion. "Uncle of the father of my father, and a very brave man. He was hard-pressed. Outnumbered and surrounded, wounded in a dozen places. As the sea-raiders were grouping for the final assault, Bormor climbed on a rock, gathered his men close around, and told them he was taking back all the prayers he had offered for victory, because our gods were frauds. He defied all the gods of the north—if such beings existed—to destroy him. And then he and his men charged into the sea-raiders and cut them to pieces. That was the turning point. After that, the sea-raiders never won another battle, and no one worshiped the old gods."

"Interesting. Still, it's good to have some kind of gods. Even those eastern monstrosities are better than no gods at all."

"A lot of people believe that the old gods will return some day."

Again they fell silent. Ambescand sensed that Daun Sheem felt the same overwhelming sensation of relief that he did: a battle between old friends had been avoided, and hundreds of lives had been spared, all by this chance encounter. There was an ominous side to their meeting, true, since it was now clear that someone had deliberately tried to set them at one another. But at this moment, Ambescand felt like laughing aloud. He could have sat on this chunk of broken stone, sipping mild, cold wine and talking of simple things, until words ran out. He was almost giddy with the feeling of deliverance from a terrible error, and he was full of euphoric confidence that whatever lay ahead, he could face it and conquer it.

As if he had read his friend's thoughts, Daun Sheem said, "It's good we met here, and not in battle. I knew you'd come south with an army before the snow fell, and once you had attacked, there'd be no avoiding a war."

"True enough. And it's lucky we happened to come here on the same night."

Daun Sheem laughed. "No luck in that, Graymantle. I've been camped here since I had word of the raid. I've learned a few things," he said, rising and starting off to his left. "Come."

They walked through the ruined streets, Daun Sheem purposefully leading the way. "Two things I must show you. I can make no sense of them. Over here," he said, guiding Ambescand to the hulk of a building. From the line of its broken wall, it appeared to have been one of the largest in the village. "This was the Inn of the Fordway. An old building, very solid. The walls didn't crumble, like the others. They fell in huge chunks. A lot of them were smashed to pieces afterward—I think I know why—but this chunk was missed."

He led Ambescand through clinging muck to where a solid slab of wall four hand-lengths in thickness and half a mark from end to end lay at an angle. One end was buried in the muck; the other rested on the ruin of the outer wall of which it had once formed a part.

"I don't see anything strange about this," Ambescand said, after inspecting the slab and its surroundings.

"The strangeness lies beneath it. You can just see it by daylight. Can you lift this?"

"Bad footing . . . but I'll try."

"You could call for some men to help you, but I think it's best if only you and I see this."

Ambescand set his feet as securely as he could in the deep,

slippery muck that had once been the hard dirt floor of a busy inn. Taking a firm grip, he straightened his back, hauling upward. The slab shifted slightly; then it gave, with a sucking sound. He held, gasping, and slowly raised it to the point where he could get his knee under it. Daun Sheem, at his side, joined in the last effort, a sharp push forward, to send the slab over the far side of the ruined wall until it pivoted of its own weight and came to rest.

In his astonishment at what lay revealed, Ambescand forgot the ache in his back and shoulders. Beneath the slab, pressed deep in the mud, were one full footprint and part of another. They had been made by feet as long as Ambescand's forearm, elbow to fingertips, and nearly half as broad. Judging from the length of the stride and the depth of the prints, they had been made by a giant.

"They're the only ones I found. I think the rest were all concealed under the rubble," Daun Sheem said.

"Purposely."

"I think so. That would explain why everything was smashed and scattered, and how. Creatures this size could hammer down walls with their bare fists."

"But why conceal their footprints? If you have a force that big and powerful, you can't hope to keep it secret for long. And you'd want your enemy to know of it, to demoralize them."

"That's right. And yet I've never heard a whisper of such a force. Have you?"

Ambescand shook his head slowly. "No."

"Did they come from nowhere? Are they the work of sorcerers? Are they demons?"

Ambescand crouched to examine the huge depressions closely. "Is it possible that these are not footprints? They could be the markings of some machine the raiders used to smash down the walls."

"They're footprints. Come. I said I had two things to show you."

Again the nomad led the way. He picked a route over the moonlit expanse of rubble, and he stopped at last by the base of a toppled chimney. Ambescand's gaze followed his pointing finger to a piece of rusted metal imbedded on its side in the mud.

Stood upright, it reached almost to Ambescand's elbow, half a mark high. It was a hand-span broad at its smaller

end, twice that at the larger, where it split to form one spiked
point and a hook, sharpened on the inner and outer edges.
The smaller end showed the markings of a break.

"I've never seen a weapon like this before. Have you?"
Daun Sheem asked.

"Never. You could gut a man the way you gut a fish, with
this hooked end."

"First you'd have to be able to lift it."

Ambescand nodded thoughtfully, studying the broken
blade. He estimated the weight of the fragment at about
four times that of his own sword, which was heavier than
the standard weapon of the guards. "To balance properly,
you'd need another quarter of a mark of blade, and a
handle a quarter of a mark long. That would make the
whole weapon a full mark high," he said. He raised his hand
in demonstration: the mark, basic unit of measurement in
the north, was the distance from the fingertips of a tall man's
upraised hand to the ground.

Daun Sheem measured with his eyes the distance between
ground and fingertips, and then he let out his breath in a
soft whistle. "If we go by our own standards, the creature
that wields such a blade must be twice the size of a man."

"And many times stronger."

They stood silent for a time, gazing in fascination at the
awesome weapon. Finally Ambescand let it fall, and it
smacked down with a flat, slapping sound. "It's almost certain that the attack was made by gigantic creatures carrying
weapons like this. Probably clubs, too, to smash down the
walls. But we don't know who leads them, or where they
come from."

"Or what they plan to do next," Daun Sheem added.

"No. You're a brave man, knowing of these creatures and
staying here all this time."

"It was my last chance to find you and show you the footprints and the broken blade. And now that I have, what
shall we do?"

"The first thing I must do is return to my guards and call
off the attack we had planned."

"A good thing. My outposts are all fully manned, and
support is less than a day's march away."

"We were to attack your home settlement, striking from
the east."

Daun Sheem's eyes widened for a moment; then he

laughed. "That might have caused me some trouble. I'm glad we met."

"So am I."

"Let's meet again before we're on the verge of fighting each other. We're getting old, you and I. I see the white in your beard, and I'm ten years older than you. Friends become more important."

"I'll send a messenger as soon as I'm back in the High City. Until we can find out more, I'd say the best course is to have patrols—yours and mine—sweep this whole region for traces of the giants. If we know where they are, they can't surprise us again."

"Do you have any idea how we can fight them?"

"None at all. We'll have to work on that."

They parted at the crossroads, Daun Sheem taking the Fordway. Ambescand heading north on the riverside road. He walked slowly, deep in thought. One problem had been replaced by another, and an element of mystery had been added. If the giant marauders were indeed products of some sorcery, it would take more than mortal strength and courage to defeat them; and he could think of no other origin for such creatures.

He knew that sorcerers were still to be found in the High City, despite the ancient enmity toward them. Duarin had been tolerant, but Duarin was the exception. Ambescand's father, and his uncle, had been unrelenting in their persecution of those suspected or accused of practicing the dark arts. It might be, he speculated, that the vengeance of those burned and broken and driven off by his forebears was now being called down on him. Adepts were said to live to a great age, and in the course of such a long life, they would learn patience. If one generation of a family escaped them, they might wait for another to come and take what revenge they could. Legends spoke of such things. This was a distinct possibility, and it fit the events well. Sorcerers would be expected to act in just such a mysterious and devious way as this, stirring up conflict between friends, confusing their judgment, summoning up giants to slay and destroy.

Yet his own experience with sorcery belied the common beliefs. He had been saved from death by Cathwar and protected in battle by Ammaranza. Cathwar had found him a fond guardian, and taught him swordsmanship, and come to his aid in the time of Duarin's madness. It was true that

Ammaranza might have used him in her own plans; but she had paid dearly for her ambition, and he had had years of happiness with Meragrand.

He turned all these things over in his mind as he walked, and he found that it was no simpler to reach clear conclusions on sorcery than on anything else, once one began thinking seriously about it. There was good and bad magic, and there were good and bad practitioners of both kinds. And the results were not always those the sorcerer had intended, so a wizard might set out to do evil and accomplish instead great good, or bring about evil in his attempt to do a good work. It was even possible—though it hardly seemed likely—that the destruction of Cutters' Ford and the appearance of these huge attackers might somehow bring about good. No man could know.

So involved was Ambescand in his ruminations that he was almost upon the dark figure standing in the middle of the road before he noticed it. He stopped abruptly, and his hand dropped to his sword hilt. Then he recognized the man who stood before him.

"Cathwar!" he cried. "You've come just when I need your help!"

"You need my help far more than you know. And I need yours. You must send your men north. Tell them to take the inland road, avoid Southmark, and assemble at Goldengrange. Ordred is prepared to receive them."

"But we must stop the army before—"

"There is no army. It's treason, Ambescand. You've been declared dead, and Feron rules as king."

Ambescand felt a sudden horror. "What of Ciantha, and our children? Are they safe?"

"Safe at present. Feron's followers have them under guard."

Ambescand covered his face with his hands and shook his head helplessly. "Feron . . . I can't believe . . ."

"It is not altogether his doing. A fellowship of sorcerers has been gathering in the High City. In all this, I see the work of Darra Jhan, Rouser of Envy; of Taerhael, the Beclouder, and Korang, the Warmaker. The others may have helped, but these three are certainly involved."

"Who are they, Cathwar?"

"I will tell you as we walk," said the wizard, turning and beckoning for Ambescand to follow. "But tell me first what happened in the ruins."

Ambescand gave a full account of all that had taken place since he had met Daun Sheem. Cathwar listened without comment, nodding from time to time. When Ambescand was done, the wizard said. "The nomad is a villainous fellow, but he is loyal to his friends. You can trust him."

"I do trust him."

"As for the rest, it's good that you saw some evidence of the power you must confront. I confess, the footprints and the blade perplex me. The destruction of your village sounds like the work of Rombonole, and yet he does not employ demons. I am puzzled. But now you will be all the more prepared."

"Prepared? To face those things?"

"I told you that when the moment came, the power would be given. It will be so. Do you recall what I told you before we entered the barrow, back on the Cape of Mists?"

You spoke of a wizard from ancient times . . . and a great war."

"When I told you those things, I believed that no one but I knew of the talisman of the Iron Mage. I was wrong. Others were already seeking it."

"How could that happen without your knowledge?"

Cathwar gave him a sidelong glance and laughed softly. "Even the mightiest of sorcerers is limited in his knowledge and his power—a fact for which the rest of you should be grateful. If it were otherwise, you'd all have been enslaved long ago. Enslaved, or worse." He walked on in silence for a short way. Then he said, "Somehow or other, I know not how, an enchanter named Cei Shalpan also learned of the truth underlying this ancient legend. He knew that it would be impossible to acquire it alone, and so he gathered a fellowship of sorcerers, each with a special sphere of magic. They swore to band together and unite their skills in a quest for the talisman, and to share its power equally when they attain it. Poor fools! The power of the Iron Mage would shrivel their evil souls to nothingness if they dared to touch it."

"Don't they realize that?"

"They're too hungry for domination and long life to reason clearly. I know how their minds work. Each one is certain that he or she can dupe the others into taking the risks, and seize the talisman when the time comes. Ammaranza was one of them, you know."

Ambescand stopped. "Ammaranza? But she . . . she was good to me, Cathwar."

"For her own purposes. Well, come along, come along. I know you feel kindly toward Ammaranza—you're inclined to excesses of gratitude, I think—but you must realize that she was part of an evil company. I know them well, and I know their magic. You've felt some of it already."

"What magic has been worked on me?"

"Korang stirred up eagerness for war in you and among your people and the nomads. Taerhael beclouded your mind so you could think only of headlong action and did not reason clearly about events, and Darra Jhan aroused envy in Feron for his own brother's happiness."

"Why do they turn their magic against me, Cathwar? What part can I play in all this?"

"I can only conjecture. They're certain that the talisman is somewhere in the northern lands. Now, it may be that they've decided that their search would be made easier if they set up their own king, one who was indebted to them —as Feron would be—for his throne. They're sensible enough to conserve their magic when they can. Or perhaps they fear that Ammaranza revealed the quest to you, and you seek the talisman for yourself."

"I'm no sorcerer, and I want nothing to do with them or the talisman or magic in any form," Ambescand said flatly.

"Unfortunate for you. The fellowship must be driven from the High City, and their power broken. You must face them and defeat them."

"I? Stand up to sorcerers?"

"You'll have all my power to protect and aid you, and other power, besides. We're not alone."

"You're better able to fight sorcerers than I am."

"It would not be wise. Not wise at all. My part in this must remain secret for a long time to come. If I do open battle against the fellowship, too much will be revealed."

"Revealed to whom? If they're defeated, what does it matter whether they know whose power defeats them? None of this makes any sense to me, Cathwar."

The wizard walked on for a time in silence. Once he appeared to be about to speak, but he checked himself. Finally, with a reluctance he did not attempt to conceal, he said, "When last I spoke to you, I told you that I sensed an evil astir in the High City. I sense it still. It's spreading throughout the northern lands, and it's an evil far beyond that company of sorcerers. Even their combined power falls far short of the thing I feel moving around us." He fell silent again, and Ambescand, filled with growing apprehension, awaited his next words.

"I fear that the old adversary of the Iron Mage is somehow involved in the quest for the talisman," Cathwar said after a time. "It's very unclear . . . I may be wrong. But if the fellowship become aware of this evil being and ally themselves with it, the struggle to destroy them might devastate the world, as it did once before. It may be that their sustained concentration on the talisman over several mortal lifetimes has somehow roused this being to awareness after ages of oblivion. I don't know. Things are so unclear . . . uncertain. Perhaps the ancient evil is already manipulating the fellowship, without their even knowing it. In any case, they must be defeated," he said, and his voice, which had been hesitant and groping, was at once firm and decisive. "I will invest you with all my power—all but what I need to sustain life. You will confront them, magic to magic. You must, and you will, and it must be soon. Well, come along, come along."

In deep night, Ambescand and Cathwar stood in the center of a torch-lit chamber. A third man had joined them. He was short and stocky, simply dressed in a well-worn brown robe of coarse weave. His nose was bent as if by a hard blow, and his sunburned skull shone like a waxed wooden bowl through his sparse brown hair. He looked like some honest but suspicious farmer, and Ambescand took him to be a servant of the wizard. Cathwar's introduction surprised him.

"This is Zandinell. He is a brother in our cause. Trust him as I do," Cathwar said.

"I will," said Ambescand, extending his hand to the second wizard.

Zandinell took the hand in a firm grip. "So, it's time to move against the fellowship, is it?"

"It is," Cathwar said.

"And this fellow will be our champion?"

"He will confront them."

"Then I wish you well, brother. Use our power wisely. Now let's be about our work."

"I'm ready. What must I do?" Ambescand asked, looking from one to the other and finally fixing his gaze on Cathwar.

Cathwar offered no explanation. Pointing to one wall, he gestured impatiently for Ambescand to move out of the way. Taking a stone from his pouch, he quickly drew an irregular seven-sided figure on the smooth floor, and he and Zandinell began to scatter powders from the same pouch in various parts of the figure. Cathwar knelt to inscribe symbols near each intersection of lines, he and Zandinell mumbling all the while in a language unintelligible to Ambescand. Cathwar measured carefully, checking distances between angles and symbols with his cincture, and when all appeared to be satisfactory, he drew two pairs of footprints in the center of the heptagon, facing each other, and a star at the center of the footprints. This done, he turned to Ambescand.

"Walk to your left. Enter the figure by crossing that line," he said, pointing, "and do not step on any lines or symbols until you reach these footprints. Place your feet in them, and the point of your sword on the star, with your left hand on the hilt and your right hand on the right crosspiece."

Ambescand followed the directions. As he fitted his feet to the marks, Cathwar took his place on the other set of footprints and gripped the sword in the same manner. Zandinell withdrew to the farthest corner of the chamber. All was still. Then Ambescand felt a wind rising all around him and rushing through the chamber; but there was no wind. The torches burned on without a shiver. And yet he felt furious motion all around him and within him; and at the heart of the headlong whirl and rush, he sensed a stillness; and in the stillness, himself. He heard the sound of deep drumming, and the roar of winds and waters; and in the heart of the noise, there was a silence; and he was in the silence. Darkness enfolded him, and brightness burst within the darkness, and light and darkness wed in a shimmering haze that hung like a veil over him. He felt a power rising like a tide within him, coursing down through his legs; pouring through his sword into his hands and up through his arms; beating like rain on his bare head and face, channeling through him; all the sources joining like confluent tributaries into one great, irresistible river in his breast, endlessly pouring, absorbed without overflow, filling him without repletion. All awareness of place, and all sense of body were lost. He became as insubstantial as a wish, as eternal as the rise and fall of the sea. He swelled, and he was so mighty he could reach out and pluck the stars from their settings in the ceiling of the world; he shrank, and he became so small he could hide in the shadow of a mote.

Then he was aware that Cathwar had slumped forward, leaning against him, hands still gripping the sword tightly. The torches were burned to smoldering stumps, and light fell in angular beams from the high, barred windows of the chamber. He took up the wizard in his arms and carried him to the next room, where he laid him on a narrow pallet. Zandinell, who stood waiting, wrapped the old man in a heavy cloak.

Cathwar seemed emptied of life. He was sunken in upon himself, pallid and dry of complexion. His half-shut eyes were lusterless.

"Break the ring," the old wizard said in a faint whisper.

"I broke it as we left it. All is nullified."

"Go quickly. The boat is at the shore."

"I'll return, Cathwar. Cling to life, and believe in me."

Cathwar's voice was almost inaudible. "Enter the city . . . with drawn sword. Never . . . let it . . . leave your hand."

"I will watch and guard him. Be victorious, brother," said Zandinell when Cathwar's eyes closed.

Ambescand left the chamber, climbing the stone steps to the barren surface of the islet. They were on Slill, the landward island of the group known as the Sisters. Far across the water was the sea wall of the High City.

A boat rocked gently at the end of a stone pier. It remained at pier-side though no rope held it. Ambescand stepped into the boat and seated himself, and the boat turned toward the city. It began to move, smoothly and at great speed, to the mainland.

CHAPTER FIFTEEN

THE TOWER AND THE WHEEL

Feron turned pale at the news. He sprang to his feet and shook his fist in the guardsman's face.

"A lie! Treason!" he cried. "Dead men don't return, and Ambescand is dead!"

"He is at the gates, my king. I saw him, and I heard his voice."

"He's dead! He and his three hundred were massacred by the nomads and easterners."

"But he stands at the western gate, and the three hundred stand behind him," the guardsman protested.

Feron turned from him with a wordless groan of fear and amazement and began to pace the floor with rapid, angry steps, gnawing furiously on his knuckle. He had seen the vision of Ambescand's death and believed it true. Now his half brother was back, alive, and what he might do to a usurper was not pleasant to contemplate.

"Keep him out, him and all his men," he told the guardsman. "This one who claims to be Ambescand is not to enter the city. Those are my orders. Go, and see that they're obeyed."

As the guardsman left, Feron summoned two runners. One he sent to gather his supporters; the other he dispatched to the sorcerers' tower. They had brought all this about with their visions and promises, and it was only fitting that they should come to his aid. They had little choice; their own skins were at stake, and in more danger than his. He could count on their magic.

He seated himself and tried to compose his wits. It came to him, in a sickening moment of realization, that the sorcerers' magic had badly failed him already, with a false vision of Ambescand's death, and their power might be no better at defending his throne than it was at far-seeing. Perhaps, he thought, starting up with terror, they had deceived

213

him from the start. Perhaps they were in league with Ambescand, or were agents of some rival power, and he, having served their purpose, was now to be cast aside. He bit on his knuckle until he broke the flesh and gasped with the sting of pain. He glanced about nervously. He had his bodyguard, and they were tough and well armed. They would be of some help. But if the entire guard went over to Ambescand, and the people followed, even his own bodyguard would surely betray him. In the end, he was alone.

He thought of Banheen. Ambescand would surely listen if Banheen appealed to him for mercy. And Ciantha, too, and the children. He had not treated them harshly; he had merely confined them and kept a watch on them. His threats had been spoken in anger; he had never intended to carry them out. Surely they knew that. If they all spoke on his behalf, Ambescand would forgive him. He dispatched a runner to fetch them, and then he settled uneasily in his chair, his mind racing, his thoughts jumbled.

When Darra Jhan entered the chamber, Feron jumped to his feet and cried, "He's at the gate! Ambescand has returned, and all—"

"He's within the High City," the sorcerer said calmly. "The guardsmen on the wall hailed him as true king and opened the gate for him, and the rest of the guardsmen and the people are flocking to him."

"They were told he was dead. Do they suspect nothing?"

"They shout about a miracle. Some say the old gods are returning, and Ambescand is their herald. They hail him as a mighty wizard."

"What are you going to do?"

"Repel him."

"That's good. Get him away, far away."

"He will not return again. Be certain of that."

"Wait, now. You mustn't kill him. I can't allow you to kill him."

The sorcerer looked darkly down on Feron, and in his cold voice he said, "We will do what must be done. Would you have him snatch away all you have? Is he to take the crown from your head as if you were a child?"

"I don't want to lose the crown."

"Then accept what must be done. Ambescand seized the throne from his half brother. Are you less daring than he?"

Feron gripped the arms of his chair hard. "No one will

ever say that of me. Do what you must. But don't fail me again."

"We do not fail."

"You showed me a vision of Ambescand's fall, and yet he lives."

Darra Jhan made a contemptuous gesture with his shrunken hand. "Ammaranza's magic countered ours. That will not happen again. We are assembling in the tower to prepare ourselves for the clash. No magic can protect a man from our combined power."

Darra Jhan turned and stalked from the chamber. Alone once more, Feron felt his brief resolve fading. He was badly frightened, and even the knowledge that the sorcerers were preparing to defend him could not restore his courage. He knew all the tales of Graymantle, and he could not imagine anything, even magic, defeating such a man—particularly if he possessed a magic of his own.

Feron reflected with growing horror on his words to Darra Jhan, words he had spoken in thoughtless haste, goaded by his fear. He moaned aloud in his futile anxiety to recall them. Now it was too late. He had unleashed the sorcerers. Ambescand would never forgive him for that.

The runner returned, and the look on the boy's face told his message before a word was out. "They're gone, my king —your father, the lady Ciantha, and her children—they're all gone!"

Feron felt as though a giant hand had reached inside him and torn out his entrails. He was lost, helplessly, hopelessly lost. It mattered little what had become of Ciantha and her children. If they had been harmed, Ambescand would avenge them, and if they had escaped, his last hope of an intercessor was gone. This had all been madness, this entire adventure. He had never really wanted to be king; he had even disliked being regent. All he wanted now was a chance to escape unhurt.

He ran to the window and looked down the broad avenue to the western gate. A crowd was assembled. The distance was too great to distinguish details, but he saw light flashing on breastplates and helmets. The crowd stirred busily, and as he looked on, it began to move toward the palace.

Feron needed to see no more. He abandoned all his faith in magic and makers of magic and in his sworn supporters, and he fell back on his last resource: flight. Flinging his crown and fur-trimmed cloak aside, he went by a back way to his private chambers. Stripping off his royal garments with desperate haste, he changed into a plain tunic, trousers, and shirt, and he replaced his embroidered slippers with stout hunting boots. Over all, he donned a hooded traveling-cloak of coarse brown stuff. Filling his pockets with purses of gold-den oaks, he left the palace by an exit that opened beyond the rear garden, and he set out at a brisk pace for the eastern gate, and the seacoast.

The hexagon tower stood near the palace, at the center of the High City, on a site of great antiquity. In the early days of the city, a tumble of stone had been unearthed on this spot, remains of a temple to some ancient and forgotten deity. The ruins had rested undisturbed until the reign of Frindiman, father of the unfortunate Aluca. Frindiman had been much influenced by signs and portents and ancient mysteries. Immediately upon his accession, he had commanded that a tower be built on the site for use by his star-readers, of whom he had scores. He spent much of his time in their company on the upper level of the tower, gazing at the ceiling of the world, and gave little attention to affairs of state or the education of his heir. When he died in a fall from the tower, he was properly mourned, but the people felt a sense of relief. Since Aluca's time, the tower had been allowed to decay.

The sorcerers had taken this tower for their own. By Feron's command, and with Ulowadjaa, Hane, and Taerhael goading the workmen, it had been refurbished to suit their purposes. Here, on the day of Ambescand's arrival, they gathered to await him.

When Darra Jhan returned from the palace, the company of eleven assembled behind the massive doors. They had chosen this spot to confront Ambescand with their power and destroy him.

"How is the king?" Bellenzor asked.

"Jellied with fear. He is a weakling beneath contempt."

"But useful. You prodded his jealousy, I trust."

"With words only. This is not a time to waste power. If Feron bolts, we will easily replace him. One of us would be more suitable than that idiot," said Darra Jhan.

"Yourself, I presume," Cei Shalpan said coldly. "Or would you prefer to be keeper of the treasures?"

Before Darra Jhan could reply, Rombonole stepped between them and said, "All this is of no importance at the
moment. Ambescand is coming, and we must be ready."

"We will attend to this woodcutter, brother. He'll pay for
this interruption in our business, and for his presumption."
Cei Shalpan turned to the four who stood side by side, facing the door. "Are you ready?"

"The moment he sets foot within the tower, I will blast all
hope from his soul," Skelbanda said. "Whatever magic protects him, he'll lose the confidence and the will to employ it."

"And as he cringes, and cowers, and seeks escape from
our wrath, I will strike him with a wasting disease. When he
tries to crawl away, Hane will shrivel his limbs," said Bellenzor in his dry, grating voice.

Jashoone pushed back a strand of hair and said, "When he
dies, I will consume his body with my flames. And so much
for Graymantle, the liberator."

"Will he come to the tower?" Aoea asked.

Bellenzor croaked, "He must. The rabble are swarming
around him, whimpering of our cruelty. They tell of broken
bodies and stolen minds, incidents of brutality and families
turned against one another. They point to our tower and cry
out to be delivered. He will come."

Waddling to the steps with the greatest speed of which his
bloated body was capable, Ulowadjaa said, "We must leave
our defenders to their work unencumbered. Come, Taerhael,
Korang. Come, Darra Jhan. Those of us who have given of
our power must withdraw. Quickly, come." And, rolling
from side to side like an overladen wagon on a bumpy road,
Ulowadjaa hoisted himself from step to step with a great puff-
ing and blowing and creaking of wood.

"We are not helpless," Darra Jhan snapped.

Without turning, Ulowadjaa said in his high voice, "Of
course not. Certainly we're not helpless. But we agreed. We
portioned out the responsibilities. I was not to face Ambescand. I kept discipline among the workmen. I've done my
part." He reached the top of the staircase, and his complaining voice was muffled by the heavy wooden floor.

"That mountain of quivering flesh must walk easily or
he'll bring the tower down around our ears," said Cei
Shalpan.

"Let him go. He's done his share," Taerhael said, starting
for the steps.

"He might be of some help against Ambescand."

Skelbanda cried vehemently, "Ambescand belongs to us! Go, all of you, and leave us to our work!"

On the second level of the tower, Korang and Darra Jhan joined the other two to await the outcome of the clash. Aoea, Rombonole, and Cei Shalpan proceeded to the uppermost platform to observe the situation in the city and bring their powers into play should the guardsmen, or the people, attempt to avenge their king. Within the confines of the tower, any exercise of their magic would be as dangerous to them as to those at whom they directed it; in the open spaces of the city, against masses of people, it would be devastating. Aoea's winds could send grown men tumbling like dried leaves before a winter blast. Rombonole could make the ground heave and split, walls fall, and buildings topple. At Cei Shalpan's bidding, the power of the storm would be unleashed upon his enemies. The three knew that no mortal, no army of mortals, could withstand them. The matter of Ambescand's return was an annoyance, nothing more. Clearly, Ammaranza had worked a self-serving magic that undid their own. But it would soon be rectified; and a display of their power would keep the people docile for a long time to come.

Aoea had positioned herself by an embrasure so as to overlook the main avenue of the city. As she watched, a solid mass of humanity moved like a slow and purposeful tide against the tower. At the head of the crowd was a tall figure. He was cloaked in gray, and a naked sword was in his hand.

"Ambescand comes," she said in her childlike voice.

The others stepped to her side to observe with her. As the mob drew nearer, several pointed fearfully to the tower, and some shook their fists at the three sorcerers and shouted words that could not be heard above the tumult.

Ambescand had gained on the others, and he marched about three marks ahead of their foremost rank. When he came near the tower, he turned, stopped, and raised his hands. The crowd came to a disorderly halt before him, and their noise diminished and died.

"I must enter alone," he cried.

A great shout went up from the massed citizens and guardsmen. They spread out to ring the tower. Again, fists were shaken at the three wizards, and undistinguishable imprecations were hurled at them. A few of the bolder people below, those on the graveled pathway, picked up stones and threw them. Instinctively, Rombonole misdirected them.

Ambescand looked up and caught sight of the three wizards standing side by side at the battlements. He studied them for a moment; then, unfixing his cloak and tossing it to a guardsman who had come to his side, he started for the door of the tower.

"He has some courage," Aoea said.

Rombonole laughed, a hard laugh that suited his hard features. "He won't have it long. Skelbanda will see to that." He paused; then he laughed again and leaned his elbows on the parapet. "I tell you, I can hardly wait to see the expressions on this mob's faces when their king and liberator comes crawling from that door looking like a bundle of dry sticks. And burns like one, as well!"

Ambescand halted before the tower door. A full mark from side to side and more than a mark in height, rimmed with iron and braced by three broad iron straps, it was made to hold the tower secure against an army. As he studied this massive portal, it swung ever so slightly inward on silent hinges. At the same time, he felt a powerful emanation, an invisible wave of poisonous hatred so intense that it was almost a tangible, viscous flow pouring over him.

Raising his sword, he stepped forward, and the unseen force rolled back before him. He touched the door with the point of the blade, and the door opened easily to admit him.

Entering, he swung the door shut behind him and set his back to it. The four sorcerers faced him, Skelbanda the foremost. Slightly behind her, on her left, were Bellenzor and Jashoone. Hane stood at her right hand.

Before he had more than a glimpse of his enemies, a mist rose and swirled around him, and he was encircled by apparitions, gaunt things with bony limbs and wasted faces, eyes hollow and black as postholes. Skinny, clawlike fingers plucked at him, loathsome things seemed to be crawling over his flesh. A wailing filled his ears, a shrill keen of despair that was like a needle of ice driven into his heart. His nostrils filled with the damp stink of the grave. He hesitated, and behind the haggard wraiths rose something huge and strong and saturated with malice, an enemy beyond his power to withstand, an enemy the very sight of which would turn his strength to water. The mist began to thin, and fade, and the

fearsome thing's outline grew ever clearer and more terrifying.

And then the sword in his hand gave a little quiver, as if
to reassure him that it was eager to be about its work. He
had the sensation of a strong, sure hand closing upon his
own, and a flood of strength and certainty poured through
him. Something greater was with him now, around him and
within him, guiding him and supporting him, and no power
on earth or beyond it could resist their conjoined force. Ambescand gave a single joyous laugh. He raised his sword and
slashed a figure in the air, and at once the things were gone
and he saw only the four sorcerers facing him.

They appeared undismayed to see him surmount the first
obstacle. They exchanged a quick glance among themselves,
and then three of them drew back a step, leaving him to the
dark lady who fixed him with her eyes.

"You've walked into our domain, woodcutter, and you
will not leave it alive," Skelbanda said. Her deep, dark eyes
were full upon him, locked with his. They shone in the light
of the torches set above the door on either side. The first two
fingertips of her right hand lay lightly on the diamond that
hung at her breast, and her left hand, raised, was reaching
out to him. "We must make an example of you, so our work
will not be disturbed again. Do you understand that? You'll
be punished, and you cannot escape. There is no escape.
Look at me, and you'll know that there is no escape, no hope
for you."

She stepped forward, her hand outstretched, fingers curved
and beckoning, her voice gentle as she articulated in soft
words the message of desolation that was in her eyes. Ambescand, too, stepped forward. His blade flashed up, and the
point touched the diamond on her breast. The crack of the
stone was drowned in Skelbanda's shrill scream. She staggered back, eyes wide, and she crumpled against the wall,
huddled, screaming uncontrollably, her hands before her face
as if to ward off some horror.

Jashoone pointed her left hand at Ambescand. A wall of
fire rose to envelop him. He swung his sword in an arc, and
the flames stood motionless and then began, slowly at first
but with gathering speed, to crawl back upon Jashoone.
Quickly, she crossed her right hand over her left, and at
once she stood encased behind a rampart of ice. Flame met
frost with a hiss like a dragon's breath, and vapor swirled

about the chamber. Ambescand turned, and before Bellenzor could cast his magic he struck the sorcerer squarely on the temple with the flat of his blade and sent him sprawling across the trembling form of Skelbanda.

Ambescand's movement had brought him near the foot of the stairs. Hane, left to face him alone, gave in to panic.

In his heart, Hane had always felt himself inferior to his fellow sorcerers. He did not command the elements or govern the emotion; his only power was to inflict agony and death. He had been the last one called to partake in the fellowship, and he well knew that if Zandinell had not scorned them and rejected their quest, the others would not have thought of him at all.

Seeing three powerful enchanters so easily swept aside, and their magic turned back against them, Hane despaired. He had used his power freely to keep the people docile and obedient; too freely, he now realized. He could not stand alone against a wizard as great as Ambescand. He had no thought but to flee.

He was closer to the door than Ambescand was. Before that dark blade could be raised against him, he was gone.

Outside, he stopped short. A wall of solemn figures enclosed him on all sides. He drew himself up and looked haughtily on the mob. This rabble was no threat to him.

"He's one of them!" a voice cried.

"The one who shrivels limbs, that's who he is!"

"He crippled my boy!"

"My husband! He shrank my husband's legs to claws!"

Folding his arms and looking from face to dirty face with contempt, Hane said, "Yes, I am he who did all these things, and more. The withering touch is my power, and whoever blocks my path I will cripple hand and foot. Make way for Hane!"

The crowd drew back a few paces; then they stopped and surged toward him again. "If a man touches me, I'll dry the life from his body!" Hane howled.

The first three men and women to reach him shrieked and fell back with shriveled talons where their hands had been. Then a rock struck Hane between the shoulders, and he staggered. A second struck him in the neck, and a third hit his knee with the sharp crack of breaking bone. He fell, and the crowd closed on him with a hungry roar.

Moments later, they drew back, silent with the realization

of their deed. Men and women looked in disbelief on their bloody hands; they glanced furtively at one another and at the patch of shredded flesh and splintered bone that lay in the open space before the tower.

In the silence, Jashoone burst from the tower door, her robes aflame. She fell to the ground, writhing, beating at the flames and screaming piteously. This time the crowd did not hesitate.

Ambescand raced up the tower steps. He gave the four who cowered on the second level no more than a passing glance, as if he knew their powers were spent and scorned to clash with them in their weakened state. He flew to the top and burst upon Aoea, Rombonole, and Cei Shalpan before they were aware of his footsteps. He said nothing. His presence attested to the defeat of those below.

"Use your power, brother!" Aoea urged Rombonole. "Bring the tower down and bury him, quickly!"

Keeping his eyes on Ambescand, Rombonole replied, "All very well for you to say. You need only ride off on a wind. I'll be buried with this woodcutter."

"I'll save you, Rombonole. Do it!"

"Call up a wind and blow him away, sister. Don't dawdle."

Stepping before the others, Cei Shalpan flung his hands high and cried out in a loud voice, intoning guttural words in a language never meant to be spoken on earth. Overhead, in the empty autumn sky, clouds began to swirl and gather. The heavens grew dark in an instant, and a monstrous smoke-colored cloud churned directly above their heads. Cei Shalpan's voice was smothered in the thunder that seemed to shake the very air around them. Ambescand stood impassive amid the din. He did not even lift his eyes. When Cei Shalpan shouted a phrase and a jagged bolt lanced downward, the dark blade leapt up to meet it. Lightning streamed from the blackness overhead, illuminating the four motionless figures in a lurid, flickering brilliance. They stood for minutes on end, and then Cei Shalpan lowered his hands and drew back, trembling. The aura of magic lightning cloaked Ambescand in an afterglow that flickered about his body before fading into the day.

The dark mass that boiled above them split and broke into fragments, and in a moment it was no more than scraps of cloud drifting westward on the sea breeze. Sunlight flooded the parapet. Cei Shalpan watched, pale, immobilized with fear, as Ambescand lowered his sword until the point was just before his eyes. He stepped back, and Ambescand matched him step for step until the sorcerer came up against the battlement. The sword point darted forward, just touching Cei Shalpan's forehead, and the wizard screamed in anguish and clasped his hands to his brow. He sank to his knees, moaning, and Ambescand turned to the others.

Aoea had begun a spell, and the wind was rising; she called forth no hurricane to blast the enemy, but a strong breeze to carry her off to safety. She stepped into a narrow crenel, her slender, childlike body fitting easily between the massive merlons, and raised her arms.

"Wait! You said you'd save me!" Rombonole cried.

Aoea fell forward into the rescuing wind, but as she did so, Rombonole sprang up, mounted the merlon, and plunged after her, clasping her about her waist. She screamed and beat at him, and all the while they sank lower and lower, spiraling down like a leaf. When they touched the ground, the waiting crowd closed upon them.

Ambescand looked down and shut his eyes, leaning his forehead against the cool stone. Wild cries rose all around him from the crowd outside and now from within the tower.

At the scrape of a footstep, he whirled, sword at the ready. Before him, at the top of the steps, a misshapen figure stood. His oversize head sat crooked on his uneven shoulders. His knees pressed against each other, and his lower legs and feet splayed outward. His gnarled, huge-knuckled hands were locked in piteous supplication.

"Save me, Graymantle," he whimpered. "They'll tear me to pieces as they did the others. Save me from them."

"You're Korang, the Warmaker."

"You know of me. You know all I've done for you," the little man said eagerly. "It was I who led you to all your victories. All your victories, Graymantle! I made you great. I did it for Ammaranza. She was special to me. When I learned of her death, I wept. Yes! I, the Warmaker, wept for her."

"Do you weep for the others? You've spilt more blood than all the armies that ever clashed in the north, Korang. You're the worst of all this evil lot," said Ambescand, approaching the sorcerer with lowered sword.

Korang shrieked as the point touched him. It shed no drop

of blood; it did not even break the skin; but it wrung from him, as it had from the others, the cry of one impaled.

A guardsman's head appeared at the opening to the stairs. "Are you all right, my king?" the man asked, gazing at him fearfully.

"Yes. It's over now."

"Are these two alive?"

"They are. Take them below. How many of the others are left?"

"Only the dark woman and the wasted man. The rest have been torn to pieces."

"I saw."

The guard lowered his eyes. "The people have suffered greatly. These sorcerers used their magic to torment those who resisted the usurper or spoke well of your rule."

Ambescand nodded. "Has Feron been found?"

"Not yet. We're searching."

"What of my wife and children?"

"No sign of them, my king. They must have escaped."

Ambescand closed his eyes and nodded, not trusting himself to speak. He dismissed the guard with a gesture. The fellow returned almost instantly with three others, and they dragged the sorcerers below. Alone, Ambescand sank to the platform.

He had used the borrowed magic, and he had used it well, but the toll was awful. The human body was too frail a vessel for such energies: the power coursing through him had been like a hurricane in a garden, or a flood bursting through the bed of a quiet stream, ripping and dislodging all before it. Even Ambescand's great strength and stamina were devastated by the effects. He tried to sheathe his sword, but his hand shook so badly that he abandoned the effort and laid the blade across his knees. He was drenched in sweat from head to foot, and his heart was pounding wildly. His head throbbed. Every muscle in his body ached, and he could not control the trembling in his arms and legs.

But worse than all the pains of his body was the desolation brought upon him by the guardsman's words. He had believed his wife and children safe. He could not believe that Feron, whatever enchantment might have been placed upon him, could be made into the slayer of his own kin. Yet they were gone, and Feron had fled, like a man who fears retribution for an unforgivable deed.

Feron was wise to fear him, Ambescand reflected. He would be found, and punished, if it took a lifetime. And the sorcerers would be punished here and now, and in a manner befitting their vile lives.

Slowly, Ambescand regained control of himself. He sat for a time on the platform, forehead pressed to the cold, rough stone of the battlement; then, sword in hand, he descended the steps. The planks of the second level were bloodstained, and the walls were spattered with crimson. He passed without a closer look and made his way from the empty tower.

The four surviving sorcerers, tightly bound, lay on the ground before the tower. Guardsmen stood near them with blades drawn. Ambescand stopped before his prisoners, and all four glared at him with hate in their eyes. Their power was gone from them; their knowledge remained.

"You'll never find it," Bellenzor said in his rasping voice. "We could not, and you have less chance than we did."

"The magic will kill you before you master it. Already, it's aged you. You'll never succeed," Skelbanda whispered.

Ambescand became aware, for the first time, of the stares his guards and the people directed to him. Ignoring them, he said to the sorcerers, "You've harmed my people and twisted the mind of one close to me. For your deeds, you deserve to die. But if you return my wife and children, I'll spare you."

"Will you free us?" Cei Shalpan demanded eagerly.

"I'll spare your lives, no more. You'll be imprisoned."

The four exchanged glances. No words passed among them, but Ambescand saw a faint smile on Skelbanda's lips. Turning her face up to him, she hissed, "They're dead! You've lost them a second time. They're dead, and you'll never see them again. There's your victory, Graymantle!"

The others joined in her mocking laughter. Two guards stepped forward to silence them, but Ambescand waved them back.

"Then you'll die," he said. Turning to the guards, he commanded that four wheels be brought to the site at once, and that the sorcerers be bound on them and their bones smashed with iron hammers. On the morrow they were to be sealed in leaden coffins, taken far out to sea, and given to the deep.

He stood apart, watching, while his sentence was carried out. By nightfall, it was over. Two of the sorcerers still moaned, but the other two were silent. He wrapped his gray cloak closer around him and waited until all sound had ceased. Only when all four were dead did he leave them, to enter his palace for the first time since his return.

Vengeance had left him feeling empty. The sorcerers had deserved their agonizing deaths, but that was over now. Their suffering was done, and they roamed the dark corridors of Shagghya with others of their kind. He lived on, and the anguish of his loss lived in him. For all his apparent good fortune, he felt himself a man accursed.

As he entered the hall of the palace, he stopped and cried out in astonishment at the sight before him. Ciantha, alive, as beautiful as ever, stood with her arms outstretched to him. He started forward as she ran to greet him, and he swept her up in his arms, joyously repeating her name. The children swarmed around them, shouting and cheering his return. Aloof, ladylike little Ketial wept daintily, while the others, even clumsy Colberane, danced for glee.

"You're alive!' Ambescand said over and over, his words like a joyous litany, embracing each of them in turn, then taking two or three in his arms at once in sheer eagerness to touch them and reassure himself that what he saw was real.

"Banheen rescued us," Ciantha said breathlessly. "He took us through tunnels below the palace. We were going to leave the city this very night and make our way to the Crystal Hills, and then Banheen heard of your return."

"They told me you were dead."

"Who told you such a thing?"

"The sorcerers. I put them to a hard death for it."

Ciantha took his hands in both of hers. "It was their last chance to hurt you. They were evil. They did terrible things to our people."

"I saw the big fat one squash a man just by pointing at him," Ordred said earnestly. "He just pointed his finger and moved his hand, like this, and the man was all squeezed up.'

"The other one, the frowning one, turned a stonecutter's hands into claws! Skinny black claws!" little Staver said, looking about with wide eyes.

"They'll do it no more. They're all dead."

Ciantha looked at him anxiously and said, "What will you do to Feron?"

He laid his hands on her shoulders and smiled down on her. "When I find him, I'll forgive him. None of this was his idea. Darra Jhan planted envy in his heart and twisted his mind."

"Is he gone, then?"

"The guardsmen have been searching the city, but they've found no trace of him. I imagine he fled when he heard I'd returned."

"He told us you were defeated. He never said it, but I think he believed you were dead," Ciantha said.

Banheen entered the hall, and at the sight of his foster son, he let out a whoop of triumph and scampered to his side with all the speed he could muster. "I knew you'd be back! I told Feron he was crazy to do what he did, but Feron never listened to me. Never listened to anyone in his life except those cursed lying magicians."

"You saved Ciantha and the children," Ambescand said, taking Banheen's hand and nearly crushing it in the excess of emotion.

Pulling his hand free, Banheen said, "Well, I couldn't leave them here. Feron wouldn't have hurt them, but those sorcerers . . . anyway, I still had the old map. Remember that map, son? The one I used to get you out of here?"

"Cathwar's map. It would have saved you, even if I'd failed. I must return to Cathwar. I don't know how long he can last."

He took a step back and saw that they, too, were staring at him. For the first time, he noticed the sadness in Ciantha's eyes, the awe on the faces of his children, and Banheen.

"What is it? What's wrong?" he asked.

Ciantha came to him, and, taking his arm, she led him to a ceremonial shield that hung on the wall. There, in the polished surface, distorted by curvature but unmistakable, he saw his image. His hair and beard were streaked with silver, and his face was as lined and seamed as an old man's. He had aged twenty years in one day.

He reached the islet of Slill well before midnight. Cathwar, corpselike and barely able to speak, lay on his pallet, heaving slow, deep breaths, like a dying man. With the aid of Zandinell, Ambescand quickly restored the seven-sided figure and carried Cathwar to the center. He set the old wizard's feet in the prints on which he had stood, took the other place, and bent the wizard's limp, bony fingers around the hilt and crosspiece of the dark sword. Cathwar swayed, barely able to hold himself erect, and Ambescand hastily undertook the enchantment that would return his magic to its proper master.

This time, the sensation was different; passive and gentle, like the coming of autumn to his soul. There was no sense of loss as he felt the power being stripped from him. It was as if he were a great, ice-covered mountain, and the ice had begun slowly melting, running down the streams and rivers, flowing ever faster until every trace was gone and only the elemental rock remained.

"It was an ordeal, wasn't it?" Cathwar said when he was strong enough to speak.

"It was. I never knew that magic could take such a toll."

"That's why you had to do it. That's part of the reason, anyway. I couldn't have lasted long enough to defeat them all."

"They defeated themselves, Cathwar. I only had to face four of them, really. The rest hung back or ran. I think if they had all attacked me together, they might have overcome. But they were not united."

Zandinell gave a little snort of disgust. "They never were. Called themselves a fellowship, but each of them was just waiting for a chance to betray the others."

Ambescand stretched and rubbed his back. "That surprised me. I never expected sorcerers to behave that way."

"Well, now you know. A sorcerer's just an ordinary man or woman underneath all the magic. Some are good, some are bad, some are brave, some are cowards. Just like soldiers, or innkeepers . . . or woodcutters," said Zandinell.

"Now I know. I'm still glad I didn't have to fight them all."

"You would have won," Cathwar said confidently. "You had a powerful magic in you, and with you. You might have died in the victory, but you would have won." The wizard paused; then he looked Ambescand directly in the eye. "But the hardest fight was with yourself, wasn't it?"

"What do you mean?"

"In the boat, coming back here after it was all over. You weren't thinking of the pain, just the power. Thinking of all the good you could do if you kept it, instead of giving it back to some half-dead old bag of bones who'd never know it if you just turned back and left him here to die."

Ambescand shook his head. His expression was pained. "Cathwar, I didn't . . . well, it occurred to me, just for a moment. But I never meant . . ."

"You came back. That's what counts."

"How did you know?"

"It's as Zandinell said: underneath all the magic, you were still an ordinary man. Better than most men, I'd say. I knew you'd come back. I knew you'd be tempted, too. But I knew you'd come back in the end."

"You trusted me with your life and all your power."

"Don't make too much out of it. I had to, so I did," Cathwar said impatiently, avoiding Ambescand's eyes. "Right now, we all need a good rest, and I think we can safely take one. It looks as though things may be quiet for a long time."

"When will I see you again?"

"I don't know. I'll find you when the time comes. Now go, and be good to your wife, and watch your children grow. Be a good king to your people."

"Come to the High City, Cathwar. Help me to be a good king."

The wizard shook his head. "I have other work. Follow your own instincts, and do what you believe is right. For a decent man, that's the best advice in the world."

Ambescand embraced the old man in parting. Cathwar protested, but he returned the embrace, and his voice was gruff with feeling when he called his last farewell from the stone pier.

The next day, Ambescand still ached in every bone and muscle. But there was work to be done, and he rose early to set about it. He did not carry his dark blade that day. As proof that peace and order had returned to the city, he went forth armed only with a silver court dagger at his belt.

He had the broken bodies of the four sorcerers placed in leaden coffins, which were then sealed shut in his presence. He gave orders to the stonemasons that the hexagon tower was to be torn down. Because it had been the setting of evil magic, it was to be demolished completely: the stones were to be smashed to bits and used as fill on the roads and the harbor mole, the iron melted and beaten into chains and manacles for traitors, the wood burned and the ashes scattered. No structure was ever again to rise on the smooth rock where the tower now loomed.

As he stood looking down on the row of leaden coffins, a man came forward from the crowd and stopped on the opposite side of them, facing Ambescand. He was a small, stout man, plainly dressed in a robe of coarse cloth, his ample paunch bulging over his belt. His sleeves were pushed up, his pudgy arms folded across his chest, and on his mild, round face, with its ruddy cheeks and bright black eyes, was the hint of a smile. A halo of fine white hair lifted and blew about his pink dome as the wind rose, and he raised his fingers to his forehead in a respectful greeting to Ambescand.

"I've come to take these away, my king," he said.

"You'll need strong men to help you."

"Oh, I have them, I have them. As I understand it, my king wishes the remains to be taken out to sea and there buried."

"So I have ordered."

"I see," the man said, and his smile became a look of mild concern.

"If you think this will be too difficult, you need not attempt it. There are others who will."

"Oh, no, my king, it's not the difficulty. No, that does not trouble me at all."

"Then say what does. Come, man, let's hear it."

The man looked uncomfortable. Wiping his brow with one forearm, he blurted, "I fear what might happen if such as these are buried at sea, my king. There are mysteries in those waters. Who knows what evil might be worked in the darkness and secrecy of the depths?"

"What you say is sensible. I've considered it myself. But it seems to me that the danger is greater if they're buried on land. We might post guards over the spot, but a sorcerer could easily get past them. If the bodies are at the bottom of the sea, it will be hard to find them."

The man nodded, but he looked no happier. "As my king orders." He scratched his pink skull; then he said, "But if I may speak . . . with all respect . . . if my king will permit . . .'

"Speak freely."

"These monstrous creatures should not be forgotten. Yet if they are not hidden away, some sorcerer as evil as they might tamper with their bones." He raised his eyes from the leaden coffins and met Ambescand's gaze. "There is an island, my king, a place shunned for its barrenness and the treacherous currents around it."

"The Stone Hand?"

"The very place, my king. Cursed in the name of all the gods for the foul deeds done there in ancient times. Let the remains of these wicked sorcerers be conveyed to the Ston

Hand, and let the curse on the island and the waters around be renewed. Call down the wrath of every forgotten god and demon in the north, so the island and all upon it may rest unhallowed while the waters roll."

Ambescand reflected on the suggestion for a moment, and then he slowly nodded his head in approval. "Can you convey them to the Stone Hand? Can any man?"

"My rowers are the strongest in the north," the man said proudly. He pointed to two towering figures who stood apart from the crowd. They were close to a mark in height, and correspondingly broad. Gray cloaks covered them from head to foot, and gray hoods, pulled forward, concealed their faces.

"Fine big fellows they are. I could use such men in my guard," Ambescand said admiringly.

"Their strength is all they have, my king. They can neither hear nor speak, and they see but poorly. They have the minds of children."

"Too bad. Well, do it, then. Take these coffins to the Stone Hand, and I'll see that it's properly cursed for all time. That was a good idea you had, and you've earned a reward."

The man ducked his head respectfully, again knuckling his forehead in a salute, and Ambescand tossed him two golden oaks—lavish payment for his service. He smiled broadly, ducking his head once more, and still once more, as the king, his work done here, left to be about other business.

The crowd drifted off once the king was gone. Before long only the stout little man and his two giant helpers were left. The stonemasons were all clustered at the foot of the tower, studying it, comparing their observations, disputing the proper method of carrying out their task. So intent were they that they did not notice the two gray giants lift the coffins, one under each arm, as easily as children would carry loaves of bread, and place them on the bed of a waiting wagon that groaned under the weight. They took their places on either side of the wagon tongue and followed at their master's back, moving with ponderous steps, like men of living stone, toward the seaward gate.

CHAPTER SIXTEEN

THE TALISMAN OF
THE IRON MAGE

*The web began with Ambescand, the child of mothers
   three,
A king's son, and a thief's son, and a greater king to be:
   He bore the timeless talisman, through days of dark
   and light,
Through times of trial and triumph, till the summons
   came at night,
   And then he rose and took the blades his honored
   ways had won—
A dark blade from the father's hand, a bright blade
   from the son. . . .*

From *The Last Deed of Ambescand*

Those of Feron's supporters who had not fled the city were
sent into exile. No blood was shed, and no force was applied.
They were given a full month to prepare for their removal
and allowed to take whatever possessions and wealth they
wished, for their exile was to be perpetual. Thus the reign of
Ambescand, born in violence, matured in peace.

Travel increased and trade flourished among the regions
of the north, and especially between each region and the High
City. Crude lumber and rare woods, metals both precious
and base, foodstuffs and hides, blocks of dressed stone, all
the bounty of forest and sea and mountain, flowed to the
heart of the kingdom. From it, in return, came the work of
the city's artists and artisans: carvings of a magical delicacy,
tools and weapons and simple household implements of great
durability and beauty, intricate works in metal and stone, fine
garments and adornments of dazzling beauty. Life was good
even among the humblest, and it showed promise of becoming ever better.

Moved as much by honest pride as by the hope of profit,
merchants ventured beyond the borders of the kingdom. A

profitable trade developed between the High City and Drylands, and there were occasional caravans to the distant east
and west, composed of merchants from every part of the
kingdom. Ambescand saw that the unity his predecessors had
striven to impose by force and terror was coming about naturally as the northlanders perceived the benefits of coopera-
tion.

All the same, the kingdom was essentially a patchwork of
separate regions with barriers both tangible and intangible
dividing them. The miners and fisher folk of the Crystal Hills
did not think in the same way as the mountaineers or foresters, nor did they live by the same values. The Headlanders
were not like any other people in the world. Ambescand
recognized the differences, and he knew that neither threats
nor force nor arguments could remove them. He was not
certain that they should be removed. Properly treated, they
might provide a stimulus to the spirit of the kingdom. He
had only to find the way, and he thought deeply on this.

His children were the key. His daughters were shy girls,
happiest in one another's company and reluctant to be long
away from the city. But his sons were born rovers, and very
popular. The people of the northlands adored·Ketial, Ingionel, and Ingellett for their beauty and gentleness, but they
loved Colberane, Ordred, and Staver as good companions.
Ambescand deliberated long, and at last he decided to put
his sons' popularity to good use by making them his vice-
gerents.

When Ketial departed to marry a nephew of old Ordred
and live in Goldengrange, Colberane traveled south with her.
After the wedding festivities, he continued southward, to the
Lake Isle, to take up his duties as master of the Southern
Forest. Later that same year, young Ordred, an ardent moun-
taineer with an interest in fortifications, was appointed keeper
of the Fastness and the Plain.

Staver presented a dilemma. He showed promise of becoming
as skilled a swordsman as either of his brothers, and an even
better archer with the short bow; but he was slight of build,
and it was clear to everyone—Staver included—that the boy's
chief strength was in his wits and not in his muscles. Even
though he was the youngest, it was Staver to whom the others
took their disputes for settlement. Ambescand therefore named
him Mage of the Crystal Hills and set for him the special task
of gathering and organizing all the books of ancient lore scat-

tered throughout the north, lest their wisdom be lost through neglect. Staver went forth eagerly in the late days of winter.

It was shortly after Staver's departure that Feron returned to the High City. On a cold, rainy morning toward the end of Lastfrost, he surrendered himself at the western gate. He was gaunt and haggard, shivering uncontrollably in the sodden, filthy rags that scarcely covered his bony frame. One of the guardsmen, moved to pity, wrapped him in his own cloak before taking him to the king. A traitor he might be, said the guardsman, but he was a king's kinsman all the same.

Feron threw himself at Ambescand's feet, so racked with sobs that his pleas for mercy were scarcely intelligible. Ambescand, when he recovered from the shock of seeing his lost half brother, jumped up, raised him to his feet, and embraced him.

"Feron, we all forgave you long ago," he said. "I've had men searching the kingdom for you from end to end. We thought you were dead."

"I hid from the searchers. I was afraid."

"I sent word everywhere that you were forgiven. Didn't you know?"

Feron nodded, sniffling and rubbing his eyes on the rough cloak. "I heard people speak of it, but I thought they were trying to trap me. I couldn't believe you'd forgive me."

"We may not share blood, Feron, but your parents were the only parents I ever knew. For their sake, I could never harm you."

"I tried to steal your kingdom. I made prisoners of your family."

"Your will was not your own. Once I knew that, how could I condemn you?"

"This is what Staver said."

Ambescand looked at him sharply, puzzled. "Staver?"

"I met him. He and a small party were traveling the coast road to Northmark. I chanced upon them while they were stopped for a rest, and I begged food of them. I didn't recognize Staver, and he showed no sign of recognizing me. I'm much changed from the man he knew. But when I heard his name spoken and was brought to him, I feared greatly."

"Staver would not harm a helpless man."

"I know that now. But I was a fugitive, and easily frightened. He bade me sit by him, and shared his own food with me. He talked of the High City, and I couldn't hide my eagerness to hear of you and the family. Staver spoke at length, and at one point, he mentioned my name. Some of his men murmured against me, and Staver spoke sharply to them, saying—as you did—that my will had been warped by the magic of Darra Jhan, and was not my own."

"Staver is wise for his years. It was good that you met him. Well, come now, there'll be time to talk soon enough. You must want a bath, and some dry clothes, and a good meal. I think you'll fit into Staver's clothing. There's quite a bit of it still here. We'll dine together at midday, just Ciantha and you and I."

Feron's eyes widened. "I threatened her, brother. Can she ever forgive my words?"

"It was Darra Jhan who threatened her, and he's paid for it. Hurry, Feron. You must be starving!" Ambescand said, smiling and leading him to the doorway.

Ciantha had indeed forgiven Feron. Even if she had not, his wandering had left marks on him that water could not wash away nor clothing conceal. His hollow, dark-ringed eyes, his gaunt face, and his broken manner would have melted her had he offended her tenfold.

They stayed long at table. For a time, the lost years seemed forgotten, as Feron poured out the story of his wanderings and then sat eager as a child to hear Ambescand tell of his battle with the sorcerers.

Feron never quite recovered from his life as a fugitive. He slept fitfully, and he had a twitch in his hands that he sometimes could not control. But the brothers were fully reconciled, and they became closer than ever. When Ciantha died of a sudden raging fever, it was Feron who consoled the distraught king in those first empty months.

The sons of Ambescand acquitted themselves well. He visited them from time to time, ostensibly on business of the state, but most of the time, while Ciantha still lived, he remained in the High City. After her death, he seemed to grow restless. He traveled much to old familiar places, and Feron always accompanied him. The inn at Riverfield was a favorite spot for them in late summer. Twice, in the spring, they made the long trip south to the territories of Daun Sheem. The nomad was cool toward Feron at their first meeting; but after downing some of the wine the brothers had brought from the north, he found himself moved by Feron's account of his fugitive years and his anecdotes of the wizards' doings. On their second visit, Daun Sheem greeted both brothers as his old friends.

Ingionel and Ingellett were married within a year of each other, and after that, Ambescand spent much time by himself. He did not seem lonely or unhappy, though he was silent and much given to recollection. In the quiet evenings by the fireside, or in his garden, or walking by the sea, he thought back on all he had seen and done, the clashes and the narrow escapes, the feats of arms and the magic, the friendship and the loyalty; he thought too of the suffering and pain and the death dealt by his hands, and he felt regret and remorse for that. It was easy enough to say that the brigands were human scum, the lowest of men, made unworthy of life by the vileness of their deeds. That might be true, but it was no comfort to him, for when he thought of the brigands, he thought of all the good men who had fallen, and their deaths fell like a shadow on his glory and made him wonder anew what purpose his own life was meant to serve. He was growing old, but his strength had not failed. There was life in him yet, and he sometimes wondered whether his true mission still lay ahead. But he quickly dismissed such thoughts as an aging man's folly.

He felt suddenly older, and prey to mortality, when the son of Daun Sheem arrived to inform him of his old friend's death. Duan Ranabas was the son's name, and he looked like a younger version of his father, but he had a solemn and sober mien completely his own. He placed a long parcel, wrapped in soft leather, into Ambescand's hands.

"This is his last gift to you, his closest friend in the northlands. He took it as a prize in the east, and he always believed it to hold great virtue," said Daun Ranabas.

Ambescand unfolded the leather, which concealed a highly polished box of an unfamiliar marble-grained wood, cornered in chased gold. Opening the case, he gave a little gasp of awe at the sight of the sword that lay within, on a bed of shining blue silk.

It looked like a moonbeam wrapped in sunlight and rainbows. The hilt and scabbard were ivory, the crosspiece silver. Fine gold wire bound the hilt and crosspiece, and on the scabbard, like a twist of fire, a train of jewel-eyed dragons wound their way. Twelve winged golden dragons with ruby eyes pursued one another down the ivory shaft, and at the bottom, mouth wide to engulf them all, a wingless dragon waited, its single emerald eye on its prey.

"The dragons represent powers of the earth and sky. The green-eyed one is the sea-dragon. He swallows all in the end," Daun Ranabas explained.

"I've never seen anything so beautiful."

"This is no decorative toy. The blade will shear a steel bar two fingers thick."

Ambescand shook his head slowly in wonderment. "It's magnificent. There are no words to describe it fitly. Or to thank you properly."

"When my father knew he was dying, he had this brought forth and commanded that it be given to you. He said that you alone were worthy of such a blade."

Ambescand drew the blade and made three swift passes in the air with it, listening appreciatively to the soft hum. Smiling ruefully at the youth, he said, "A wonderful sword, truly. But I fear there'll be no more campaigning for me."

"You must have it all the same. It was his wish."

"No man could refuse it, Daun Ranabas."

When he had done admiring the splendid gift, Ambescand went to a chest and took out a box. Presenting it to his visitor, he said, "This is something you must have. It was your father's, and mine, and now it should be yours."

The youth looked on the gold and silver goblet with its bowl of sweetwood. "He spoke of this once, when I was a child. It holds a magic against poison, does it not?" he said.

"It will protect against poison, that's true. But I want you to have it for the memories, not the magic."

That night they passed the goblet back and forth between them often, and for a time Ambescand felt as if his old friend were with him again. He liked this young man and hoped he would stay to meet and befriend his own sons. But Daun Ranabas was eager to return to his heritage now that his promise was fulfilled, and he was on his way all too soon.

On the third night after Daun Ranabas' departure, Cathwar appeared in Ambescand's chambers at night. He bore a great sword in a scabbard of plain iron, with an iron crosspiece in the form of soaring wings that rose on either side of the plain hilt. He looked weary, but his voice was strong.

"One more task, and then our work is done," he said.

Ambescand looked up from his place by the fireside. He rubbed his eyes and smiled. "First Daun Ranabas comes to me with a sword, and then you. You're both too late. My days as a swordsman are past, Cathwar. Give the blades to my sons."

"This task is yours: not to wield a blade, but to forge the blades of deliverance."

"I'm no armorer," Ambescand said.

"You spent many a day at Vurner's forge when you were a boy in Long Wood. You'll remember enough to do the work that must be done. You must bring your own sword and the two that were given you by Daun Sheem. The blades must be reforged, and new substance added to them. Come, and quickly. I will tell you all."

"Where are we going, Cathwar? I can't simply disappear from the palace," said Ambescand. But even as he protested, he was taking up the blades.

"The forge lies deep below the palace. We will work at night and be done in three days. No one need know. Come, Ambescand."

Stooping, Cathwar entered the high fireplace and seemed to vanish. Ambescand, following, saw that one wall had swung back. Cathwar stood in the opening, his staff glowing in his hand like a torch. When Ambescand had passed through and the door had thumped softly shut behind him, Cathwar led the way down a corridor to another corridor, thence to staircases and passages whose existence Ambescand had never suspected. He had thought he knew the city and the palace intimately, but now it seemed to him that five times as much of the palace must lie beneath the ground as above, and little of it was familiar to him.

They stopped at last before a great iron door at the end of a passage deep below the palace. Cathwar drew a key from the recesses of his black robe, and, unlocking the door, he flung it wide. Within, a forge glowed like sunset against one wall of the modest chamber. An anvil rested in the center of the chamber, and the tools of the swordsmith hung upon the walls and stood by the anvil.

"What magic will you work here, Cathwar?" Ambescand asked as he gazed around the forge.

"The most important magic of our lives, I think," Cathwar replied. He was inspecting the forge and the fuel piled high on both sides of it.

"More important than the battle against the sorcerers?"

"That was one small skirmish in a great war that has scarcely begun," said Cathwar. "Here, help me with this. Put coal on."

Ambescand shoveled coal from the pile until Cathwar told him to stop. The wizard spread the fresh coal, carefully laid on chalky white twigs from a separate pile in what appeared to be a pattern, and then fanned the fire until it was burning brightly. Ambescand looked on, curious.

"I've never seen that white wood before. Is it part of your magic?"

Cathwar let out a little dry snort of laughter. "Not everything I do is magic. That's just good fuel. It's dredged up in Mistlands. It absorbs virtue from those waters. Dry it properly, and it's useful in working metals."

"What is it called?"

Cathwar frowned and mumbled, "Some fool named it *wizard-bone.*" He turned his attention to the fire for a time; then, stepping back from the heat, he said to Ambescand, "Long ago, I told you I feared a struggle to come. Now I know that what is to come will be worse than I ever suspected."

"But the sorcerers were crushed."

"They were pawns. I think the power that stirred them might even have meant for them to be defeated. That will give you some idea of its might . . . and its subtlety. We may have been used ourselves. I don't know. It's all dark to me."

"What has this to do with the forge?"

"We've done all we can, and it's not enough, not nearly enough. The enemy is growing stronger, and his strength will go on growing beyond our lifetimes. But there will be one last battle. Men of your blood, doing your work, will face the dark power. I think they'll win, with our help."

"After we're dead?"

"Long after," said Cathwar, looking into the flames.

"Cathwar . . ." Ambescand began, and when the wizard turned to him, he blurted, "you were an old man when I first met you, and I was a boy. Now I'm old, but you seem no older. Don't you age, Cathwar? Don't wizards die?"

"You saw them torn to tatters and broken on the wheel. We die, right enough. But it's only the body that has to die. The magic can live on." When Ambescand shook his head confusedly, the wizard went on, "Some men leave children behind, or works, or knowledge, or an empire. We leave our magic. That's why you and I are here. It's you who'll pass the magic on, and it will go to three who won't be born for many generations."

"I have no magic to give, Cathwar."

The wizard pointed to the dark blade at Ambescand's side. "Since your youth, you've borne with you a greater magic than mine; greater than that of the fellowship of sorcerers you vanquished."

"This sword?"

"The crosspiece."

Ambescand drew the sword and studied the crosspiece in the firelight. It was a simple bar of iron, square in cross section, hammered into a rude ball at each end. It looked no more magical than a clod of dirt.

"Do you recall, when we entered the grave mound, I told you of a wizard from ages past?" Cathwar went on. "And of a certain object, a talisman hidden in the mound, the repository of all his magic?"

"I remember."

"The talisman is the crosspiece of your sword."

"Why didn't you tell me? You let me go through life with this power at my fingertips, and you never told me of it. Why not, Cathwar? Did you think me so unworthy?"

"If you were unworthy, you would never have laid a hand on that sword."

"Then why was I never told?"

"You never suffered for not knowing," Cathwar said wearily.

"I suffer now, Cathwar, because now I know the truth: I'm a fool and a dupe. I was a foolish young man, and now I'm a foolish old king. Everyone deceived me, all through my life." Ambescand slammed his blade home in its scabbard with a clang. "I thought I had a high destiny, but I was born to be used by everyone. You used me, Cathwar. Ammaranza used me, and Duarin."

"When they tried, they brought about their destruction. You live."

"True," Ambescand admitted. "But what about you, Cathwar?"

"A greater power guides us both. And if that jars your pride," said the wizard, his eyes blazing, "then you truly are a fool. There's more honor in serving a good cause than in being king for no better cause than one's own glory, and you've served the cause of humankind as no man has ever done before. You'll serve it here, at this forge, and you'll go on serving it when you're nothing but a memory and a legend."

Ambescand smiled and shook his head at the words. "No, Cathwar. I know you mean to cheer me, but I'll never be a legend, and I know that. My life and my deeds have not the makings of legend. People will hear my name and laugh at my foolishness, if they remember me at all."

"You'll be known to future generations as a sage, a wizard of great power, a warrior none could withstand. Songs will be sung of your deeds, and men will sit among the ruins, in a dark time, and take courage from the legend of Ambescand."

"Why do you mock me?"

"I do not mock. I say what will be."

"I fought no armies, Cathwar, only bands of murderous brigands. The magic I wielded was not my own, and you know that well. As for being a sage . . . all I know is that I never knew anything," said Ambescand bitterly.

"Some would call that wisdom."

"I would not."

"When fighting was inevitable, you fought and won; when it was unnecessary, you avoided it with honor. You bore sorrow without losing hope. You sought no power, but when it was thrust upon you, you ruled for the good of all, wisely and honestly. When magic was given into your hands, you used it well. You've been a good man, a brave man, and the time will come when the north needs the memory of such a man to keep its spirit alive," said Cathwar.

"They have Tallisan, and Pytrigon, and the ancient kings. They have no need of me."

"Nevertheless, you are chosen. Why you and no other, I cannot say. The power that governs such things is beyond my understanding."

"But it makes no sense, Cathwar."

"Believe," said a hollow, rustling voice behind them.

Ambescand whirled to face the speaker, turning and drawing his sword with all the speed of his youth. He saw a shimmering oval of light, slowly fading, and within it, the form of a man gradually taking on solidity. A sudden sensation of recognition flooded through him; he had been in the presence of this being before, though he had never seen him. He felt Cathwar's hand fall gently on his forearm, and he sheathed his sword.

The apparition was wholly formed now, and only a faint, steady luminescence remained, emanating from the figure like heat from an ember. He was a venerable man; he looked no older than Cathwar and Ambescand, but there radiated from him an aura of great antiquity, and great goodness. He was clad in a simple robe of gray. His long beard and hair were gray, and his eyes, under thick gray brows, were gray also. All of him but his pale face and hands was the color of cold iron.

"Believe," he said again, in a voice like the sea-wind over stones.

"I know you. I've never seen you, but I know you."

"I was with you in the tower. You wear my magic at your side."

"The Iron Mage," Cathwar whispered.

"Now the time comes for my magic to be passed on to other hands. You must prepare it."

"Why me? Why me, of all men, Mage?"

The voice of the Iron Mage came rustling dry and hollow down a wind from beyond the boundaries of time and space. It was a voice from an age of dying light; from a dry and barren world, a place of ruins where only shadows dwelt and all was forgotten. And yet, for all the desolation in that voice, it held a note of triumph, as if it proclaimed victory after long suffering.

"You are the crossing-point of forces out of a lost age. Born to no magic of your own, you possess a far rarer gift: you are the focus for the magic of others. Like the wick that allows the oil to burn without itself being consumed, you are the vessel of magic too powerful for any sorcerer to possess. Do not ask why, Ambescand. It must be so, and it is so," said the thin voice.

"What must I do, mage?" Ambescand asked humbly.

"The power I overcame is astir in the world once more, and a long, cruel war lies before us. When the last battle comes, three brothers must confront the old enemy, wielding the very blades you carried to this chamber. Fused in those blades will be your blood and my magic, hammered into their steel at this forge, these three nights, by your hand."

Ambescand nodded sadly. "I had hoped to leave my sons a legacy of peace."

"Someday there may be peace, but first will come the struggle," said the Iron Mage.

"It sounds as though there will be much suffering."

"There is always suffering. Think back on your own life, Ambescand, and you will know that men were not born for joy."

Ambescand made no reply. In the silence, Cathwar said, "The forge is ready."

Ambescand turned and looked weary-eyed at the glowing forge. He removed his tunic and then began to untie his shirt. He felt the touch of the Iron Mage on his shoulders, and strength began to flow into his sagging, aged muscles. He knew it would be taken from him when the work was done, but it felt good to have his youthful vigor alive in him once more.

For three successive nights and days, Ambescand labored at the forge. When he was done, the three swords that lay before him appeared no different from the ones he had taken up at Cathwar's summons: a straight blade, gleaming bright, mounted in gold and ivory; a curved blade, its mountings black and silver; and the dark and massive Iron Angel, with its sweeping winged crosspiece. But the swords were forever changed. All now bore his blood, beaten into the glowing metal drop by drop, and all held a portion of the talisman of the Iron Mage.

When his task was done, Ambescand looked to the ancient mage. "What will become of these blades, and of me? Am I permitted to know?" he asked.

"You may see what is to come. I can show, but I cannot explain, and you may be happier knowing nothing."

"I want to know."

The Iron Mage reached into his robe and drew forth a round pendant of dull dark iron, hammered thin. He took it in his fingertips and held it away from him, murmuring low in a language unknown to Ambescand.

The metal began to brighten, as if the sun were rising within it, and soon it was as clear as a window opening on a summer sky. Ambescand moved closer, and he saw the faint reflection of his face, lined and weary, reddened from the heat of the forge, framed in lank white hair and beard.

The face blurred, and grew faint, and was gone. Then, as

through a veil of distance, he saw gray-robed giants moving through a forest, long, hooked blades slashing rhythmically, and frightened men and women in headling flight before them.

That scene faded, and again Ambescand saw only the dim image of his face, reflected as if in a window. He glanced at the Iron Mage, but the wizard did not meet his troubled eyes.

When he looked upon the disc again, a new scene lay before him, dimmer and less distinct than the first had been. He could see three figures on a low rise, their swords drawn and crossed, points raised to the sky, while a glowing ribbon of light, a beam of infinite power, played upon the blades.

The mist stirred and swirled, and the three swordsmen were gone. Ambescand saw only his own face, wide-eyed.

"My sons! Were those men my sons?" he cried.

"Look," said the Iron Mage.

This time the disc was as milky as sea-mist, all but opaque. Ambescand leaned closer, stared hard, and saw, beneath the obscuring streamers of pale luminosity, figures wandering in a dark wood, lost to all other living beings; yet as he watched, and felt their utter isolation, Ambescand felt also a sense of dread for a hostile power that lay all around them life a dark sea around an isle of light.

The mist covered all, and the metal grew dark and dull again. The Iron Mage let it fall from his fingers and turned from Ambescand to where the swords lay. Placing his pale and bony hands on each blade in turn, he began a low chant in the same unknown language he had used to bring to life the iron disc. Though he was consumed with curiosity about the meaning of the visions he had been given, Ambescand knew better than to interrupt the spell the old wizard was weaving, and he kept his silence.

"Take them, Cathwar, and guard them well until the day comes," said the Iron Mage, his dry voice fading. The light that encircled him had begun to dim, and he to grow fainter in outline, almost transparent, as if his very substance were being drawn away. He turned his attenuated face to the king. "Farewell, Ambescand. Your work is done. Rest now, and know you will be called upon no more."

"Farewell, mage."

"You are a brave man. My blessing is with you," said the Iron Mage in a voice as faint as the rustle of a distant forest on a summer night. The glow faded, and he was gone, and

Ambescand was a weary old man, exhausted to the point of pain, aching from head to foot.

"I'll take you to your chambers. You need a long rest," said Cathwar as he bound up the blades in casings of soft leather.

Ambescand, too weak to protest the offer of aid, struggled to lace his tunic. "I've done what you once did, Cathwar. I've given away all my power." He sighed wearily and added, "But mine will never come back."

"It will do a great deed in the time to come."

"I hope so. And all this time, I never knew I had it."

They made their slow way upward, pausing at intervals for Ambescand to rest and regain his breath. Down gloomy passages and dark corridors, up endless-seeming flights of stone steps they walked, and they emerged at last in Ambescand's chambers. He collapsed full length on his bed, where he lay motionless. After a time, he asked in a weak voice, "What of you, Cathwar? Will we meet again?"

"I think not. The Iron Mage placed a powerful concealment on these blades, but even so, they must be carefully hidden and constantly guarded."

"And only you can guard them."

"Only I," Cathwar agreed. "It is odd where life brings us. You, a king, become an armorer, and I, a wizard, must be a guard."

"We do as we must."

"So we do. Farewell, Ambescand, and my thanks. You have been a good friend," said the wizard.

"Good-bye, Cathwar," said Ambescand faintly.

The old wizard looked about and saw a cloak thrown over a chair. He took it up, and, like a father with his child, he spread it over the sleeping king. Then, concealing the three blades under his own cloak, he slipped silently through the hidden opening in the fireplace.

CHAPTER SEVENTEEN

NIGHTFALL, DARK, AND DAWN

Ambescand's first act when he was recovered from his labors was to send messengers to the Lake Isle, and the Fastness, and the Crystal Hills. But before the first of his sons could reach the High City, he lay weak and helpless, felled by the same mysterious fever that had taken the life of his Ciantha.

He did not surrender to his sickness; he fought it. Though much of his great strength was lost, much remained, and the healers and mediciners who came and went at all hours were amazed by the old king's stubborn resistance.

Feron stayed by the bedside in the king's gloomy bedchamber and listened to his brother's disjointed talk of deceptions and delusions and evil powers lurking ready to pounce and destroy with a blasting power from beyond this world. Though the voice was weak and the breathing rapid, the words were vivid, and Ambescand spoke with great urgency and conviction. Feron, who had never been a courageous man, shuddered at his words, and he looked fearfully into the dark corners and called for more light. But he remained at his brother's side.

On the third night, the fever broke. The king ate, and he spoke with his brother for a time, and then he fell into a profound, quiet sleep. As Ambescand lay resting easily, his breathing regular and deep, Feron allowed himself to doze off in his chair. He snapped awake abruptly in the dead of night, chilled by some alien presence, and he heard his brother's voice. Turning to the bed, he started and gave a choked cry of horror. Hovering just above Ambescand's chest, about head-high, was a ball of pale violet light, and Ambescand was speaking to it.

As Feron gazed, the light moved and folded in upon itself, and before his eyes it became a semblance of a human face. Feron bit his knuckle and grew pale. For a moment, he was paralyzed by his fear. Then, very slowly, he forced himself to his feet.

"Begone, whatever you are!" he cried in a quivering voice. "You're the evil power that killed Ciantha, the one he spoke of in his sickness . . . I won't let you take him. Go! Leave him now!"

A low and hateful hissing, like the sound of drenched embers, filled the air around him. He snatched a massive candlestick from the tabletop and brandished it like a mace. "Begone murderer! Leave him, or I'll pound you to pieces!" Feron cried.

"No, Feron," said Ambescand weakly. "Stay apart—this is no quarrel of yours."

"You're my brother."

"This is an old enemy of mine. It's Hane . . . returned from Shagghya . . . for his revenge."

"Then he must face the two of us, brother," said Feron, with a resolute step forward. "He'll have no revenge on you if I can stop him."

"Feron, stop! Stay! He'll destroy you if you interfere!" Ambescand cried, his voice cracking. He raised himself and clutched at Feron's arm, and his grip was firm.

"I know Hane well," Feron said calmly. "He was a sneaking coward when he lived, the least of all his fellowship in magic and in all else. I have no fear of Hane. Let me go."

"Feron . . . brother . . . he's more powerful than he was in flesh and blood. Would you rush to your death?"

"Death? I don't see death," said Feron, and in his eyes was a light that Ambescand had never seen in them before. "I see redemption. Don't deny me my last chance to be a man. Release me and let me do what I must."

"Feron . . ." Ambescand began, but his voice failed when he looked in those eyes. His grip on Feron's arm relaxed.

"Don't sorrow for me, brother. Rejoice!" Feron cried. And, raising the candlestick high, he dashed forward. He swung with all his might at the ball of glowing violet, but his blow met no resistance, and he staggered and went sprawling headlong on the flagstones.

Scrambling to his feet, he raised the candlestick once more. The violet light flickered, like distant summer lightning, and Feron staggered back, clutching at his chest. The candlestick clattered to the floor. Feron gave a soft, choked cry and fell to his knees, then onto his side, gasping and moaning.

The face in the violet light turned to Ambescand, its features twisted into a smile.

"You've failed again, Hane," said Ambescand evenly, easing from the bed. "You were sent to kill me, not my brother. I've beaten the fellowship again." He was on his feet now, steadying himself against the bed while he fumbled under his pillow. He drew forth the little dagger of Ammaranza and held it before him as he took one slow step, then another. "I did the thing I was born to do, Hane. So did Feron, I think. But you failed, you and all the rest. Kill me or not, you'll never change that."

Ambescand raised his dagger and slashed at the violet light. It flared, and a pain cut through his lungs, as if he had inhaled fire and seared his insides to charred husks. He bent over, clawing at his chest, gasping with the shock of pain. The burning flowed within him, moving out like tributary streams from the inferno in his chest which itself grew ever hotter and more agonizing. His head grew light, and he was dizzy from the pain. He staggered and almost fell. Before him, the light hovered, as if watching. Through narrowed, pain-bleared eyes, Ambescand could distinguish the twisted, smirking face within the sphere of light. The sound of low laughter came from everywhere in the room, as if the very air were mocking him. The pain intensified, and he felt his life being consumed within him like straw in a fire. With his last strength, he drew himself erect and flung his dagger into that jeering face; then he sank to his knees, succumbing to the holocaust that raged inside him.

Hane's laughter grew louder, and the violet glow descended to hover by the fallen king. Then, abruptly, the laughter ceased and the violet light paled. A brighter light, purest white, began to fill the room, drowning Hane's in its own radiance. The violet winked out, and Ambescand heard one shriek like the cry of a crushed rodent, and then there was silence. The pain was gone, and in its place was an overwhelming, all-comforting sensation of peace.

The bodies of Ambescand and Feron were discovered in the morning, side by side on the cold stone floor of the king's bedchamber. Their hands were tightly clasped, as if they had sought to strengthen each other in the final moment.

Fear and suspicion coursed through the palace like a cold wind. The great king of the north was dead, and no one knew what might befall his people. Before the sun had set, rumors had spread through the High City, and fear lay like a mist in all the streets and byways. A plot, some said, and only the beginning of the slaughter. Poison, said others. A curse, and the working of foul magic, said still others. A few maintained that Feron, having wormed his way back into the king's favor, had at last taken this opportunity to avenge his disgrace; others held just as strongly that Ambescand, with his dying strength, had at last punished Feron for his usurpation. And there were those who simply glanced at the spot where the dark tower had stood and murmured a prayer to the old forgotten gods.

Staver arrived in the High City that very night, and by morning the rumors were quelled. The king and his half brother had died of a consuming fever: so Staver declared, and there was no one who would gainsay him. When his brothers arrived and saw the bodies, they added the force of their words to Staver's.

The people of the High City began to breathe more easily, and even to smile at their former fears. After all, they said to one another, kings die just as you and I. Ambescand was an old man, his great strength eroded by the years, and Feron was wasted by his wanderings. A powerful fever could easily claim both men at one stroke. And so the people put their fears to rest and mourned their king and his half brother, and life seemed to go on much as it always had. Instead of one weak and aged king, they now had three strong young ones, close-knit and experienced in ruling. The kingdom was safe.

For Colberane, Ordred, and Staver, things were not so simple. They conferred long and sat late into the night, seeking answers to some troubling questions. Ambescand had disappeared from his chambers for three days, and no one had seen him leave or return. His great dark blade had vanished; the scabbard lay empty on a chest. He had summoned his sons just before falling ill, as if he had seen some foreshadowing of his end. These were all facts, indisputable; but the sons of Ambescand wondered how these facts were related, and what they signified.

Colberane and Ordred found the circumstances curious, but not terribly disturbing. Swords can be lost; men can wish to withdraw from their world for a time, and an aging man may seek to put his affairs in order. It was not well to create mysteries and then worry oneself over them, they said.

But Staver seemed to think that something more was involved here. He was the youngest of the three, but even he was past his youth by this time. In his years in the Crystal Hills he had studied deeply and learned much, and he spoke to his brothers of things he had found.

"I've read a prophecy said to be from the time of the sorcerer-kings. It tells of three brothers, rulers in the north, who will confront an evil from the dawn of time," he said.

"We're not the first three brothers to rule in the north," Ordred pointed out.

"No, but there's more to the prophecy. These three brothers will be the sons of a man who had three mothers—and that's what once was said of Ambescand. Don't you remember?"

"'The son of three mothers will father three sons . . .' I remember that much," said Colberane. "What's the rest of it?"

"'With their hands on his blood they will shake the world when they are long dead and their names forgotten,' or something like that," Staver said.

"That's a fine lot of gibberish, if you ask me. All this prophecy business is gibberish. I know you take it seriously, brother, but I can't. After something has come about, anyone can dig up some old writing and twist it in all directions until it says what he wants it to say, but what good is it all?"

"Sometimes it tells what will be, Ord."

"Think of what you just recited!" Ordred said irritably. "Long after we're dead and forgotten, we'll put our hands in our father's blood and shake the world. What a pack of nonsense!"

"It doesn't have to be exactly like that. Prophecies don't speak directly. Ambescand didn't really have three mothers, but three women treated him as their own son."

"That's different. There's no way that dead men can put their hands in another dead man's blood. That's nonsense."

"It's *on* his blood, Ord, not *in* it."

"That's even sillier! You can put your hand *in* someone's blood, but how . . . ? Oh, let's not waste our time quibbling, brother."

"Perhaps we just don't understand the prophecy. There's another part to it that might make better sense to you. It tells of a sword that will disappear and return as three. Now, you can't deny that Ambescand's sword has disappeared," said Staver.

Colberane quickly retorted, "If one sword returns as three, they're going to be mighty small swords. But it hasn't returned, not threefold, or tenfold, or any other way."

"Staver, you worry me," Ordred said, leaning forward and clasping his brother's arm. "I think you've been up there in the cold and darkness for too long."

"That's right," Colberane broke in. "You stay indoors all day, reading old books, and you're beginning to sound like an old book yourself. It's not healthy, Staver."

"Come to the Fastness. We'll do some climbing, hunt rockgoats, camp out under a good clear sky, and count the stars. You'll soon forget all this and be your old self again," said Ordred.

"Ord's got the right idea. You were always the smartest one, Staver, but there's such a thing as too many books. You need a change. Visit Ord and then come south and stay at the Citadel for a season. We might even visit Daun Ranabas."

Staver looked from one concerned face to the other, and then he smiled and nodded his head. Sighing, he said, "Perhaps you're right. I really hope you are. If these prophecies are true, there's much suffering in store for the northlands. War and disease . . . monstrous creatures like nothing we've ever seen before . . . dissolution of the kingdom and a scattering of the people . . . it will be as if the kingdom had never existed."

"Aren't there any good prophecies in those books of yours?" Ordred asked.

"Well, the three brothers will defeat the evil power in the end. At least, I think they will. The wording is difficult. The prophecy may be speaking of two different sets of brothers."

"We've had enough talk of prophecy," Colberane declared. "We're at peace with our neighbors now, the guard is strong, and the north is prospering. Nobody's seen any monsters, and no one's sick. If those terrible things ever do come about, it will be long after our time. Let's do our best to run the kingdom well and leave the future to our children."

Colberane's sound common sense prevailed. While Ordred remained in the High City, the other brothers returned to their own domains. The following summer, Staver kept his promise and spent the season with Ordred at the Fastness. In the fall, he proceeded south to visit Colberane.

He found it good to be with his brothers again, to talk late into the night about family memories that a ruler could speak of to no one else. The company of his brothers' families pleased him greatly. He resolved to delay his own marriage no longer.

On a journey to the Headland, he had met a wise and fair lady named Devan, only daughter of an old family. His short visit—to examine and copy some rare volumes—became an extended stay, and when he finally left the Headland, he and Devan were betrothed. He had hoped to complete his work of gathering the old wisdom before marrying, but now, seeing his brothers' happiness, he recognized his own solitude and felt himself a fool for waiting.

He traveled homeward in the early summer, through a prosperous countryside where every man was at peace with his neighbor and no one feared danger in the night, or on lonely paths. Everywhere, Staver was received with affection and gratitude. When he returned at last to his home in the Crystal Hills, his perspective had changed, and he had moved closer to Colberane's view: the prophesied sorrows seemed too remote and unlikely to allow them to overshadow present happiness.

Devan and Staver married in the autumn, and their first child, a daughter, was born at the end of the following year. It seemed for a time as though this child, whom they named Meradaina, would grow up in a better world than anyone living had ever hoped to see. Then came the first raid in the south, and all the bright promise began to fade.

A second attack followed the first before Coleberane's forces could set out to defend their lands. The only tracks from the burned and blood-soaked villages led southward, to Drylands.

Some days after, while the people of the Southern Forest were fortifying their homes and arming themselves, news began to reach them of events in Drylands. Daun Ranabas had been struck by a raging fever as he sat at dinner with his closest friends. He had died before the night was out, and he had named no successor. Out of nowhere, a figure who called himself Radin Am-Gaharis, The Blade of Vengeance, arose to lead the nomads against the northern kingdom, claiming that the three kings of the north had murdered Daun Ranabas by magical means and calling for vengeance paid in blood.

The next raids on Colberane's territory were turned back,

but the threat of war remained. As soon as word reached them, Ordred and Staver began preparations to assist their brother. At this point came the first raid in the north, where a new enemy had risen. The exiled adherents of Feron, having brooded long over the crushing of their ambitions, now sought to avenge themselves on their conqueror's sons. Their forces struck at the villages in the mountains near the Fastness, and on the Plain, and at the southernmost settlements in the Crystal Hills.

Thus began the long brutal age that ended in the sundering of the kingdom. No great battles were fought—only a succession of fierce encounters that slowly bled the strength from the forces of the sons of Ambescand. It was an ongoing war with no decisive victories and no crushing defeats. When things seemed blackest, an unexpected success would raise everyone's hopes; when things looked best, a sudden reversal would dash all prospects. But nothing was final. Always the balance teetered back and forth, with permanent advantage to neither side. It seemed almost as though some inhuman power meant the killing and the destruction to go on until nothing remained to be won and no one survived to win it. No leader had appeared among the exiled nobles, and the nomad raids continued after the death of Radin Am-Gaharis at the terrible battle of Lost Lake. Without leaders, there could be no parleys, no treaties, no truce; only war, year after weary year.

Colberane died in the Citadel on the Lake Isle, worn out by ceaseless struggle, weakened by the wounds sustained in years of battle. Ordred fell in an ambush on the road to Northmark. Staver lived to a great age, secluded in the Crystal Hills, while the fighting passed to other hands: his son Tapran, wielder of the great ax Jembre, inscribed with signs of potency; the sons of Ordred and Colberane; the husbands of their daughters; and the sons of those sons after them, who led the forces long known as the armies of Ambescand.

In the shuttered silence of his retreat, surrounded by volumes of ancient lore, Staver sought the reason for the fighting, for he had come to believe that its cause lay outside the wills and tempers of men. He sensed an evil power at work in the north, spreading like slow poison to touch every life and every plot of ground, moving outward like a pestilent cloud. But he could not name it, or identify its origin, or fathom its motive. An ancient, nameless evil; something older than civilization, older than myth and legend, older than man; this he felt and feared. And yet he had also the feeling of a countering force present in the north, a power for good out of the forgotten ages, rising and gathering its strength for the final encounter. He sought the answer until he had no more strength, and his eyes were darkened with his searching, and then one still night, weak with the fading of his hopes, he rested his head on his thin arms and went to sleep at his book-cluttered table and never awoke again.

With the death of the last son of Ambescand, the people of the northland lost heart. They did not doubt the courage and battle prowess of Tapran and his cousins, but they felt the loss of a bulwark. Many fled to the west, over the mountains to Long Wood and the Headland, and among those who fled were some of Ambescand's own descendants.

The way was hard. Some crossed safely and settled in Long Wood or disappeared into Mistlands to the south. Others were harried, attacked, and pursued through the mountains only to be ambushed on the far side. The survivors made their way to the Headland, where their tales spread such fear that soon afterward the Headlanders destroyed the bridge that was their only link to the rest of the kingdom and erected nine watchtowers along the Fissure, which formed their southern boundary.

Now, throughout the north, the tide turned in favor of the mysterious enemy. One after another, the strongholds fell. A sickness came upon the High City, killing all who stayed until too few remained alive to bury the dead. Foul weather and blight ravaged the fertile plain, and soon the farmlands lay barren and the crofts stood empty under the sullen skies. The Fastness was besieged by an army. It held out for nine hard years and then fell through betrayal.

War did not touch the Citadel on the Lake Isle, nor did blight or sickness lay waste to the land or strike down the people. But a despair came over them and crushed their spirit. Their voices sank to hushed whispers, and their songs were stilled. They ceased to smile and love and look to the morrow, and they lost all hope. One winter's end, the Citadel's last inhabitants wandered off, aimless and listless, into the forests, and the enemy's forces entered the gates unopposed.

Only the Crystal Hills withstood the power that had swept over the kingdom, and now all the enemy's strength was turned north, against this last redoubt of the descendants of

Ambescand. Monstrous gray beings, manlike but not men, strong and soulless, were in the force that marched to the northern cape. They crossed the long chain of bridges by stealth and fell upon the guardians in all their ferocity.

Fierce was that battle, and merciless. The invaders were driven off at last, but the price of victory was terrible. It took perilous magics to repulse the gray men, who were invulnerable to mortal weapons, and the defeat of the human invaders cost dearly in blood. Of those who had dwelt in the Crystal Hills, three of every four lay dead.

In their retreat, the invaders destroyed the bridges linking the Crystal Hills to the mainland. This promised some safety, but the survivors had lost as much in spirit as they had in blood and bone. It was clear to them that all the north, save the Crystal Hills, had fallen to the power of the enemy, and they were so reduced in number and so weakened that they could scarcely hope to survive, much less carry on the struggle.

In desperation, they turned to their mage. He had saved them from the gray men, and now they begged him to bring them to a place of safety. With the wisdom passed on by Staver, and gleaned from his books, the mage transported them to another plane of existence, leaving this world to the enemy. But something of them never truly left; with the passing years, the desire to return and fight once more for their kingdom and their mage grew ever stronger, binding them to this world with an unbreakable chain.

The sundering of the kingdom was complete. The High City and the Fastness and the Citadel on the Lake Isle were strongholds of the enemy now. Scattered fugitives huddled on the Plain, and in the Southern Forest, and in Long Wood, where they lived in constant fear of attack. Those who had fled to the Headland were forever separated from the mainland, for nothing could cross the Fissure, and no boat could survive the raging waters that battered and raced wildly beyond the outer shores.

In the separation, old ties were broken and forgotten, wilfully dismissed from memory because of the shame and bitterness they recalled. Children were told nothing of the kingdom, and the very name of Ambescand became almost legendary, like the Snow Moon, and the Burnt Man, and the Green Folk. Even language changed—not so much as to impede communication, but enough to mark a speaker as one from outside, and therefore suspect.

And so generation succeeded generation. The power of the conquering enemy became entrenched, and to most of the people of the north, it seemed as though things had been this way since time beyond memory and would be so always.

All hope of deliverance was not lost, nor did all resistance die. Little bands of foresters kept the memories alive as best they could, and some were so bold as to strike back at their conquerors whenever an opportunity presented itself. They learned to hide and survive; to fight with bow and ax against the enemy's armored swordsmen; to wait. From time to time —so it was said—a figure they called the Dark Prophet appeared among them. She gave the power that guided their foe a name—the Cairnlord—and promised a day when three brothers bearing blades of great power would come to lead them against his legions and restore the old kingdom. Men believed the prophecy, and clenched their wills, and abided for that day.

In the fullness of time, an aged man came to the Headland. He was bowed with years, his face scored by time and suffering, and he bore in his arms a long bundle wrapped in soft leather. He moved slowly, deliberately, like a man at the end of his strength. But hope was in his ancient eyes, and he had about him the air of a man whose mission is near its fulfillment.

He sought out one Vannen, a landholder who lived remote from his neighbors, and gave him the three blades forged by Vannen's own remote forebear. To Vannen's wife Ciantha, a beautiful woman with bright red hair and green eyes, he gave a greater gift. A few days after his arrival, Ciantha went away with the old man, to take up his magic and his mission. She was seen no more on the Headland.

Cathwar's work was done now, and he could rest at last. But the task of Ciantha, and Vannen, and their three sons, was only beginning.

For the deliverance of the north was at hand. Its story is the story of Colberane, Ordred, and Staver, the sons of Vannen and Ciantha, and those who followed them. The story of Ambescand is done.